C000094969

Pocket Guide
to
Classic Books

For my Mother
with all my love

The Pocket Guide to Classic Books

Maureen Hughes

REMEMBER WHEN

First published in Great Britain in 2010 by
REMEMBER WHEN
An imprint of
Pen & Sword Books Ltd
47 Church Street
Barnsley
South Yorkshire
S70 2AS

ISBN 978 1 84468 061 0

A CIP catalogue record for this book is available from the British Library

Typeset by S L Menzies-Earl

Printed and bound by CPI UK

Pen & Sword Books Ltd incorporates the Imprints of Pen & Sword
Aviation, Pen & Sword Maritime, Pen & Sword Military, Wharncliffe
Local History, Pen & Sword Select, Pen & Sword Military Classics, Leo
Cooper, Remember When, Seaforth Publishing and Frontline Publishing

For a complete list of Pen & Sword titles please contact
PEN & SWORD BOOKS LIMITED
47 Church Street, Barnsley, South Yorkshire, S70 2AS, England
E-mail: enquiries@pen-and-sword.co.uk
Website: www.pen-and-sword.co.uk

Contents

Acknowledgements

I WOULD FIND it difficult to work if I didn't have the support of those I love and often wonder how they cope trying to get my attention when I am lost under a mound of books – in fact, how do they find me? So again in this, my latest book, I would like to say thanks to my family; to my husband Gwyn, thank goodness he is the family chef because I would never find the time and so no one would eat if it was left up to me; to my daughter, Vicky, the voice of reason when things go wrong; to my son Kieran who, living miles away, has been patiently content with just sporadic 'sightings' of his mother. Thank you to my four gorgeous grandchildren, Kristian, Aaron, Ellis and Harry, who grow ever more adorable by the day and to Paula and Aisha who play such a special role in my family. More thanks too, to my in-laws, Marian and Tom, my cousin Michael, my lifelong school-friend Jo and my friend Carol, who have to be so patient when 'I just don't have the time!' Then last, but certainly not least, there is my agent Hilary, of Straight Line Management, who stands on the firing line fielding off all problems so that I can just get on with it! Over the years she has become not just a good agent but a good friend too, so, 'Thanks Hilary!' Indeed, thanks to you all for making it possible for me to do the job I love so much – writing – because without your support I wouldn't even want to write, for although it means a lot to me, it does actually only come a poor second to those I love.

I would also like to express my thanks too to various people who have helped me 'out of the kindness of their hearts!' Many professionals in their field have given me their knowledge, expertise and help, but more importantly they have given me – a complete stranger in some cases – their precious time, all without which my job would have been far more difficult, so a huge thank you to those individuals. Some, however, as is the way of man, went that extra mile; so Fraser Elgin, Christine De Poortere (from Great Ormond St Hospital Children's Charity), Sr Christina Kenworthy Brown, Lars Bo Jensen, Ian Collier, Dr Lynn Forest-Hill (Education Officer, Tolkien Society), Andrew Gasson (Chairman of the Wilkie Collins Society and author of *Wilkie Collins – an Illustrated Guide*), Chris 'Willy' Wilson (*Brendan Behan*), David Perdue (David Perdue's Charles Dickens' page),

Susan Hubbard (creator of www.seekingjaneausten.com web site), Dr Michael Ward (author: *Planet Narnia*) an extra special 'Thank you' goes to all of you for whom nothing was too much trouble; I stand in awe at your knowledge and dedication to your own particular subject area and am grateful that you were so willing to share that knowledge with me. And finally to Fiona Shoop, my editor at Remember When – 'We have made it this far; and after three books are still talking to each other; here's to many more! Thank you, Fiona.'

Photograph Credits

Portrait of Jane Austen	Reproduced with kind permission of Jane Austen Centre, Bath
One of Jane Austen's former homes in Bath	Susan Hubbard of www.seeingjaneausten.com
Jane Austen Festival	Reproduced with kind permission of Jane Austen Centre, Bath
Chawton Cottage	Susan Hubbard of www.seeingjaneausten.com
8 College Street	Susan Hubbard of www.seeingjaneausten.com
Haworth Parsonage	Andrew Hollingsworth, Yorkshire Tourist Board
The Wild Brontë Country	Steven Gillis
The Yorkshire Village of Haworth	Andrew Hollingsworth, Yorkshire Tourist Board
Gads Hill House	Reproduced with kind permission of Gads Hill School
Michael Ward	Reproduced with kind permission of William Clayton
Mother reading to her children	Reproduced with kind permission of Ms Xuejing Song
Students Studying	Reproduced with kind permission of Miss Charlotte Elston
Statue of Peter Pan	Photo by courtesy of Gt Ormond Street Hospital Children's Charity
J K Rowling	J P Masclet
Alfred Nobel	The Nobel Foundation

## Chapter One

Welcome to the World of Classic Books

Introduction

THOSE OF you who have read my first two books – *The Pocket Guide to Musicals* and *The Pocket Guide to Plays and Playwrights* – will, I am sure, have picked up the enormous influence my wonderful mother had upon every aspect of my life. However, due to the era in which she was born (the 1920s), a childhood plagued with ill health, and the premature death of her own mother when she was just 11 years old, my mother's education was very limited and was brought to an abrupt end when she was just 13 years old. As a consequence she always considered herself uneducated. I know better for she was actually a very intelligent lady with a thirst for knowledge and a respect for the arts, both of which she thankfully passed on to me. I owe her so much and often wonder what (had she been born at a different time and when opportunities were more readily available) she would have achieved. Maybe she would have been a brain surgeon or a great scientist for she had that level of intelligence but it is something I will sadly never know. However, something she did achieve, and to which I aspire, was to treat everyone as equal: she saw neither social nor cultural divide, nor did she consider academics as the intelligent elite. "Knowledge is for everyone," she would say, "there isn't an exclusivity clause attached to it, all that requires attention is the accessibility to that knowledge." And so I believe that she would have been delighted to know that I was attempting to open up the world of the Classics to everyone, everywhere. So Mum, this is for you.

This woman, I am proud to call my mother, wanted me to have all the opportunities denied to her and so exposed me to both the theatre and classical literature at a very early age. Each Christmas my stocking always had a least one classic book and a copy of *Pears Encyclopaedia*. This had an enormous impact upon me, but probably not quite in the way she expected, nor indeed intended. I know that she hoped I would voraciously devour books at the speed of light and be an authority on the Classics – bless her; don't you just love the optimism and belief of mothers! However, this time it slightly misfired and I grew up with a fascination for encyclopaedias, especially children's encyclopaedias, and even now this is the first section I make for in any bookshop! I am not sure, however, whether it is a reflection of my appetite for knowledge, the simplicity of my mind, or simply a deep-rooted desire to revert to my childhood! As for the Classics, to be honest they were always more of an uphill struggle for me, but I so wanted to please my mother that I did read all she bought me. When I look back I realise that I enjoyed a book far more when she had told me, not only the story beforehand, but when she had described the author or the times in which the author lived – in the most theatrical and vividly imaginative way one could ever imagine of course! I thought little of this when I was younger but later when I began teaching English Literature, and without even realising it, I found that I approached each piece of work from the same perspective as my energetically, theatrical mother all those years previously. I stimulated my pupils' interest by giving them a taster for the work, by telling them about the author and the times in which they lived. For most this was enough and they went on to read the book or, if it was a book we were studying, then this was of enormous help to them. For those not naturally inclined to be 'bookish' they told me it was an easier way for them to feel at least a little knowledgeable and so the seeds for this *Pocket Guide* – sown by my mother all those years ago – were starting to grow and now will hopefully blossom and give both enjoyment and knowledge to others.

Although, thanks to my mother, I am now relatively well read, I can by no means match up to the literary prowess of many and, more importantly in my case, I cannot match up to that of my adored younger cousin Michael whom I swear has read every book ever written; though when sanity prevails I realise this cannot be true! However, when feelings of inadequacy and ignorance creep through the window, good sense it seems just storms right out through that front door and I am then left alone with those all too familiar feelings of being the sole inhabitant of a cultural wilderness, where nothing will grow in my seemingly infertile mind. It's then that I can recall all the various snippets of information fed to me by my mother and suddenly I don't feel quite so stupid after all, because I know something if not everything – you see a little knowledge is not a dangerous thing; it can be a saviour, it has certainly been mine at times!

This book, therefore, is for all those people who like me have found themselves in a situation where all around them appear to be better read. I hope, that after reading this, never again will they feel totally inadequate and want to curl up in embarrassment, knowing that their smiling and nodding during discussions on a particular book is fooling no one, not even themselves. After reading *The Pocket Guide to Classic Books* they may not be able to discuss the works in any depth of course, but they will have a basic foundation enabling them to nod with some conviction and hopefully it will do for the reader what my mother did for me and encourage them to go on and read the classics – if not, then there are lots of fascinating encyclopaedias out there – I know, because most of these I have read with the passion my mother desired from me at the sight of a book!

The World of Books is for Everyone

What Makes a Classic?

WRITING a book on classical literature I thought would be interesting, fun, stimulating and lots of other things beside; I never thought for one moment that it would be confusing; I was soon to realise just how far from the truth that initial thought had been.

Surely, before beginning this work, all I had to do was to establish exactly who and what would be included in the book and take it from there. What could be difficult about that? In my naivety, it seemed quite straight forward to me, and trust me, naivety is the correct word to use here.

The initial confusion set in when I asked myself the all-important question: 'What makes a book a **classic book** and not just another book?' I soon realised that I didn't actually know the answer to this question. But that didn't worry me too much as I felt sure someone would know. Right? Wrong! This, it would seem, is a question without an answer and further more it also seemed that I had opened a can of worms. Friends argued amongst themselves when asked, teachers were embarrassed that they didn't know and academics were all quite certain that they did know! The trouble here, however, was that none of them agreed with each other – and, more to the point, none of this helped me at all. Just as I was beginning to think that if there was no answer then it really didn't matter at all, my friend Jess threw me into a total state of panic:

> "If you're having problems then try thinking of it in terms of a radio/interview question: 'So, Ms Author, what is it that actually makes a book a classic book?' ... Because" she said, "believe me, that is the question they will all ask you."

Now I had to have an answer, and there wasn't one. She went on:

> "I reckon then that you have to define it first for yourself; first draw up some parameters e.g. a classic has to be 'x' years old, or whatever, and then work within those parameters."

Things were finally looking up. Wrong again. Because every time I drew up 'some parameters' I kept moving the goal posts – yes I did say I kept moving them! Eventually I realised that this was my clue, my answer to the unanswerable. At the outset I couldn't see the tunnel, let alone the light; now suddenly it was becoming a little clearer, the tunnel was in sight and a chink of light was penetrating the darkness, and all thanks to the fact that there is no correct and definitive answer.

The penetrating light was the realisation that there are obviously some books which without doubt are very popular now, but you know instinctively that they won't pass the test of time and be read in their thousands hundreds of years hence. So this quickly became one of the original defining parameters: 'The Test of Time'. However I reconsidered when I looked at some books, which are centuries old and which academics would label a classic, and yet equally I knew were not being read by the universal thousands today. Can you see the circle I was circumnavigating; the treadmill I was on? It was clear that my defining parameters would have to have some liquid fluidity.

It was then that I decided the only way to proceed was by following my own instincts and include what I felt to be correct, the reason for this being that if this is a question without an answer, then who is there to prove me wrong? So, if you don't find what you are looking for in my book I do apologise but equally I do hope you enjoy reading about the entries I have chosen to include.

Once this decision had been taken and the task had become a lot clearer I was now, I hoped, about to write an enjoyable and informative *Pocket Guide to Classic Books*. Only one more hurdle to jump and that was where should I start? Another difficult decision to take and one that I know will not please everyone, but never-the-less it had to be taken and so I decided to start in the Fifteenth Century; the reason for this being mainly because I thought the appeal would be greater than if I started with earlier works, and let's face it there is little point in self indulgent writing, is there? I wanted to write what – hopefully – people would want to read, so please enjoy.

Maureen Hughes

Chapter Two

The Literary Giants

ACH SEPARATE genre of the arts, be it theatre, opera, literature – or whatever – is generally headed by a 'giant' of its field. This is someone who has achieved the top level of attainment, someone to whom other gifted individuals can aspire and someone upon whom the rest of us can simply gaze in awe and with total admiration knowing that they have achieved where many fail.

So many writers, so many greats and so many giants, meant that which to select for inclusion in this section was not an easy decision, but one that had to be taken. So, after extended deliberation you will find below my final decision, together with an explanation, for of course this is only my own humble opinion. However, on this occasion I am quite confident that most will agree with me and the only problem will be that you as the reader will want to add others, as to be honest I did too!

THE BRONTËS are included on the grounds that they are a family of writers; this in itself is a gigantic and incredible achievement and so justifies their place in this section.

JANE AUSTEN qualifies quite simply because it seems to me that even those not interested in literature can, if asked the question, 'Who wrote *Pride and Prejudice?*' answer correctly with Jane Austen. And finally –

CHARLES DICKENS I felt had to be included because just as Shakespeare created fantastic words, which have lived on and come to life through the years, Dickens created fantastically colourful characters who have survived the test of time with some even evolving into adjectives – we all know, for example, what kind of person you are if you are called a Scrooge!

Now, before someone asks me why I haven't included the Bard, then it is quite simply because I have an entire section devoted to William Shakespeare in the predecessor to this book, *The Pocket Guide to Plays and Playwrights*, and *The Pocket Guide to Classics* is primarily, though not exclusively, devoted to novelists.

The World of Jane Austen
1775 – 1817

Works by Jane Austen include:
Emma • *Lady Susan* • *Mansfield Park* • *Northanger Abbey* •
Persuasion • *Pride and Prejudice* • *Sense and Sensibility* •

JANE AUSTEN: The Woman and Her Life

• Jane Austen was born on 16 December 1775 in the little village of Steventon, Hampshire to the Reverend George Austen and his wife Cassandra (née Leigh)
• She was the second daughter and seventh child in a family of eight children
• It was a close knit family where, throughout Austen's life, the two sisters Jane and Cassandra were close friends; their father was a scholar who encouraged learning in his children; their mother had a sharp wit and was famed for her impromptu stories, and all of the family loved acting, an interesting fact considering how well Austen's work lends itself to dramatisation for both stage and screen
• It was around 1787 that Austen began to write

7

- In 1801 the Austen family moved to Bath
- Her father died in 1805, after which the family moved several times before finally settling in Chawton, near Steventon, in a large cottage provided by Austen's brother Edward
- Although she never married, the style in which her novels were written would suggest that she had experienced the feelings of love at its height and love in its depths, but there is no concrete evidence to confirm this, probably due in part to the fact that after her death her sister, Cassandra, censored which of her personal letters survived and which did not – leading us now, of course, to wonder why!
- In 1816 Austen began to suffer from ill health
- Jane Austen died on 18 July 1817 with one novel, *Sanditon*, still incomplete
- She was buried in Winchester Cathedral

THE AUSTEN CHILDREN [Jane Austen's brothers and sisters]

There were eight children in the Austen family:

1. James {1765-1819} was the first born and followed his father into the ministry
2. George, {1766-1852} the second child, was born handicapped and after being placed with, and brought up by, others he was generally never spoken about as so often happened at that particular time in history when the handicapped were looked down upon as second class citizens
3. Edward {1767-1852} came next; he was adopted by one Thomas Knight
4. The fourth son, Henry {1771-1850} served in the army, went into banking and then finished his career as a member of the clergy – as with his father and older brother James before him
5. Cassandra{1773-1865} was the fifth child, but first daughter, born into the Austen family and grew up to be Jane's closest friend in adulthood
6. Son number five was Francis (Frank) {1774-1865} who became an Admiral in the Royal Navy
7. Jane {1775-1817} made her appearance as child number seven; little did any of the family realise her great destiny in the world of literature
8. The sixth son, and final child, to be born to the Reverend George Austen and his wife Cassandra was Charles {1779-1852} who, like his older brother Frank , also joined the Navy

BRIEF SYNOPSES OF MAJOR WORKS BY JANE AUSTEN

Emma

As a pretty, wealthy and self-satisfied young woman who it would appear has everything, Emma Woodhouse indulges herself by matchmaking among her friends and neighbours, rather unsuccessfully though! After a series of embarrassing errors she herself finds marital happiness with George Knightly, a mature and protective local squire.

Mansfield Park

This is considered to be the most serious of Austen's novels and shows how strength of character and a moral outlook will eventually win the day. Fanny Price is the niece of Sir Thomas Bertram and is taken in as a child to be cared for in his family home – her own family not enjoying the same level of financial stability. Against all odds she grows into a kind and caring adult and eventually marries Sir Thomas Bertram's son Edmund, her cousin.

Northanger Abbey

A tale of the consequences when one allows fantasy and reality to become entwined; this is the story of Catherine Morland, a young and avid reader who falls in love with a wealthy young man, Henry Tilney. Henry takes Catherine to Northanger Abbey, the Tilney family's seat. However, influenced by the fact that she is an avid reader of Gothic novels she erroneously imagines that Henry's father, General Tilney, is somehow involved in a criminal mystery and is consequently mortified when her suspicions are discovered. She is sent home in disgrace but is eventually reunited with the man she loves.

Persuasion – **Published posthumously**

Anne Elliot had once been in love with Captain Frederick Wentworth but had been persuaded not to marry him because he did not have the correct social status. However, seven years later things have changed and he has returned from the Napoleonic Wars with both money and an acceptable social rank in the Navy; he is now accepted by Anne's father and his circle of snobbish friends. Anne realises that she still loves Wentworth and eventually they are reunited – after a few detours and a near miss with the young woman, Louisa Musgrove, that is!

Pride and Prejudice

Probably the best known and most loved of all Austen's novels, this tells the story of Mr and Mrs Bennett who live with their five daughters at Longbourn in Hertfordshire. Their second daughter, Elizabeth Bennett, is a high-spirited young woman who is attracted to Fitzwilliam Darcy, a rich and aristocratic landowner, who clearly is attracted to her too. However, external forces in the form of **pride and prejudice** intervene to keep the pair apart. Elizabeth has a great deal of **pride** and self-respect and detests – is **prejudiced** – against Darcy because he is quite simply a snob, and behaves like one; whilst on the other hand Darcy is very **proud** of his rank and social standing and is **prejudiced** against what he perceives to be the vulgarity of the Bennett Family. But fate intervenes and presents the pair with a set of circumstances, which draw them closer together.

Sense and Sensibility

The deceased Henry Dashwood had left his estate to his son John, thus leaving his widow and her daughters, by a previous marriage, in financial difficulties. His intention had been that his son would take care of his stepmother and her daughters, but John is far too selfish for this. Marianne, the most sensible daughter, becomes infatuated with John Willoughby who on the face of it seems to be a kind and romantic lover, but in reality is nothing but an unscrupulous fortune hunter and who deserts her for an heiress. She then settles for an unromantic marriage to a man 20 years older than her, but who is reliable. Meanwhile, Elinor, Marianne's older sister has long been in love with Edward Ferrers and so with patience and understanding, with regards to his mistakes, she finally wins her man.

EXPERIENCE YESTERDAY'S WORLD OF JANE AUSTEN TODAY

We read their books and temporarily live the lives of their characters; we perhaps wonder too about the domestic surroundings which inspired our favourite writers to pen their masterpieces. Well the wonderful thing is that in many cases we can now actually visit those inspirational homes that our writers have long since vacated, for many have been lovingly preserved for us to enjoy. In the case of Jane Austen, for example, she lived in various towns and various houses many of which can still be seen today, so you can in fact take a 'Jane Austen National Tour' if you wish!

Steventon

Jane Austen was born in the Hampshire village of Steventon where her father was the rector; she lived there until she was 25 years old. Sadly, though, the family home is no longer standing.

Bath

The Regency town of Bath in Somerset is the town most frequently associated with Jane Austen. Although she was neither a native nor a particularly long term resident in the town, it has, with its Regency-style architecture, become synonymous with the name Austen and as a town itself is clearly very proud of this fact, and rightly so too.

Austen paid two extended visits to Bath towards the end of the Eighteenth Century, and from 1801-1806, the city of Bath actually became her home. The Jane Austen Centre in Gay Street is now a permanent exhibition centre dedicated to her and tells the story of her 'Bath experience' where she wrote two of her novels, *Northanger Abbey* and *Persuasion* which are both largely set in the town of Bath. The town is now almost as it was when Austen lived there; the houses where she lived are still there and the settings for her two novels can still be seen too, either independently or by taking part in a guided tour organised by The Jane Austen Centre.

4, Sydney Place – former home of Jane Austen in Bath

In addition to this permanent dedicated centre, each year at the end of September Bath holds the exciting 'Jane Austen Festival', where residents and visitors can, if they wish, dress in Regency-style costumes to experience the feel of the period and celebrate the life and works of Austen. The festival opens with a spectacular costumed parade followed by nine days of Austen inspired events such as country fairs, soirées, theatre, concerts, walking tours, food and dancing and is well worth a visit for Austen lovers – or indeed Austen lovers to be.

THE JANE AUSTEN FESTIVAL

Jane Austen Festival Bath

Chawton Cottage

Chawton Cottage in Chawton, Hampshire is in fact the home most associated with Jane Austen and where she spent the last eight years of her life until just a few weeks before her death in 1817. It belonged to her brother, Edward, who gave it to his widowed mother and sisters rent-free for the rest of their lives. It was here that she wrote *Emma*, *Mansfield Park* and *Persuasion* as well as revising *Northanger Abbey*, *Pride and Prejudice* and *Sense and Sensibility*. This house is now a Jane Austen Museum.

Jane Austen's Home in Chawton, Hampshire

Winchester

Austen spent her final weeks in Winchester, lodging at 8 College Street, a house which still stands today, though privately owned. She was in Winchester seeking medical advice for the illness that was to shortly prove fatal.

It was whilst staying here at 8 College Street,
Winchester that Jane Austen died

AND FINALLY

• All of Jane Austen's novels were published anonymously
• The Prince Regent of the time, later to become George IV, was a great Austen fan and at his request *Emma* was actually 'respectfully dedicated' to him
• Her novels are a beautiful reflection of the English country gentry of her time
• Some of Austen's novels started their lives under another title for example:
> *Sense and Sensibility* was originally entitled *Elinor and Marianne*
> *Pride and Prejudice* was originally entitled *First Impressions*
> *Northanger Abbey* was originally entitled *Susan*

And so now we move on to other Giants in the field of Literature, and this time it is not one Giant but a family of Giants.

The World of The Brontë Sisters

The Brontës are one of the most famous family of writers of all time and comprises of not only Charlotte, Emily and Anne but also of their brother Branwell and their father the Reverend Patrick Brontë, for they too saw their works in print.

Patrick Brontë 1777-1861 was the father of this extraordinary family
Maria Branwell 1783-1821 was the mother of this extraordinary family
Patrick Brontë married **Maria Branwell** 29th December 1812

Together Patrick and Maria had six children but sadly, as so often happened in earlier centuries, not all of their children survived into adulthood.

1. Maria	1814-1825	was the first daughter who died whilst she was still a child
2. Elizabeth	1815-1825	the second daughter was born the year after Maria and died just a few days after her
3. Charlotte	1816-1855	the third daughter Charlotte survived into adulthood and went on to became the only Brontë child to marry when she married Arthur Bell Nicholls
4. Patrick Branwell	1817-1848	was the only son born to Patrick and Maria

5. Emily Jane	1818-1848	Emily was the third daughter and fourth child in the Brontë family
6. Anne	1820-1849	was the final child and completed this historic, literary family

Family Background

Because the Brontës were unique as a family of writers the way in which we look at their lives must surely be different too and so instead of the usual bullet format, we have here a prose overview.

Patrick Brontë was not, as one would expect from the ë in the surname, from some far off Romantic East European culture but actually originated from Ireland where the family name was Bunty and not Brontë; he chose the more impressive name of Brontë when he arrived in England to go up to St John's College, Cambridge. Perhaps he had some sort of premonition that his

Three sisters, three talents, three giants

family name was to be immortalised by his children, and let's face it Brontë does sound like a wonderfully, romantic, exotic and literary name after all.

In 1820 the Brontë family arrived and settled in the Yorkshire town that was to become synonymous with the family name – Brontë of Haworth – where they lived in the Parsonage. In later years, as their literary genius became universally recognised, they became known as the 'Brontës of Haworth' and the surrounding countryside became known as 'Brontë Country' with their former home now preserved as the Brontë Parsonage Museum. Visiting the museum and the surrounding countryside is what can only be described now as an 'Experience of the Senses'. The Brontë legacy is such that you can almost smell and feel their works as you stand high in the Pennines surrounded by their literary history.

Tragedy was never far away from the Brontë family and began when the young children lost their mother, Maria, in 1821. Her place in the home was taken by Maria's sister, Elizabeth Branwell, who moved into the Parsonage to care for her young nieces, nephew and their father Patrick. Only a few years later though death struck again, this time claiming the lives of the two eldest girls, Maria and Elizabeth. The death of these girls who never reached an age at which they could perhaps write their own novels leaves one wondering whether they too might have aspired to literary heights, given the opportunity; that is a question, however, that will remain forever unanswered except by conjecture, but my guess is that they too would indeed have written great novels – but then I am a romantic at heart.

THE BRONTË NOVELISTS

The Brontë children, encouraged by their father, developed a voracious appetite for books and whilst still children wrote their own miniature books, complete with miniature writing, for Branwell's toy soldiers to 'read'. Whilst the surviving Brontë girls grew up to be governesses and teachers, Branwell was not blessed with the same drive and focus and, though a talented artist, he fell into bad ways and sadly took the destructive road of alcohol and drug abuse.

The writing career of the sisters began with a book of poetry, aptly called *Poems*, which they wrote using the pseudonyms of Currer, Ellis and Acton Bell and for which they used their own money to finance the publication. It was not the success they hoped it would be with only two copies sold but, and all budding novelists take note, they carried on regardless and undeterred (if not immediately successfully) and ventured into the realms of the novel, a realm that was to become their own kingdom.

Charlotte's first attempt at novel writing was a novel called *The Professor* which, although rejected by several publishing houses, received praise enough for Charlotte to continue with her writing and produce *Jane Eyre* which was published in 1847, quickly followed by Emily's *Wuthering Heights* and Anne's *Agnes Grey* in the same year. But still the true identity of the Brontë sisters was a closely guarded secret, though speculation was now rife. Eventually their identity was revealed and the rest is, as they say, history with Charlotte now on her way to literary success as too were Emily and Anne. Happiness and success were, however, to be short lived for within a space of nine months Charlotte Brontë lost her brother Branwell and her two sisters, Emily and Anne, to the killer disease tuberculosis.

Charlotte found comfort and solace in her writing and eventually happiness in a marriage to her father's curate, the Reverend Arthur Bell Nicholls. In what had become true, tragic Brontë style though, her happiness was short lived for she died just a few weeks before her 39th birthday. To compound the tragedy she was, at the time of her death, in the early stages of pregnancy. Her father lived on for a further six years having survived not only his wife but all six of his children too. His death brought this remarkable family to an end, for there were no descendants to take up the pen and write on into the sunset.

THE BRONTË NOVELS OF:

ANNE BRONTË
Agnes Grey

This novel tells us the story of Agnes, a rector's daughter, who works as a governess, first for the Bloomfield family and their undisciplined children and then for the Murrays. In her second position she finds the eldest child, Rosalie, to be everything she is not. The contrast in characters culminates in the contrast of outcomes when Rosalie marries ambitiously, but unhappily, whereas the gentle and modest Agnes finds happiness with the curate, Mr Weston.

The Tenant of Wildfell Hall

This novel is narrated by farmer Gilbert Markham who has fallen in love with a young widow, recently arrived in the neighbourhood with her son Arthur. Mystery surrounds the widow though, who on the surface of it appears to have a rather strange relationship with her landlord, Lawrence.

However, it is in fact an innocent relationship for Lawrence is actually her brother and had offered her sanctuary in Wildfell Hall when, in fear for the safety of her son, she was forced to flee from her husband, Arthur Huntingdon, who had fallen into a seedy lifestyle of drink and infidelity. She later returns to her husband to nurse him through a fatal illness, which after his death leaves her free again and without ties.

CHARLOTTE BRONTË

Jane Eyre

As a penniless orphan Jane Eyre is taken care of by her heartless aunt Mrs Reed, who sends her away to Lowood School where, after some unhappy years, she eventually becomes a teacher. Following this she is appointed as governess to Adèle at Thornfield Hall, who is the illegitimate daughter of Mr Rochester. Jane's time at Thornfield is constantly disturbed by some 'unknown' presence and by the fact that she is forbidden to visit a certain part of the house. Eventually, Jane and Mr Rochester fall in love and plan to marry. On the eve of their wedding, however, tragedy strikes when Jane's veil is torn by an unknown mad woman, who it turns out is Rochester's insane wife. It transpires that it is she who is the unknown presence in the house and that she in fact lives in the forbidden part of the house too. Jane flees from Rochester and Thornfield Hall and survives near death on the moors, after which she is taken in by the caring Rivers family who it turns out are her cousins. She also discovers that she has inherited money and is on the point of accepting second best in love by marrying her cousin the Reverend St John Rivers when a telepathic call from Rochester takes her back to Thornfield Hall. Here she finds the Hall destroyed by fire and Rochester blinded trying to save his wife. Jane and Rochester are reunited in love and his sight partially returns.

The Professor

William Crimsworth teaches English at a girls' school in Brussels and whilst there he falls in love with Frances Henri. The Protestant Frances is at odds with the Catholic Headmistress, Zoraide Reuter, who makes a play for Crimsworth. Resisting the manipulating Mlle Reuter, Crimsworth resigns his post at the school, finds another one and then marries Frances.

Shirley

Set in Yorkshire at the time of the Luddite riots, Robert Gérard Moore persists in introducing the latest labour-saving machinery with the result that there is an attempt to destroy his factory by fire, as well as an attempt on his life. Trying to solve his financial problems Robert proposes to the heiress, Shirley Keeldar – despite the fact that he really loves his cousin Caroline Helstone, and she him. Shirley angrily rejects him for she is in love with Robert's brother, Louis. Eventually, all is resolved in the love tangle and both couples are united with the person they love.

Villette

Lucy Snowe, a poor and plain girl teaches at a girl's school in Villette where the headmistress, Madame Beck, is very capable, though somewhat unscrupulous. Whilst at the school, Lucy falls in love with John Bretton, the very handsome English doctor who works at the school. It is a love, however, that is unreturned. Eventually she gradually falls in love with the despotic – though good-hearted – cousin of Madame Beck, Professor Paul Emanuel, and through his generosity she becomes mistress of her own school. He is called away to work abroad leaving the reader to wonder whether he ever returns to marry Lucy.

EMILY BRONTË
Wuthering Heights

This story of two families – the Earnshaws and the Lintons – is related by two characters, Lockwood and Ellen 'Nelly' Dean, and tells of the all-consuming and passionate love between Catherine Earnshaw and Heathcliff; a love which destroys them both, and all around them. Heathcliff had been brought to Wuthering Heights by the then owner, a kind Mr Earnshaw, where he was brought up as Earnshaw's own son. Of Earnshaw's two other natural children, his headstrong daughter, Catherine, becomes a devoted friend to Heathcliff, whereas his son, Hindley, resents him. After his father's death, Hindley mistreats Heathcliff and Catherine marries within her station, despite loving Heathcliff. Revenge and love dominate this story, which revolves around the two families and their children. Only death is able to reunite the two lovers.

THE BRONTË COUNTRY

There is a part of Yorkshire that IS the Brontës and so it is no surprise to know that it is actually called the Brontë Country. It is an area in the North of England which straddles the West Yorkshire and East Lancashire

It was the wild moors that was to be the inspiration behind
much of the Brontë output

Pennines, a windswept area of moors and heather with a wild, chilling and haunting feel to it. This is the bleak landscape and backdrop which inspired the Brontës' work; walking across this moorland one can almost hear Heathcliff and Cathy call out in desperation to each other.

Haworth is a hilltop village not far from Bradford and set on the Pennine Moors; it is where the Brontë sisters wrote most of their work, whilst living at the Parsonage adjacent to the Haworth Church where their father was the parson. They lived at the Haworth Parsonage between the years 1820-1861.

EXPERIENCE YESTERDAY'S WORLD OF THE BRONTË SISTERS TODAY

As a Yorkshire lass myself and an avid reader it was therefore inevitable that I would be drawn to Brontë country; it was a long time ago now but I can remember the visit as though it was yesterday and can honestly say that I could feel and almost see these remarkable sisters all around me.

Here it is possible to take a walk around their former home and soak in the surrounding and pervading countryside. By visiting Haworth one can learn so much more about the family whilst also experiencing the wild countryside, which was a great stimulating force on their lives; here at first hand you can experience the moors and the haunting, echoing emptiness which draws in visitors to all its mysterious cruelty. For those who have never experienced the pull of moorland, I have to tell you that it is quite unique and riveting; almost like a magnet it pulls its victims – or lovers – into its clutches. It is interesting to note that the Brontë sisters were drawn too, to the North Yorkshire seaside town of Scarborough, which itself sits on the edge of the North Yorkshire Moors, also wild and consuming in its intensity. Anne Brontë, the youngest of the three sisters actually died in Scarborough and is buried in St Mary's churchyard, overlooking the sea.

And so we now move on to one of the greatest creator of characters who has ever lived, Charles Dickens.

The Yorkshire Village of Haworth

21

The World of Charles Dickens
1775 – 1817

Charles Dickens

Major Works by Charles Dickens include:
Barnaby Rudge • Bleak House • David Copperfield • Dombey and Son • Great Expectations • Hard Times • Little Dorrit • Martin Chuzzlewit • Mystery of Edwin Drood (The) • Nicholas Nickleby • Old Curiosity Shop (The) • Oliver Twist • Our Mutual Friend • Pickwick Papers (The) • Tale of Two Cities (A)

CHARLES DICKENS: The Man and his Life
• Dickens was born Charles John Huffam Dickens on 7 February 1812 in Portsmouth, England to John and Elizabeth Dickens
• He was educated at Giles School in Chatham, Kent and Wellington House Academy, London
• In 1824 his father was sent to prison for debt, as a result of which Dickens was withdrawn from school and sent to work in a blacking factory, where

he stuck labels on bottles, an experience that left both physical and mental scars, and one which was to haunt him for the rest of his life – this bottle factory appears in his largely autobiographical novel *David Copperfield*

• At 15 – and his schooling at an end – he became a clerk in a solicitor's office whilst studying shorthand in the evenings

• In 1829 he became a freelance reporter at Doctor's Commons Courts

• In 1830 Dickens met and fell in love with Maria Beadnell, the daughter of a banker, but in 1833 the relationship ended, probably because her parents did not think him a good match. A rather unflattering version of her later appeared in his novel *Little Dorrit*

• In 1833 he began contributing stories to magazines and newspapers

• In 1834 he adopted the soon to be famous pseudonym of 'Boz'; the first series of *Sketches by Boz* was published in 1836

• In 1835 Charles Dickens met and became engaged to Catherine Hogarth, marrying her in 1836; they went on to have 10 children together before separating in 1858

• In 1836 as well as marrying Catherine Hogarth he also became editor of *Bentley's Miscellany*

• It was the success of his novel *The Pickwick Papers* that allowed Dickens to become a full-time writer – whilst in true workaholic fashion, still continuing with his journalistic and editorial work

• In 1846 he became the founder-editor of the *Daily News*

• Dickens was well known for giving public readings of his works, the first of which he gave in 1853 – probably it was his great love for the stage and his own expertise as an actor that made his readings so animated, lively and thus popular

• He was a great personal friend of that other great Victorian writer, Wilkie Collins, and in 1856 they worked together on the stage play *The Frozen Deep*. In the same year Dickens bought Gad's Hill, an estate he had admired since childhood; he paid just £1,790 for the property

• In 1857 Dickens' company performed *The Frozen Deep* and when a young actress, Ellen Ternan, joined the same company; it is said that Dickens fell in love with her

• In 1858 he became a professional public reader – that is he was paid for his readings – and in the same year he and Catherine separated

• He lived in London between the years 1822 to 1860 after which he moved to his country house of Gad's Hill near Chatham in Kent, where he continued to live until his death

• In 1865 Dickens and Ellen Ternan were badly shaken up in a railway accident whilst returning from a holiday in Paris. Ten people were killed

and forty injured in this accident, which had a profound and long-term effect upon Dickens
• Many say that his gruelling reading tours took such a strain on his health that they were a major contributing factor to his relatively early death at the young age of 58, for he was not a 'quiet' reader but a 'performing' reader who threw himself wholeheartedly into the performance in hand, carrying on almost compulsively even when he was unwell
• Charles Dickens died on 9 June 1870 at Gad's Hill, near Chatham, Kent; quite typically after a full day's work; the cause of death was a stroke
• He is buried in Westminster Abbey

OTHER WORKS BY CHARLES DICKENS INCLUDE:

Charles Dickens had a great love for Christmas and so it naturally followed then that he wrote many great works based on and around the theme of Christmas. Such works include:

Christmas Books
Battle of Life (The)
Chimes (The)
Christmas Carol (A)
Cricket on the Hearth (The)
Haunted Man (The)

Christmas Stories
Christmas Tree (A)
Doctor Marigold
George Silverman's Explanation
Going into Society
Haunted House (The)
Holiday Romance
Holly Tree (The)
Hunted Down
Magic Fishbone (The)
Message from the Sea (A)
Mrs Lirriper's Legacy
Mrs Lirriper's Lodgings
Mugby Junction
No Thoroughfare
Nobody's Story

DISCOVER MORE ABOUT HISTORY

Wharncliffe Books are an imprint of Pen & Sword Books who now have over 2000 titles in print covering all aspects of history. Wharncliffe specialise in local history and have a number of leading titles in print. 2008 has seen the launch of two new imprints in the Wharncliffe name, True Crime and Transport. These books will cover all aspects of crime and transport, both on a local and national scale. If you would like to receive more information and special offers on your preferred interests along with our standard catalogue, please complete and return this card (no stamp required in the UK). Alternatively, register online at www.pen-and-sword.co.uk. Thank you. **PLEASE NOTE: We do not sell data information to any third party companies.**

Mr/Mrs/Ms/Other................ Name..

Address..

....Postcode.........................

Email address..

LOCAL HISTORY		TRANSPORT		TRUE CRIME	
Guides	☐	Railways	☐	Foul Deeds	☐
Industrial History	☐	Cars	☐	Conmen/Hoaxes	☐
Family History	☐	Buses/Trams	☐	Serial Killers	☐
Nostalgia	☐	Canals	☐	ALL THE ABOVE	☐

Website: www.pen-and-sword.co.uk • Email: enquiries@pen-and-sword.co.uk
Telephone: 01226 734555 • Fax: 01226 734438

Wharncliffe Books

FREEPOST SF5

47 Church Street

BARNSLEY

South Yorkshire

S70 2BR

Perils of Certain English Prisoners (The)
Poor Relation's Story (The)
Seven Poor Travellers (The)
Somebody's Luggage
To Be Read at Dusk
Tom Tiddler's Ground
What Christmas Is as We Grow Older
Wreck of the Golden Mary (The)

Further Works include:

American Notes
Child's History of England (A)
Dinner at Poplar Walk (A)
Lazy Tour of Two Idle Apprentices (The) {with Wilkie Collins}
Life of Our Lord (The)
Mudfog Papers (The)
Pictures from Italy
Sketches of Young Couples
Sketches of Young Gentlemen
Uncommercial Traveller (The)

A BRIEF SYNOPSIS OF THE MAJOR NOVELS

Charles Dickens' novels are not only full of some of the most colourful characters in literature but, as one would expect of one of the greatest writers of all times, they are brim full of excitement in the form of gripping storylines. In addition to the plots one can only describe his sub plots as a 'cacophony of sub plots'! He was master in the art of creating suspense and a desperate need in the reader to read on. This was probably because his works were first serialised before they appeared in book form, which of course meant that he had to ensure his readers returned for the next instalment by leaving the previous on a cliffhanger.

Dickens was a social and intensely sensory writer, so expertly drawn are his characters that one can virtually 'see' them come to life on every page, and so intimate is his description of Victorian life that the sights and the smells are almost tangible to the reader, giving a uniquely graphic and accurate insight into that particular era in history. He was a true master of his craft allowing the reader to reach out to touch, feel, hear, smell and see his story; in fact one could say that reading the novel is almost a secondary experience.

Below you will find 'a very short' synopsis of Dickens' major works; to write a full synopsis of course would be almost akin to writing a standard novel!

Barnaby Rudge	This is one of two historical novels – the other being *A Tale of Two Cities*, written by Dickens and deals with murder and the Gordon Riots. Barnaby Rudge is himself a simple man trapped in complex times.
Bleak House	The story of a long-drawn-out court case where no one is the winner as at the conclusion of the tale the court costs swallow up all the available monies.
Christmas Carol (A)	A moral tale in which Ebenezer Scrooge is a bitter miser who is shown the error of his ways one bleak Christmas when he experiences three separate visits from the three ghosts of Christmas Past, Present, and Future. The tale concludes with Scrooge being a reformed character.
David Copperfield	This novel, written in the first person, is in part autobiographical and charts the life of David Copperfield from his birth through to the harsh treatment meted out by his stepfather and culminating in the happiness he eventually found with Agnes, the sensible young woman he met earlier in his life.
Dombey and Son	The core of this novel is the fact that Paul Dombey is disappointed when his first child is a girl, for he wants only a son and as a result he despises his daughter, Florence. His second child though is a son, Paul Jr, but Paul Jr is weak and dies in childhood. Paul Dombey is later reconciled with his daughter.
Great Expectations	Pip, an orphan, helps the escaped convict, Magwitch, who is later transported to Australia where he becomes a wealthy man and prospers. Magwitch anonymously funds Pip to become a gentleman but in becoming a gentleman he then forgets those who matter. Pip falls in love with the heartless Estella (who turns out to be Magwitch's daughter) and is destined to experience much

	before he discovers the value and identity of true wealth.
Hard Times	Thomas Gradgrind runs a school based on uncompromising principles, which includes lack of frivolity. So when he catches his children, Louisa and Tom, peeping into a circus he is very angry as he considers this a frivolous way of life. He takes an abandoned 'circus child' into his school in the hope of redeeming her. It takes years of 'hard times' to soften Thomas Gradgrind's approach to life.
Little Dorrit	Amy Dorrit is forced to care for her impoverished father in a debtors' prison in this rags to riches – and back again – story.
Martin Chuzzlewit	This is one of Dickens' lesser known novels and focuses on the greed of old Martin Chuzzlewit's relatives, especially on Mr Pecksniff, who are hoping to inherit his wealth.
Mystery of Edwin Drood (The)	This is a murder mystery and will always, in fact, remain a mystery for Dickens died before he completed it. The story is of the murder of Edwin Drood and who dunnit – which only one man knows – Charles Dickens – and which he took to the grave with him, for he died after completing chapter 22 in which he never gave us the answer!
Nicholas Nickleby	The story of a young man attempting to care for his mother and sister after the death of his father, despite opposition in the guise of help from his unscrupulous Uncle Ralph.
Old Curiosity Shop (The)	Nelly Trent and her grandfather, who has lost everything to gambling, are in debt to the evil Daniel Quilp from whom Nell's grandfather has borrowed money. Trying to escape from Quilp's clutches they wander the countryside exhausted and hungry. Finally 'Little Nell' dies, exhausted by the ordeal, and her heartbroken grandfather dies soon after.
Oliver Twist	Young Oliver is born in the workhouse and

27

	destined to a life of hardship. He makes his way to London where he is taken in by Fagin and his gang of thieves before eventually being rescued and adopted by the kindly Mr Brownlow.
Our Mutual Friend	John Harmon is the son of a wealthy dust contractor and the heir to his father's fortune, but only if he agrees to marry Bella Wilfer. After his father's death it takes his supposed drowning, a case of mistaken identity and marrying Bella – as another man – before the family fortune comes his way.
Pickwick Papers (The)	This novel revolves around a group of eccentric travellers and their stories.
Tale of Two Cities (A)	Set in the time of the French Revolution the plot focuses on two lookalikes who both love the same woman, Lucie. Of the two men, Carton is the irresponsible one who has little ambition and who drinks too much and yet it is he who gives his life to save the life of Darnay – the better of the two suitors.

DICKENSIAN CHARACTERS

Dickens is as well known for the 'drawing' of his characters as for the novels themselves. In fact some of his characters have actually entered the English language. You do not need to have read *A Christmas Carol* to know that you are obviously considered a mean and tight individual when the word Scrooge is attributed to you every time you reluctantly contribute to yet another office collection! Some say that his characters are not characters, but caricatures; frankly, who cares because they are so vividly 'drawn' that they come alive on the page and penetrate the reader's mind, illustrating the story with such an exciting visual verbosity and colour that anyone shown a picture of the character in question would recognise him/her immediately; a rare quality achieved by very few writers. In addition, Dickens based many of his characters on his own family or on people he knew which gives them a feeling of personal intimacy.

CHARACTER	BOOK	COMMENTS
A Artful Dodger	*Oliver Twist*	Real name Jack Dawkins, he is the most successful thief in Fagin's gang and shows Oliver how to pick pockets.

CHARACTER	BOOK	COMMENTS
B		
Barbary, Miss	*Bleak House*	Godmother who raised Esther and who is later revealed to be her aunt.
Barkis	*David Copperfield*	A carrier who is in love with Peggotty, David Copperfield's nurse, (nanny); His catchphrase is 'Barkis is willin'. He and Peggotty are later married.
Barnacles	*Little Dorrit*	Name of the family that controls Circumlocution Office where nothing ever gets done and everything just goes 'round and 'round in circles.
Bates	*Oliver Twist*	He is one of the boys in Fagin's London gang.
Belle	*Christmas Carol (A)*	Ebenezer Scrooge's lost love and fiancée whom the Ghost of Christmas Past takes him to visit so that he might see the life he could have had with her.
Bet	*Oliver Twist*	Nancy's friend who is plunged into madness after identifying Nancy's body.
Biddy	*Great Expectations*	She is in love with Pip but he ignores her as his own fortunes improve. He later realises that he loves her only to find that she has married someone else.
Billickin, Mrs	*Mystry of Edwin Drood (The)*	A cousin of Mr Buzzard.
Blackpool, Stephen	*Hard Times*	A worker at Bounderby's Mill who is falsely accused of a bank robbery and who dies before his name is cleared.
Bounderby, Josiah	*Hard Times*	A 'self-made man' who says he was abandoned as a child but in fact it was he that abandoned his own mother and later his wife.
Brownlow, Mr	*Oliver Twist*	A kind old gentleman who rescues Oliver and later adopts him.
Bullseye	*Oliver Twist*	Bill Sykes' dog.
Bumble, Mr	*Oliver Twist*	He is the parish Beadle at the workhouse where Oliver Twist is born.
C		
Carker, James	*Dombey and Son*	He embezzled money from the firm when he was younger and so is called 'the junior' despite being the elder brother.
Carton, Sydney	*Tale of Two Cities (A)*	It is his resemblance to Charles Darnay that allows him to take Darnay's place on the guillotine, thus saving his life.

CHARACTER	BOOK	COMMENTS
Cheeryble Brothers	Nicholas Nickleby	The benevolent business men, Charles and Edwin (Ned), who befriend and employ Nicholas Nickleby and his family.
Cheeryble Frank	Nicholas Nickleby	Nephew of the Cheeryble Brothers, he marries Kate Nickleby.
Chick, Louisa	Dombey and Son	She is the sister of Paul Dombey Sr. His catch phrase is: 'Make an effort'.
Chillip, Dr	David Copperfield	The physician who attended Clara Copperfield at the birth of her son, David Copperfield.
Chuffey	Martin Chuzzlewit	Devoted old clerk of Anthony Chuzzlewit.
Chuzzlewit, Martin	Martin Chuzzlewit	Son of Martin Sr with whom he falls out over the love he feels for Mary Graham; they are later reconciled and young Martin marries Mary Graham.
Chuzzlewit, Old Martin	Martin Chuzzlewit	Martin's grandfather who is suspicious of his hypocritical relatives.
Claypole, Noah	Oliver Twist	Assistant at Sowerberry's with whom Oliver fights.
Clennan, Arthur	Little Dorrit	After losing everything in a banking scam Arthur is imprisoned in Marshalsea where Amy cares for him when his health fails him. The novel comes to an end with the marriage of Arthur and Amy.
Cratchit, Bob	Christmas Carol (A)	Father of Tiny Tim and underpaid, overworked employee of Ebenezer Scrooge – until the reformation of Scrooge's character.
Creakle, Mr	David Copperfield	The cruel Headmaster of Salem House School to which the Murdstones sent David Copperfield.
Crewler, Sophy	David Copperfield	She married Traddles, David Copperfield's old school friend from Salem House; and whom he described as 'the dearest girl in the world'.
Crisparkle, the Revd Septimus	Mystery of Edwin Drood (The)	The kindly and good-natured minor canon of Cloisterham Cathedral.
Cruncher, Jerry	Tale of Two Cities (A)	Messenger for Tellson's Bank who also moonlights as a grave robber.

D

CHARACTER	BOOK	COMMENTS
Darnay, Charles	Tale of Two Cities (A)	He is tried for treason but is acquitted due to his resemblance to Sydney Carton. Carton later saves Darnay's life when he takes his place on the guillotine after he is arrested by the revolutionaries.

CHARACTER	BOOK	COMMENTS
Dartle, Rosa	*David Copperfield*	She is in love with Steerforth and is also a companion to his mother. When Steerforth was a child he marked her face by throwing a hammer in a fit of temper.
Dedlock, Lady	*Bleak House*	The wife of Sir Leicester Deadlock she is, unknown to her husband, the mother of Esther Summerson. When her secret is discovered she runs away and is found dead by her daughter.
Defarge, Ernest	*Tale of Two Cities (A)*	A leader among the revolutionaries.
Dennis	*Barnaby Rudge*	He was the hangman and one of the leaders of the no-popery riots.
Dick, Mr	*David Copperfield*	The eccentric lodger at the home of David's aunt, Betsey Trotwood, and one upon whose 'wisdom' she seems to bizarrely depend.
Dombey, Florence	*Dombey and Son*	Florence is the unwanted and neglected daughter of Paul Dombey and sister of Little Paul, whom she nurses when he is ill.
Dorrit, Amy	*Little Dorrit*	The daughter of William, she was born in the debtors' prison.
Dorrit, William	*Little Dorrit*	Father to Amy, Fanny and Edward he is also a long term inmate of Marshalsea debtors' prison.
Doyce, Daniel	*Little Dorrit*	He is the inventor of some mechanical wonder for which he is unable to get a patent in the Circumlocution Office, though he later successfully sells his invention abroad.
Durdles	*Mystery of Edwin Drood (The)*	The drunken stonemason who engraves tombstones for Cloisterham Cathedral.

E

Emily	*David Copperfield*	Mr Peggotty's niece and childhood friend of David who comes under the spell of Steerforth, David's 'dubious' friend.
Estella	*Great Expectations*	Estella is the woman Pip adores but she knows only how to ill-treat men and then when she marries she receives a taste of her own medicine.

F

Fagin	*Oliver Twist*	Probably one of the most well known of Dickens' characters (immortalised in the film and stage musical *Oliver*), he runs a

CHARACTER	BOOK	COMMENTS
Flite, Miss	*Bleak House*	gang of thieves and it is into his hands that Oliver falls when he runs away to London. An elderly, eccentric woman who owns a large number of tiny birds which she says will be released on 'the day of judgement'.
Fred	*Christmas Carol (A)*	The kind-hearted nephew of Scrooge and son of his adored sister, Fan. It is to his home that the Ghost of Christmas Present takes Scrooge.

G

CHARACTER	BOOK	COMMENTS
Gargery, Joe	*Great Expectations*	Joe, a blacksmith, is the husband of Pip's sister who mistreats both of them.
Ghost of Christmas Future	*Christmas Carol (A)*	This ghost shows Scrooge what could become of the sick child Tiny Tim and of himself too if he doesn't change his ways.
Ghost of Christmas Past	*Christmas Carol (A)*	This ghost takes Scrooge on a journey to remind him of the sad and lonely life he led as a child, thus showing him how he became the man he became.
Ghost of Christmas Present	*Christmas Carol (A)*	This ghost lets Scrooge experience the joy to be had as part of a family when he takes him to watch the Cratchits and the family of his nephew Fred celebrate Christmas. He is also taken to see the children, Ignorance and Want – those who need the wealthy, such as himself, to help ease their suffering.
Gradgrind, Thomas	*Hard Times*	The father of Thomas and Louisa and a man of high principles.
Gradgrind, Louisa	*Hard Times*	She is the eldest daughter of Thomas; she marries Bounderby, a man she doesn't love and who she later leaves to return to her father.
Gradgrind, Tom	*Hard Times*	He is the son of Thomas and is employed by Bounderby's bank from whom he steals.
Gummidge, Mrs	*David Copperfield*	She is the widow of Mr Peggotty's former partner, who had died in poverty, and is forever wailing that she is 'a lone lorn creetur'.

H

CHARACTER	BOOK	COMMENTS
Haggage, Dr	*Little Dorrit*	The graphically described dirty doctor at the Marshalsea prison who delivered Amy Dorrit.
Haredale, Geoffrey	*Barnaby Rudge*	He is suspected of being the killer of his

CHARACTER	BOOK	COMMENTS
Harmon, John	*Our Mutual Friend*	brother, Rueben, and so spends his life tracking down the real killer. Alias John Rokesmith, alias Julius Handford, he is the son of a wealthy dust contractor and heir to his fortune but only if he agrees to marry Bella Wilfer.
Havisham, Miss	*Great Expectations*	A bitter old woman who has never recovered from her experience of being jilted at the altar years before and who even continues to wear her wedding dress.
Hawk, Sir Mulberry	*Nicholas Nickleby*	Business associate of Ralph Nickleby, he flees to France after he kills Verisopht in a duel.
Headstone, Bradley	*Our Mutual Friend*	A schoolteacher who becomes obsessed with one of his pupils' sisters. She, however, is not interested, a fact which leads to attempted murder.
Heep, Uriah	*David Copperfield*	Probably the original slimy creep who was continually professing to be 'ever so 'umble' whilst he was in fact a two-faced villain.
Higden, Betty	*Our Mutual Friend*	She runs a 'minding school' for orphans and other children and has a deep-rooted fear of the workhouse.

J

CHARACTER	BOOK	COMMENTS
Jaggers, Mr	*Great Expectations*	Lawyer to Miss Havisham and Magwitch.
Jarley, Mrs	*Old Curiosity Shop (The)*	The proprietor of a travelling waxworks show.
Jarndyce, John	*Bleak House*	Jarndyce is the owner of Bleak House who adopts Esther Summerson.
Jasper, John	*Mystery of Edwin Drood (The)*	The uncle of Edwin Drood and a man with a drug habit, he has feelings for Edwin's fiancée but no one will ever know the outcome of this tale for Dickens died before he completed the book.
Jellyby, Mrs	*Bleak House*	Mrs Jellyby might be involved with many charities but she nevertheless neglects her large family.
Joe (the fat boy)	*Pickwick Papers (The)*	Mr Wardle's servant who has the ability to fall asleep at anytime – unless, that is, he is eating!
Jupe, Sissy	*Hard Times*	The abandoned 'circus child' who is taken in by Gradgrind.

CHARACTER	BOOK	COMMENTS
K		
Kenge	*Bleak House*	Known as 'Conversation Kenge', he is the solicitor for John Jarndyce.
Kenwigs	*Nicholas Nickleby*	Nicholas tutors the three daughters of the Kenwigs family who are neighbours of Newman Noggs.
Krook	*Bleak House*	Krook, otherwise known as the Lord Chancellor, collects courtroom documents. He is a drunken and illiterate individual.
L		
La Creevy, Miss	*Nicholas Nickleby*	The cheerful little miniature painter in the Strand from whom the Nicklebys lease lodgings.
Lammie, Alfred and Sophronia	*Our Mutual Friend*	A society couple who each marry incorrectly thinking that the other has money.
Landless, Neville and Helena	*Mystery of Edwin Drood (The)*	These are twins. Neville in a set-up, quarrels with Drood which results in him being a suspect after Drood disappears.
Leeford, Edward (aka Monks)	*Oliver Twist*	He is the half-brother of Oliver who attempts to corrupt him so that he alone might inherit all of their father's property.
Lillyvick ,Mr	*Nicholas Nickleby*	To the dismay of the Kenwigs – who had hoped to inherit his money – he secretly marries Henrietta Petowker.
Littimer	*David Copperfield*	He is the manservant of Steerforth and is involved in the elopement of Steerforth and Emily.
M		
Maggy	*Little Dorrit*	The granddaughter of Mrs Bangham and a faithful friend to Amy Dorrit.
Magwitch, Abel	*Great Expectations*	The father of Estella, Magwitch is also a convict whom Pip helps after he escapes from the prison ship. He is also the one who uses his fortune to increase Pip's expectations.
Manette, Dr Alexandre	*Tale of Two Cities (A)*	He was a prisoner in the Bastille for 18 years.
Manette, Lucie	*Tale of Two Cities (A)*	Daughter of Dr Manette, married to Charles Darney.

CHARACTER	BOOK	COMMENTS
Marchioness (The)	*Old Curiosity Shop (The)*	This is the name Dick Swiveller gives to the little servant who is kept locked away below stairs and whom he later marries.
Marley, Jacob	*Christmas Carol (A)*	Jacob Marley, the former partner of Ebenezer Scrooge, is dead but comes back to haunt Scrooge, for when he was alive he, like Scrooge was a miser and is now paying the price for it in the afterlife. He hopes to persuade Scrooge to mend his ways.
Micawber, Wilkins	*David Copperfield*	David lodges with Mr Micawber who always spends more than he earns and ends up in the debtors' prison. Before his fortune eventually turned, his catch phrase was 'Something will turn up'.
Mowcher, Miss	*David Copperfield*	She was the hairdresser and manicurist to Steerforth; she was also a dwarf.
Murdstone, Edward	*David Copperfield*	The stepfather of David and second husband of his mother Clara. He is a cruel man who treats David badly, sends him away to school and later to work in a bottle factory.
Murdstone, Jane	*David Copperfield*	She is Edward's sister, a hard, stone-faced woman who moved into David's childhood home when her brother , Edward, married David's mother.

N

CHARACTER	BOOK	COMMENTS
Nancy	*Oliver Twist*	One of the most famous of the Dickensian heroines, probably due to the films and musical based on the novel. Nancy is part of Fagin's gang when she befriends Oliver; she is also the girlfriend of evil Bill Sykes.
Neckett, Mr	*Bleak House*	The Sheriff's Officer, generally referred to as Coavinses, the name of the sponging house which he keeps.
Nell's Grandfather	*Old Curiosity Shop (The)*	He has a secret gambling habit and to fund this borrows money from the evil Quilp.
Nemo	*Bleak House*	The law-writer.
Nickleby, Nicholas	*Nicholas Nickleby*	Trying to take care of his mother and sister after his father's death he turns to his Uncle Ralph who brings nothing but trouble to the Nickleby family.
Nickleby, Kate	*Nicholas Nickleby*	Sister of Nicholas.
Nickleby, Mrs	*Nicholas Nickleby*	Mother of Nicholas and Kate, she is rather

CHARACTER	BOOK	COMMENTS
		muddleheaded and naive; she is also unaware of much that is going on around her.
Nickleby, Ralph	*Nicholas Nickleby*	The evil, unscrupulous uncle of Nicholas and Kate and father of Smike.
Nipper, Susan	*Dombey and Son*	Florence Dombey's maid, she is dismissed when she confronts Paul Dombey about his treatment of Florence.
Noggs, Newman	*Nicholas Nickleby*	Ralph's clerk and a close friend of Nicholas; he is also an alcoholic.
Nubbles, Kit	*Old Curiosity Shop (The)*	A shop boy at the Old Curiosity Shop, which is owned by Little Nell's grandfather, he is devoted to Little Nell.

P

CHARACTER	BOOK	COMMENTS
Pardiggle, Mrs	*Bleak House*	A lady 'distinguished for rapacious benevolence'.
Peggotty, Clara	*David Copperfield*	The archetypal nanny to whom David was devoted. Her loyalty to David and his family never wanes.
Peggotty, Daniel	*David Copperfield*	Clara Peggotty's brother who lives in an upturned boat on the beach at Yarmouth.
Pegler, Mrs	*Hard Times*	Bounderby's mother, whom he deserted.
Pelt, Soloman	*Pickwick Papers (The)*	A shady lawyer engaged by Tony Weller.
Pickwick, Samuel	*Pickwick Papers (The)*	Samuel Pickwick travels around England, seeking out adventures with his friends.
Pip	*Great Expectations*	Pip is brought up and mistreated by his older sister Mrs Joe Gargery. He helps the escaped convict Magwitch who later becomes his secret benefactor.

Q

CHARACTER	BOOK	COMMENTS
Quilp, Betsey	*Old Curiosity Shop (The)*	Unlike her husband she is a kind soul; after his death she happily remarries.
Quilp, Daniel	*Old Curiosity Shop (The)*	Quilp is the evil dwarf who lends money to Nell's grandfather. He later drowns in the Thames.

R

CHARACTER	BOOK	COMMENTS
Radfoot, George	*Our Mutual Friend*	He exchanges identities with John Harmon, which leads to his eventual death.
Rudge, Barnaby	*Barnaby Rudge*	A simple straightforward boy who falls in with a bad crowd and as a result becomes involved in the Gordon Riots. He is later

CHARACTER	BOOK	COMMENTS
Rudge, Barnaby Sr	*Barnaby Rudge*	sentenced to death but with the help of Gabriel Varden is granted a reprieve. Barnaby's father, Mary's husband, and Reuben Haredale's murderer.

S

CHARACTER	BOOK	COMMENTS
Sapsea, Thomas	*Mystery of Edwin Drood (The)*	A pompous auctioneer and mayor of Cloisterham.
Sawyer, Bob	*Pickwick Papers (The)*	A medical student who was the drinking buddy of Benjamin Allen.
Scrooge, Ebenezer	*Christmas Carol (A)*	A miser who is taught the error of his ways when his dead partner, Jacob Marley, sends three Ghosts to visit him.
Sikes, Bill	*Oliver Twist*	A vicious thief and the object of Nancy's affections, he murders Nancy when he discovers that she has been helping Oliver and is later killed himself in an accident whilst being pursued by the police.
Skewton, The Honourable Mrs	*Dombey and Son*	She is the mother of Edith Granger and is 70 years old, though she tries to appear much younger by the heavy, over-use of cosmetics.
Smike	*Nicholas Nickleby*	Smike was abandoned as a child at Dotheboys Hall school where he was appallingly treated by the evil Squeers; he is the secret son of Ralph Nickleby and dies of TB.
Snevellici, Mr, Mrs and Miss	*Nicholas Nickleby*	Actors in Crummles' Company.
Snodgrass, Augustus	*Pickwick Papers (The)*	A member of the Pickwick Club who fancies himself as a poet – though he has not actually written any poetry!
Snubbin, Mr Serjeant	*Pickwick Papers (The)*	Counsel for the defendant in Bardell v Pickwick.
Soloman, Daisy	*Barnaby Rudge*	The Parish clerk and bell ringer at Chigwell.
Sowerberry	*Oliver Twist*	An undertaker for whom Oliver is sent to work when he is still a child.
Sparkler, Edmund	*Little Dorrit*	A man of limited ability and talents he offers marriage to all sorts of different and unsuitable young ladies before finally marrying Fanny Dorrit; they lose everything in the Merdle banking scam.
Sparsit, Mrs	*Hard Times*	Housekeeper of Bounderby, she is a busybody who causes problems between

CHARACTER	BOOK	COMMENTS
Spenlow, Dora	*David Copperfield*	Bounderby and his wife, Louisa. She is the wife of David Copperfield and he tries to teach her how to keep house, but fails miserably as she is a giddy and spoilt scatterbrain. Dora dies young.
Squeers, Fanny	*Nicholas Nickleby*	The daughter of Wackford Squeers from whom she has inherited a nasty disposition. She falls in love with Nicholas, though not he with her!
Squeers, Wackford	*Nicholas Nickleby*	He is the proprietor of Dotheboys Hall, a school where unwanted boys are sent – for him to mistreat. Nicholas becomes an assistant master there and after seeing the evil ways of Squeers, he thrashes him.
Stareleigh, Mr Justice	*Pickwick Papers (The)*	The judge in the case of Bardell v Pickwick.
Steerforth, James	*David Copperfield*	An arrogant, self-centred charmer who fools most, including David, into admiration of him.
Stryver	*Tale of Two Cities (A)*	Another man in love with Lucie Manette.
Summerson, Esther	*Bleak House*	Esther is brought up by her aunt: after the death of her aunt she is adopted by John Jarndyce which later leads to a very complicated love life!
Swiveller, Dick	*Old Curiosity Shop (The)*	After putting the half-starved servant girl, The Marchioness, through school he marries her.

$\mathcal{T}$

CHARACTER	BOOK	COMMENTS
Tigg, Montigue	*Martin Chuzzlewit*	He is a con man who works under the two names Tigg Montigue and Montigue Tigg.
Tiny Tim	*Christmas Carol (A)*	The sickly youngest child in the Cratchit family.
Tox, Lucretia	*Dombey and Son*	She loves Paul Dombey Sr but after his first wife's death he marries someone else. Despite this she remains loyal to him throughout.
Traddles, Tommy	*David Copperfield*	David's best friend at Salem House School who frequently takes a beating.
Trent, Nelly	*Old Curiosity Shop (The)*	Known as Little Nell she helps her grandfather escape the clutches of evil Quilp but dies as a result of the hardships they endure.
Trotter, Job	*Pickwick Papers (The)*	Alfred Jingle's servant.
Trotwood, Betsey	*David Copperfield*	David's eccentric aunt who, though strange, has a heart of gold.

CHARACTER	BOOK	COMMENTS
Tulkinghorn	*Bleak House*	Lawyer to the Dedlock family he is murdered by Hortense, Lady Dedlock's former maid, when he discovers her mistress's secret and tries to make personal gain from it.
Tungay	*David Copperfield*	Creakle's one legged assistant, (he has a wooden leg) at Salem House School.
Tupman, Tracy	*Pickwick Papers (The)*	A member of the Pickwick Club, with an eye for the ladies.
Turveydrop, Mr & Prince	*Bleak House*	Mr Turveydrop owns a dance Academy where his son, Prince, gives dancing lessons.
Twist, Oliver	*Oliver Twist*	One of the most famous of Dickens' characters, which in itself is strange because he is also one of the most normal and ineffectual characters, having no strange idiosyncrasies. He was born in a workhouse where he uttered the famous words, "Please Sir, I want some more."

$\mathcal{U}$

CHARACTER	BOOK	COMMENTS
Varden, Gabriel	*Barnaby Rudge*	An honest locksmith, owner of the Golden Key and saviour of Barnaby Rudge.
Venus, Mr	*Our Mutual Friend*	He is a taxidermist and a general practitioner in bones; he is in love with Pleasant Riderhood who, originally despising his occupation, finally relents and marries him.
Veneering, Hamilton and Anastasia	*Our Mutual Friend*	A High Society couple who throw regular dinner parties. It is at one of these parties that the story of John Harmon is discovered.

$\mathcal{W}$

CHARACTER	BOOK	COMMENTS
Wegg, Silas	*Our Mutual Friend*	A one-legged impudent old rascal.
Weller, Samuel	*Pickwick Papers (The)*	Mr Pickwick's devoted servant.
Wemmick	*Great Expectations*	He is the clerk to Mr Jaggers, the lawyer.
Westlock, John	*Martin Chuzzlewit*	A one-time pupil of Mr Pecksniff.
Wickfield, Agnes	*David Copperfield*	David's true love, she becomes his second wife after the death of Dora.
Wickfield, Mr	*David Copperfield*	The father of Agnes and lawyer to Betsey Trotwood whose over indulgence in wine makes him very vulnerable to the slimy ways of Uriah Heap.

CHARACTER	BOOK	COMMENTS
Wilfer, Bella	*Our Mutual Friend*	Old Harmon's will states that his son, John, should marry Bella if he is to gain
Willet, John	*Barnaby Rudge*	The host of the Maypole Inn.
Winkle, Nathaniel	*Pickwick Papers (The)*	his inheritance; he disappears but they later meet, fall in love and marry anyway. A member of the Pickwick Club he travels around with Samuel Pickwick and his friends. Winkle falsely claims to be a sportsman.
Wren, Jenny	*Our Mutual Friend*	This is the business name of the doll's dressmaker; her real name being Fanny Cleaver.

SOME MEMORABLE DICKENSIAN QUOTATIONS

There are great writers and there are 'great' writers. Those who belong in the second category are there because they write more than a great story, craft more than wonderfully visual characters and use the English language in a more unique and special way than is the norm. They are in that second category because they have left, or will leave, behind a legacy that goes beyond the book itself. If it were the book that was merely their legacy then surely its riches would be confined to those who had actually read the work. However, the legacy these writers leave behind is the fact that their works become intrinsically entwined in the lives of future generations, irrespective of whether they have an interest or knowledge of the written word. Many lines from the 'greats' become a part of our vernacular and so the man in the street who might consider himself poorly read is actually, without realising it, quoting lines from great literary works; that indeed is a very special legacy. Now browse through the lines below and perhaps discover that you have for years been using lines first penned by Dickens as a part of your everyday speak!

A

...accidents will occur in the best-regulated families...	*David Copperfield*
A dangerous quality, if real; and a not less dangerous one, if feigned	*Dombey and Son*
...am as light as a feather, I am as happy as an angel, I am as merry as a schoolboy. I am as giddy as a drunken man	*Christmas Carol (A)*
Annual income twenty pounds, annual expenditure	*David Copperfield*

nineteen six, result happiness. Annual income
twenty pounds, annual expenditure twenty pounds
ought and six, result misery

Anything that makes a noise is satisfactory to a
crowd

A word in earnest is as good as a speech

Old Curiosity Shop (The)

Bleak House

B

Barkis is willin'

David Copperfield

C

Change begets change

Martin Chuzzlewit

D

Darkness is cheap, and Scrooge liked it
Death doesn't change us more than life

Christmas Carol (A)
Old Curiosity Shop (The)

F

...for gold conjures up a mist about a man, more
destructive of all his old senses and lulling to his
feelings than the fumes of charcoal

...for not an orphan in the wide world can be so
deserted as the child who is an outcast from a living
parent's love.

Nicholas Nickleby

Dombey and Son

G

God bless us every one

Christmas Carol (A)

H

Heaven above was blue, and earth beneath was
green; the river glistened like a path of diamonds
in the sun; the birds poured forth their songs from
the shady trees; the lark soared high above the
waving corn; and the deep buzz of insects filled the air

Heaven knows we need never be ashamed of our
tears, for they are rain upon the blinding dust of
earth, overlying our hard hearts

He did each single thing, as if he did nothing else
He was bolder in the daylight – most men are

Nicholas Nickleby

Great Expectations

Dombey and Son
Pickwick Papers (The)

I

I don't profess to be profound; but I do lay claim to
common sense

I had considered how the things that never happen,
are often as much realities to us, in their effects, as
those that are accomplished.

David Copperfield

David Copperfield

I hope that real love and truth are stronger in the end than any evil or misfortune in the world.	*David Copperfield*
In a word, I was too cowardly to do what I knew to be right, as I had been too cowardly to avoid doing what I knew to be wrong	*Great Expectations*
In the majority of cases, conscience is an elastic and very flexible article	*Old Curiosity Shop (The)*
In truth, no men on earth can cheer like Englishmen...	*Little Dorrit*
It is a far, far, better thing that I do, than I have ever done; it is a far, far, better rest that I go to, than I have ever known.	*Tale of Two Cities (A)*
It is a melancholy truth that even great men have their poor relations.	*Bleak House*
It is a most miserable thing to feel ashamed of home.	*Great Expectations*
It is good to be children sometimes, and never better than at Christmas, when its mighty Founder was a child himself.	*Christmas Carol (A)*
It was a harder day's journey than yesterday's, for there were long and weary hills to climb; and in journeys, as in life, it is a great deal easier to go downhill than up	*Nicholas Nickleby*
It was one of those March days when the sun shines hot and the wind blows cold: when it is summer in the light, and winter in the shade	*Great Expectations*
It was the best of times, it was the worst of times	*Tale of Two Cities (A)*
...I was not aware at first to whom I had the pleasure of objecting	*David Copperfield*
I went away, dear Agnes, loving you. I stayed away, loving you. I returned home, loving you!	*David Copperfield*
I will die here where I have walked. And I will walk here, though I am in my grave. I will walk here until the pride of this house is humbled	*Bleak House*
I will honour Christmas in my heart, and try to keep it all the year. I will live in the Past, the Present, and the Future. The Spirits of all Three shall strive within me. I will not shut out the lessons that they teach. Oh, tell me I may sponge away the writing on this stone!	*Christmas Carol (A)*

L

Love is in all things a most wonderful teacher	*Our Mutual Friend*
Loves and Cupids took to flight afraid, and Martyrdom had no such torment in its painted history of suffering.	*Dombey and Son*
Love, though said to be afflicted with blindness, is a vigilant watchman	*Our Mutual Friend*

M

Mrs Joe was a very clean housekeeper, but had an exquisite art of making her cleanliness more uncomfortable and unacceptable than dirt itself	*Great Expectations*
My advice is, never do tomorrow what you can do today. Procrastination is the thief of time	*David Copperfield*
Mystery and disappointment are not absolutely indispensable to the growth of love, but they are, very often, its powerful auxiliaries	*Nicholas Nickleby*

N

Never...be mean in anything; never be false; never be cruel	*David Copperfield*
No one who can read, ever looks at a book, even unopened on a shelf, like one who cannot	*Our Mutual Friend*

O

Once a gentleman, and always a gentleman	*Little Dorrit*

P

Peggotty!...Do you mean to say, child, that any human being has gone into a Christian church, and got herself named Peggotty	*David Copperfield*
Pride is one of the seven deadly sins; but it cannot be the pride of a mother in her children, for that is a compound of two cardinal virtues – faith and hope	*Nicholas Nickleby*

R

Rich folks may ride on camels, but it ain't so easy for 'em to see out of a needle's eye	*Martin Chuzzlewit*
...Ride on! Rough-shod if need be, smooth-shod if that will do, but ride on! Ride on over all obstacles, and win the race!	*David Copperfield*

S

...she indulged in melancholy – that cheapest and most accessible of luxuries	*Dombey and Son*
Surprises, like misfortunes, seldom come alone	*Oliver Twist*

T

Take nothing on its looks; take everything on evidence. There's no better rule	*Great Expectations*
The children of the very poor are not brought up, but dragged up	*Bleak House*
The flowers that sleep by night, opened their gentle	*Old Curiosity Shop (The)*

eyes and turned them to the day. The light, creation's mind, was everywhere, and all things owned its power	
The plain rule is to do nothing in the dark, to be a party to nothing underhanded or mysterious, and never to put his foot where he cannot see the ground	Bleak House
…there are books of which the backs and covers are by far the best parts	Oliver Twist
There can be no disparity in marriage like unsuitability of mind and purpose	David Copperfield
'The school is not quite deserted,' said the Ghost. 'A solitary child, neglected by his friends, is left there still.'	Christmas Carol (A)
The sun does not shine upon this fair earth to meet frowning eyes, depend upon it	Nicholas Nickleby
The Sun himself is weak when he first rises, and gathers strength and courage as the day gets on	Old Curiosity Shop (The)

W

When we came within sight of the sea, the waves on the horizon, caught at intervals above the rolling abyss, were like glimpses of another shore with towers and buildings	David Copperfield
Whether I shall turn out to be the hero of my own life, or whether that station will be held by anybody else, these pages must show.	David Copperfield

Y

You do not know…what men have done to win it [gold], and how they have found, too late, that it glitters brightest at a distance, and turns quite dim and dull when handled	Barnaby Rudge
You will profit by the failure, and will avoid it another time	Little Dorrit

DICKENS THE SOCIAL WRITER

So we now can appreciate Charles Dickens gave us gripping story lines, eccentric and colourfully vivid characters as well as a wealth of memorable quotations. But in addition to all of this he is also recognised as the quintessentially Victorian author; a social author who through his writings has ensured that we have a permanent reminder of life in his time.

He also wrote a great deal from his own personal experiences, meaning that his work as well as in some cases being a cathartic piece was also a social and historical documentation of Victorian life. We find that Dickens himself 'appears' in works such as *Oliver Twist*, *David Copperfield*, *Bleak House* and *Hard Times*. Dickens' father, Charles, seemed to have an inbuilt incapacity for financial management, the result being that the family had first-hand experience of life in a Victorian debtors' prison and so he was acutely aware of the miseries suffered by the poor; of interrupted educational opportunities and of the plight of child labourers. For when his family hit hard times – brought on by his father's inadequacies – his education had been halted and he had been forced to work as a young boy in a blacking factory.

As with many writers, Dickens' observational, mental stockroom was full of characters and events extracted from his life. *David Copperfield* features the ever optimistic Mr Micawber, a gentleman with no sense where money is concerned but who is always sure that 'something will turn up' and who is drawn from Dickens' own somewhat impecunious father. His mother appears as the querulous Mrs Nickleby in *Nicholas Nickleby*, whilst the rejection he felt when considered an unsuitable suitor for Maria Beadnell manifests itself in the novel *David Copperfield* in the form of Dora Spenlow and again in the character Flora Finching in *Little Dorrit*.

Dickens' beloved home at Gad's Hill House which is now an independent school

EXPERIENCE YESTERDAY'S WORLD OF CHARLES DICKENS TODAY

You can enjoy and feel the Dickensian world today by visiting the Charles Dickens Museum in London, which is situated at 48 Doughty Street and is the only surviving London home of Dickens. Here you will find four floors of paintings, rare editions, manuscripts, original furniture and many other items relating to the life of Charles Dickens.

Dickens might only have lived in Doughty Street for a comparatively short period of time (1837-1839) but it was nevertheless in this house that he penned some of his greatest works, including *The Pickwick Papers, Oliver Twist* and *Nicholas Nickleby*. Imagine being able to stand in the house that first rang with those immortal words, 'Please, Sir, I want some more' and to be able to soak up the atmosphere of the inspirational surroundings. The following successes of these works meant that his financial position was such that he could afford to move to more larger premises, which would be more suited to his growing family's needs and so after the birth of their third child, the Dickens family moved to a new home at 1 Devonshire Terrace, Regents Park, London. Sadly though it is not possible to visit this house for it was demolished in 1959, a fate which almost befell Doughty Street in 1923, until it was saved by the Dickens Fellowship who raised the mortgage and bought the freehold so that future generations might enjoy the past world of Dickens.

However, of all his homes Charles Dickens' heart was firmly in the hearth of Gads Hill Place, a house he saw and longed for as a child and one which, when he achieved financial success he was able to buy, and where he ended his days. This house, however, is now an independent school called Gads Hill School with not really option to visit, unless you wish to send your children there to be educated. Imagine just how the knowledge of the literary heights achieved by one of its previous occupants must inspire all those young people to enjoy the fine education now on offer there, and how fitting that the final house of a master of the English language should now be a school to educate future generations of possible literary scholars.

AND FINALLY

• As with many writers both before and after him, Dickens had a great affinity with the stage and in fact very nearly became an actor himself and so ever the actor, he was known as the best after dinner speaker of his age
• Much of Dickens' work first appeared serialised in magazines before being published in book form. This meant that the masses – unable to afford the price of a book – could read and enjoy his writings; even the illiterate populace could enjoy his works as his colourful writing lent itself so admirably to many stage versions at the time
• His novel *A Christmas Carol* was both conceived and written within a few weeks
• His novel *The Mystery of Edwin Drood* was unfinished when he died

Chapter Three

Looking for Information

This is a section of browsing opportunities which I hope will whet your appetite for further exploration into the world of the classics. After reading about the literary giants then you could be forgiven for thinking that it's all down hill from here and that everyone else is second best! Not so, for Literature is the 'Land of Giants', as you are about to witness for yourself in this section. I hope that here you will find your favourite author and perhaps many others you have never come across before, or perhaps never even heard of for that matter. For ease of reading they are organised according to the century in which they lived. Of course, many straddle two centuries and so I have put them into the one I think they belong. So, if you don't find your own personal favourite where you expect to find them, then try looking in the neighbouring century.

As we move on to discover, century by century, the greatest writers that ever lived, or that are in fact still living, we must also pause to take a brief look at the life in those centuries, for the way in which people behaved or were expected to behave in times gone by is crucial to the accurate construction of a written piece, whether the piece depicts life 20 years ago or 200 years ago. There are certain rules and conventions, some written and some passed down orally, which dictate the correct and acceptably polite way to behave in society and then there are sub divisions in all societies, such as professions and clubs, where the rules become more specific to them and them alone. These rules, which are laid down according to time and place, generally come under the heading of 'etiquette'.

These influences upon each of us are to be found not only in present events but in anything preceding today, for our past life shapes the way in which we think and behave; equally so future events, which represent both our hopes and fears, play a part in the shaping of present day man; we may live today, but we are actually the products of yesterday and tomorrow.

I am not who I am,
But who I was
And who I will be
Anon

All writers must first, therefore, have a basic knowledge about the times in which their novels are set, the times in which their characters lived; they should appreciate the expectations and constraints of each era. For it is these expectations and constraints together with the political climate, national and personal cash flow, social status, the education system, new discoveries and inventions, the place of women in society and so on that actually determines 'The correct way in which to behave'.

There always has been – and I daresay always will be – a correct way in which we are expected to behave in certain situations. This varies from century to century of course and yet still has one basic rule from which all other rules evolve and that is to treat others as you wish to be treated. The word etiquette itself actually dates back from Seventeenth Century France where King Louis XIV used small placards or 'etiquettes' to remind his guests at court of the expected and correct rules of behaviour. The oldest guide to etiquette, however, was surprisingly written circa 3550BC by the Egyptian philosopher Ptah-Hotep and listed rules of behaviour to be passed down from one generation to the next. Whilst in America, the father of American etiquette was actually George Washington (1732-1799), who compiled a list of *Rules of Civility and Decent Behaviour In Company and Conversation*. This was based on earlier rulebooks from France and England though interestingly many of Washington's rules remain in use to this day. So if you read through these rules below you will find that many are pertinent to today, whilst others give a real feel for Eighteenth Century manners and expectations; but above all you will find them a fascinating and entertaining read that will serve to remind you of the true and actual force of simple and straightforward good manners. Take these rules back in time, or take them forward, they will still work:

Rules of Civility and Decent Behaviour in Company and Conversation – George Washington

1. Every action done in company ought to be with some sign of respect to those that are present.
2. When in company, put not your hands to any part of the body not usually discovered.
3. Show nothing to your friend that may affright him.
4. In the presence of others, sing not to yourself with a humming voice, or drum with your fingers or feet.

5. If you cough, sneeze, sigh, or yawn, do it not loud but privately, and speak not in your yawning, but put your handkerchief or hand before your face and turn aside.

6. Sleep not when others speak; sit not when others stand; speak not when you should hold your peace; walk not on when others stop.

7. Put not off your clothes in the presence of others, nor go out your chamber half dressed.

8. At play and attire, it's good manners to give place to the last comer, and affect not to speak louder than ordinary.

9. Spit not into the fire, nor stoop low before it; neither put your hands into the flames to warm them, nor set your feet upon the fire, especially if there be meat before it.

10. When you sit down, keep your feet firm and even; without putting one on the other or crossing them.

11. Shift not yourself in the sight of others, nor gnaw your nails.

12. Shake not the head, feet, or legs; roll not the eyes; lift not one eyebrow higher than the other, wry not the mouth, and bedew no man's face with your spittle by [approaching too near] him [when] you speak.

13. Kill no vermin, or fleas, lice, ticks, etc. in the sight of others; if you see any filth or thick spittle put your foot dexterously upon it; if it be upon the clothes of your companions, put it off privately, and if it be upon your own clothes, return thanks to him who puts it off.

14. Turn not your back to others, especially in speaking; jog not the table or desk on which another reads or writes; lean not upon anyone.

15. Keep your nails clean and short, also your hands and teeth clean, yet without showing any great concern for them.

16. Do not puff up the cheeks, loll not out the tongue with the hands, or beard, thrust out the lips, or bite them, or keep the lips too open or too close.

17. Be no flatterer, neither play with any that delight not to be played withal.

18. Read no letter, books, or papers in company, but when there is a necessity for the doing of it, you must ask leave; come not near the books or writings of another so as to read them unless desired, or give your opinion of them unasked, also look not nigh when another is writing a letter.

19. Let your countenance be pleasant but in serious matters somewhat grave.

20. The gestures of the body must be suited to the discourse you are upon.

21. Reproach none for the infirmities of nature, nor delight to put them that have in mind of thereof.

22. Show not yourself glad at the misfortune of another though he were your enemy.

23. When you see a crime punished, you may be inwardly pleased; but [damaged manuscript] show pity to the suffering offender.

24. Do not laugh too loud or too much at any Public Spectacle.

25. Superfluous compliments and all affectation of ceremonies are to be avoided, yet where due they are not to be neglected.

26. In pulling off your hat to persons of distinction, as noblemen, justices, churchmen, etc., make a reverence, bowing more or less according to the custom of the better bred, and quality of the persons; among your equals expect not always that they should begin with you first; but to pull off the hat when there is no need is affectation, in the manner of saluting and re-saluting in a word keep to the most usual custom.

27. Tis ill manners to bed one more eminent than yourself be covered, as well as not to do it to whom it is due. Likewise he that makes too much haste to put on his hat does not well, yet he ought to put it on at the first, or at most the second time of being asked; now what is herein spoken, of qualification in behavior or saluting ought to be taking place and sitting down for ceremonies without bounds are troublesome.

28. If any one come to speak to you while you are sitting, stand up, though he be your inferior, and when you present seats, let it be to everyone according to his degree.

29. When you meet with one of greater quality than yourself, stop, and retire, especially if it be at a door or any straight place, to give way for him to pass.

30. In walking the highest place in most countries hand; therefore place yourself on the left of him whom you desire to honor: but if three walk together the middle place is the most honorable; the wall is usually given to the most worthy if two walk together.

31. If anyone far surpasses others, either in age, estate, or merits [and] would give place to a meaner than himself, the same ought not to accept it, [save he offer] it above once or twice.

32. To one that is your equal, or not much inferior, you are to give the chief place in your lodging, and he to whom it is offered ought at the first to refuse it, but at the second to accept though not without acknowledging his own unworthiness.

33. They that are in dignity or in office have in all places precedency, but whilst they are young, they ought to respect those that are their equals in birth or other qualities, though they have no public charge.

34. It is good manners to prefer them to whom we speak before ourselves, especially if they be above us, with whom in no sort we ought to begin.

35. Let your discourse with men of business be short and comprehensive.

36. Artificers and persons of low degree ought not to use many ceremonies to lords or others of high degree, but respect and highly honor them, and those of high degree ought to treat them with affability and courtesy, without arrogance.

37. In speaking to men of quality do not lean nor look them full in the face, nor approach too near them at left. Keep a full pace from them.

38. In visiting the sick, do not presently play the physician if you be not knowing therein.

39. In writing or speaking, give to every person his due title according to his degree and the custom of the place.

40. Strive not with your superior in argument, but always submit your argument to others with modesty.

41. Undertake not to teach your equal in the art himself professes; it [damaged manuscript] of arrogance.

42. Let thy ceremonies in Courtesy be proper to the Dignity of his place with whom thou converses for it is absurd to act the same with a Clown and a Prince.

43. Do not express joy before one sick in pain, for that contrary passion will aggravate his misery.

44. When a man does all he can, though it succeed not well, blame not him that did it.

45. Being to advise or reprehend any one, consider whether it ought to be in public or in private, and presently or at some other time; in what terms to do it; and in reproving show no signs of cholor but do it with all sweetness and mildness.

46. Take all admonitions thankfully in what time or place soever given, but afterwards not being culpable take a time and place convenient to let him know it that gave them.

47. Mock not nor jest at a thing of importance. Break no jests that are sharp, biting, and if you deliver anything witty and pleasant, abstain from laughing thereat yourself.

48. Where in [wherein] you reprove another be unblameable yourself, for example is more prevalent than precepts.

49. Use no reproachful language against any one; neither curse nor revile.

50. Be not hasty to believe flying reports to the disparagement of any.

51. Wear not your clothes foul, or ripped, or dusty, but see they be brushed once every day at least and take heed that you approach not to any uncleanness.

52. In your apparel be modest and endeavor to accommodate nature, rather than to procure admiration; keep to the fashion of your equals, such as are civil and orderly with respect to time and places.

53. Run not in the streets, neither go too slowly, nor with mouth open; go not shaking of arms, nor upon the toes, nor in a dancing [damaged manuscript].

54. Play not the peacock, looking everywhere about you, to see if you be well decked, if your shoes fit well, if your stockings sit neatly and clothes handsomely.

55. Eat not in the streets, nor in your house, out of season.

56. Associate yourself with men of good quality if you esteem your own reputation; for 'tis better to be alone than in bad company.

57. In walking up and down in a house, only with one in company if he be greater than yourself, at the first give him the right hand and stop not till he does and be not the first that turns, and when you do turn let it be with your face towards him; if he be a man of great quality walk not with him cheek by jowl but somewhat behind him but yet in such a manner that he may easily speak to you.

58. Let your conversation be without malice or envy, for 'tis a sign of a tractable and commendable nature, and in all causes of passion permit reason to govern.

59. Never express anything unbecoming, nor act against the rules before your inferiors.

60. Be not immodest in urging your friends to discover a secret.

61. Utter not base and frivolous things among grave and learned men, nor very difficult questions or subjects among the ignorant, or things hard to be believed; stuff not your discourse with sentences among your betters nor equals.

62. Speak not of doleful things in a time of mirth or at the table; speak not of melancholy things or death and wounds, and if others mention them, change if you can the discourse; tell not your dream, but to your intimate.

63. A man ought not to value himself of his achievements or rare qualities [damaged manuscript] virtue or kindred.

64. Break not a jest where none take pleasure in mirth; laugh not alone, nor at all without occasion; deride no man's misfortune though there seem to be some cause.

65. Speak not injurious words neither in jest nor earnest; scoff at none although they give occasion.

66. Be not forward but friendly and courteous, the first to salute, hear, and answer; and be not pensive when it's a time to converse.

67. Detract not from others, neither be excessive in commanding.

68. Go not thither, where you know not whether you shall be welcome or not; give not advice [without] being asked, and when desired do it briefly.

69. If two contend together take not the part of either unconstrained, and be not obstinate in your own opinion; in things indifferent be of the major side.

70. Reprehend not the imperfections of others, for that belongs to parents, masters, and superiors.

71. Gaze not on the marks or blemishes of others and ask not how they came. What you may speak in secret to your friend, deliver not before others.

72. Speak not in an unknown tongue in company but in your own language and that as those of quality do and not as the vulgar; sublime matters treat seriously.

73. Think before you speak; pronounce not imperfectly, nor bring out your words too hastily, but orderly and distinctly.

74. When another speaks, be attentive yourself; and disturb not the audience. If any hesitate in his words, help him not nor prompt him without desired; interrupt him not, nor answer him till his speech has ended.

75. In the midst of discourse [damaged manuscript] but if you perceive any stop because of [damaged manuscript]; to proceed: If a person of quality comes in while you're conversing, it's handsome to repeat what was said before.

76. While you are talking, point not with your finger at him of whom you discourse, nor approach too near him to whom you talk especially to his face.

77. Treat with men at fit times about business and whisper not in the company of others.

78. Make no comparisons and if any of the company be commended for any brave act of virtue, commend not another for the same.

79. Be not apt to relate news if you know not the truth thereof. In discoursing of things you have heard, name not your author always; a secret discover not.

80. Be not tedious in discourse or in reading unless you find the company pleased therewith.

81. Be not curious to know the affairs of others, neither approach those that speak in private.

82. Undertake not what you cannot perform but be careful to keep your promise.

83. When you deliver a matter do it without passion and with discretion, however mean the person be you do it to.

84. When your superiors talk to anybody neither speak nor laugh.

85. In company of those of higher quality than yourself, speak not 'til you are asked a question, then stand upright, put off your hat and answer in few words.

86. In disputes, be not so desirous to overcome as not to give liberty to one to deliver his opinion and submit to the judgment of the major part, specially if they are judges of the dispute.

87. [damaged manuscript] as becomes a man grave, settled, and attentive.

88. [damaged manuscript] predict not at every turn what others say.

89. Be not diverse in discourse; make not many digressions; nor repeat often the same manner of discourse.

90. Speak not evil of the absent, for it is unjust.

91. Being set at meat scratch not, neither spit, cough, or blow your nose except there's a necessity for it.

92. Make no show of taking great delight in your the table; neither find great delight in your victuals; feed not with greediness; eat your bread with a knife; lean not on the table; neither find fault with what you eat.

93. Take no salt or cut bread with your knife greasy.

94. Entertaining anyone at table it is decent to present him with meat; undertake not to help others desired by the master.

95. If you soak bread in the sauce, let it be no more than what you put in your mouth at a time and blow not your broth at table; let it stay till it cools of itself.

96. Put not your meat to your mouth with your knife in your hand; neither spit forth the stones of any fruit pie upon a dish nor cast anything under the table.

97. It's unbecoming to heap much to one's meat keep your fingers clean; when foul wipe them on a corner of your table napkin.

98. Put not another bite into your mouth till the former be swallow; let not your morsels be too big.

99. Drink not nor talk with your mouth full; neither gaze about you while you are a drinking.

100. Drink not too leisurely nor yet too hastily. Before and after drinking wipe your lips; breathe not then or ever with too great a noise, for it is an evil.

101. Cleanse not your teeth with the tablecloth, napkin, fork, or knife; but if others do it, let it be done without a peep to them.

102. Rinse not your mouth in the presence of others.

103. It is out of use to call upon the company often to eat; nor need you drink to others every time you drink.

104. In company of your betters be not [damaged manuscript] than they are; lay not your arm but [damaged manuscript].

105. It belongs to the chiefest in company to unfold his napkin and fall to meat first; but he ought then to begin in time and to dispatch with dexterity that the slowest may have time allowed him.

106. Be not angry at table whatever happens and if you have reason to be so, show it not but on a cheerful countenance especially if there be strangers, for good humor makes one dish of meat and whey.

107. Set not yourself at the upper of the table but if it be your due, or that the master of the house will have it so, contend not, lest you should trouble the company.

108. If others talk at table be attentive but talk not with meat in your mouth.

109. When you speak of God or his Attributes, let it be seriously; reverence, honor and obey your natural parents although they be poor.

110. Let your recreations be manful not sinful.

111. Labor to keep alive in your breast that little spark of celestial fire called conscience.

Some of the social expectations in earlier centuries are quaint, amusing, and sometimes even downright ridiculous, but knowledge of them is necessary for the writer in order that he can stamp his work with a seal of 'authenticity'. Other influences upon a writer and his work, in addition to those mentioned earlier, include the questions of conflict. Was there a war, for example? If so then there would, almost certainly, be a lack a marriageable young men – especially if the war was pre 1945 – which in turn would affect the behaviour of the women. Was the government of the day a dictatorship? Was the reigning monarch self-centred and squanderous, which would beg the question:

To whom are the riches directed;
For whom are the riches intended?
Anon

In earlier centuries how the life of the poor compared to the lives of the more wealthy members of society would have a similar bearing on an author's work – for state handouts are a fairly recent luxury! Everything about the century in question would and could affect the writer and in turn his work; telling a good story is of course excellent, but set against a backdrop of authenticity, it could become a masterpiece – a classic even!

In addition to discovering more about the writers themselves and the times in which they lived, in this section you will also discover more about the works they have written, immortal lines they have given us, characters they have created, homes they have lived in, awards they have won and so on.

Although primarily we will be looking at writers post Fifteenth Century, there are of course pre-Fifteenth Century writers who just cannot be ignored, Geoffrey Chaucer for example being one of them, and so before starting the main body of the piece there is, shall we say rather aptly, a sort of prologue, as a tribute to Geoffrey Chaucer and his works.

Literature in pre-Fifteenth Century England was in English, Latin and French and the actual writing itself was done by hand (by scribes) with the first printed book not appearing until 1476. This was also when English assumed the modern form – except in spelling, of course – which was not fully standardised until after Dr Johnson's *Dictionary* of 1755.

During Chaucer's time most writing was in French, for writers in this era had to be maintained by the church, or by secular patrons, who spoke French. The kings of England also spoke French rather than English, with the first King of England to insist that court business be conducted in English being King Henry V (1413-1422). Much Middle English writing, therefore, derives from French, which in turn derives from the classical language of Latin.

Interestingly it is Geoffrey Chaucer who is credited with being the first English poet to write only in English, though it would be a long time after his death before the ease and wit evident in his work would once again emerge.

Geoffrey Chaucer
c1342/3 – 1400

Major Works by Geoffrey Chaucer include:
Boece and Troilus and Criseyde • *Book of the Duchess (The)* •
Canterbury Tales (The) • *House of Fame Legend of Good Women (The)* •
Palamon and Arcite • *Parlement of Fowls* • *Troilus and Criseyde* •

GEOFFREY CHAUCER: The Man and His Life

We must at this point remember that, when dealing with individuals born centuries ago, we cannot attribute with absolute certainty any fact to any particular individual, not even details of parentage; there was no DNA then remember! Official records in those times were very lacking in detail and accuracy, if they existed at all that is. Therefore, much of our knowledge is academic conjecture, theoretical assumptions and the result of the piecing together of the smaller nuggets of information we do have, and deciding where each particular piece fits to actually allow us to glimpse the bigger picture. However, the interesting fact is that the opening lines to *The Canterbury Tales* is thought by many to be the starting point for English Literature.

• Chaucer was born in the early 1340s, generally thought to be 1342/3
• He was probably the son of John and Agnes Chaucer who were known to be wine merchants in London at that time, which made for quite a comfortable and privileged English middle-class life; his social standing in the class structure of society would mean that he had royal connections too
• Although British, the name Chaucer is actually derived from the French word *chaussier*, meaning a maker of footwear
• In the mid 1360s, probably 1365/6 Chaucer married Philippa Pan – at least that's who we think he married! And we also think – though cannot be sure – that they had four children, two sons and two daughters
• As well as being a great literary figure he was also a prominent public figure of his time, working as a diplomat, a civil servant and as a courtier; such positions gave him great social status and the opportunity to travel on diplomatic missions at a time when 'the ordinary man' rarely left the town of his birth
• In 1374 he was appointed controller of customs in the port of London.
• From July 1389 to June 1391 Chaucer was Clerk of the King's Works – which made him responsible for the upkeep of Royal Buildings and Estates – during which time he was robbed on several occasions and once even beaten, which is probably the reason for his holding the position for such a short time!
• Geoffrey Chaucer died in the year 1400
• In the mid 1500s, in recognition of his literary status, Chaucer's body was moved to Poets' Corner in Westminster Abbey, London

AND FINALLY

• In his day Chaucer was as well known for his literary translations as for his own original works; one fine example of this is his translation of the French poem *Roman de la rose*
• But of course his pièce de résistance, and the work for which he will always be remembered is *The Canterbury Tales*, which is 17,000 lines long and is written in prose and verse of various metres – though predominantly in rhyming couplets

The Canterbury Tales

In his work *The Canterbury Tales* Chaucer tells the story of a band of travellers on a pilgrimage to the shrine of Thomas À Beckett, at Canterbury Cathedral. The pilgrims meet in the Tabard Inn in Southwark where Harry Bailly, the Host of the Inn, suggests that each of these travelling pilgrims tell four tales, two on the way to Canterbury and two on the way back, believing that this will shorten the journey. He suggests he travels with them and says that the teller of the best tale will win a free supper upon their return.

The tales themselves are linked together by exchanges between the travelling pilgrims, in addition to the prologues and epilogues of each tale. Chaucer's *The Canterbury Tales* probably has the most famous opening lines in English Literature:

> Whan that Aprille with his shoures soote
> The droghte of March hath perced to the roote,
> And bathed every veyne in swich licour
> Of which vertue engendred is the flour

The translation into modern English of which is:

> *When April with his showers sweet with fruit*
> *The drought of March has pierced unto the root*
> *And bathed each vein with liquor that has power*
> *To generate therein and sire the flower*

The actual Tales themselves are as follows:

Knight's Tale (The)	Physician's Tale (The)
Miller's Tale (The)	Pardoner's Tale (The)
Reeve's Tale (The)	Shipman's Tale (The)
Cook's Tale (The)	Prioress's Tale (The)
Man of Law's Tale (The)	Chaucer's Tale of Sir Thopas
Wife of Bath's Tale (The)	Tale of Melibeus (The)
Friar's Tale (The)	Monk's Tale
Summoner's Tale (The)	Nun's Priest's Tale (The)
Clerk's Tale (The)	Second Nun's Tale (The)
Merchant's Tale (The)	Canon's Yeoman's Tale (The)
Squire's Tale (The)	Manciples Tale (The)
Franklin's Tale (The)	Parson's Tale (The)

These tales are then immediately followed by Chaucer's closing 'Retracciouns' in which he takes leave of his book.

A BRIEF SYNOPSIS OF FOUR OF THE TALES

Sadly I cannot give a brief outline of more than four of the tales in a book which itself is ruled by word count but, working on the theories that 'anything is better than nothing' and 'less is more', this should be both fine and acceptable, unless of course your glass is half empty and not half full, then you almost certainly won't be happy!

Knight's Tale (The)

This is the story of two love rivals, Palamon and Arcite, their love for Emelye and how when they compete in a tournament to win her love a victory suddenly becomes a tragedy. Palamon is defeated in the tournament and at the very moment of his victory, Arcite is thrown by his horse and dies. Palamon and Emelye are then later united.

Miller's Tale (The)

This tale is more vulgar tale than The Knight's Tale and is one of deception. A young student by the name of Nichols persuades Alison, the younger wife of his landlord, to sleep with him. He keeps the landlord out of the way by telling him that another great biblical flood is coming and to wait safely for the flood he must hide suspended in a tub from the rafters; he adds to this that he must tell no one in case they label him mad. Another man also 'likes' Alison and after various farcical situations, the landlord cuts himself down from the rafters and when trying to explain what he was doing up there in the first place he is indeed, as predicted, pronounced a mad man!

Wife of Bath's Tale (The)

A knight in King Arthur's court rapes a woman and, as a punishment, is set the task of finding out what women really want, 'more than anything else'. If he fails in this task, which he has one year and one day to complete, then it is deemed that he must die. After a year and still no answer the Knight meets an old hag who says she will give him an answer and tells him that what women want most is 'to have sovereignty over their husband'. And so he has the answer, but at a price, for in return for the answer to his question he must marry the ugly old woman! Because she is so ugly though the Knight is unhappy and so she gives him the choice of her being ugly and faithful or beautiful and unfaithful. He in turn gives her the choice to become whatever would bring the most honour and happiness to her and as a result she becomes fair and faithful – and so they live happily ever after!

Pardoner's Tale (The)

Radix malorum est cupiditas or 'greed is the root of all evil' is the theme of this tale of three drunken and debauched men who set out to find and kill Death, whom they believe is to blame for the death of their friend and the deaths of all other people. An old man tells them that they will find him at the foot of a tree but when they get there they find gold coins instead and forget about Death. One man sets off to find food and drink, while the other two stay behind secretly plotting to kill him when he returns. Meanwhile the one who had left to find food and drink poisons the wine that he is bringing back for his companions. On his return he is killed as planned; the two killers then drink the poisoned wine and die as a result. So the three men did indeed find Death and exactly where they had been directed, for there he was at the foot of the tree in the guise of greed.

And so we leave Chaucer and pre-Fifteenth Century literature behind as we move on to look at writers of the classics century by century.

The Fifteenth Century

Life in the Fifteenth Century

• Although there are no official dates for the term, 'The Medieval Period', in history, it is generally considered to have come to an end during the Fifteenth Century, (in England usually thought to be around 1485)
• The Fifteenth Century is known as the age of exploration and discovery
• Many people in the Fifteenth Century still believed that the earth was flat and thought that ships could therefore sail off the edge! Even those who knew it was round believed it to be much smaller that it is and so when the Americas were finally discovered it was quite a surprise to them
• Food was served in a long trencher and diners merely dived in, using their hands and fingers to scoop up the food; in wealthy households the trencher was made from metal, whereas in the poorer households it was merely a hollowed out piece of bread which was used to hold the food
• Cutlery was still primarily used for cooking food, whilst fingers were used for eating it!

• In the Fifteenth Century it was acceptable for men to wear hats to the table in order to keep their hair out of the food
• Water, because it was so polluted, was rarely drunk, instead beer and ale were the preferred beverages
• Glass was very expensive and so if you were lucky enough to have glass windows and wanted to move house, then you took your windows with you!
• There were no drains and all rubbish was thrown onto the streets – including sewage
• Tradesmen tended to live and work in the same street as each other and so for example in many towns butchers and slaughterhouses could be found on the same street, generally called The Shambles. An example of just such a street can be found in the centre of the historica city of York, where the cramped and overhanging style of housing can also be viewed first hand
• Only about one third of the population could read and write
• Up until this point in history, and the arrival of the printing press, all books had either been handwritten by scribes or at best printed by the use of wood blocks
• Henry VI was less than a year old when he became King in 1422

Popular Writers of the Fifteenth Century

Writer	Date	Works include
Machiavelli, Niccolò Italian Little is known of Machiavelli's early life but he later became known for his attacks upon the church. His name has now become the adjective 'Machiavellian' meaning using clever trickery or amoral methods to achieve a goal, particularly a political goal.	1469-1527	Discourses on Livy Florentine Histories (The) Prince (The)
Malory, Thomas (Sir) British Now here is a writer surrounded by mystery and conjecture, for Malory's true identity is actually uncertain although many believe him to be of Welsh descent. He is also believed to be Sir Thomas Malory of Newbold Revel, Warwickshire, who was a knight before 1442.	c. 1400s	Le Morte d'Arthur

The Sixteenth Century

Life in the Sixteenth Century

• The Sixteenth Century saw the introduction of 'new' foods such as potatoes, apricots and tomatoes

• It was thought that fresh fruit was bad and so fruit was only eaten if it was cooked

• In the Sixteenth – and the following Seventeenth – Century the professional occupations were not considered suitable occupations for women. If a woman did work, then she was expected to take up employment in domestic service, or at the very least in some related household activity

• A hundred years later and water was still not fit to drink and therefore alcohol was still considered the safer beverage

• It was a century of economic crisis, for although England economically flourished it was at the expense of the poor, who got poorer, whilst the rich got richer

• Poverty had become a problem and with no state handouts available then the only option for those in dire need was to beg. However, begging was frowned upon, except for those who were either old or disabled. The outcome of this ruling was that some of the very poor, and therefore desperate people, pretended to be disabled; any able-bodied person caught begging was whipped until blood was drawn. For those caught more than once then the punishment became even more severe.

• There were also strict laws against those who were too lazy to work, ranging from flogging to death

• In the Sixteenth Century honey was used to sweeten food

• Cruel sports were acceptable, sports such as dogfighting, cockfighting and pig baiting

• Football was also popular but with fewer rules than today – in fact anyone and everyone could join in and so it was a bit of a free-for-all

• Public hangings of criminals was a popular form of entertainment

• For those in poor health, being sick and subjecting oneself to treatment during this century was often more dangerous that the actual sickness itself and operations killed rather than saved most sick patients as anaesthesia was so primitive

• The progress of medicine in the Sixteenth Century was hampered by superstition and a deep-rooted fear of the church. Therefore study of the true human form was rarely possible, although by the middle of the century human corpses – generally those of executed criminals – were studied; gravediggers were also used to supply the demanding medical research market

• Henry VIII, who acceded to the throne at the age of 19, soon became one of the most memorable monarchs of all time

• When Catherine of Aragon failed to produce a male heir for Henry VIII, he asked Rome for a divorce so he could marry Anne Boleyn. Rome hesitated, Anne fell pregnant and Henry went ahead anyway. Thereafter, as most people now know, he eventually went on to have a total of six wives

• In this century the churches were ransacked by the crown and their possessions seized

• The luxury of chairs to sit upon was for the wealthy, the poor had to be content with stools

• Latin was still considered the language of literacy and in 1589 Spenser's *Faerie Queen* was a revelation as it opened up the possibility of using the English language in prose

• Education in the Sixteenth Century was selective, not in the academic terms with which we are now familiar, but on social terms. If you were wealthy and male then you could expect a good education; if you were poor then the best you could hope for was the opportunity to learn to read and write. If, however, you had the misfortune to be both poor and female then chances were you would be illiterate

• One of the most outstanding monarchs in history reigned during this century – Elizabeth I

Popular Writers of the Sixteenth Century

Writer	Date	Works include
Cervantes, Miguel de Spanish Cervantes was the fourth of seven children and little is known of his education except that he did not go to university. The work for which he will always be remembered, *Don Quixote*, has been translated into more than 60 languages.	1547-1616	*Don Quixote* *La Galatea* *Labours of Persiles and Sigismunda (The),* *A Northern Story*

63

The Seventeenth Century

Life in the Seventeenth Century

• The Seventeenth Century saw the birth of banking and The Bank of England in 1694, which is sometimes known as the 'Old Lady of Threadneedle Street'

• Forks 'arrived' in Europe as an item of cutlery

• Girls fortunate enough to be educated were actually educated in the 'necessities' of life rather than in the academic subjects. They were expected to be expert needlewomen and to have at least a basic knowledge of music rather than to be accomplished mathematicians, for example

• In the early part of the Seventeenth Century those who could afford it were able to have water piped directly into their homes and in the latter half of the century oil lamps were used to light the streets, thus making them a much safer place to be late at night

• 1665 saw the famous outbreak of the Bubonic Plague, also known as the 'Black Death'. Bubonic plague was a problem as no one realised that it was the fleas on the rats that were responsible for passing it on to humans when they bit them. The bodies of those killed by the plague were generally buried outside of the cities and towns in an attempt to halt the spread of the disease

• In the following year of 1666, fire raged through London destroying more than 13,000 houses

• The poor found that housing, even for them, was becoming more luxurious and they could now expect to have houses built of stone or brick instead of the cold and draughty wood from which they were previously constructed; they could also expect a chimney in the roof to let out the smoke, instead of the former customary hole in the roof

• Furniture in this century made great strides forward with the appearance of the first real armchairs

• Clothes were restrictive, hot and stuffy, at the beginning of the century when men wore starched collars called ruffs, and women wore frames made out of wood or whalebone under their dresses. Things changed throughout the hundred years, not necessarily becoming more comfortable as there was always rather a lot of clothing to wear – although not in the underwear department, for women didn't wear knickers!

• This was the century in which the first English newspaper was printed

• School life was hard with long hours and severe corporal punishment being the order of the day

- Transport was both uncomfortable and dangerous. Those who wanted to travel long distances did so at their peril by riding in stagecoaches which were both uncomfortable and frequently targeted by notorious highway men. For more local travel, the wealthy were carried around the towns in sedan chairs; the poor, however, had no choice but to walk
- Toothbrushes became a 'must-have'
- People married much earlier in life during the Seventeenth Century with it being as early as 14 for boys and 12 for girls, although such married couples were not allowed to live together until they were considered mature enough
- Families were initially much larger but, with a high infant mortality rate, few children survived into adulthood
- In England a man could beat his wife with a switch, provided it was no thicker than his thumb (hence the saying 'rule of thumb')
- Boys and girls were dressed alike until the age of six years
- Meat was eaten in abundance by those who could afford it; the poor ate vegetables; and still no one from any class drank water, as it remained unsafe to do so
- Actors were treated as scum – unless they were superstars – and were even refused burial on consecrated ground. For this reason an actor often took a stage name to protect his identity, a tradition which has continued to the present day – though not for the same reasons
- Rubbish of every kind was thrown onto the streets and so began the custom of a man walking on the outside of the lady, for then when rubbish was thrown from an upstairs window it was more likely to land on him, as were the splashes from the carriages travelling along the rough and muddy roads

Popular Writers of the Seventeenth Century

Writer	Date	Works include
Bunyan, John British Bunyan was the son of a travelling tinker. His life was tinged with sadness for when he was just 15 years old his mother died, his sister died and his father remarried – all within a period of two months. After his own marriage, when he was about 20 years old his first daughter Mary was born blind, and approximately 10 years and three more children later his wife died.	1628-1688	*Grace Abounding* *Life and Death of Mr Badman (The)* *Pilgrim's Progress (The)*

Writer	Date	Works include
Defoe, Daniel British Born in London, Defoe was of Flemish descent – the family name was Foe – and his father was a butcher. He is known for writing in the first person, a technique which enabled him to penetrate the minds of his characters. In his lifetime he wrote around 250 books, pamphlets and journals, was married for 47 years and had eight children.	1660-1731	*Moll Flanders* *Robinson Crusoe* *Roxana*
Pepys, Samuel British The son of a tailor, Pepys did not let his humble start in life prevent him from becoming one of the most important men of his time and one of the greatest writers of all time. Educated at Magdalene College, Cambridge, he is chiefly known for his diary which gives us an insight into the life of Restoration London 1660 to 1669.	1633-1703	*Pepys' Diary*

The Eighteenth Century

Life in the Eighteenth Century

• It wasn't until this century, and after Dr Johnson's *Dictionary*, that English spelling was fully standardised
• Royal Ascot began in 1711
• The wealthy – and therefore the powerful – were generally the landowners
• In 1789 the River Thames froze over in some areas of London
• In the early Eighteenth Century gin was extremely cheap and readily available, thus giving rise to an epidemic of gin drinkers. The problem was solved mid century when a tax was imposed on the sale of gin
• It was still only the children of the upper classes who could be assured of

a decent education; children from poorer families were expected to work for the family from a very early age
• In many European countries the punishment for those caught pickpocketing was to have their fingers cut off – and this included children too
• The rules of dining were considered to be very important, for it was at the dinner table that young ladies would be most likely to meet their prospective husbands
• At a dinner party the host would sit at the foot of the table, whereas, the hostess would sit at the head of the table
• After a meal the ladies retired to the drawing room whilst the men stayed behind to continue their drinking and to talk to each other
• A bride in the Eighteenth Century would not sew the last stitch on her wedding dress until it was time for her to leave for the church, for fear of bringing bad luck
• It was in this century that the famous landscape gardener Lancelot Brown who when looking at a piece of land coined the phrase 'it has great capabilities'; as a result he soon became known as Capability Brown
• The wealthy lived in large luxurious mansions, the poor lived in just two or three rooms, whilst those living in extreme poverty were condemned to exist all together in just one room
• Public executions remained a popular form of entertainment

Popular Writers of the Eighteenth Century

Writer	Date	Works include
Austen, Jane British Austen was born in Steventon, Hampshire to Reverend George Austen and Cassandra. She was one of eight children – six boys and two girls – who grew to be a fine analytical, realistic observer of Regency England. (See Separate Entry)	1775-1817	*Northanger Abbey* *Pride and Prejudice* *Sense and Sensibility*
Boswell, James British (Scottish) Boswell was in part educated at home and	1740-1795	*Life of Johnson L.L.D* *(The)*

Writer	Date	Works include
later at Edinburgh University. He is renowned for his great friendship with Samuel Johnson, a man more than 30 years his senior.		
Choderlos de Laclos, Pierre Ambrose François French He was born in Amiens, France, the son of a government official. After a spell in the army he married Marie-Soulange Duperré – who was the eldest child in a family of 22 children. Later in life he joined the army again and under Napoleon rose to the rank of general.	1741-1803	*Des Femmes et de leur Éducation* *Les Liaisons Dangereuses*
Cooper, James Fenimore American He was born in the US as the twelfth child of Elizabeth (née Fenimore) and William Cooper, (the founder of Cooperstown). His early career was as a sailor, but he resigned after the death of his father. In 1811 he married Susan Augusta De Lancey with whom he went on to have seven children. He died in 1851, followed a few months later by his wife and is now generally recognised as America's first National novelist.	1789-1851	*Deerslayer* *Last of the Mohicans (The)* *Pioneers (The)*
Fielding, Henry British Fielding was born in Glastonbury, Somerset as the eldest child in a large family and was not only a novelist but in the earlier years of his career a playwright and a journalist too. His sister, Sarah, was also a writer and the two siblings were very close. In later life, ill health led Fielding to the warmth of Portugal a journey he immortalised in *The Journal of a Voyage to Lisbon*. He died and was buried in Portugal.	1707-1754	*Amelia* *Joseph Andrews* *Tom Jones*
Goldsmith, Oliver Irish	1730-1774	*Vicar of Wakefield (The)*

Writer	Date	Works include
Goldsmith was born the son of the Reverend Charles Goldsmith an Anglo-Irish clergyman and was educated at Trinity College, Dublin. He then left Ireland for Europe and became a member of the artistic set which included the likes of Samuel Johnson and David Garrick. Like many of his contemporaries he was renowned in a variety of artistic fields such as essayist, dramatist and poet, and not exclusively as a novelist.		
Johnson, Samuel British Often referred to as Dr Johnson, Samuel was born in Lichfield, Staffordshire the son of a bookseller; this gave him the formative exposure to a constant supply of books. He was later educated at Pembroke College, Oxford but due to financial difficulties failed to graduate. In 1735 he married Elizabeth Porter; her death in 1752 caused him intense grief and in fact during his lifetime it would appear that he was frequently attacked by periods of mental stress. He is best remembered for his dictionary, which took him nine years to complete and was finally finished in 1755.	1709-1784	*Dictionary of the English Language (A)* *History of Rasselas, Prince of Abyssinia (The)* *Lives of the English Poets (The)*
Lamb, Charles British Charles, who was educated at Christ's Hospital, was one half of the well-known brother and sister authors of *Tales from Shakespeare* which retold Shakespeare's plays especially for children. He also wrote under the pseudonym Elia for *London Magazine*.	1775-1834	*Adventures of Ulysses (The)* *Mr Leicester's School* *Tales from Shakespeare*
Lamb, Mary British Mary was one half of the well-known brother and sister authors of *Tales from*	1764-1847	*Mr Leicester's School* *Poetry for Children* *Tales from Shakespeare*

Writer	Date	Works include
Shakespeare which retold Shakespeare's plays especially for children. Hers was a poor family and, unlike her brother, she received little formal education but helped support the family by taking on domestic chores and supporting her invalid mother. In 1796, in a fit of madness, she stabbed and killed her mother. Declared temporarily insane she was committed to the care of her brother Charles. Her mental illness recurred several times and after the death of Charles, whom she survived by 13 years her health deteriorated.		
Peacock, Thomas Love British Born in Weymouth, Dorset, as the only child of Samuel and Sash Peacock, he left school at 13 years old. He started his career by writing verse but later realised that his real talent was in the writing of fiction. His marriage to Jane Gyrffydh was touched by sadness when, after the death of their second child – they had four children – Jane suffered a breakdown and died seven years later.	1785-1866	*Gryll Grange* *Headlong Hall* *Nightmare Abbey*
Radcliff, Ann British Ann Radcliff was born in London, the only child of William and Ann Ward. Ann who married William Radcliff in 1787 was probably one of the most reclusive writers of her time. Despite being more successful than many of her artistic contemporaries little is known of her or her life with much left to speculation and conjecture.	1764-1823	*Italian (The)* *Mysteries of Udolpho (The)* *Romance of the Forest (The)*
Richardson, Samuel British Richardson was born in Derbyshire and – though not confirmed – it is widely believed he was educated at The Merchant Taylor's	1689-1761	*Clarissa or the History of a Young Lady* *Pamela* *Sir Charles Grandison*

Writer	Date	Works include
School in London. He started his working life as a successful printer, but his domestic life was incredibly sad by today's standard of life expectancy. He had six children by his first wife, five of whom died before they were ten years old; his wife then died followed by his sixth child. He married again and went on to have another six children, four of whom survived their father.		
Rousseau, Jean-Jacques French (Swiss born) Rousseau was born in Geneva the son of Isaac and Suzanne; his mother died 10 days after his birth and so he spent his early years in the care of his father, a watchmaker. He later became a great and influential philosopher of his time.	1712-1778	*Confessions (The)* *Émile: or, on Education* *Julie: or, the New Eloise*
Sterne, Laurence British Although Sterne was English, he was in fact born in County Tipperary, Eire the son of Roger and Agnes Sterne. He was educated at Cambridge and after graduating he took holy orders and became vicar of Sutton-on-the-Forest, North Yorkshire. In fact he had a family history of careers of the cloth, his great grandfather being an Archbishop of York and his uncle an Archdeacon of Cleveland.	1713-1768	*Sentimental Journey (A)* *Tristram Shandy*
Swift, Jonathon Irish Swift was born in Dublin, Ireland of Anglo-Irish descent, his father having died before his birth. He was educated at Trinity College, Dublin and in 1695 was ordained as a priest in the Anglican Church. His great masterpiece, *Gulliver's Travels*, was originally published under the title *Travels into Several Remote Nations of the World* and was not published under Swift's own name either. This work is divided into four volumes.	1667-1745	*Gulliver's Travels* *Tale of a Tub*

Writer	Date	Works include
Wollstonecraft, Mary British A contemporary of other great literary figures of her time such as William Blake and William Wordsworth, Wollstonecraft was born the daughter of a farmer and considered to be one of the first feminists. She had two children and died just 11 days after the birth of her second daughter, Mary.	1759-1797	*Vindication of the Rights of Woman (A)* *Wrongs of Woman (The)*

The Nineteenth Century

Life in the Nineteenth Century

• Although by this point the UK was travelling further along the road of democracy, initially very few men – and no women – were allowed to vote

• Most families in this century were considered to be working class; to be considered of higher status a person was expected to employ at least one servant and, as a matter of interest, that was generally a female servant too

• In this century a child failing to achieve in his schoolwork was often made to sit in the corner of the room wearing a conical-shaped hat; the letter D was written on the hat signifying that the child in question was considered to be a 'dunce'. This tradition actually spilled over into the next century, the hat finally being dropped, as was the stool, so that the 'dunce' was merely made to stand in the corner, facing the wall in disgrace

• Working conditions for the poor were appalling in Nineteenth Century with abusive child labour prevalent; for example, in the first half of the century children as young as five worked underground and young boys were made to climb up chimneys in order to clean them

• In the early Nineteenth Century only the wealthy had flushing toilets for it was not until later that they came into common usage

• The poor at this time were sent to the workhouse, a hard institute designed as a detriment to poverty! Here families were forced to live apart and subjected to strict rules and hard labour

• Watching a criminal being hanged for his crime continued to be regarded by many as a 'good day out'

• The father was considered to be the 'Head of the Family' and all family members were expected to obey him

• Although divorce was made legal by the mid Nineteenth Century, it was in reality a very rare occurrence

• In the second half of the century the middle classes had a separate bathroom built in their houses, whilst the poorer working classes bathed in a tin bath placed in front of an open fire for warmth. Although gradually phased out, this primitive tin bath still actually remained in use, in working-class homes, well into the first half of the Twentieth Century

• It was in this century that the Scottish inventor, Alexander Graham Bell was born and invented the telephone – one can't help but wonder at what he would have made of mobile phones!

• It was in the Nineteenth Century that birthday cakes became popular, fish and chip shops opened, convenience foods arrived in cans and jars, and chocolate became a favourite

• Courting in this century was more relaxed than in previous centuries, but in contrast to the present there were unbreakable rules – in fact today the word 'courting' is virtually obsolete in itself

• A young girl at this time was merely a 'wife-in-training' rather than an individual in her own right and so was usually chaperoned when socialising with the opposite sex

• There was a well-defined pecking (class) order in evidence in the Nineteenth Century and one was expected to socialise, and in fact marry, within one's own station

• Sex outside of marriage was taboo

• An academically gifted woman was frowned upon: in fact learning for females was generally frowned upon

• Women often carried a fan, supposedly to keep them cool, but all women knew how to get across a message to an attractive man by the way in which she held or used her fan; for example, to flick the fan in a swift manner was to tell a gentleman that she was an independent woman, whereas if she flicked in a slower, more restrained manner then that would signify that she was out of bounds!

• Small waists for women were very fashionable and achieved by the excrutiatingly painful use of the corset

• Archery was considered a suitable sport for women as it was thought to be ladylike

• Women finally began to wear knickers

• The Nineteenth Century was the century of Florence Nightingale and the century in which medicine made great advancements. In the second half of the century women were even allowed to qualify as doctors

Popular Writers of the Nineteenth Century

Writer	Date	Works include
### *A* Alcott, Louisa May American Alcott was born in Pennsylvania, USA to Amos Bronson Alcott and Abigail May Alcott. Louisa's early life was very much influenced by her father's inability to provide financial stability for his family and as a result she eventually became the sole provider for her family.	1832-1888	*Aunt Jo's Scrap Bag* *Jo's Boys* *Little Women*
Andersen, Hans Christian Danish Although Andersen was born into poverty he was able to get an education when one Jonas Collins raised money to help him, and thus he progressed to the University of Copenhagen and later became a prolific teller and writer of tales. * See additional separate entry	1805-1875	*Emperor's New Clothes (The)* *Snow Queen (The)* *Ugly Duckling (The)*
### *B* Balzac, Honore de French Considered to be one of the greatest writers of all time he wrote prolifically after a difficult start in life. He was born in Tours, France, the son of Anne Charlotte Laure Sallambier and Bernard François Balssa. It would seem that his mother possessed little maternal instinct and so he spent much of his childhood separated form his family. He studied law at the Sorbonne but aspired to be a writer.	1799-1850	*Eugenie Grandet* *Hated Son (The)* *Research of the Absolute (The)*
Baum, L. Frank American Lyman Frank Baum was born to Benjamin	1856-1919	*Father Goose* *Wonderful Wizard Of Oz (The)*

Writer	Date	Works include
and Cynthia Ann Stanton Baum in Chittenango, New York, the seventh child in a family of nine children; his was a very religious family. Baum was not a healthy child and so was educated at home. He later became a writer and after the enormous success of *The Wonderful Wizard of Oz* he went on to write a further 13 Oz books.		
Blackmore, R.D. British His full name was Richard Dodderidge Blackmore and he was born on 7 June 1825 in Longworth, Berkshire, England. He was educated at Exeter College, Oxford after which he was called to the bar but ill health ended his career. His first novel was *Clara Vaughan* but it was his third novel *Lorna Doone* that was to be the most successful of his 14 novels.	1825-1900	*Clara Vaughan* *Lorna Doone* *Maid of Sker (The)*
Braddon, Mary Elizabeth British Braddon was born in London and whilst still a child her parents separated. Her first career was that of an actress – whilst she wrote her first works – eventually retiring from the stage to become a full-time writer. She eventually became well known – notorious – for her sensational novels, which were written during a very straight-laced time in history.	1835-1915	*Lady Audley's Secret* *Aurora Floyd* *Mary*
Brontë, Anne, Charlotte & Emily British An extraordinary family of writers who became famous for their skilled writing and in turn made an area of Yorkshire famous for being their home to the extent that it later became known as the 'Brontë Country' and they collectively became 'the Brontës of Haworth'.	1820	*Jane Eyre* – Charlotte Brontë *Tenant of Wildfell Hall* – Anne Brontë *Wuthering Heights* – Emily Brontë

Writer	Date	Works include
All of the Brontë children, and there were six of them, died young – as did their mother. These three sisters however left behind for us a legacy of seven classic books. *See separate entry		
Burnett, Frances Hodgson British Born Frances Eliza Hodgson in Manchester, she was the third of five children. After the death of her father Edwin in 1852 her mother, Eliza, moved the family to America where following her mother's death she became the main provider for her siblings. She wrote more than 50 books and several stage plays.	1849-1924	*Little Lord Fauntleroy* *Little Princess (A)* *Secret Garden (The)*
C		
Carroll, Lewis British Lewis Carroll was the pseudonym for Charles Lutwidge Dodgson. A shy child, he was the third of eleven children born to the Rev Charles Dodgson and his wife, Frances Jane Lutwidge. As well as a writer Carroll was also a mathematician and an accomplished photographer.	1832-1898	*Alice's Adventures in Wonderland* *Hunting of the Snark (The)* *Through the Looking Glass*
Collins, Wilkie British Wilkie Collins was the son of the well-known landscape painter, William Collins. He became one of the great Victorian writers and an expert on the writing of suspense and mystery. He was a prolific writer of his age but has often been overshadowed in popularity by his great friend Charles Dickens. He had a great interest in the stage and in fact wrote a play *The Frozen Deep* for Charles Dickens's amateur company, and in which Dickens himself played the lead. One can only assume then that he would have been thrilled to see *The Woman in*	1824-1889	*Man and Wife* *Moonstone (The)* *Woman in White (The)*

Writer	Date	Works include
White adapted as a stage musical with music by the great Twentieth Century composer, Andrew Lloyd Webber.		
Conrad , Joseph British Conrad, real name Józef Teodor Konrad Korzeniowski, is British of Polish descent. He lost both parents as a child and was brought up by an uncle; it was in 1886 that he became a British subject. His life at sea and his life in the tropics were influential in his literary outpourings. He was married to Jessie George, by whom he had two children.	1857-1924	*Lord Jim* *Nostromo* *Secret Agent (The)*
D Dickens, Charles British Charles Dickens, born to John and Elizabeth Dickens in Portsmouth, was and is one of the greatest writers of all time. He wrote several classic masterpieces despite his formal education coming to an abrupt end when he was just 15 years old. As well as writing his books, he also took great delight in performing excerpts from them, and toured extensively in Europe and America for this sole purpose. *See separate entry	1812-1870	*David Copperfield* *Oliver Twist* *Tale of Two Cities (A)*
Dostoevsky, Fyodor Russian His name in full was Fyodor Mikhaylovich Dostoyevsky and he was born in Russia the second son of a doctor, Mikhail, and his wife Maria Dostoyevsky. He was educated at home and at a private school before being sent to the Academy for Military Engineers, though he had no interest in things military. His life was plagued by epilepsy and a	1821-1881	*Brothers Karamazov (The)* *Crime and Punishment* *Idiot (The)*

Writer	Date	Works include
compulsion to gamble which often saw him write frantically in order to secure an advance to pay off his gambling debts.		
Doyle, Arthur Conan (Sir) British Charles Altamont and Mary Foley had 10 children of which Arthur Conan was the second – his full name being Arthur Ignatius Conan Doyle. A man of great intellect, Arthur Conan Doyle was educated at Edinburgh University where he qualified as a doctor, a skill which would later infiltrate his novels. Although dominated by his creation, Sherlock Holmes, Conan Doyle was so much more and wrote so much more. He married twice and had three children.	1859-1930	*Adventures of Sherlock Holmes (The)* *Study in Scarlet (A)* *White Company (The)*
Dumas père, Alexandre French Dumas, the father, was both a novelist and a dramatist. Initially a lawyer, he turned his artistic leanings towards the stage to write what would now be classed as rather crude and melodramatic works. When he then turned his attention to writing novels he found success and recognition came his way more than it did for his dramatic works.	1802-1870	*Black Tulip (The)* *Count of Monte Cristo (The)* *Three Musketeers (The)*
Dumas fils, Alexandre French The son of the 'father' he was both a novelist and a playwright, but unlike his father before him he was more successful in the dramatic field. Unlike his father in another field too, whose works were historical, the son preferred to work in the present. He was in fact the illegitimate son of Alexandre Dumas père.	1824-1895	*La Dame aux Camélias*

Writer	Date	Works include
E Eliot, George British First things first – George was in fact a woman called Mary Ann (or Marian) Cross née Evans; it is said that she adopted a male pseudonym to ensure her intellectual works were taken seriously. The youngest of five children born to Robert and Christiana Evans, her love of literature was always there, particularly during the years she cared for her sick father until his death.	1819-1880	*Middlemarch* *Mill on the Floss (The)* *Silas Marner*
F Faulkner, William American In full his name was William Cuthbert Faulkner, though in fact his original surname was actually Falkner. He was the eldest of four sons born to Murry and Maud Falkner. He married Estelle Oldham with whom he had a daughter, Jill. As well as novels he also wrote for the screen, but only for financial reasons and only out of necessity for his love was in the books he wrote. He died of a heart attack at the age of 64.	1897-1962	*Absalom Absalom!* *As I Lay Dying* *Sound of Fury (The)*
Flaubert, Gustave French Flaubert was born into a middle-class medical family; his father, Achille Cléophas Flaubert, was a surgeon and clinical professor whilst his mother was the daughter of a doctor. Initially he studied law but ill health forced him to give up and concentrate on his writing and as a result he became rather reclusive.	1821-1880	*L'Education Senti-mentale* *Madame Bovary* *Trois Contes*

Writer	Date	Works include
Forster, E.M. British Forster's father died when he was a baby and so his mother and paternal aunts were left to raise him alone. He was educated at Tonbridge School in Kent and later at Kings College, Cambridge. After leaving Cambridge he decided to devote his life to writing.	1879-1970	*Howards End* *Passage to India (A)* *Longest Journey (The)*
G Grahame, Kenneth British Grahame was born in Scotland but was brought up by his grandmother in England after being orphaned at an early age. Lack of money prevented him taking advantage of a university education and so until his retirement he worked at the Bank of England. He married Elspeth Thompson, with whom he had one son. As well as his masterpiece, *The Wind in the Willows*, Grahame also wrote journalistic articles, essays and stories.	1859-1932	*Wind in the Willows (The)*
Gaskill, Elizabeth English Gaskell was born Elizabeth Cleghorn Stevenson, the daughter of a Unitarian minister and also married a Unitarian minister, William Gaskell with whom she had six children. She was a great friend of Charlotte Brontë and after Brontë's death went on to write her biography. Inevitably, and like many, many writers Gaskell, left one of her works unfinished, the work thought by some to be her finest, *Wives and Daughters*.	1810-1865	*Cranford* *Life of Charlotte Brontë* *Sylvia's Lovers*
Grimm, Brothers Grimm, Jakob Ludwig Grimm, Wilhelm Karl German	1785-1863 1786-1859	

Writer	Date	Works include
Two remarkable brothers who collected and recorded on paper traditional folk tales, generally underlying each with a moral, to pass on to future generations. *See Separate Entry		
Galsworthy, John British The eldest son of John Galsworthy, a solicitor, and Blanche Bailey, he was educated at Harrow and later at New College Oxford where he studied law, being called to the bar in 1890. His intention was to specialise in marine law and with that in mind he took a trip around the world – writing won him over in the end though. He used the pseudonym John Sinjohn for his first works. Galsworthy, also a playwright, is primarily known for his sequence of novels, *The Forsyte Saga*.	1867-1933	*Country House (The)* *Forsyte Saga (The)* *Freelanders (The)*
H Hawthorne, Nathaniel American Hawthorn was brought up in Salem where he lived with his mother and two sisters at his uncle's house, his father having died when he was a young boy. He was educated at Bowdoin college and, before distinguishing himself as a novelist, he became a great writer of short stories, though this brought him little in the way of wealth or recognition.	1804-1864	*House of the Seven Gables (The)* *Scarlet Letter (The)* *Twice-Told Tales*
Hugo, Victor French Born Victor-Marie Hugo he was the third son of Joseph-Léopold-Sigisbert Hugo, a general in Napoleon's army. He studied at the Pension Cordier and the Lycée Louis-le-Grand. His studies in law did not interest him but writing and politics did and so he went on to	1802-1885	*Les Miserables* *Man Who Laughs (The)* *Notre-Dame de Paris*

Writer	Date	Works include
be a poet, novelist, dramatist and one of the most important figures in French Literature as well as being a politically active French citizen throughout his life.		
Hughes, Thomas British He was born in Berkshire and educated at Rugby School, the setting and inspiration for his most famous novel *Tom Brown's Schooldays*, and later went up to Oriel College, Oxford which was to inspire his less successful novel *Tom Brown at Oxford*.	1819-1875	*Tom Brown's Schooldays* *Tom Brown at Oxford*
J James, Henry American James was born in the US in 1915 and then became a British subject, with the result that both sides of the Atlantic can in some part lay claim to this man of genius. A studious child he was home schooled in his early years prior entering Harvard Law School. He first became an exceptional writer of short stories before embarking on full-length novels, of which he went on to write 20 before he died in London.	1843-1916	*Portrait of a Lady (The)* *Daisy Miller* *Ambassadors (The)*
Jerome, Jerome K British He was born Jerome Klapka Jerome in Staffordshire and was the youngest of four children. Unlike many of his contemporaries he did not enjoy a university education but instead left school at the age of 14 to begin a series of jobs in an early life that was dominated by a riches to rags existence. By the age of 16 both his parents had died and by 18 he embarked on an unsuccessful career as an actor. He died in 1927 survived by his wife Ettie and daughter Rowena.	1859-1927	*Idle Thoughts of an Idle Fellow (The)* *My Life and Times* *Three Men in a Boat*

Writer	Date	Works include
K		
Kipling, Rudyard British Born Joseph Rudyard Kipling in India, he was the son of John Lockwood Kipling and Alice Macdonald who brought him to England as a child and left him for five years at a foster home. He didn't return to India until 1882. He married Caroline Balestier in 1892 and became known for his short stories, his poems and especially for his works for children, more than he did for his novels.	1865-1936	*Jungle Book (The)* *Kim* *Just So Stories*
Kingsley, Charles British Son of Charles Kingsley Sr and Mary Lucas Kingsley, he was educated at Magdalene College, Cambridge, and was both a clergyman himself and the son of a clergyman. Known as a Christian Socialist he was later appointed Professor of Modern History at Cambridge and tutor to the Prince of Wales, whilst retaining his heart and voice for the working classes. He married Frances Grenfell in 1844.	1819-1975	*Greek Fairy Tales for My Children* *Water Babies (The)* *Westward Ho!*
L		
Lever, Charles Irish Lever was born and raised in Dublin. He was educated at Trinity College, Cambridge and in 1831 qualified as a doctor of medicine. He was a great raconteur, a gift which helped ease his financial situations, as he led an excessive lifestyle, and his anecdotal style of writing is the style for which he is remembered. In 1842 he became the editor of Dublin University Magazine and became a great traveller, eventually dying in 1872, in Trieste, Austria-Hungary (now in Italy).	1806-1872	*Charles O'Malley* *Dodd Family Abroad (The)* *Harry Lorrequer*

Writer	Date	Works include
## *M*		
Marryat, Captain British This is a genuine title, for Captain Frederick Marryat was a naval captain and so committed to the sea that he actually 'ran away to sea' several times before being allowed to officially embark on his naval career. He began writing whilst at sea and even after resigning his commission to concentrate on writing he retained the title for his works, many of which centred on the sea.	1792-1848	*Children of the New Forest* *Mr Midshipman Easy* *Peter Simple*
Melville, Herman American Melville was born the third child of Allan and Maria Melville's eight children. His father died when he was 12 years old and his mother was left to bring up the eight children alone; it was then that Melville went out to work and led an adventurous life, adventures upon which he drew upon to write. Sadly, not achieving the success he so desired he had a breakdown. In 1847 he married Elizabeth Shaw with whom he went on to have four children.	1819-1891	*Moby Dick* *Omoo* *Typee*
## *N*		
Nesbit, E. British Always known only as E. Nesbit, though her full Christian name was Edith, she became renowned for her children's novels and before she died had penned numerous books for children in addition to her other writings. A committed socialist throughout her life, together with her husband she was among the founder members of the Fabian Society – the precursor to the Labour Party.	1858-1924	*Railway Children (The)* *Story of the Treasure Seekers (The)* *Wouldbegoods (The)*

Writer	Date	Works include
P Pushkin, Alexander Russian Born into a Russian aristocratic family with the full name and correct spelling of Aleksandr Sergeyevich Pushkin he is the Russian writer who is – by some – credited with the responsibility of being the founder of Russian Literature. He led a privileged life and was fluent in French. He became revolutionary in his beliefs and writings and as a result was exiled.	1799-1837	*Bronze Horseman (The)* – Poem *Eugene Onegin* – Verse Novel *Queen of Spades (The)* – Short Story
S Scott, Walter (Sir) British Born in Edinburgh, Scott was the son of a solicitor. At the age of 18 months polio left him lame though not unable to pursue his education at Edinburgh University, marry, have four children, and achieve great literary success. He is remembered by many for writing his early 'Waverly' novels anonymously and revered for his moral and decent attitude to life. *See separate entry	1771-1832	*Guy Mannering* *Ivanhoe* *Rob Roy*
Stowe, Harriet Beecher American Born Harriet Elizabeth Beecher, Stowe will always be remembered as the 'brave' author of *Uncle Tom's Cabin*, through which she condemned slavery to such a degree that it has actually been held to 'blame' as one of the causes for the American Civil War. So powerful was the message of *Uncle Tom's Cabin* that to read or own the book in the South of America was extremely dangerous. She was one of four children born to the congregational minister, Lyman Beecher, and grew up with an intense	1811-1896	*Uncle Tom's Cabin* *Mayflower (The)* *Minister's Wooing (The)*

Writer	Date	Works include
belief in right and wrong which was perpetuated when she married clergyman, Calvin Ellis Stowe.		
Sewell, Anna British Although Sewell wrote only one book, it was so successful and enjoyed such critical acclaim that she rightly sits in a list of classic writers. Injured when she was very young, Sewell was unable to lead a full life and her lack of mobility meant she relied on horse and carriage to transport her. Out of this grew a love and compassion for horses and the inspiration for her novel in which she humanised the horse to tell the tale.	1820-1878	*Black Beauty*
Shelley, Mary British Mary Wollstonecraft Godwin was born in London, the second daughter of literary parents, William Godwin and Mary Wollstonecraft. Her mother died soon after Mary's birth and her father remarried, which brought her little happiness. She was home schooled and had the fortune to mix with great literary figures of the time. She married the poet Percy Bysshe Shelley, thus becoming Mary Shelley, but her life was touched by sadness, the sadness of losing children, suffering miscarriages, and later the death of her husband in a sailing accident.	1797-1851	*Frankenstein* *Last Man (The)* *Fortunes of Perkin Warbeck*
Stevenson, Robert Lewis British Full name was Robert Louis Balfour Stevenson, he was born in Edinburgh as the only son of Thomas Stevenson, a civil engineer, and Margaret Isabella Balfour; was educated at Edinburgh University. His first	1850-1894	*Kidnapped* *Strange Case of Dr Jekyll and Mr Hyde (The)* *Treasure Island*

Writer	Date	Works include
area of study was engineering but he abandoned this to study law and although called to the bar in 1875 he never actually practiced but announced that he wanted to be a writer instead. In 1880 he married American divorcee Fanny Vandegrift Osbourne. Robert Louis Stevenson's life – like many writers – was plagued with ill health.		
Spyri, Johanna Swiss Born Johanna Louise Heusser in Hirzel, Switzerland she was the fourth of six children born to Joh Jak Heusser and Meta Schweizer. In 1852 she married Johann Bernhard Spyri and together they had one son who sadly died before he was 30 years old – in the same year as his father. *Heidi*, the most famous of Spyri's books has sold over 50,000000 copies in over 50 countries.	1827-1901	*Heidi* *Heimatlos* *Leaf from Vrony's Grave (A)*
Stendhal French Stendhal was born Marie-Henri Beyle in Grenoble in France and used Stendhal as one of his many pseudonyms. His father, Chérubin Beyle, was a barrister; his mother died when he was only seven years old. His later life then revolved around his army career, his writings and women, women, women.	1783-1842	*Armance* *Charterhouse of Parma (The)* *Red and the Black (The)*
Stoker, Bram Irish Bram (short for Abraham) Stoker was the third of seven children born in Dublin, Southern Ireland to Abraham Stoker and Charlotte Thornley, and was educated at Trinity College Dublin. As a child he was unable to walk but he grew up to be an outstanding athlete when at University. He married	1847-1912	*Dracula* *Lady of the Shroud (The)* *Mystery of the Sea (The)*

Writer	Date	Works include
Florence Balcombe, with whom he had one son. For nearly 30 years Stoker worked as business manager in the Lyceum Theatre for Sir Henry Irving. Although he also wrote many novels and short stories it is for one novel only that he is actually remembered, and that is his famous horror story, *Dracula*.		
T Thackeray, William Makepeace British Thackeray was born in Calcutta, India returning home to England after the death of his father, Richmond Thackeray. He was educated at Charterhouse Public School and later at Trinity College, Cambridge. He married Isabella Gethen Creagh Shawe with whom he went on to have three daughters, one of whom died in infancy. His wife later went insane and never recovered, though she actually survived her husband.	1811-1863	*Vanity Fair* *Pendennis* *History of Henry Esmond (The)*
Tolstoy, Leo Russian Born into an aristocratic Russian family Tolstoy's – full name Lev Nikolayevich, Count (Graf) Tolstoy – early years were filled with sadness when first his mother, Mariya Nikolayevna née Princess Volkonskaya died before he was two years old, followed by his father Nikolay Ilich, Count Tolstoy, in 1837. He was educated at home and at the University of Kazan – though here he failed to gain a degree and went on to live a life of debauchery, before he eventually married and together with his wife went on to have 13 children.	1828-1910	*War and Peace* *Anna Karenina*
Trollope, Anthony British Trollope came from a good family background	1815-1882	*Barchester Towers* *He Knew He Was Right* *Warden (The)*

Writer	Date	Works include
but without the money to sustain that which was expected of suchm and so his education at Harrow and Winchester was a somewhat miserable experience and his life made uneasy by the lack of money. He enjoyed a long and successful career working for the Post Office, which necessitated him writing early in the mornings. Despite what was in essence two jobs, he was, by any standard, most prolific in his literary outpourings		
Twain, Mark American Mark Twain, real name Samuel Langhorne Clemens, was born in Florida Missouri, the sixth child of John and Jane Clemens. His father died when he was eleven and at that point Twain's formal education ceased. Family circumstances meant that he was not destined to enjoy further education beyond the age of 13 years. He married Olivia Langdon in 1870 and nine months later they had a son, who sadly died before he was two years old; three daughters then followed.	1835-1910	*Adventures of Huckleberry Finn Adventures of Tom* *Sawyer (The) Innocents Abroad (The)*
𝒱 Verne, Jules French Jules Verne was born in Nantes, France and was the eldest in a family of five children; at just 11 years of age he ran away to sea before later being sent away to study law in Paris. His heart, however, was not in a legal career but in literature and the theatre. He was later to be heralded by some as the father of science fiction.	1828-1905	*20,000 Leagues Under the Sea, (Parts 1 & 2) Around the World in Eighty Days Journey to the Centre of the Earth (A)*
𝒲 Wilde, Oscar Irish	1854-1900	*Picture of Dorian Gray (The)*

Writer	Date	Works include
Primarily a dramatist, Wilde actually wrote only one novel, but such was, and is, the popularity of both his novel and the writer himself that he has earned the right to be included in this prestigious list of novelists. He was born into an Irish literary family with both his father and mother published writers and educated at Trinity College, Dublin and Magdalen College, Oxford. He was well known for his intelligent wit and flamboyance with his life ending, as he had lived it, in dramatic fashion when on his deathbed he converted to Roman Catholicism.		
## 2 Zola, Émile French Zola, full name Émile-Édouard-Charles-Antoine Zola, was born in Paris though he spent his early years and his youth in Aix-en-Provence, southern France. His father died in 1847 throwing him and his mother into poverty, a situation which continued into adulthood. In 1870 Zola married Gabrielle-Alexandrine Meley, this was a lifelong marriage despite a 14-year affair which resulted in two children. Zola was renowned as a defender of truth and justice and a champion of the poor and downtrodden.	1840-1902	*La Débâcle* *Les Rougon-Macquart* (consisting of 20 volumes) *Thérèse Raquin*

The Twentieth Century

Life in the Twentieth Century

• There was more progress made in this century than in any other, both in terms of technological advancements and in social awareness
• At the beginning of the century women worldwide were considered

second class citizens and of little consequence; by the turn of the century, however, women were equal to men and serving as world leaders
• At the beginning of the century children could leave school at the age of 14 years, but by the end of the century the school leaving age had risen to 16 years with the majority of young people voluntarily remaining in education until they reached the age of 18, and in many cases 21 years old
• The 1940s saw the introduction of the highly controversial 11-plus examination, (sometimes called the scholarship examination). The children who passed this exam. Went on to continue their education at a grammar school, which was supposedly for the academic elite; the 'failures' went on to a secondary school which concentrated on the less academic approach to study
• Until the latter half of the century corporal punishment was permitted – even encouraged – within schools
• Sweets were a luxury at the beginning of the century and although they became more readily available in the 20s and 30s they were then subjected to rationing during the Second World War. By the end of the century there were sweets galore and they were more of a necessity than the luxury they once were
• On a global awareness level the world had become smaller with the richer countries striving to help the poorer 'third world' countries
• Family structures and expectations changed. The extended family began to disappear as more opportunities to travel and relocate surfaced; one parent families became acceptable as did divorce and towards the end of the century the stigma of being homosexual finally began to diminish
• On the downside, whilst the poorer members of society were helped through a system of benefits, it was a system which lent itself to fraudulent claims and, some believe, a lazy attitude to work and life
• The Twentieth Century saw an influx of labour saving devices in the home and, in general, living conditions gradually improved throughout the hundred years. For example, at the beginning of the century bathrooms were a luxury, not a necessity, and outside toilets were the 'norm'
• At the beginning of the century most people shopped at small local shops as opposed to the American-style hypermarkets popular at the close of the century
• There was a revolution in clothes and fashion. In 1900 women still wore long dresses, no bra, and knickers that that reached the knee – and even below. Skirts then became shorter, so did knickers, and the bra arrived. Men, whose underwear in the Nineteenth Century had practically covered their entire body, were introduced to the joys of the Y-fronts and other liberating fashions until eventually total freedom was acheived, where any style was acceptable for both sexes

- The availability and manufacture of artificial fibres, such as nylon and polyester, had a huge impact on the fashion industry
- Technological advancement was incredible during this century with the arrival – or the ready availability – of making life both easier and more enjoyable for the masses:
  - Personal Travel: family cars – traffic lights – catseyes – driving tests – parking meters – seat belts – aeroplanes – hovercraft – buses
  - Communication Devices: telephones – mobile phones – email
  - Leisure: foreign travel – cinemas – radio – TV – video recorders – computers and Internet
- Medicine joined the progress march when the National Health Service was formed in 1948, when antibiotics were discovered and with the realisation that man could transplant a human organ from the body of one man to another. It was a neverending march too which continues to this day
- The contraceptive pill, which became readily available in the 1960s, meant that both sexes had a new found sexual freedom never before experienced and women had control over their own lives
- International wars claimed millions of lives and weapons became not only more destructive but more cruel too in their destruction
- The liberation of women marched forward with the Sex Discrimination Act of 1970s making it illegal to discriminate against women in employment, education and training

Popular Writers of the Twentieth Century

Writer	Date	Works include
A Adams, Douglas British Born Douglas Noel Adams, the son of Christopher and Janet he was educated at Cambridge University where he gained a degree in English Literature. He became well known and respected for his series of books, *The Hitchhiker's Guide to the Galaxy*, featuring the intergalactic adventures of Arthur Dent, Ford Perfect, Zaphod Beeblebrox and Marvin the paranoid android, which began as a radio	1952-2001	*Hitchhiker's Guide to the Galaxy (The)* *Life, the Universe and Everything* *Restaurant at the End of the Universe (The)*

Writer	Date	Works include
series and sold over fifteen million copies in his lifetime. Adams died at the tragically young age of 49 taking with him the genius that could have given so much more to the world of literature.		
Amis, Kingsley British Oxford-educated Amis was born in London as Kingsley William Amis. The Second World War, during which he served in the Royal Corps of Signals, interrupted his education, which he finally completed when he was awarded a degree in English. He spent his life writing and in a variety of teaching positions and was knighted in 1990, becoming Sir Kingsley Amis.	1922-1995	*Lucky Jim* *One Fat Englishman* *Old Devils (The)*
Anderson, Sherwood American Anderson was one of seven children born in Camden, Ohio to Irwin McClain Anderson and Emma Jane Smith. A disrupted childhood meant that his education was sporadic and incomplete. In 1904 he married Cornelia Lane with whom he went on to have three children before they divorced. He later married Tennessee Mitchell, another marriage doomed, but eventually he found happiness with his fourth partner, Eleanor Copenhaver. Sherwood Anderson became a master in the art of short story telling.	1876-1941	*Dark Laughter* *Marching Men* *Windy McPherson's Son*

B

Writer	Date	Works include
Barrie, J.M. British Sir James Matthew Barrie will be forever remembered as the creator of Peter Pan. His life was influenced greatly at the age of	1860-1937	*Auld Licht Idylls* *Little Minister (The)* *When a Man's Single*

Writer	Date	Works include
six by the tragic death of his brother and by the equally tragic effect it had on his mother. He longed for the tranquility of the years prior to this event, perhaps regretting that he ever grew up? In 1894 Barrie married Mary Ansell, a marriage which was childless and, it is said, unconsummated. When he completed his studies at Edinburgh University he settled into a life of writing – primarily for the stage. He bequeathed his Peter Pan works to Great Ormond Street Hospital for Sick Children.		
Bainbridge, Beryl British Born Beryl Margaret Bainbridge in Liverpool, England and educated at the Merchant Taylors School she was made a Dame in 2000. Married twice, she is as renowned for her endearing eccentricities as she is for her powerful writing which has to date resulted in five separate nominations for the Booker Prize – each though being unsuccessful.	1934-	*According to Queeney* *An Awfully Big* *Adventure* *Dressmaker (The)*
Bellow, Saul American In 1913 Bellow's parents emigrated from Russia to Canada where he was then born in 1915 as the fourth child of Abraham and Lescha Bellow. As a child he was ill and like many writers he lived in his own imaginary world; aged eight the family moved to Chicago and in 1924 his mother died. He was educated at the Universities of Chicago and North western and, in addition to his writing career, went on to become a university lecturer as well as serving as a Merchant Marine in the Second World War.	1915-2005	*Adventures of Augie* *March* *Humboldt's Gift* *Mr Sammler's Planet*
Blyton, Enid British	1897-1968	*Famous Five* *Malory Towers* *Secret Seven*

Writer	Date	Works include
Enid Mary Blyton was born in East Dulwich, London. A trained teacher, she is one of the most published authors of books for children and by the time of her death had published over 600 novels, plays, poems and short stories. In 1924, she married her first husband, Hugh Pollock, with whom she had two daughters. In 1943 she was married for a second time to surgeon, Kenneth Darrell Waters. Enid Blyton has been subjected to much criticism over the years, and for many reasons; but the fact remains that she is single-handedly responsible for introducing many children to the joys of reading.		

C

Writer	Date	Works include
Christie, Agatha British Dame Agatha Mary Clarissa Christie, née Miller, was educated at home by her mother and was destined to become one of the most prolific writers ever with sales of her works exceeding 100 million and translations into 100 languages. She worked as a nurse during the First World War, which was when she started writing. As well as novels Christie also wrote for the stage and her works have been adapted for both film and TV. It was she who was responsible for creating such enduring characters as Hercule Poirot and Miss Marple.	1890-1976	*Death on the Nile* *Murder at the Vicarage* *Mysterious Affair at Styles (The)*
Chesterton, G. K. British Gilbert Keith Chesterton was born in London and educated at St Paul's School, but despite going on to further education failed to get a degree and yet he was a man of huge diverse and often reactionary views and opinions. During his lifetime he was friends with many of the literary greats and wrote about them too.	1874-1936	*Charles Dickens: A Critical Study* *Everlasting Man (The)* *Innocence of Father Brown (The)*

Writer	Date	Works include
Crompton, Richmal British Richmal Crompton, real name Richmal Crompton Lamburn, was born in Bury, Lancashire and read Classics at Royal Holloway College before teaching Classics at Bromley High School in Kent. After a severe bout of polio she gave up teaching to become a full-time writer. Although she wrote books for grown-ups, she will be forever remembered as the creator of the William series of books, of which she wrote 38.	1890-1969	*Just William* *More William* *William the Conqueror*
D Dahl, Roald British Roald Dahl was born in Wales despite the fact that both his parents were Norwegian. He was one of those rare individuals who had a passionate and all consuming interest in everything – including chocolate! Dahl married twice and had five children. Although his life was tinged with tragedy he refused to let it be his destruction and instead became a champion for those less unfortunate. *See separate entry	1916-1990	*Charlie and the Chocolate Factory* *James and the Giant Peach* *Tales of the Unexpected*
F Ferber, Edna American Edna Ferber was born in Kalamazoo, Michigan as the daughter of Jacob Ferber, a Hungarian-born Jewish storekeeper and his Milwaukee-born wife, Julia Neumann Ferber. Her writing career started when she was appointed editor of her High School magazine after which she became a reporter on a local newspaper. There then followed a successful career as a full-time writer with her books being adapted both for stage and screen.	1885-1968	*Ice Palace* *Showboat* *So Big*

Writer	Date	Works include
Fitzgerald, F. Scott American Born Francis Scott Key Fitzgerald he was educated at Princeton but let a broken love affair ruin his early social and academic promise and it soon became apparent that love was to be a determining factor in his life. He later found happiness with his wife Zelda and together they had a daughter Frances, nick-named 'Scottie'. The bubble bursting though with his heavy drinking and Zelda's mental breakdown. His final love, Sheilah Graham, remained with him until his early death of a heart attack at the age of 44 years old.	1896-1940	*Beautiful and the Damned (The)* *Great Gatsby (The)* *This Side of Paradise*
Fleming, Ian British A name synonymous with the character James Bond, Fleming, full name Ian Lancaster Fleming, was born into a privileged life of wealth and social status. He struggled though to become a person in his own right, always living it seemed in the shadow of his successful father (who died just before Ian was nine) and brilliant elder brother, Peter. Money played a significant part in his life, which he lived to the full; some would say that he was James Bond as he worked at one time as a successful spy.	1908-1964	*James Bond Books (The)* include: *Casino Royale* *Goldfinger* *On Her Majesty's Secret Service* *Chitty Chitty Bang Bang*
Forster, E.M. British Born Edward Morgan Forster, the son of Alice Clara née Whichelo and Edward Morgan Llewellyn Forster. It was his mother and aunts who brought him up as his father died soon after he was born. He was educated at Kings College, Cambridge and was able to lead a life dominated by his desire to write and, being personally wealthy, not by the need to earn a wage.	1879-1970	*Howards End* *Passage to India (A)* *Room with a View (A)*

Writer	Date	Works include
Frank, Anne German Anne Frank was a young Jewish girl who chronicled her family's two years in hiding during the German occupation of the Netherlands in a diary which became a piece of classic literature. The family were eventually discovered and Anne died in Bergen-Belsen concentration camp, near Hanover, Germany in 1945.	1929-1945	*Diary of Anne Frank (The)*
G Golding, William British William Golding, born in Cornwall, was educated at Marlborough Grammar School and later at Brasenose College, Oxford where he read Science before transferring courses to English Literature. Married with two children he was knighted by Queen Elizabeth II in 1988.	1911-1993	*To the Ends of the Earth (Trilogy)* *Lord of the Flies* *Free Fall*
Greene, Graham British Born in Berkhampstead, Hertfordshire to Charles Greene and Marion Raymond Greene he was educated at Balliol College, Oxford where he became a prolific student writer. He worked as copy editor for *The Times* and in 1927 he married Vivien Dayrell-Browning. His first novel was *The Man Within*. Many of his novels later became screenplays and in fact one, *The Third Man*, existed in reverse in that it started out as a screenplay and then became a novel. Greene's life was plagued by a serious mental disorder, which may have aided or hindered his output; a question we cannot answer.	1904-1991	*Brighton Rock* *England Made Me* *Power and the Glory (The)*

Writer	Date	Works include
H		
Hardy, Thomas British He was the eldest of four children born to Thomas Hardy and Jemima (née Hand). His early years were, as happens with so many writers – as previously mentioned – plagued with ill health and as a result he did not start school until he was eight years old. His early adult years were spent working in architecture and in 1874 he married Emma Lavinia Gifford, who was to be his wife for 38 years; two years after her death he married Florence Dugdale.	1840-1928	*Far From the Madding Crowd* *Jude the Obscure* *Tess of the d'Urbervilles*
Heller, Joseph American The film version of Catch-22 brought fame to Joseph Heller who was born in Brooklyn, USA and who. during WW II, served with the US Air Force. He studied at both the universities of Columbia and Oxford before becoming a teacher for a short time.	1923-1999	*Catch-22* *God Knows* *Something Happened*
Huxley, Aldous Leonard British Born into a financially well off and artistically successful family Huxley, was educated at Eton and Balliol College, Oxford. Eye problems, which were to be the curse of his life, struck him when he was 16 years old preventing him from both pursuing a career as a scientist and fighting in the First World War. He, therefore, worked for the War Office, taught, and worked as a critic. Huxley, who was a friend of novelist D.H. Lawrence, also wrote travel books, histories, poems, plays, and essays.	1894-1963	*Brave New World* *Crome Yellow* *Do What You Will*
Hartley, L.P. British	1895-1972	*Boat (The)* *Go-Between (The)* *Hireling (The)*

Writer	Date	Works include
Leslie Poles Hartley was born in Cambridgeshire and educated at Harrow and Balliol College, Oxford. He spent the early years of his working life as a fiction reviewer; his first book *Night Fever* was a collection of short stories and was published in 1924 with his full-length novel *The Shrimp and the Anemone* was not published until 1944. He was awarded the CBE in 1956.		
Hemingway, Ernest American Born Ernest Miller Hemingway, the first son of Clarence Edmonds Hemingway, a doctor, and Grace Hall Hemingway. After graduating from high school he worked as a reporter. During the First World War he worked as an ambulance driver for the American Red Cross and was decorated for heroism.	1899-1961	*Farewell to Arms (A)* *For Whom the Bell Tolls* *Old Man and the Sea (The)*
J Joyce, James Irish Full name was James Augustine Aloysius Joyce, he was born in Dublin, Eire, the son of John Stanislaus Joyce and Mary Jane Murray. He was educated at Belvedere College, a Jesuit grammar school in Dublin, and later at University College, Dublin. He later gained recognition for his experimental use of language.	1882-1941	*Finnegans Wake* *Portrait of the Artist as a Young Man (A)* *Ulysses*
James, Henry American Born in New York, Henry James was the second of the five James children. In his early years he travelled extensively in America and Europe, schooled by tutors and governesses. Later he enrolled at Harvard Law School but dropped out to concentrate on his writing.	1843-1916	*Ambassadors (The)* *Portrait of a Lady (The)*

Writer	Date	Works include
A prolific writer, he wrote 20 novels as well as numerous stories, plays and travel sketches before he died in England, the country where he had become a British citizen in 1915.		

K

Writer	Date	Works include
Kafka, Franz German Franz Kafka was born into a middle-class Jewish family, the son of Julie Löwy and Hermann Kafka. He was a paradoxical figure, quiet, intellectual and solitary whilst at the same time a charming and humorous individual. During the day he had an office job with the nights devoted to writing. He had a poor relationship with his domineering father and little belief in his own abilities, to such an extent that before his death from TB in 1924 he requested that all his unpublished manuscripts be destroyed, a request which fortunately, for future generations, was ignored by his literary executor.	1883-1924	*Brief an den Vater* (Letter to Father) *Castle (The)* *Trial (The)*

L

Writer	Date	Works include
Le Carré, John British *See separate entry	1931-	*Most Wanted Man (A)* *Spy Who Came in from the Cold (The)* *Tinker, Tailor, Soldier, Spy*
Lessing, Doris British Born Doris May Taylor in Persia – now Iran – to British parents she later moved, with her parents, to Southern Rhodesia – now Zimbabwe. Her formal education came to an end at the age of 14 after which she embarked upon a series and variety of jobs. Her first marriage was to Frank Charles Wisdom in 1939, with	1919-	*Golden Notebook (The)* *Summer Before Dark (The)*

Writer	Date	Works include
whom she had two children. Her second in 1945 was to Gottfried Lessing with whom she had another child before their divorce in 1949. After this divorce she came to Britain where she has lived ever since. Lessing is a politically motivated writer and a communist.		
Leroux, Gaston French Leroux was born in Paris where he also studied law. Upon the death of his father he inherited a large sum of money, which he quickly squandered, and so found that he had to work for a living; this he did by working as a journalist, travelling extensively to report from all over the world before devoting his life to writing. He became known for detective fiction but will always be remembered as the author of *The Phantom of the Opera*, a novel which has been adapted as both a film, and a stage and film musical.	1868-1927	*Mystery of the Yellow Room (The)* *Perfume of the Lady in Black (The)* *Phantom of the Opera (The)*
London, Jack American It is widely believed that Jack London was in fact the son of astrologer and journalist William Chaney, who deserted Jack's mother, Flora, before he was born: she then married Jack London before her young son was a year old. Largely self-educated, he was an avid reader and in early adulthood he had a variety of jobs before he became a full-time writer. He married twice, first to Bess Maddern with whom he had two children and then to Charmian Kittredge with whom he had just one child who died before she was even two days old. Jack London himself died very young, at just 40 years of age.	1876-1916	*Call of the Wild (The)* *Sea Wolf (The)* *White Fang*
Lewis, C.S. British	1898-1963	*Lion the Witch and the Wardrobe (The)* *Out of the Silver*

Writer	Date	Works include
Clive Staple Lewis was born in Belfast and after the death of his mother was educated at boarding school. After fighting in the Second World War he went up to Oxford to read Classics and then on to be a tutor at Magdalen College and later a Professor at Cambridge University. He was a friend and contemporary of Tolkien – the meeting of two great minds and intellects. C. S. Lewis is best remembered for his work *The Chronicles of Narnia*.		*Planet* *Screwtape Letters*

M

Writer	Date	Works include
Márques, Gabriel José García Columbian Márques was born in Aracataca, in a tropical region of northern Colombia. He was initially brought up by his grandparents who were a huge influence on his early life. Márques began to read law before working as a journalist. He married Mercedes Barcha Pardo in 1958 and in 1959 their first son, Rodrigo, was born with their second son, Gonzalo, born in 1962	1928-	*Love in the Time of Cholera* *Of Love and Other Demons* *One Hundred Years of Solitude*
Milne, A.A. British Alan Alexander Milne was born in London and educated at Cambridge University. He began his career by writing for newspapers and magazines, becoming the assistant editor for the famous magazine *Punch* whilst still in his twenties. In 1913 he married Daphne de Selincourt and in 1920 their son Christopher Robin was born. In the final years of his life A.A. Milne became an invalid; he died in 1956.	1882-1956	*Lovers in London* *Red House Mystery* *Winnie-the-Pooh*
Maugham, Somerset British Full name of William Somerset Maugham, he was orphaned at the age of 10 and consequently raised by an uncle. In 1897 he	1874-1965	*Cakes and Ale* *Moon and Sixpence (The)* *Of Human Bondage*

Writer	Date	Works include
qualified as a doctor and it was upon his experiences as a doctor that he drew to write his first novel *Lisa of Lambeth*. It was the resulting success of this novel that encouraged him to give up medicine and become a writer. During the First World War he worked as a secret agent and after the war he bought a home in France, which was to become his home until he died at the great age of 91 years.		
Morrison, Toni American Born Chloe Anthony Wofford in Ohio, USA, the second of four children of George Wofford and Ramah Willis Wofford, she studied humanities at Howard and Cornell Universities, which was then followed by an academic career. She made her debut as a novelist in 1970 and has since been showered with both nominations and awards for her writing in which she has portrayed the life of black Americans and their struggle to find cultural identity.	1931-	*Beloved* *Jazz* *Song of Solomon*
Mitchell, Margaret American Although the author of just one novel, its extraordinary commercial success rightly earns Margaret Mitchell a place in this list. Published in 1936 *Gone with the Wind* took the world by storm and within six months had sold 1,000,000 copies. In 1937 Mitchell was awarded the Pulitzer Prize. *Gone with the Wind* was sold throughout the world and translated into numerous languages, made into a film, and many years later into a stage musical. If Margaret Mitchell had not been tragically killed in a road accident in 1949 who knows what other great novels she might have written; sadly thoughwe will never know the answer.	1900-1949	*Gone with the Wind*

Writer	Date	Works include
N Nabokov, Vladimir American Born in Russia as Vladimir Vladimirovich Nabokov into an established aristocratic family, his father, V.D. Nabokov, was also a writer and was politically active in the Russia of that day. Nabokov was educated at Trinity College, Cambridge from where he graduated with a first class honours degree. He married Véra Evseyevna Slonim with whom he went on to have one son. His writing included novellas, poetry and scientific papers on entymology.	1899-1977	*Lolita* *Mashenka* *Speak, Memory*
O Orwell, George British George Orwell is the pseudonym of Eric Arthur Blair. He was born in India, the only son of Richard Walmsley Blair and Ida Mabel Blair, and was brought to England when he was just one year old. Academically brilliant, he won a scholarship to Eton but later chose not to go to University. He was a committed socialist but was afraid of communism; his books were a reflection of his political beliefs and fears. In 1943 he became literary editor of the left-wing magazine, *The Tribune*. Orwell died of tuberculosis in 1950.	1903-1950	*Animal Farm* *Nineteen Eighty-Four* *Road to Wigan Pier (The)*
P Potter, Beatrix British Beatrix Potter was the eldest of two children born to Rupert and Helen Potter. Her family life was one of privilege and as a result she was educated at home by a series of governesses. As a result of this she led a somewhat solitary life in which her pets became her 'missing' school	1866-1943	*Tale of Jemima Puddle Duck (The)* *Tale of Mr Jeremy Fisher (The)* *Tale of Peter Rabbit (The)*

Writer	Date	Works include
friends. In adult life she suffered heartbreak when her fiancé, Norman Warne, died just a few weeks after their engagement. She then remained single until she married her solicitor at the age of 47 years. *See Separate Entry		

R

Writer	Date	Works include
<u>Remarque, Erich Maria</u> <u>German</u> Born Erich Paul Remark in Osnabrück, Germany as the son of Peter Franz Remark and Anna Maria Remark, he was a bright and musical child who at the age of 18 was conscripted into the German army. He married and divorced Ilse Jutta Zambona – twice. He married for a third time to Paulette Goddard, a marriage which lasted until his death. He was not a prolific writer and his reputation rests mainly on his novel, *All Quiet on the Western Front*.	1898-1970	*All Quiet on the Western Front* *Arc de Triomph* *Road Back (The)*
<u>Rushdie, Salman</u> <u>British</u> Salman (Ahmed) Rushdie was born in Bombay, India into a Muslim family and was later educated at Cambridge University. Born in the East and educated in the West gave him the bio-cultural input into his work for which he has become renowned. His work *The Satanic Verses*, in which certain passages were interpreted by some Muslims as blasphemous, brought upon him the notorious death sentence or fatwa – which actually brought upon him more fame and success!	1947-	*Midnight's Children* *Satanic Verses (The)* *Shalimar the Clown*

S

Writer	Date	Works include
<u>Steinbeck, John</u> <u>American</u>	1902-1968	*Grapes of Wrath* *Of Mice and Men* *Winter of Our*

Writer	Date	Works include
He was born John Ernst Steinbeck in California, America as the only boy in a family of four children. Although he studied at Stanford University he did not take a degree but instead worked for some time as a labourer, an experience which was to prove useful in his later writing.		*Discontent (The)*
Shute, Nevil Australian (British born) Born Nevil Shute Norway in Ealing, Middlesex, England, he was the younger son of Arthur Hamilton Norway and Mary Louisa Gadsden. Educated at Shrewsbury Public School he later went up to Balliol College, Oxford. Shute displayed an early fascination with airplanes and after university he fittingly became an aeronautical engineer. In 1931 he married Frances Mary Heaton with whom he had two daughters. Dissatisfied with Britain after the Second World War, he settled in Australia. During his lifetime Nevil Shute wrote 24 novels and an autobiography.	1899-1960	*On the Beach* *Pied Piper* *Town Like Alice (A)*
T Tolkien, J.R.R. British John Ronald Reuel Tolkien was born in Bloemfontein, South Africa but came to England at the age of four. He read English at Oxford where he gained a first. He later became a university lecturer but it was his love of language and myths that were to influence his writing when he created *The Hobbit* to entertain the four children from his marriage to Edith Bratt. His most successful work *Lord of the Rings* has inspired not only a screen adaptation but also a stage musical.	1892-1973	*Fellowship of the Ring (The)* *Hobbit (The)* *Return of the King (The)* *Two Towers (The)*

Writer	Date	Works include
W Waugh, Evelyn British In full, Evelyn Arthur St John Waugh, was born into a London literary family. His father was a publisher and literary critic and his younger brother was a writer. Waugh was educated at Lancing College, Sussex, later going up to Hertford College, Oxford to read History. In 1928 he married Evelyn Gardner; it was a marriage that was to last only a few months, by which time had she left him for another man. Divorce was out of the question since his conversion to the Roman Catholic faith but by 1936 he managed to have the marriage annulled, leaving him free to marry Laura Herbert the following year and with whom he went on to have seven children. He died on Easter Day in 1966.	1903-1966	*Decline and Fall* *Handful of Dust (A)* *Sword of Honour* *(a trilogy)*
Wells, H.G. British Herbert George Wells didn't have the easiest start in life with the threat of poverty never far away. His education was limited though compensated for by his voracious appetite for books. After a series of menial jobs he won a scholarship to study Biology with the result that he later became a science teacher. He married his cousin Isabel Mary Wells in 1891 but it was an unhappy marriage and they separated in 1894. In 1895 he then married his second wife Amy Catherine Robbins with whom he later had two sons. From humble beginnings he rose to heights of recognition for both his writing and his international political voice.	1866-1946	*History of Mr Polly (The)* *Time Machine (The)* *War of the Worlds*
White, E.B. American	1899-1985	*Charlotte's Web* *Stuart Little* *Trumpet of the Swan*

Writer	Date	Works include
White, full name Elwyn Brooks White, was born in New York, America where he was reputedly a shy child growing into an equally shy adult. After graduating from Cornell University he began his lifelong career as a magazine writer. It was after his retirement that he started writing the children's books for which he became famous. He married Katherine Sergeant Angell, *The New Yorker*'s first fiction editor.		*(The)*
Wodehouse, P.G. British In full, Pelham Grenville Wodehouse; he was the third son born to Eleanor (née Deane) and Henry Ernest in Guildford, Surrey and was educated at Dulwich College. He initially worked in a bank but after just two years he resigned and in the same year his first novel, *The Pothunters*, was published heralding an exciting and varied career in writing which took him across the pond and into the world of films as well as literature. In 1955 he became a US citizen and in 1975 was knighted by the Queen.	1881-1975	*Code of the Woosters (The)* *Summer Lightning* *Ukridge and Uncle Fred in the Springtime*
Woolf ,Virginia British Woolf was born into a child-dominated family. Her father, Leslie Stephen, had three children from a previous marriage and her mother, Julia Margaret Cameron, had one child from her previous marriage and together they had a further four children. At the age of 13 Virginia entered a nine-year period of tragedy during which time she lost both her parents and her half-sister.	1882-1941	*Mrs Dalloway* *To the Lighthouse*

BRIEF BIOGRAPHIES OF SELECTED WRITERS

When someone becomes well known for doing a certain thing then it is often difficult to see the real person behind the mask of achievement. We think we know famous people, but we don't; we know what they want us to know and see only what they choose to show us, or indeed even what the media feel the need to feed us, and so I hope that maybe you will find a little peep into the other world of just a selected few writers will be both informative and fascinating.

Louisa May Alcott
1832-1888

Well known Works include:

Aunt Jo's Scrap Bag • *Eight Cousins* • *Flower Fables* •
Garland for Girls (A) • *Good Wives* •*Hospital Sketches* •
Jack and Jill • *Jo's Boys* • *Little Men* • *Little Women* • *Lulu's Library* •
Modern Mephistopheles (A) • *Moods* • *Old Fashioned Girl* •
Rose in Bloom •*Spinning Wheel Stories* • *Under the Lilacs* •
Work: A Story of Experience • *Works* •

LOUISA MAY ALCOTT: The Writer and the Woman

• Louisa May Alcott was born in Germantown, Pennsylvania, in 1832 as the daughter of Amos Bronson Alcott and Abigail May
• She had three sisters: Anna, Elizabeth and May
• Alcott was, in the main, educated at home by her father
• She was a tomboy, just like her character Jo in *Little Women*; the character which she based on herself
• Her father, an idealist with somewhat unconventional ideas, was not a good family provider and his daughter soon realised that she must find a way to supplement the family income
• Alcott, as her mother before her, believed in the abolition of slavery and in women's rights
• She wrote short stories and poetry for magazines before embarking on full-length novels
• *Flower Fables*, Alcott's first book was published in 1854
• A total of over 30 books and collections of stories were eventually published

• She was never well again after contracting typhoid from an unsanitary hospital where she had volunteered as a nurse when the American Civil War began
• Louisa May Alcott died on 6 March 1888 and was buried in Sleepy Hollow Cemetery in Concord

EXPERIENCE YESTERDAY'S WORLD OF LOUISA MAY ALCOTT TODAY

The most permanent of the past Alcott homes is now a National Historic Landmark and open for the public to visit today and this is Orchard House in Concord, Massachusetts, USA where the family lived from 1858 to 1877. It is also where Louisa May Alcott wrote, and where she set, her most famous and classic novel *Little Women*. A fascinating place to visit, Orchard House has changed very little since the Alcotts were in residence and in fact more than 75% of the furnishings were actually owned by the Alcott family themselves. A visit to this house is a step back in time and a step into the mind and heart of Louisa May Alcott herself.

AND FINALLY

• Alcott's writing career began with poetry and short stories which were published in popular magazines of the time; she was 35 years old before her publisher suggested to her that she should write a novel for girls; the result being *Little Women*
• Louisa May Alcott died just two days after her father

Wilkie Collins
1824-1889

Major Works by Wilkie Collins include:

Antonina • Armadale • Basil • Black Robe (The) • Blind Love •
Dead Secret (The) • Evil Genius (The) • Fallen Leaves (The) •
Guilty River • Hide and Seek • Jezebel's Daughter •
Law and the Lady (The) • Legacy of Cain (The) • Man and Wife •
Memoirs of the Life of William Collins Esq (The) • Moonstone (The) •
Mr Wray's Cash-Box • My Miscellanies • New Magdalen (The) •

No Name • *Poor Miss Finch* • *Queen of Hearts (The)* •
Rambles Beyond Railways • *Rogues Life (A)* • *Two Destinies (The)* •
Woman in White (The) •

WILKIE COLLINS: The Man and his Life

• William Wilkie Collins was born on 8 January 1824 to artist William Collins and his wife Harriet (née Geddes) in Marylebone, London as the elder of two boys; his younger brother Charles was born in 1828
• His father was the well-known landscape artist and portrait painter
• His middle name – which he adopted as his pen name – was taken from his godfather, the Scottish painter, Sir David Wilkie
• He was educated at The Maida Hill Academy and after that at Cole's Boarding School in London; he left school altogether at the age of 16 years to work in the office of a London tea merchant
• Until the recent discovery of an earlier piece of work, *Volpurno*, it was always thought that 1843 was the year which saw the publication of his first work with *The Last Stage Coachman* appearing in *Illuminated Magazine* of that year.
• In the year 1846 Collins became a law student at Lincoln's Inn and was called to the Bar in 1851
• Charles Dickens and Wilkie Collins met for the first time in 1851 and formed what was to be a lifelong friendship, cemented not only by their love of writing but by their love of theatre too
• In 1847 his father William Collins died; Collins first book was a biography of his father
• In 1853 Collins and Charles Dickens made together the first of what was to be many tours abroad
• Collins and Dickens also collaborated on a play *The Frozen Deep*, but more than writing plays together and enjoying a mutual love of all things theatrical, they also played in lead roles opposite each other when *The Frozen Deep* opened in 1857
• Wilkie Collins worked extensively as a journalist including writing articles for Dickens' magazines *Household Words* and *All the Year Round*
He led a flamboyant lifestyle, not dissimilar to many celebrities today, eating and drinking to excess and travelling extensively. He eventually took copious amounts of opium – but only to ease the symptoms of ill health – as well as enjoying the company of many other like-minded people
• His private life was somewhat daring for Victorian times, for in 1858 he began an unconventional relationship with a widow by the name of

Elizabeth Caroline Graves, (though always referred to as Caroline). This relationship was to last most of their lives, except for one, peculiar but fascinating hiccup

• Graves had one daughter from a previous marriage; the daughter's name was Elizabeth Harriet – she was known, however, by the name of 'Carrie'

• The interesting hiccup occurred when Caroline Graves – mid relationship with Collins – married another man! Collins himself had, in fact, already begun a relationship with another woman called Martha Rudd, so perhaps it was for that reason that Caroline moved out; or maybe she gave him an ultimatum of marriage? We will never know for certain, although it would appear now that Collins had no intention of marrying anyone, as despite having three children with Martha Rudd, he did not marry her either! But whoever was to blame and for whatever reason this hiccup appeared, each of their new relationships did not stand the test of time and so it would seem that Collins and Graves were clearly destined to be together as, three years later, they were reunited once more and went on to spend the rest of their lives together, finally being buried beside each other. However, Collins did not let go of his relationship with Martha Rudd entirely and so had a relationship with the two women until his death. Although Rudd never lived with Collins – that honour belonging Graves – he did house her a few streets away under the name of Dawson, and actually visited her himself under the name of Mr William Dawson, barrister at laws. We are talking Victorian times here, and even in the Twenty-first Century maintaining two such relationships, so publicly, would be frowned upon. Of course Collins and his ladies did not have the problems of press intrusion as we do today and so seemed to have 'pulled it off', though why anyone of them would want to share, is beyond me, but it does make for interesting reading

• It must be noted that Collins always provided for his children during his lifetime and made generous provision for them in his will, as well as for Martha and Caroline. The sad conclusion to this tale though is that the solicitor embezzled the money and left both ladies and their children financially distressed

• In 1860 Collins' younger brother, Charles, married Charles Dickens' younger daughter, Kate

• In 1868 Wilkie Collins' mother died after dedicating her life to her family; this was a death that hit Wilkie Collins very hard

• In 1873 his younger brother, Charles, died thus leaving Wilkie Collins as the sole surviving member of his immediate family

• In 1884 Collins became a founder member of The Society of Authors

• In June of 1889 Wilkie Collins suffered a fatal stroke

• In 1999 his first novel *Iolani*, which in 1844 had been rejected by several publishers, was finally published, over 100 years after his death

OTHER WORKS BY WILKIE COLLINS INCLUDE:

Works written in collaboration with Charles Dickens include:
Lazy Tour of Two Idle Apprentices (The)
No Thoroughfare
Perils of Certain English Prisoners (The)

Short Stories by Wilkie Collins include:
After Dark [a collection of six short stories]
Little Novels [a collection of 14 short stories]
Queen of Hearts (The) [a collection of 10 short stories]

Plays by Wilkie Collins include:
Miss Gwilt [the stage title of *Armadale*]
Black and White [in collaboration with Charles Fechter]
Court Duel (A) [adapted from the French by Collins]
Dead Secret (The)
Evil Genius (The)
Frozen Deep (The)
Lighthouse (The)
Man and Wife
Message from the Sea (A) [in collaboration with Charles Dickens]
Moonstone (The)
New Magdalen (The)
No Name
No Thoroughfare [in collaboration with Charles Dickens]
Rank and Riches
Red Vial (The)
Woman in White (The)

AND FINALLY

• During his life-time Wilkie Collins wrote over 100 non-fiction pieces, more than 60 short stories, 30 novels, and at least 15 plays
• His first book published was a tribute to his deceased father and was entitled, *Memoirs of the Life of William Collins*

• As well as being a prolific writer, like his friend Charles Dickens, he loved to tread the boards – just as Shakespeare before them

• Although most people are aware of the recent adaptation of Collins' novel *The Woman in White* into a stage musical, Collins had in fact made his own stage adaptation in 1871

• Collins suffered from rheumatic gout and neuralgia which severely affected his eyes and was the reason for his excessive intake of opium, which was reputedly to relieve the pain and nothing else

• His first novel, *Iolani*, was rejected – and as I keep saying: 'Struggling novelists, take note and never give up'

• Wilkie Collins was only 5'6"tall

• It is said that the sudden meeting of the character Walter Hartright with the mysterious 'Woman in White' in the novel of the same name was inspired by a real life event in Collin's own life in which he was apparently accosted by a woman in flowing white gowns when he was strolling home one evening. True or not we will never know, but as they say: 'There is always some element of fact in every work of fiction'

Sir Arthur Conan Doyle
1859-1930

Major Works by Sir Arthur Conan Doyle include:
(So prolific was Doyle that even his major works
have to be categorised)

Actor's Duel and The Winning Shot (An) • *Conan Doyle Stories (The)* • *Croxley Master (The)* •*Danger! and Other Stories* • *Doings of Raffles Haw (The)* • *Dreamers (The)* • *Firm of Girdlestone: A Romance of the Unromantic (The)* • *Great Shadow (The)* • *Green Flag and Other Stories of War and Sport (The)* • *Hound of the Baskervilles (The)* •*Last Galley: Impressions and Tales (The)* • *Mystery of Cloomber (The)* • *Parasite (The)* • *Round the Fire Stories* • *Round the Red Lamp: Being Facts and Fancies of a Medical Life* • *Sign of Four (The)* • *Strange Studies from Life* • *Study in Scarlet (A)* • *Surgeon of Gaster Fell (The)* • *Tales of Adventure and Medical Life* •

Tales of Long Ago • Tales of Pirates and Blue Water •
Tales of Terror and Mystery • Tales of Twilight and the Unseen •
Tragedy of Korosko (The) • Valley of Fear (The) • White Company (The)

Sherlock Holmes Short Story Collections include:
Adventure of Sherlock Holmes (The) • Case-Book of Sherlock
Holmes (The) • Complete Sherlock Holmes Story (The) • His Last Bow •
Memoires of Sherlock Holmes (The) • Return of Sherlock Holmes (The)

Professor Challenger Stories:
Disintegration Machine (The) • Land of Mist (The) • Lost World
(The) • Poison Belt (The) •Professor Challenger Stories (The) •
When the World Screamed

SIR ARTHUR CONAN DOYLE: The Writer and the Man

• Arthur Ignatius Conan Doyle was born on 22 May 1859 in Edinburgh, Scotland, though of Irish descent, to Charles Altamont Doyle and Mary (Foley)

• His father was a chronic alcoholic and so from the age of nine other members of the Doyle family paid for his education at a Jesuit boarding school – where sadly he failed to find happiness

• He was devoted to his mother and inherited many of her qualities for she too was a voracious reader and a master storyteller

• During his unhappy years at boarding school he would enthral his peers with his expert storytelling. He wrote regularly to his mother whilst away from home and continued to do so until her death

• When Doyle was in his teens his father was committed to a mental asylum

• Although artistic and creative by nature the young Doyle decided to study medicine and with this in mind went to Edinburgh University where his contemporaries were J.M. Barrie and Robert Louis Stevenson. It was here he penned his first story, *The Mystery of Sassasa Valley*, heralding what was to be an illustrious career in writing

• In 1881 he was awarded a Bachelor of Medicine and Master of Surgery Degree from the University of Edinburgh

• After graduation he spent the next few years practising medicine and struggling to achieve success as a writer

• In 1885 he married Louisa Hawkins and together they went on to have two children – a boy and a girl – before she died in 1906

• In 1888 he had his first success with his novel *A Study in Scarlet*, and so began a serious dichotomy in the literary career of Arthur Conan Doyle. On the one hand he wrote the hugely commercially successful works featuring Sherlock Holmes, whilst on the other he wrote his more serious works of novels, plays and poems, which he believed would bring him success

• It wasn't until 1891 that Doyle decided to abandon his medical career in favour of a writing career

• In 1893 – against popular outcry – he killed off his successful creation Sherlock Holmes in his novel *The Final Problem*, which in his eyes freed him from the constraints of the character Holmes, thus leaving him free to write what he believed would be far superior works

• Sherlock Holmes made another appearance though in 1901 in his supremely popular work *The Hound of the Baskervilles* and again in 1903 with the serialisation of *The Return of Sherlock Holmes*

• He was knighted in 1902 by King Edward VII for his services to the crown during the Boer War

• His wife Louisa died of tuberculosis in his arms on 4 July 1906; he had nursed her through this illness since 1893 when she was given only a few months to live

• On 18 September 1907 Arthur Conan Doyle married Jean Leckie, a woman he had discreetly loved during the long illness through which he loyally cared for his wife. With Jean he then went on to have another two sons and a daughter

• The First World War brought tragedy when it claimed several members of his family – his son, his brother, two brothers-in-law and two nephews

• Later in his life he developed an almost obsessive interest in science fiction and spiritualism

• Sir Arthur Conan Doyle died after a full and furious life on 7 July 1930 surrounded by his family; his final words to his wife were quite simply, "You are wonderful."

OTHER WORKS BY SIR ARTHUR CONAN DOYLE INCLUDE:

Plays

Brigadier Gerard
Brothers
Duet. A Duologue (A)
Fires of Fate (The)
House of Temperley (The)

Jane Annie or the Good Conduct Prize (with J.M. Barrie)
Pot of Caviare (A)
Question of Diplomacy (A)
Sherlock Holmes (with William Gillette)
Speckled Band (The)
Story of Waterloo (The)

Pamphlets

Case of Mr. George Edalji (The)
Case of Oscar Slater (The)
Debate with Dr. Joseph McCabe (A)
Early Christian Church and Modern Spiritualism (The)
Great Britain and the Next War
In Quest of Truth
Our Reply to the Cleric
Psychic Experiences (reprint)
Spiritualism and Rationalism
To Arms!
Treatment of our Prisoners (The)
War in South Africa: Its Cause and Conduct (The)

Verse

Guards Came Through and Other Poems (The)
Songs of Action
Songs of the Road

Works on the War and Spiritualism

Civilian National Reserve
Edge of the Unknown (The)
New Revelation: or, What Is Spiritualism? (The)
Our American Adventure
Spiritualism – Some Straight Questions and Direct Answers
British Campaign in France and Flanders, 1914-1918 (The)
Coming of the Fairies (The)
Crime of the Congo (The)
German War (The)
Great Boer War (The)
Immortal Memory (The)
Outlook on the War (The)
Wanderings of a Spiritualist (The)

World War Conspiracy (The)
Western Wanderings
Word of Warning (A)

AND FINALLY
- Sir Arthur Conan Doyle was a volunteer physician in the Boer War
- Early on in his career he was more recognised on the other side of the pond than on this
- Doyle was a man of high principles who could not tolerate injustice and who fought publicly on at least two occasions for those who had been wronged
- He made two unsuccessful attempts to enter politics

Thomas Hardy
1840-1928

Works by Thomas Hardy include:
Changed Man and Other Tales (A) • *Desperate Remedies* • *Far from the Madding Crowd* • *Group of Noble Dames (A)* • *Hand of Ethelberta (The)* • *Jude the Obscure* • *Laodicean (A)* • *Life's Little Ironies* • *Mayor of Casterbridge (The)* • *Pair of Blue Eyes (A)* • *Return of the Native (The)* • *Romantic Adventures of a Milkmaid (The)* • *Tess of the d'Urbervilles* • *Trumpet Major (The)* • *Two on a Tower* • *Under the Greenwood Tree* • *Well-Beloved (The)* • *Woodlanders (The)*

THOMAS HARDY: The Writer and the Man
- Thomas Hardy was born on 2 June 1840 at Higher Bockhampton near Dorchester, Dorset as the eldest of four children born to Thomas Hardy, a stonemason, and Jemima (née Hand)
- His early years were spent growing up in an ancient stone cottage on the edge of Dorset heathland; he was educated at the local village school

• He later continued his education at school in the nearby county town of Dorchester
• After leaving school he was apprenticed to John Hicks, a local architect
• In 1862 he continued his architectural career in the London office of Arthur Blomfield – though his heart was in writing and not in architecture
• His first and lasting love was poetry, but his poetry failed initially to attract the attention he craved and so it was with some reluctance that he turned to writing prose in the hope that through this he may be able to earn a living. It wasn't, however, until 1873 that he was able to make his dream a reality
• In 1874 Hardy married Emma Lavinia Gifford, though it was hardly a match made in heaven
• In 1885 he designed and built Max Gate, a family home in which he was to write some of his best loved novels including: *The Mayor of Casterbridge*, *The Woodlanders*, *Tess of the d'Urbervilles* and *Jude the Obscure*; as well as three collections of short stories, *Wessex Tales*, *A Group of Noble Dames* and *Life's Little Ironies*
• In 1912 Emma Hardy died suddenly bringing to an end a marriage in which the two partners lived almost unaware of the other's existence
• In 1914 Hardy married Florence Emily Dugdale, a woman 38 years his junior
• Thomas Hardy died on 11 January 1928 at the age of 87 years

AND FINALLY
• During his lifetime Hardy wrote almost a thousand published poems and 14 published novels
• His heart is buried in his home parish churchyard at Stinsford, Dorset; his ashes, however, are in Poets' Corner in Westminster Abbey, London

Hardy's Short Story Collections include:
Changed Man and Other Tales (A)
Group of Noble Dames (A)
Life's Little Ironies
Wessex Tales

Poems
Dynasts (The) [a poetic drama, though never intended for performance]

Human Shows
Late Lyrics and Earlier
Moments of Vision
Poems of the Past and the Present
Time's Laughingstocks
Wessex Poems

Henry James
1843-1916

Works by Henry James include:

Ambassadors (The) • American (The) • Aspern Papers (The) • Awkward Age (The) • Beast in the Jungle (The) • Beldonald Holbein (The) • Bostonians (The) • Chaperon (The) • Confidence • Coxon Fund (The) • Daisy Miller • Death of the Lion (The) • Diary of Man of Fifty (The) • Europeans (The) • Glasses • Golden Bowl (The) • In the Cage • International Episode (An) • Ivory Tower (The) • Lessons of the Master (The) • Nona Vincent • Other House (The) • Pandora • Pension Beaurepas (The) • Portrait of a Lady (The) • Princess Casmassima (The) • Private Life (The) • Pupil (The) • Sacred Fount (The) • Turn of the Screw (The) • Washington Square • Watch and Ward • What Maisie Knew • Wings of the Dove (The)

HENRY JAMES: The Writer and the Man

• Henry James was born in New York, USA in 1843 as the second of five children – four boys and a girl – born to Henry James Sr and his wife, Mary

• James' father was an intellectual theologian with very forward thinking beliefs

• The James children were extraordinarily well travelled and as a consequence of this had exceptionally good linguistic skills, in comparison to other children of their time. This was because their father believed that an extensive and comprehensive education could only be achieved through first hand experiences and the observations of such, rather than from the confines of

traditional education, which is actually a rather unusual and bohemian approach for the era in which they lived
• At the age of 19 years James enrolled at The Harvard Law School, but he was more interested in reading and in writing short stories than in the study of law
• For almost a decade he wrote only short stories before embarking on his first full length novel
• In 1876 Henry James moved to London where he fitted well into the London literary society of the time, mixing with gigantic names such as Robert Louis Stevenson and Robert Browning
• In 1897 James moved to the quiet English location of Rye in Sussex
• It was in 1915 he became a British citizen
• Henry James died on 28 February 1916 and his ashes were interred at the Cambridge Cemetery in Massachusetts, United States; in 1976 a memorial stone was placed for him in the Poets' Corner of Westminster Abbey, London

OTHER WORKS BY HENRY JAMES INCLUDE:

Plays
Pyramus and Thisbe
Still Waters Change of Heart (A)

Works of Non Fiction include:
French Poets and Novelists
Hawthorne
Italian Hours
Little Tour in France (A)
Middle Years (The)
Notes of a Son and a Brother

Short Stories include:
Author of Beltraffo (The)
Brooksmith
Bundle of Letters (A)
Covering End
Daisy Miller
Diary of a Man of Fifty (The)
Figure in the Carpet (The)

Flickerbridge
Friends of the Friends (The)
Greville Fane
Jolly Corner
Julia Bride
Light Man (A)
Louisa Pallant
Madame de Mauves
Madonna of the Future (The)
Marriages (The)
Mrs. Medwin
Passionate Pilgrim (A)
Point of View (The)
Real Thing (The)
Romance of Certain Old Clothes (The)
Sir Edmund Orme
Story In It (The)
Story of It (The)
Tree of Knowledge (The)

AND FINALLY

• Henry James never married for, whilst ostensibly being an outgoing and gregariously sociable adult, he kept 'involvement' at arm's length
• Henry James' novels have been extensively adapted for both stage and screen with more than 40 films alone made based on his novels

James Joyce
1882-1941

Works by James Joyce include:

Chamber Music • Dubliners • Exiles • Finnegans Wake • Pommes Pennyeach • Portrait of the Artist as a Young Man (A) • Stephen Hero • Ulyssees

JAMES JOYCE: The Writer and the Man

- James Joyce was born on 2 February 1882 in Dublin, Ireland
- He was the eldest of 10 surviving children born to John Stanislaus Joyce and May Murray
- As a child Joyce had a predominantly Jesuit education in addition to being educated at home – more or less by himself with the help of his mother
- In 1898 he went on to Dublin University where he studied modern languages
- After university he left Ireland to study medicine in Paris but was soon to return home when his mother became ill
- James Joyce's mother died in 1903 but his father lived on until 1931
- In 1904 he met Nora Barnacle who was to become his partner and later his wife; they went on to have two children together, Georgio and Lucia
- In 1904 he left Ireland to live in Europe where he then spent most of his life
- Sadly his daughter suffered from grave mental problems necessitating her eventual committal to a mental institution in Paris
- In 1932 his grandson was born
- James Joyce died on 13 January 1941 and was buried in Zurich

OTHER WORKS BY JAMES JOYCE INCLUDE:

Works of Non Fiction
Critical Writings of James Joyce (The)
Letters of James Joyce, Volumes 1, 2 & 3

Short Stories
Araby
Boarding House (The)
Two Gallants
May Goulding
What is a Ghost?

AND FINALLY

- At one point negotiations over particular passages in *The Dubliners* resulted in the publisher withdrawing his offer to publish – albeit only temporarily
- Joyce did not believe in the institution of marriage and so when he

met someone with whom he wanted to share his life, Nora Barnacle, he was forced to leave Ireland, a country of strong Catholic morals. To protect his inheritance rights, however, James and Nora were finally married in 1931
• Whereas many writers can produce a book in a year, some even in months, Joyce was a writer who would take many, many years to produce the final draft of some of his works, having proofed and rewritten numerous times

Rudyard Kipling
1865-1936

Major Works by Rudyard Kipling include:

All the Mowgli Stories • *Captains Courageous* • *Diversity of Creatures* • *Elephant, the Hare and the Black Cobra (The)* • *Five Nations* • *Gypsy Trail (The)* • *Indian Tales* • *Jungle Book (The)* • *Just So Stories for Little Children* • *Kim* • *Life's Handicap* • *Light That Failed (The)* • *Man Who Was: And Other Stories (The)* • *Puck of Pook's Hill* • *Rewards and Fairies* • *Second Jungle Book (The)* • *Something of Myself* • *Stalky & Co* • *Story of the Gadsbys (The)* •

RUDYARD KIPLING: The Writer and the Man

• Joseph Rudyard Kipling was born on 30 December 1865 in Bombay, India, the son of John Lockwood Kipling and Alice (née) MacDonald
• His family background was very impressive; his father was an artist and a scholar who was also curator of Lahore Museum. Through his mother he had, as they say, connections, for two of her sisters married the Nineteenth Century painters Sir Edward Burne-Jones and Sir Edward Poynter, whilst her third sister married Alfred Baldwin meaning that she became the mother of Stanley Baldwin – the future Prime Minister, whilst Alice herself, of course, became mother to one of the most famous, and prolific writers of all time – Rudyard Kipling
• Kipling's sister, also called Alice but known as Trix, was born in 1868

• Kipling's early childhood was idyllically happy until, at the age of five years, he and his sister were taken to Southsea in England where they were then left with foster parents; his childhood happiness ended on that fateful day
• He was initially educated at a small private school in Southsea
• At the age of 12 years he started at The United Services College at Westward Ho!
• In 1882 he left school and set sail for India where he was to become a journalist; it wasn't until 1884 that his sister followed him
• In 1892 Rudyard Kipling married Carrie Balestier, the sister of Walcott Balestier who was a great friend of Kipling's and a collaborator with him on the novel *The Naulahka*. Sadly, Walcott Balestier died in the same year that his sister married his friend
• The Kiplings lived for a while in America
• Rudyard and Carrie Kipling went on to have three children, though sadness followed when his daughter, Josephine, died when she was just six years old and his son John was reported as missing in action during the Second World War when he was only 18 years old
• In 1907 he was awarded the Nobel Prize in Literature
• In 1926 Kipling received the Gold Medal of the Royal Society of Literature, which only Scott, Meredith, and Hardy had been awarded before him
• Rudyard Kipling died in 1936 and his ashes were then laid in Poets' Corner in Westminster Abbey

OTHER WORKS BY RUDYARD KIPLING

Kipling wrote numerous collections of short stories; here you will find just some of these collections by title, and in addition you will also find a few selected named stories taken from the various collections. There is just not the space to list all of his works and in fact one wonders however he himself found the time to write them all and so I stand back in wonder, admiration and awe at the marvels of such a fertile mind and fine intellect.

Short Story Collections include:

Actions and Reactions
Day's Work (The)
In Black and White
Land and Sea Tales
Life's Handicap

Limits and Renewals
Many Inventions
Plain Tales from the Hills
Soldiers Three
Traffics and Discoveries
Wee Willie Winkie and Other Child Stories

Short Stories include

As Easy as ABC
At the End of the Passage
Baa Baa Black Sheep
Beginning of Armadillos (The)
Beyond the Pale
Bisara of Pooree (The)
Bridge Builders (The)
Butterfly That Stamped (The)
Bumbling Well Road
Cat that Walked by Himself (The)
Children of the Zodiac
Crab that Played with the Sea (The)
Dayspring Mishandled
Dream of Duncan Parreness (The)
Elephant's Child (The)
Gate of the Hundred Sorrows (The)
How the Alphabet was Made
How the Camel Got His Hump
How the First Letter Was Written
How the Leopard Got His Spots
How the Rhinoceros got His Skin
How the Whale Got His Throat
Maltese Cat (The)
Man Who Would Be King (The)
Mary Postgate
Pig
Return of Imray (The)
Story of Muhammad Din (The)
Wish House (The)

Poetry Collections include:

Barrack Room Ditties

Departmental Ditties and Other Verses
Five Nations (The)
Seven Seas (The)
Years Between (The)

Individual Poems include:
Ballad of East and West (The)
Female of the Species
Five Nations (The)
Fuzzy-Wuzzy
Gunga Din
If
Legend of Evil (The)
Power of the Dog (The)
Recessional
Ritual of the Calling of an Engineer (The)
Widow at Windsor (The)
Soldier, Soldier
Tommy
When Earth's Last Picture is Picture
Absent Minded Beggar (The)
Bell Bouy (The)

Works of Non Fiction include:
American Notes
France at War
Letters of Travel
Sea Warfare
Fringes of the Fleet (The)
From Sea to Sea
Irish Guards in the Great War (The) – Volumes I & II
Book of Words (A)
Something of Myself
Souvenirs of France

EXPERIENCE YESTERDAY'S WORLD OF RUDYARD KIPLING TODAY

One can also visit The National Trust property of Bateman's Burwash, Etchingham, East Sussex which was the home of Rudyard Kipling from 1902 to 1936. It is a Seventeenth Century house and with its many oriental rugs and artifacts is an obvious reflection of the author's strong associations with the East. Most of the rooms are pretty much as Kipling left them, including his own book-filled study; it is also possible to view the original illustrations for *The Jungle Book* and see his 1928 Phantom Rolls Royce.

AND FINALLY

• Kipling was twice offered and twice refused a Knighthood
• He was the first Englishman to be awarded the Nobel Prize for Literature
• This 'And Finally' section is going to end on a different note to all other 'And Finally' sections, for here I am going to include an entire poem by Rudyard Kipling; not only one of his most well-known poems, but possibly one of the most well-known poems of all time

IF

If you can keep your head when all about you
Are losing theirs and blaming it on you;
If you can trust yourself when all men doubt you,
But make allowance for their doubting too;
If you can wait and not be tired by waiting,
Or, being lied about, don't deal in lies,
Or, being hated, don't give way to hating,
And yet don't look too good, nor talk too wise;
If you can dream – and not make dreams your master;
If you can think – and not make thoughts your aim;
If you can meet with triumph and disaster
And treat those two impostors just the same;
If you can bear to hear the truth you've spoken
Twisted by knaves to make a trap for fools,
Or watch the things you gave your life to broken,
And stoop and build 'em up with wornout tools;
If you can make one heap of all your winnings
And risk it all on one turn of pitch-and-toss,
And lose, and start again at your beginnings
And never breath a word about your loss;
If you can force your heart and nerve and sinew
To serve your turn long after they are gone,
And so hold on when there is nothing in you
Except the Will which says to them: "Hold on!"
If you can talk with crowds and keep your virtue,

Or walk with kings – nor lose the common touch;
If neither foes nor loving friends can hurt you;
If all men count with you, but none too much;
If you can fill the unforgiving minute
With sixty seconds' worth of distance run –
Yours is the Earth and everything that's in it,
And – which is more – you'll be a Man, my son!

D.H. Lawrence
1885-1930

Major Works by D.H. Lawrence include:

Aaron's Rod • *Boy In The Bush (The)* • *Escaped Cock (The)* •
Kangaroo • *Lady Chatterley's Lover* • *Lost Girl (The)* •
Mr Noon Part I and Part II • *Plumed Serpent (The)* •
Rainbow (The) • *Sons and Lovers* • *St Mawr* • *Trespasser (The)* •
Virgin And The Gipsy (The) • *White Peacock (The)* • *Women in Love* •

D.H. LAWRENCE: The Writer and the Man

• David Herbert Lawrence was born on 11 September in the year 1885 in the mining town of Eastwood, Nottinghamshire, England. He was the fourth child born to Arthur Lawrence and Lydia Beardsall
• His father was a miner, starting in the mines at the age of just 10 years, and his mother was a former school teacher
• The Lawrence family home life was a troubled one with a discontented mother and a bitter, heavy drinking father
• Lawrence was not a healthy child, but a frail individual who did not join in the boisterous games with the other boys, which lead to a childhood of bullying
• Despite his difficult background, Lawrence won a scholarship to Nottingham High School
• After leaving Nottingham High School in 1901 he began work for a surgical appliances manufacturer in Nottingham
• Actively encouraged by his mother after a bout of pneumonia, he later

started work as a pupil-teacher at a local school
- In 1906 he then became a student teacher at the University College, Nottingham during which time his first short story was published
- After graduating from Nottingham University he took up a teaching post in Croydon
- 1909 saw the publication of his poems in the English Review
- In 1910 Lawrence's mother, Lydia, died
- Following his own illness Lawrence returned to Nottinghamshire where he fell in love with the wife of his former professor, Frieda von Richthofen; the pair then left England for Germany
- Lawrence and Frieda married in 1914 and eventually settled in Cornwall, but it was at the time of the First World War and the pair suffered at the hands of those who were suspicious of an English man married to a German woman in such turbulent times
- The treatment he received in his own country during this period was the cause of him leaving his homeland and in effect becoming somewhat of a wanderer
- In 1924 his father died
- Probably his most well known novel is that of *Lady Chatterley's Lover* which was heavily criticised and then banned for its sexual content. What annoyed Lawrence was the fact that *Lady Chatterley's Lover* was the object of wide scale pirating throughout Europe after the ban
- Lawrence never really enjoyed full health in his lifetime which was prematurely cut short when he died on 2 March 1930 in Vence, France at the age of 44 years

OTHER WORKS BY D.H. LAWRENCE INCLUDE:

Poetry

Amores
Birds, Beasts And Flowers
Fire and Other Poems
Last Poems
Look! We Have Come Through!
Love Poems and Others
Nettles
New Poems
Pansies
Tortoises

Short Story Collections
England, My England and Other Stories
Glad Ghosts
Ladybird, The Fox, The Captain's Doll (The)
Love Among The Haystacks and Other Pieces
Prussian Officer and Other Stories (The)
Rawdon's Roof
Sun
Woman Who Rode Away and Other Stories (The)

Plays
Widowing of Mrs Holroyd (The)
Touch and Go
David
Fight for Barbara (The)
Collier's Friday Night (A)
Married Man (The)
Merry-Go-Round (The)

In addition D.H. Lawrence also wrote travel pieces, essays and translations.

EXPERIENCE YESTERDAY'S WORLD OF D.H. LAWRENCE TODAY

For D.H. Lawrence lovers then a visit to the D.H. Lawrence Birthplace Museum is a must for it is, as the name implies, the birthplace of D.H. Lawrence. Here at 8a Victoria Street, Eastwood, Nottinghamshire you can enjoy a guided tour of Lawrence's very first home in Eastwood, seeing at first hand exactly in what kind of environment he lived and wonder what inspired the outpourings of such a great man.

AND FINALLY

• *Lady Chatterley's Lover*, the novel D.H. Lawrence wrote in 1928 and was banned from sale in the UK until 1960, finally sold 200,000 copies on the first day

John Le Carré
1931-

Major Works by John Le Carré include:

Absolute Friends • Call for the Dead • Constant Gardener (The) • Honourable Schoolboy (The) • Little Drummer Girl (The) • Looking Glass War (The) • Mission Song (The) • Most Wanted Man (A) • Murder of Quality (A) • Naïve and Sentimental Lover (The) • Night Manager (The) • Our Game • Perfect Spy (A) • Russia House (The) • Secret Pilgrim (The) • Single & Single • Small Town in Germany (A) • Smiley's People • Spy Who Came in from the Cold (The) • Tailor of Panama (The) • Tinker, Tailor, Soldier, Spy •

JOHN LE CARRÉ: The Writer and the Man

• John Le Carré was born on 19 October, 1931 in Poole, Dorset as David John Moore Cornwell, the son of Richard Thomas Archibald Cornwell and Olive Cornwell

• He has one sister and one brother

• His relationship with his parents was rocky; his father was a con man and spent time in jail; his mother abandoned him when he was very young and he was 21 years old before they became reacquainted

• Le Carré was educated at Sherborne School, the University of Berne and Lincoln College, Oxford from where he graduated with a first class honours degree in Modern Languages

• He married Alison Sharp in 1954 and together they had three sons

• At one point in the 1950s Le Carré taught at Eton Public School

• He was a member of the British Foreign Service from 1959-1964, a period in his life which gave him a first-hand insight that was to prove most useful when he began to write novels on espionage

• It was in 1961 that he started writing novels

• After his divorce from Alison, Le Carré went on to marry Valerie *Jane* Eustace – known by her second name – with whom he had a fourth son

• He has four sons and twelve grandchildren

• He lives in Cornwall, England

AND FINALLY

John Le Carré cannot type but writes in longhand

C.S. Lewis
1898-1963

Major Works by C.S. Lewis include:

Abolition of Man (The) • *Beyond Personality* • *Discarded Image (The)* • *Great Divorce (The)* • *Out of the Silent Planet* • *Perelandra* • *Pilgrims Regress (A)* • *Screwtape Letters (The)* • *Screwtape Proposes a Toast* • *That Hideous Strength Till We Have Faces: A Myth Retold* • *Vivisection*

The Chronicles of Narnia

Horse and his Boy (The) • *Last Battle (The)* • *Lion, the Witch and the Wardrobe (The)* • *Magician's Nephew (The)* • *Prince Caspian* • *Silver Chair (The)* • *Voyage of the Dawn Treader* •

C.S. LEWIS: The Writer and the Man

• Clive Staples Lewis was born as the second son of Albert and Florence (née Hamilton) in Belfast, Northern Ireland on 29 November 1898
• His brother, Warren, was born in 1895
• The Lewis family were very religious in their ways and in their outlook on life: his grandfather was a minister, his father wrote evangelical pamphlets and his mother was the daughter of a clergyman
• His was an educated family where learning was valued and so he was consequently given an early grounding in Latin and French by his mother, who herself was a great intellect; the more mundane subjects were attended to in the educationally formative years by a governess
• Tragedy hit the Lewis family in 1908 when Lewis' mother died of cancer
• Within a few weeks of his mother's death he was sent off to join his older brother, Warren, at Wynyard School in Watford, England. It was not a happy experience for either of the boys; the school eventually closed in 1911
• After a short spell at another school, he finally arrived at Cherbourg School in Malvern – a much happier time for him then began
• Lewis later won a scholarship to Malvern College and once more school became an unhappy place for him; it was during this period in his life that he abandoned his childhood Christian faith
• In 1917 he went up to University College, Oxford

• He also served in the first World War and was wounded in 1918
• In May 1925, Lewis was elected a Fellow of Magdalen College, Oxford, as tutor in English Language and Literature. He remained there for 29 years after which, in 1954, he left for Magdalene College, Cambridge
• 1931 was a turning point for C.S. Lewis for it was in that year he became a Christian; one evening in September, Lewis had a long talk on Christianity with J.R.R. Tolkien, who was a devout Roman Catholic, and Hugo Dyson; at this point in time he did not believe that Jesus Christ was the Son of God – the following day, he did
• In 1933 *The Pilgrim's Regress: An Allegorical Apology for Christianity, Reason and Romanticism* was published. In the same year the 'Inklings' was formed; it being a close, if not exclusive, tight knit circle of like-minded friends who for the following 16 years met in Lewis' room at Magdalen College on Thursday evenings and before lunch on Mondays or Fridays at the Eagle and Child pub in Oxford. Another member of this club was J.R.R. Tolkien
• In 1935 Lewis agreed to write the volume on Sixteenth Century English Literature for the Oxford History of English Literature series. Published in 1954, it became a classic
• In 1946 Lewis was awarded honorary Doctor of Divinity by the University of St Andrews
• In 1950 came the defining moment in the life of Lewis with the publication of *The Lion, the Witch and the Wardrobe*, for this was the work that was to bring him to the masses, thus making his voice one to be heard – always important for one of strong Christian beliefs
• In June, 1954, he accepted the Chair of Medieval and Renaissance Literature at Cambridge
• In 1956 he married Joy Davidman Gresham at Oxford Registry Office, a woman he had met during a trip to Canada and who was 15 years his junior. It was said that it was partly inspired by his books that in 1948 that she had converted from Judaism to Christianity. At the time of their marriage she was desperately ill with bone cancer and was predicted to live only a few months more. Lewis married her so that she would be granted British citizenship and therefore not deported back to Canada. After a bedside ceremony her life was – it seemed miraculously – extended until 1960 when she died after a trip to Greece
• In 1961 *A Grief Observed* – an account of the suffering Lewis endured after the death of his wife – was published under the pseudonym of N.W. Clerk
• C.S. Lewis himself died one week before his 65th birthday on 22 November 1963

OTHER WORKS BY C.S. LEWIS INCLUDE:

Non Fiction
Allegory of Love
Broadcast Talks
English Literature in the 16th Century
Mere Christianity
Personal Heresy (The)
Problem of Pain (The)
Reflections on the Psalms
Rehabilitations
Shall We Lose God in Outer Space
Studies in Medieval and Renaissance Literature
Weight of Glory (The)

Short Stories include:
Adventures of Eustace (The)
Ministering Angels
Shoddy Lands (The)

AND FINALLY

• In 1941 *The Guardian* newspaper published 31 *Screwtape Letters* in weekly instalments for which Lewis was paid £2 per letter; he gave the money to charity

• C.S. Lewis' nickname was Jack, and this is how he was always known to his friends

POSTSCRIPT – Do The Chronicles of Narnia hold a hidden secret?

Many years ago a lecturer in English Literature told me that a well-written and well-constructed piece of fiction should consist of many layers, the first layer being quite simply the 'story layer' – and a good story is after all the initial motivating force. Underneath that first layer, however, there may be further layers; these can be in social studies, historical analyses, political theories and so on. These deeper layers may be discovered and further analysed either by students of literature or simply by the enthusiastic reader, bringing the fiction to life and conveying a hitherto hidden meaning and understanding of the work. In their obscurity these secondary layers can in fact become a stimulating challenge to the scholar for occasionally in one of the hidden layers there can be what is sometimes referred to as a secret code, a puzzle woven into the plot to stretch even the most intelligent academic – and probably entertain the author too, as he watches the search and listens to the theories! This is especially true in the case of C. S. Lewis for he loved secrets, secrets which he would keep even from his closest friends and so the idea that *The Chronicles of Narnia* successfully held a secret for so long would have delighted Lewis.

Since the Chronicles were first published in the 1950s many have searched but none have found, well to be honest that's not strictly true. Many have searched and many have claimed to have found an underlying, secret or code hidden in Lewis' work, but generally this is just a case of wanting to find something and twisting and turning the text to fit in with the reader's desire rather than the writer's intent.

MEET DR MICHAEL WARD

Dr Michael Ward

Michael Ward is an Anglican clergyman and leading expert on the works of C.S. Lewis. He has a degree in English from Oxford, a degree in Theology from Cambridge and a PhD from St Andrews.

Dr Ward claims that he really has found a secret, a governing and imaginative scheme underlying the Narnia chronicles. He believes that C.S. Lewis deliberately constructed *The Chronicles of Narnia* out of the imagery of the seven heavens. (According to astronomers, before Copernicus in the Sixteenth Century the seven heavens contained the seven planets, which revolved around Earth and exerted influences over people and events, and even the metals in the Earth's crust.)

One might well ask why no one had noticed this hidden secret until now. Well it is quite simply because no one thought that there was a further layer and assumed it stopped at the second level, where could be found the obvious Biblical allegories or suppositions – about which Lewis himself had spoken quite openly. The fact that the secret was in the stars didn't seem possible as Lewis was a devout Christian and most thought that astrology and Christianity were unlikely, if not damned, bedfellows. But that is because Christian beliefs are looked upon in a superficial way by many; and this misunderstanding thus leads scholars down wrong paths. Some, though, did spot the connection but failed to follow it through with the same investigative intensity and passion as that of Dr Ward. Another reason seemed to prohibit further delving and that was Tolkien, who dismissed the Chronicles as mishmash – and who was going to argue with the great man! Although recognised as a man of gigantic intellect and master of research, Lewis was not known as the gifted and imaginative writer as was his close friend J.R.R. Tolkien. Maybe now that will all change.

Is there a secret code? Read *Planet Narnia* by Michael Ward and decide for yourself!

EXPERIENCE YESTERDAY'S WORLD OF C.S. LEWIS TODAY

This is a more difficult one for although there is a house to be seen, it is not a museum and so tours of the house, The Kilns in Oxfordshire, are by strict appointment only. It belongs to The C.S. Lewis Foundation and it is intended by them that it is respected as a quiet place of study, fellowship and creative scholarly work, much in the manner that characterised Lewis' own period of residency there. Here you will find serious seminars and pre-arranged guided tours for international students of Lewis' work.

George Orwell
1903-1950

Major Works by Geoge Orwell include:

Animal Farm • *Burmese Days* • *Clergyman's Daughter (A)* •
Coming Up for Air • *Down and Out in Paris and London* •
Homage to Catalonia • *Inside the Whale* •
Keep the Aspidistra Flying • *Nineteen Eighty-Four* •
Road to Wigan Pier (The) • *Shooting an Elephant*

GEORGE ORWELL: The Writer and the Man

• On 25 June in 1903 George Orwell was born as Eric Arthur Blair in Bengal, India to Richard Walmesley and Ida Mabel (née Limousin) Blair; he had two sisters

• His mother was of French extraction

• Orwell won a scholarship to Eton and upon leaving he joined the Indian Imperial Police in Burma, which was then a British colony. He soon realised how much the Burmese resented being ruled by the British and later was able to recount his experiences in his novel *The Burmese Days*

• At the beginning of 1928 he resigned his career in the police force in order to become a full-time writer

• Despising the separation of people by race, creed and class he decided to live for a time as a sort of vagabond in the slums of Paris and London which resulted in his first book *Down and Out in Paris and London*

• Before the publication of *Down and Out in Paris and London* in 1933 he took the name George Orwell

• In 1936 he was commissioned to write an account of poverty among unemployed miners in the North of England; the result being *The Road to Wigan Pier*

• He married Eileen O'Shaughnessy and they had one adopted son, Richard Horatio

• Once a part of the British Imperial establishment into which he was born he became, with maturity, first an anarchist and then a rebellious socialist

• In 1936 he travelled to Spain to fight for the Republicans against Franco's Nationalists where he was then forced to flee in fear of his life from Soviet-backed communists who were suppressing revolutionary socialist dissenters

• Unlike many socialists of his generation he did not take the leap from socialism to communism; in fact he had a fear and dread of communism and wanted to expose the failings of a communist society in a simple story-based novel that could be easily understood by all generations and societies – *Animal Farm*. At first publishers were reluctant to publish such a critical piece of work though it is now widely read as the classic it has become

• In 1943 he became literary editor of the *Tribune*, a left wing socialist paper. At this period in his life, as well as writing novels, he was also a serious journalist

• His wife Eileen died on 29 March 1945

• In 1949 he married his second wife Sonia Bronwell

• He died of tuberculosis in a London hospital on 21 January 1950 although he had suffered ill health for many years

AND FINALLY

• The name Orwell came from the River Orwell in East Anglia

• His books generally have an underlying political theme

• The last pages of Orwell's novel *Nineteen Eighty-four* were written in a remote house on the Hebridean island of Jura

Sir Walter Scott
1771-1832

Works by Sir Walter Scott include:

Abbot (The) • *Anne of Geierstein* • *Antiquary (The)* • *Betrothed (The)* • *Black Dwarf (The)* • *Castle Dangerous* • *Count Robert of Paris* • *Fair Maid of Perth (The)* • *Fortunes of Nigel (The)* • *Guy Mannering* • *Heart of Midlothian (The)* • *Ivanhoe* • *Kenilworth* • *Monastery (The)* • *Old Mortality* • *Peveril of the Peak* • *Pirate (The)* • *Quentin Durward* • *Redgauntlet* • *Rob Roy* • *Saint Ronan's Well* • *Talisman (The)* • *Waverley* • *Woodstock* •

Sir Walter Scott

SIR WALTER SCOTT: The Writer and the Man

• Scott was born in Edinburgh on 15 August 1771 as the ninth child of Walter Scott and Anne Rutherford
• Of the 12 children born to Scott's parents only five survived early youth
• In 1773 he contracted polio which left him lame in his right leg
• As a child he was privately educated before attending the High School of Edinburgh and Kelso Grammar School
• He was later educated at Edinburgh University, though ill health interrupted his studies he eventually decided to read law; qualifying as a lawyer in 1792 he was admitted to the Faculty of Advocates
• He was indentured to his father during the year 1785-1786
• In 1797 he married Charlotte Carpentier with whom he went on to have four children, two boys and two girls
• His wife Charlotte was of French descent
• On 16 December 1799 he became Sheriff-Deputy of Selkirkshire, an office he held until his death in 1832
• In the year 1806 he was appointed Principal Clerk of Session, a position he held until 1831
• The law profession provided him with a steady income throughout his life and was a profession he continued alongside his writing career
• In 1809 he became half owner of John Ballantyne's publishing company,

which collapsed in 1813. The company's assets were then bought by Archbald Constable and Co. who remained his publishers until 1826

• In 1811 Scott bought a small farm on the banks of the Tweed – Abbotsford; he moved into his new home in 1812

• 1814 saw the publication of the first of the Waverley novels – 26 more followed – though no one knew he was the author

• In 1820 he accepted a baronetcy and in the same year he was also elected President of the Royal Society of Edinburgh

• In 1822 it was Sir Walter Scott who was responsible for organising the visit of George IV to Edinburgh

• In 1826 he became insolvent and with an admirable display of great honour he pledged the future income from his publications to a trust in order that he might repay his creditors. He then began to work excessively, to the detriment of his health. To add to his distress his wife also died in the same year

• In 1827 Sir Walter Scott finally admitted authorship of the Waverley novels

• In 1829 his health started on a downward spiral culminating in his death on 21 September 1832

OTHER WORKS BY SIR WALTER SCOTT ALSO INCLUDE:

Poetry

Apology for the Tales of Terror (An)
Bridal of Triermain (The)
Field of Waterloo (The)
Harold the Dauntless
Lady of the Lake (The)
Lay of the Last Minstrel (The)
Lord of the Isles (The)
Marmion
Minstrelsy of the Scottish Border
Rokeby
Visions of Don Roderick (The)

Miscellaneous Prose

Letters of the Malachi Malagrowther
Letters on a Demonology and Witchcraft

Life of Napoleon Bonaparte (The)
Paul's Letters to His Kinsfolk
Tales of a Grandfather

AND FINALLY

• Scott built himself a castle and filled it with real antiques – not fake
• He was renowned for writing at tremendous speed and had an assistant to copy out and correct his manuscripts
• When there was a proposal to discontinue Scotland's distinctive banknotes, it was Scott who helped to save them
• Adaptations of Scott's work for the stage were a huge success during his lifetime
• Many operas have been composed on the Waverley Novels, particularly *Lucia di Lammermoor* and *Ivanhoe*
• Scott's early novels were published anonymously, or under pseudonyms, until the year 1827 when he admitted to his authorship at a public dinner

Robert Louis Stevenson
1850-1894

Major Works by Robert Louis Stevenson include:

Beach of Falesa (The) • *Black Arrow: A Tale of Two Roses* •
Kidnapped • *Master of Ballantrae (The)* • *Meaning of
Friendship (The)* • *Memoir of Fleeming Jenkin* • *Prince Otto* •
Sea Fogs (The) • *Strange Case of Dr Jekyll and Mr Hyde (The)* •
Treasure Island • *Underwoods* • *Weir of Hermiston* • *Will O' The Mill* •

ROBERT LOUIS STEVENSON: The Writer and the Man

• Born Robert Lewis Balfour Stevenson on 13 November 1850, he was the only son of engineer Thomas Stevenson and his wife, Margaret Isabella Balfour

• He later changed the spelling of his name to the French version of Louis, the name by which he is of course now well known

• His father was a lighthouse engineer, as were his ancestors and so it was always assumed that he would follow in their footsteps, but Stevenson's leanings were artistic rather than scientific and from an early age he yearned to be, and knew he would be, a writer

• Ill health marred regular schooling for Stevenson but he did attend Edinburgh University where it was expected that he would follow in his father's footsteps and become a lighthouse engineer, but instead he studied law

• Stevenson was called to the Scottish Bar as an Advocate in 1875, though he never actually practised law, announcing that he wanted to become a writer

• By nature he was not only a writer but he was an unconventional, bohemian-styled rebel too, whose journey through life seemed to be constantly blighted by ill health and, some would say, his non-conformist attitudes to life in general

• In 1876 when he was in the South of France, Stevenson met Fanny Vandegrift Osborne a married American woman who made a huge impression on him

• In 1879 he travelled to America to join Fanny, who was now divorced from her husband, and they married in 1880

• Shortly after his marriage he was reconciled with his parents, from whom he had been estranged for quite some time, when with his new wife and his stepson, Lloyd, he returned to British shores

• In 1887 his father Thomas Stevenson died

• His continual ill health and the search for a cure – or at least respite – frequently took him away from his native Scotland. He journeyed to the warmer climate of the South of England and further afield to the South of France and America, culminating in 1888 in an extended excursion sailing the South Seas, where he in fact spent the rest of his life and which were to be the stimulus for further great writing. In fact all his journeys fed his writings either in descriptive narratives or as settings for his novels

• Robert Louis Stevenson died tragically young in 1894, aged just 44 years

OTHER WORKS BY ROBERT LOUIS STEVENSON INCLUDE:

Non Fiction

Across the Plains: With Other Memories and Essays
Amateur Emigrant (The)

Footnote to History (A): Eight Years of Trouble in Samoa
Memories and Portraits
Old and the New Pacific Capitals (The)
Silverado Squatters (The)
Travels with a Donkey in the Cevennes
Vailima Letters

Short Story Collections
New Arabian Nights
Merry Men and Other Tales and Fables (The)
South Sea Tales

Poetry
Child's Garden of Verses (A) [this includes the famous poem *My Shadow*]
Songs of Travel and Other Verses
Underwoods

AND FINALLY
• Stevenson's first novel *Treasure Island* has never been out of print since it was first published
• Stevenson lived his life plagued by ill health and in constant fear that the dreaded tuberculosis would get him. As a consequence of this – in fact – very rational fear, he travelled far and wide in search of a cure or at the very least in search of a way of keeping the tuberculosis at bay. Ironically it was not the illness he so dreaded that was to finally end the life of this genius for he actually died as a result of a cerebral haemorrhage

There is no way I could conclude this section without including that very special poem which is a part of most children's childhood, evoking picturesque and often poignant memories, individual to each child. For me, I can remember my mother pointing out my shadow and saying "Look! There he is, it's your friend, your shadow." No matter how many times she said those words, they held a sort of magic and the shadow became a real person. However, if you are one of the few not familiar with this poem then please read it and pass it on to your children; creating magic for them to pass on to the next generation.

My Shadow

I have a little shadow that goes in and out with me,
And what can be the use of him is more than I can see.
He is very, very like me from the heels up to the head;
And I see him jump before me, when I jump into my bed.
The funniest thing about him is the way he likes to grow –
Not at all like proper children, which is always very slow;
For he sometimes shoots up taller like an India-rubber ball,
And he sometimes goes so little that there's none of him at all.
He hasn't got a notion of how children ought to play,
And can only make a fool of me in every sort of way.
He stays so close behind me, he's a coward you can see;
I'd think shame to stick to nursie as that shadow sticks to me!
One morning, very early, before the Sun was up,
I rose and found the shining dew on every buttercup;
But my lazy little shadow, like an arrant sleepy-head,
Had stayed at home behind me and was fast asleep in bed.

Jonathan Swift
1667-1745

Major Works by Jonathan Swift include:
Gulliver's Travels • *Modest Proposal (A)* • *Tale of a Tub (A)* •

JONATHAN SWIFT: The Writer and the Man

• Jonathan Swift was born on 30 November 1667 in Dublin, Ireland, as the second son born to Jonathan Swift Sr and Abigail Erick
• His father died before he was born, leaving his wife, daughter and unborn son in the care of his brothers
• When he was a year old Swift was taken to England for three years by his nurse; so as well as having no father, he was just a baby when he was parted from his mother in his formative years
• As a child, Swift was educated at Kilkenny School in Ireland

• In 1682 he went to Trinity College, Dublin
• In 1686 he was granted his Bachelor of Arts Degree *speciali gratia* (by special favour), a term often used to describe a degree when a student's record failed
• In 1710 Swift's mother died
• Swift later went to live and work in England as secretary to Sir William Temple and as tutor to eight-year-old Esther Johnson, whom he nicknamed Stella
• When Esther Johnson grew up she became his closest female friend and they corresponded regularly
• In 1692 Swift gained an MA from Oxford University; the same year as his first major work *An Ode to the Athenian Society* was published
• In 1694 he left the service of Sir William Temple and returned to Ireland where he was ordained as a deacon in the Protestant Church of Ireland
• He returned to Temple's employ in 1696 and began to write another of his greatest works *A Tale of a Tub,* though it wasn't actually published until 1704 – and even then anonymously
• In 1702 he was awarded the degree of Doctor of Divinity by Trinity College, Dublin
• In 1716 it was rumoured that Swift and his lifelong friend Stella had married, though this never was and never has been been proved to be true and is thought by most to be just that – a rumour
• In 1728 Stella died, an incident which naturally had a profoundly distressing effect upon Swift
• He was declared of unsound mind and memory in 1742 and was thereby confined to his house
• He died in 1745 leaving the little wealth he had accrued to finance the building of a house for the mentally ill

OTHER WORKS BY JONATHAN SWIFT INCLUDE:

Journal to Stella

Poetry

An Ode to the Athenian Society
Beautiful Nymph Going to Bed
Cassinus and Peter
Grand Questions Debated (The)
Lady's Dressing Room (The)

On His Deafness
Strephon and Chloe
Verses on the Death of Dr Swift
Windsor Prophecy

Satirical Works
Battle of the Books
Polite Conversation

AND FINALLY
• Swift suffered from Ménière's disease throughout his life, a disease which caused him dizziness and deafness
• Many people over the years have thought Swift's work offensive and to betray his misanthropic view on life, especially when one considers his obsession with the body and its functions; his sanity is sometimes brought into question at a date earlier than 1742

William Makepeace Thackeray
1811-1863

Works by Thackery include:
Adventures of Philip (The) • *Book of Snobs (The)* • *Catherine* •
FitzBoodle Papers (The) • *Great Hoggarty Diamond (The)* •
History of Henry Esmond Esq (The) • *Paris Sketch Book (The)* •
Pendennis • *Love the Widower* • *Luck of Barry Lyndon (The)* •
Men's Wives • *Newcomes (The)* •
Vanity Fair • *Virginians (The)* •

WILLIAM MAKEPEACE THACKERAY: The Writer and the Man
• Thackeray was born in Calcutta, India, as the only son of Richmond Thackeray who worked for The East India Company

- His father died in 1815 and the following year he was sent home to England; he was never to return to India
- His mother remarried in 1817 and then joined her son in England in 1820
- Thackeray went to Charterhouse School in London in 1822 where reputedly he was not happy
- He went up to Trinity College, Cambridge, but left without taking a degree
- He also studied art, both in London and in Paris
- In 1836 he married an Irish girl by the name of Isabella Shawe and together they had three daughters, one of whom died during childbirth. After the birth of their third daughter, Minnie, Isabella displayed signs of depression which then sealed her fate but which today may have been recognised as post-natal depression and successfully treated. But not so in that era and therefore as a result she had a complete mental breakdown from which she never recovered; she attempted suicide by throwing herself into the Irish Sea from a ferry and thereafter had to be constantly watched
- Thackeray nursed Isabella and took her to the continent in search of cures, but all in vain and she was eventually nursed privately, though tragically wanted nothing to do with her children and barely recognised her husband
- Before finding success, security and fame with *Vanity Fair* Thackeray inherited and lost £20,000 and also failed an early attempt at journalism before going on to be a prolific journalist
- His novel *Vanity Fair* was serialised in 1847-1848 bringing him instant fame and fortune
- Thackeray stood as an unsuccessful parliamentary candidate in 1857
- In 1860 he became the editor of *The Cornhill Magazine*
- He died suddenly in 1863 leaving, as did Dickens, an unfinished novel, the title of which is *Denis Duval*
- A commemorative bust of him was subsequently placed in Westminster Abbey

OTHER WORKS BY WILLIAM MAKEPEACE THACKERAY INCLUDE:

Short Stories
Lovel the Widower
Shabby Genteel Story (A)

He also wrote extensively for various periodicals.

AND FINALLY

• In his time Thackeray was second only in fame to Charles Dickens who was at one time a friendly rival until they quarreled in what became famously known as the 'Garrick Club Affair'
• Thackeray was a competent sketcher and had a great association with *Punch*, contributing caricatures, articles and humorous sketches
• He was also renowned for his lectures, 'The English Humourists of the Eighteenth Century', and 'The Four Georges', which he also delivered in America

Leo Tolstoy
1828-1910

Major Works by Leo Tolstoy include:
Anna Karenina • *Death of Ivan Ilyich (The)* •
Kreutzer Sonata (The) • *Resurrection* • *War and Peace* •

LEO TOLSTOY: The Writer and the Man

• Leo Tolstoy was born into Russian Aristocracy in 1828 as Lev Nikolayevich, Count (Graf) Tolstoy (also spelt Tolstoi) on the family estate about 130 miles south of Moscow, Russia
• He was one of four children born to Nikolay Ilich, Count Tolstoy, and his wife Mariya Nikolayevna, née Princess Volkonskaya
• Both of Tolstoy's parents died when he was a child, his mother before he was two years old and his father in 1837, followed by his grandmother 11 months later and his aunt Aleksandra in 1841; yet despite all of this tragedy, Tolstoy was later to describe his childhood as idyllic
• He was educated at home but later, in 1844, he entered the University of Kazan to study first oriental languages and then law, though he left in 1847 without a degree
• During his younger days he led a somewhat wild way of life
• In 1851 he joined the army and later fought in the Crimean War, after which he resigned

• In 1852 his first piece *Childhood* was accepted for publication, a successful piece which was soon followed by *Boyhood* and them by *Youth*
• In 1862 Tolstoy married Sofia (Sonya) Andreyevna Behrs with whom he went on to have 13 children. She was a great help to him in organising and transcribing his writing, though theirs was not a happy marriage and became more and more unhappy as time progressed
• He soon came to realise that he had a real interest in teaching and so opened a school on his own estate for peasant children. His methods were progressive and liberal – no examinations and no punishments
• Tolstoy was excommunicated from the Russian Orthodox Church in 1901
• In the final years of his life he searched for a religion/belief/truth, the meaning of living a good life and so imposed a strict way of living upon himself and others too. Remembering the debauchery of his early life made it all the more remarkable when he became a pacifist and when he gave up meat, tobacco, alcohol and preached chastity. His new moral stance attracted interest from all over the world, including from Mahatma Gandhi
• The closing chapters of Leo Tolstoy's life were filled with sadness and so different to that of the opening chapters where, despite the tragedies of numerous deaths, he was happy
• Death was just around the corner when at the age of 82 he was estranged from all of his family except one daughter
• They were on their way to a monastery when he fell ill at the railway junction of Astapovo; and so it was here that Leo Tolstoy, Novelist, Story Writer, Educationalist, Political Writer, Religious Writer and Philosopher died

OTHER WORKS BY LEO TOLSTOY INCLUDE:

For the Stage
Power of Darkness (The)
Fruits of Enlightenment (The)

Short Stories
After the Ball
Boyhood
Childhood
Cossacks (The)
Death of Ivan Ilyich (The)

Devi (The)
Family Happiness (A Novella)
Father Sergius
Hadji Murat
I Cannot be Silent
Kreutzer Sonata (The)
Landowners Morning (A)
Master and Man
Polikushka
Raid (The)
Three Deaths
What Men Live By
Youth

AND FINALLY

• In 1947 Tolstoy started keeping a diary, which he continue throughout his life

• He used the royalties from his novel *Resurrection* to pay for the transportation of a persecuted religious sect, the Dukhobors, to Canada

Mark Twain
1835-1910

Works by Mark Twain include:

Adventures of Huckleberry Finn • Adventures of Tom Sawyer (The) • American Claimant (The) • Connecticut Yankee in King Arthur's Court • Diary of Adam & Eve (The) • Following the Equator • Guilded Age (The) • Innocents Abroad (The) • Life on the Mississippi • Man that Corrupted Hadleyburg (The) • Mysterious Stranger (The) • Personal Recollections of Joan of Arc • Prince and the Pauper (The) • Roughing It • Tom Sawyer Abroad • Tom Sawyer Detective • Tramp Abroad (A) • Tragedy of Pudd'nhead Wilson (The) • What is Man •

MARK TWAIN: The Writer and the Man

• Mark Twain was actually born Samuel Langhorne Clemens in Florida, America, the son of John Marshall and Jane Lampton Clemens and the sixth of their seven children

• His father died in 1847 and so it was that his formal education came to an end

• His father's early death meant that he started work whilst in fact still a child, first by delivering papers and then as an errand boy; these menial jobs were followed by a series of other menial positions of employment

• In 1857 he became an apprenticed (club) riverboat pilot on the Mississippi river

• In 1859 he earned his steamboat pilot licence which allowed him to work as a river pilot on the Mississippi river until the Civil War closed the river

• It was in 1863 that Clemens adopted the name by which we all know him today – Mark Twain. Mark Twain is interestingly an old riverboat term meaning the line between safe water and dangerous water

• His first big break came when his short story *Jim Smiley and His Jumping Frog* was published in papers across the country

• He married Olivia Langdon in the year 1870 and together they went on to have one son and three daughters; his son, Langdon, died in infancy and two of his daughters died before Twain himself

• His wife, Olivia (Livy), died after a serious illness which lasted two years

• Mark Twain died suddenly on 21 April 1910 survived only by his daughter Clara

AND FINALLY

• Read any one of those wonderful books of quotations that, at the moment, are so popular with most readers and I can almost guarantee that you will come across several pearls of wisdom said to have emanated from the lips of Twain

H.G. Wells
1866-1946

Major Works by H.G. Wells include:

Ann Veronica • *Croquet Player (The)* • *First Men in the Moon (The)* • *History of Mr Polly (The)* • *Invisible Man (The)* • *Island of Doctor Moreau (The)* • *Kipps* • *Love and Mr Lewisham* • *Men Like Gods* • *Modern Utopia (A)* • *Mr Britling Sees it Through* • *New Machiavelli (The)* • *Time Machine (The)* • *Tono-Bungay* • *War of the Worlds (The)* • *When the Sleep Wakes* • *Wonderful Visit (The)* • *World of William Clissold (The)* •

H.G. WELLS: The Writer and the Man

• H.G. Wells was born on 21 September 1866 in Bromley, Kent to Joseph Wells and Sarah, née Neal

• His father was a shopkeeper dealing in china

• Wells was educated at Bromley Academy which was a private school for tradesmen's sons run by Thomas Morely

• In 1880 Wells had to leave school when his parents were unable to meet the school fees.

• Then started a period of work in retail shops, which he hated but which became the background and inspiration for novels such as *Kipps* and *The History of Mr Polly*

• With his mother's financial support he was able to able to return to education and further his studies

• He eventually studied biology at the Normal School (later the Royal College) of Science, in South Kensington, London, where T.H. Huxley was one of his teachers

• In 1887 he failed his final examination in geology and left without a degree

• Despite this he managed to gain teaching positions and eventually gained his BSc

• He married his cousin Isabel Wells

• A period of ill health in 1893 forced him to leave teaching and concentrate on freelance journalism and short story writing

• At about the same time his first marriage ended and he set up home with Amy Catherine (Jane) Robbins

• In 1895 the pair married and went on to have two sons together
• Sadly his second marriage did not bring him contentment and he went on to have, what were at the time, two scandalous affairs, the first with Amber Reeves who bore him a daughter and the second with Rebecca West who bore him a son
• His wife Catherine died in 1927 and he then went on to have further liaisons including ones with Odette Keun and Baroness Moura
• In his lifetime, despite his constant self-awareness of possible world catastrophe, he still retained his belief in social equality and world peace
• H.G. Wells died on 13 August1946

OTHER WORKS BY H.G. WELLS INCLUDE:

Short Story Collections
Country of the Blind and Other Stories (The)
Complete Short Stories

Works of Non Fiction
Outline of History (The)
Short History of the World (A)
Shape of Things to Come (The)
Experiment in Autobiography
Mind at the End of its Tether
Anticipations
Discovery of the Future (The)

AND FINALLY
• As with many famous writers Wells was a member of the Socialist Fabian Society in London, although he did quarrel with the Society's leaders – among them George Bernard Shaw
• His son Anthony West (by Rebecca West) also became a writer

A BRIEF SYNOPSIS OF POPULAR CLASSIC BOOKS

There is an age old saying to which, to be honest, I have never fully subscribed, and that is: 'A little knowledge is a dangerous thing.' That implies that an all or nothing approach to learning is the only way; if that was the case then I am afraid there would be an awful lot of frustrated students in the world, for not everyone is capable of intense study, nor indeed wants to study in great depth. But most people do enjoy the acquisition of knowledge, to a lesser or greater degree. Therefore, a little knowledge can be both satisfying and final for some, whilst for others it can whet the appetite for further exploration of whatever subject is in question. It is with this in mind that you will find here a brief synopsis of some of the more popular classic books so that you may say either: 'Ah, so that's what that book is all about then,' and feel quite satisfied in the little knowledge you have now acquired. Or there again you may say: 'Now that sounds like a good read,' and promptly go out and buy the book. Either way that little knowledge has not been a dangerous thing, but instead has served a purpose for both points of view and that surely can only be a good thing?

Novel	Author	Synopsis
A		
Adam Bede	George Eliot	The story of a young man in love and all that can happen to one in such a tragic state.
Ann Veronica	H.G. Wells	The story of a young girl who defies her father and rebels against conventional morality by running away with the man she loves.
Adventures of Sherlock Holmes (The)	Sir Arthur Conan Doyle	Stories of the detective whose art of deduction solves many a crime.
Adventures of Huckleberry Finn	Mark Twain	Huckleberry Finn lives with his father who is a drunk and one day he decides to fake his own death and run away into a life of adventures.
Adventures of Tom Sawyer (The)	Mark Twain	The adventures of a young and mischievous boy growing up in Missouri.
Alice's Adventures in Wonderland	Lewis Carroll	Alice follows a 'rabbit in a hurry' down a hole and into a wonderland of characters.
American (The)	Henry James	The story of a self-made millionaire whose forthright nature is in direct contrast with the cunning and arrogant family of French aristocrats whose daughter he wants to marry.

Novel	Author	Synopsis
All Quiet on the Western Front	Erich Maria Remarque	Set in the First World War this novel looks at the daily relentless lives of the soldiers in the trenches with a feeling that they have no past or future, but have only today.
And Then There Were None	Agatha Christie	This is a murder mystery from the point of view of ten characters – who each in turn are murdered until none remain.
Animal Farm	George Orwell	A political book which can be enjoyed by children on a simple level before they become politically aware of its profound meanings and the fact that it is based on the story of the Russian Revolution and its betrayal by Joseph Stalin.
Anna Karenina	Leo Tolstoy	The stories of three families; the Oblonskys, the Karenins, and the Levins are interwoven throughout a novel which – on a superficial level – explores the meaning of true love and sees Anna's realisation only when it is too late to prevent her own suicide.
Around the World in Eighty Days	Jules Verne	Phileas Fogg is a coolheaded English man who makes a bet that he can travel around the world in 80 days – at that time an almost impossible task. He succeeds with just ten minutes to spare.

B

Beau Geste	Wren, P.C.	This is the first of Wren's foreign legion novels, and tells the story of the three Geste brothers who, when a family jewel goes missing, wrongly fall under suspicion of theft and so join the foreign legion.
Beloved	Toni Morrison	This winner of the Pulitzer Prize for fiction is actually based on the tragic true story of a runaway slave who when recaptured kills her own infant daughter in order to spare her a life of slavery.
Black Tulip	Alexandre Dumas, père	Set in the Seventeenth Century this is the story of Cornelius van Baerle, a humble grower of tulips whose only wish is to grow the perfect specimen of the tulip negra. When his godfather is murdered, Cornelius

Novel	Author	Synopsis
		is caught up in the politics of the time, is imprisoned and faces a death sentence. His jailor's daughter Rosa, though, holds the key to his survival and his chance to produce the perfect tulip.
Bluest Eye (The)	Toni Morrison	The story of a black girl, obsessed with white perception and standards of beauty, who longs to have blue eyes.
Brave New World	Aldous Huxley	Here we see a life far into the future where the World Controllers have created the ideal society; everyone is happy through use of genetic engineering, brainwashing plus recreational sex and drugs. Only one man, Bernard Marx, longs to break free.
Brighton Rock	Graham Greene	A novel set in Brighton's violent, criminal underworld, which revolves around the ambitions of a 17-year-old boy who wants to run a successful gang.

C

Novel	Author	Synopsis
Call of the Wild (The)	Jack London	A novel in which the protagonist is a dog called Buck who reverts to his natural instincts when he finds himself working as a sled dog.
Catcher in the Rye	J.D. Salinger	Trials, tribulations and realisations of Holden Caulfield, a young boy, as he grows up.
Charlotte's Web	E.B. White	The charming story about Wilbur the Pig and his friend Charlotte, a spider who could spell.
Charterhouse of Parma	Stendhal	Fabrice, a young aristocrat, returns to the court of Parma after the Battle of Waterloo, enters the church, has an affair, kills a rival, goes to prison, is pardoned, falls in love, has another affair and a child. His lover and child die, he soon follows.
Children of the New Forest	Captain Marryat	Children who are used to an aristocratic way of life, learn the values of a more simple life in the New Forest when, after escaping from the Roundhead soldiers, they are brought up by a gamekeeper.

Novel	Author	Synopsis
Clarissa: or The History of a Young Lady	Samuel Richardson	A work in eight volumes and over one million words this is the story of a young woman, Clarissa, who is helped to escape from the man her parents want her to marry by the unscrupulous – but fascinating – Lovelace. He eventually drugs and rapes her; she temporarily loses her sanity whilst, overcome with remorse, he is killed in a duel by Clarissa's cousin.
Count of Monte Cristo (The)	Alexandre Dumas, père	Edmond Dantès the reader is taken along his journey of a wrongful trial, his search for justice, revenge, and ultimately riches, forgiveness, and love
Cranford	Elizabeth Gaskell	Set in the 1830s this is a series of linked sketches depicting the life of ladies in a quiet country village. It is based on Knutsford in Cheshire where Mrs Gaskell spent her childhood.
Crime and Punishment	Fyodor Dostoevsky	A contradiction of motives and theories convince a young man, Raskolnikov, that he can solve all his problems by murdering an old pawnbroker.

D

Novel	Author	Synopsis
Daniel Deronda	George Eliot	Gwendolen Harleth marries for money and position, despite the fact that her husband has a long-term mistress with whom he has children. Daniel Deronda is an idealistic young man with great influence over Gwendolen, but after her husband's death he, in fact, marries someone else!
Don Quixote	Miguel de Cervantes	Don Quixote imagines that he has been called upon to roam the world on his old horse and accompanied by his Squire Sancho Panza in search of adventures.
Dr Jekyll and Mr Hyde (The Strange Case of)	Robert Louis Stevenson	A medical experiment means that Dr Jekyll becomes his other self, Mr Hyde with an increasing and destructive regularity.
Dracula	Bram Stoker	A Transylvanian vampire makes his way to England where he victimises innocent people to gain the blood he needs to live.

Novel	Author	Synopsis
ℰ		
Eight Cousins	Louisa May Alcott	After the death of her father Rose is sent to live with her aunts and seven male cousins in a story of one girl's survival against all the odds – and so many boys!
ℱ		
Far From the Madding Crowd	Thomas Hardy	The story of the beautiful and impulsive Bathsheba Everdene and the marital choices she makes.
Farewell to Arms (A)	Ernest Hemmingway	The tragic love story of an American Lieutenant and an English nurse during the first World War.
For Whom the Bell Tolls	Ernest Hemmingway	Set during the Spanish Civil War, where Jordan's doomed mission is to blow up a bridge in order to aid a coming Republican attack. After he blows up the bridge he is wounded and heroically makes his retreating comrades leave him behind.
Forsyte Saga (The)	John Galsworthy	This is a sequence of novels set at the turn of the Nineteenth/Twentieth century which look at the lives of three generations in the same upper-middle class family and their attitude to recently accrued wealth.
𝒢		
General in his Labyrinth (The)	Gabriel Garcia Márques	This is a fictionalised biography of Simon Bolivar, the hero of Latin American independence.
Go-Between (The)	L.P. Hartley	The central figure is a 12-year-old boy who carries letters between two people having an affair and, not understanding the complexities of adult relationships, inadvertently causes a tragedy.
Golden Bowl (The)	Henry James	Maggie marries Amerigo, an impoverished Italian Prince, who is actually having an affair.
Grapes of Wrath (The)	John Steinbeck	The bitterness of the Great Depression is portrayed in this epic account of the journey made by an emigrant farming family from the

Novel	Author	Synopsis
		dust bowl of the West to the 'Promised Land' of California.
Gulliver's Travels	Jonathan Swift	Divided into four volumes, each tells the story of Lemuel Gulliver who, having embarked on a voyage, finds himself for various reasons in strange lands.
		Book 1: In this the first, and most well known of the four books, he finds himself in the land of Lilliput, where he is a giant in a land of little people just six inches high.
		Book 2: In the second book he is in Brobdingnag, a land of giants and where he is looked after by a nine-year-old girl called Glumdalclitch.
		Book 3: Finds him on the floating island of Laputa, a land of absent-minded inhabitants engaged in ridiculous pastimes.
		Book 4: The final book finds the hero in Houyhnhnms, a land of virtuous horses. But also on this land live the despicable Yahoos – who it transpires are in fact human beings.
Guy Mannering	Walter Scott	Harry Bertram, son of the laird of Ellangowan in Dumfriesshire, is kidnapped as a child and taken to Holland. Behind the plot is Glosin who hopes to get his hands on Ellangowan if there is no heir.

H

Novel	Author	Synopsis
Hand of Ethelberta (The)	Thomas Hardy	Ethelberta marries the son of the house where she is a governess but is then widowed at 21. Keen to maintain the social position her marriage gave, she tries hard to conceal the fact that she is related to the butler!
He Knew He Was Right	Anthony Trollope	Louis Trevelyan becomes insanely jealous when another man pays attention to his wife Emily Rowley. He absconds with their son and has a complete mental breakdown. He dies shortly after an attempted reconciliation.

Novel	Author	Synopsis
Heart of Midlothian (The)	Sir Walter Scott	Based on two historical incidents, the Porteous Riots and the story of Isobel Walker.
Heidi	Johanna Spyri	A little orphan girl penetrates the heart of her bitter grandfather.
Herzog	Saul Bellow	Moses Herzog's second wife is having an affair with his close friend which drives him to the brink of suicide.
History of Henry Esmond, Esq (The)	William Makepeace Thackeray	Set against a backdrop of the late Seventeenth, early Eighteenth Century England this is the story of Henry Esmond, who is in love with Beatrix, but marries her mother!
Pendennis	William Makepeace Thackeray	This is a portrait of a young man documenting his experiences and the temptations he faces as he makes his way through life.
Hitchhiker's Guide to the Galaxy (The)	Douglas Adams	Arthur Dent and Ford Perfect escape Earth seconds before it is destroyed and then they hitchhike their way around the Universe searching for the answers to the question of life.
Hobbit (The)	J.R.R. Tolkien	The hobbit, Bilbo, was quite happy at home until the wizard, Gandalf, arrived with a band of dwarves. Bilbo then found himself in a dangerous quest which leads him to the treasure of Smaug, the dragon.
Hound of the Baskervilles (The)	Sir Arthur Conan Doyle	It seems that there is a killer hound on the loose until Sherlock Holmes is called in to discover the truth, that the hound is greed in human form.
Howards End	E.M. Forster	A story of class warfare between a wealthy family, two cultured sisters, and a man living in relative poverty. The object of their war is the country house, Howards End.
Hunchback of Notre Dame (The)	Victor Hugo	Wrongly accused of murder, Esmeralda is held prisoner in Notre Dame Cathedral by Frollo where the hunchback, Quasimodo, saves her from execution and kills the evil Frollo.

Novel	Author	Synopsis
ɒ		
Idiot (The)	Fyodor Dostoevsky	Dostoyevsky's intention was to create a protagonist with 'a truly beautiful soul' and to trace his fate as he came into contact with brutal reality, and so the innocent epileptic Prince Myshkin - the idiot – is drawn into a web of violent and passionate relationships leading to blackmail, betrayal and murder.
Island of Dr Moreau (The)	H.G. Wells	The story of a mad scientist who transforms animals into human creatures – Beast Creatures.
Ivanhoe	Sir Walter Scott	Wilfred of Ivanhoe is a supporter of the Norman King Richard and is courting Lady Rowena, both unforgivable in his father's eyes. It is a story of romance and righteousness and a story in which Robin Hood appears too, as Locksley.
ɟ		
Jane Eyre	Charlotte Brontë	The story of a young orphan girl left to find her way in the world; a story of personal survival and the conquering qualities of a love shrouded in mystery.
Journey of the Plague Year (A)	Daniel Defoe	Supposedly narrated by an eye witness to the Great Plague it describes in vivid detail the devastation and terror experienced by Londoners as the plague took a grip.
Jude the Obscure	Thomas Hardy	An ordinary man dreams of becoming a scholar and sets out to achieve this. He falls in love with a married woman and together they are ostracised from society with tragic results. Jude never becomes a scholar.
Jungle Book (The)	Rudyard Kipling	A human baby is abandoned in the jungle where he is raised by a family of wolves; he is educated by a black panther and a bear.
Just So Stories	Rudyard Kipling	It is said that the title of this book came about because when Kipling told his own children stories they wanted them telling each time the same, or as they said 'Just So'.

Novel	Author	Synopsis
K		
Kangaroo	D.H. Lawrence	This is a novel based on Lawrence's visit to Australia in which he took in the Australian landscape and life.
Keep the Aspidistra Flying	George Orwell	A bookseller's assistant abhors the shallow materialistic ways of the middle classes but yet reconciles himself to that life when he marries the girl he loves.
Kenilworth	Sir Walter Scott	Published in the year of the Coronation of George IV this is the story of Elizabeth and her favourite Leicester, and of the betrayal and murder of Leicester's wife.
Kidnapped	Robert Louis Stevenson	Set at the time of the Jacobite Rebellions and in the Scottish Highlands where the young hero David Balfour is attacked and kidnapped.
Kim	Rudyard Kipling	A novel which brings India to life through the story of orphan Kimball O'Hara and his personal life as a vagabond, through his adoption and his aptitude for the secret service.
L		
Lady Chatterley's Lover	D.H. Lawrence	The sensational story of Lady Chatterley's affair with the gamekeeper Oliver Mellors.
Lady Susan	Jane Austen	The story consists of letters written chiefly between Mrs Vernon and her mother, Lady de Courcy, and between Lady Susan (widow of Mr Vernon's brother) and her London friend Mrs Johnson.
Last Days of a Condemned (The)	Victor Hugo	The story of a condemned man's last day and a vehicle for Victor Hugo to launch his own protest against the death penalty.
Last of the Mohicans (The)	James Fenimore Cooper	Adventures of the wild frontier life, drawing vivid pictures for the reader of the American Indians and the pioneers.
Legend of Montrose (A)	Sir Walter Scott	This is a novel based on an episode in the Earl of Montrose's 1644 campaign to raise Scotland for Charles I against the forces led by the Marquis of Argyle.

Novel	Author	Synopsis
Life of Charlotte Brontë	Elizabeth Gaskell	Exactly what its title says, this is a warm and compassionate look at the life of Elizabeth Gaskell's dear and personal friend Charlotte Brontë, this novel was at the request of Charlotte's father Patrick.
Light that Failed (The)	Rudyard Kipling	The story of a painter who is going blind and who is rejected by the woman he loves.
Lion, the Witch and the Wardrobe (The)	C.S. Lewis	Lucy, a Second World War evacuee, stumbles through a wardrobe into the magical land of Narnia, a land of nymphs, fauns, centaurs and talking animals. She learns that the land is ruled by a cruel White Witch and can only be freed by the good Lion, Aslan, and Lucy and her three siblings.
Little Lord Fauntleroy	Frances Hodgson Burnett	This is the story of a little American boy called Cedric who became an English Lord.
Little Princess (A)	Frances Hodgson Burnett	Sarah Crew arrives in London from India. At her new school she is treated like a princess; things change though with the death of her father after which she is forced to live in the attic with the servants.
Little White Bird (The)	J.M. Barrie	This novel serves as an introduction to Peter Pan and tells the story of a wealthy bachelor and a boy named David whom he takes for walks in Kensington Gardens where he tells him about Peter Pan who can be found in the Gardens at night.
Little Women	Louisa May Alcott	The story of the four March sisters, Meg, Jo, Beth and Amy growing up in mid 1800s America.
Longest Journey (The)	E.M. Forster	The plot centres on Rickie Elliot, a schoolmaster and aspiring writer who was born lame and the relationship he has with Stephen Wonham, his healthy pagan half-brother. It is whilst saving Stephen's life that Rickie dies.
Lord Jim	Joseph Conrad	Jim once behaved in a cowardly way but redeems himself and when a situation once again presents itself where he can flee and live, or die with honour, he chooses the latter.

Novel	Author	Synopsis
Lord of the Flies	William Golding	A psychological study into what happens when a group of young boys are marooned on a desert island and tribal survival instincts take over.
Lord of the Rings	J.R.R. Tolkien	Mythological tales about Middle Earth with Hobbits, Elves, Orcs and other mythological creatures.
Lorna Doone	R.D. Blackmore	Set in the late Seventeenth Century it tells the tale of the Doone family who terrorise Exmoor and kill John Ridd's father. He then discovers a child, Lorna, who has been kidnapped by the Doones; they grow up to love each other. She, it emerges, is of noble blood. (It is interesting to note that some of the characters are based on real people.)
Love in the Time of Cholera	Gabriel Garcia Márques	Two couples find love – one couple the young and traditional; the other couple are old and in their twilight years.
Lucky Jim	Kingsley Amis	A successful future in a University History department looks assured for Jim Dixon but first he must survive a weekend at Professor Welch's, give a lecture on Merrie England, and resist the beautiful girlfriend of his hosts awful son, Bertrand.

M

Novel	Author	Synopsis
Madame Bovary	Gustave Flaubert	Emma Bovary is the wife of a doctor who relieves the boredom and emptiness of her life by living beyond her means and embarking on adulterous affairs.
Man Who Laughs (The)	Victor Hugo	Set in the Seventeenth Century this is a tale of the English people's fight against feudalism.
Marble Faun	Nathaniel Hawthorne	Three American art students in Italy become somehow involved – to a greater or lesser degree in the murder of an unknown man
Mayor of Casterbridge (The)	Thomas Hardy	Michael Henchard determinedly rose from workman to mayor until the calculating Donald Farfrae ruins him.
Middlemarch, a Study of Provincial Life	George Eliot	This is a novel of multiple plots in which Dorothea Brooke is unhappily married to

---

Novel	Author	Synopsis
		the elderly pedant, Mr Casaubon, with disastrous consequences. The friendship she has with Will Ladislaw keeps her sane. Casaubon dies and his will states if she marries Ladislaw she loses her fortune. Love wins over the money!
Midnight's Children	Salman Rushdie	This is the story of Saleem Sinai who was born on the stroke of midnight on the day that India was granted independence and so we see a new India through this new life.
Mill on the Floss	George Eliot	A story which centres on the two children of Mr Tulliver, Tom and Maggie, and the expectations and bigotry of the times which lead to the two being separated until flood descends upon the town and Maggie heroically rescues her brother, leading to a momentary reconciliation before the two are drowned.
Millennium Hall	Sarah Scott	A sheltered community is created for the elderly, disabled, female or otherwise unfortunate persons, by women who are themselves tired of men.
Moby Dick	Herman Melville	Aboard the whaler, *Pequod*, Captain Ahab and his crew are out to find and kill the snow-white sperm whale, known as Moby Dick, a whale that had cost Ahab his leg on a previous voyage. The novel culminates when Moby Dick charges the boat which sinks, killing all but the narrator of the tale.
Moll Flanders	Daniel Defoe	The story of the daughter of a woman who had been transported to Virginia for theft soon after the birth of her child. The story tells of her seduction, marriages and of her visit to Virginia where she finds her mother and discovers that she has unknowingly married her own brother.
Most Wanted Man (A)	John Le Carré	This is the story of a half-Chechen, half-Russian bastard Muslim refugee called Issa (a name that means Jesus) who is pursued by competing security services, afraid that he might unleash fundamentalist mayhem upon the country.

Novel	Author	Synopsis
Mr Midshipman Easy	Captain Marryat	Jack Easy, the son of a wealthy gentleman, has been brought up to believe all men are equal which causes him no end of problems!

N

Novel	Author	Synopsis
Nineteen Eighty-Four	George Orwell	Set in an imaginary future where the world finds itself dominated by three totalitarian, warring police states.

O

Novel	Author	Synopsis
Of Mice and Men	John Steinbeck	This tragedy follows the story and misadventures of two Californian ranch hands, Lennie and George.
On the Beach	Nevil Shute	A novel which looks at the effects of an atomic war and the subsequent complete destruction of the entire human race.
One Flew Over the Cuckoo's Nest	Ken Kesey	A disturbing tale of life in a mental home and the vulnerability of the inhabitants.
One Hundred Years of Solitude	Gabriel Garcia Márques	A novel which follows the trials and tribulations, and the ups and downs of several generations of the Buendia family from the time they found the fictional village of Macondo in South America.

P

Novel	Author	Synopsis
Passage to India (A)	E.M. Forster	Despite their cultural differences Cyril Fielding (British) and Dr Aziz (Indian) are friends, until Aziz is wrongly accused of sexual harassment.
Picture of Dorian Gray (The)	Oscar Wilde	Dorian Gray has a portrait of himself which ages instead of him. He destroys the portrait which then turns young as he ages.
Pied Piper	Nevil Shute	John Howard is holidaying in the South of France at the beginning of the Second World War and promises his friends that he will take their children back to England with him. Along the way he meets several other children and his little band grows.
Pilgrim's Progress (The)	John Bunyan	Written as the author's dream this allegorical piece is a symbolic vision of the

Novel	Author	Synopsis
		good man's – Christian – journey through life.
Portrait of a Lady (The)	Henry James	Isabel Archer is the American Lady of the piece who refuses two proposals of marriage to then find herself – influenced by the sinister Madame Merle – married to the vile Gilbert Osmond, who is only interested in her money.
Portrait of an Artist as a Young Man (A)	James Joyce	The journey and development of Stephen Dedalus from early boyhood through to manhood and the realisation of his own destiny.
Power and the Glory (The)	Graham Greene	A weak and alcoholic priest tries to fulfill his priestly duties in rural Mexico at a time when the church is outlawed and the constant threat of death is ever present.
Pride and Prejudice	Jane Austen	The story of young ladies in search of husbands.
Prince and the Pauper (The)	Mark Twain	Two boys, alike in all ways except that one is heir to the throne of England and the other belongs to the poor of the nation, decide to switch clothes – for fun! But fate has other ideas and they are each thrown into the other's world to taste the reality of life on the other side of the fence.

$\mathcal{R}$

Novel	Author	Synopsis
Railway Children (The)	E. Nesbit	A kind old gentleman regularly travels on the 9.45 train and waves at three children whose father has been wrongly imprisoned. It is he who helps prove their father's innocence.
Red and the Black (The)	Stendhal	Julien Sorel is an intelligent, sensitive, ambitious youth who uses seduction as a means to further his career. The book ends when he is executed for the attempted murder of one of the women he had seduced.
Rob Roy	Sir Walter Scott	This is the story of the son of an English merchant, Frank Osbaldistone , who travels to the Scottish Highlands to collect a debt stolen from his father. (Interestingly Rob Roy himself is not the central character in this novel.)

169

Novel	Author	Synopsis
Robinson Crusoe	Daniel Defoe	The story of Robinson Crusoe's mental and physical survival when he is shipwrecked on an island.
Rose and the Ring (The)	William Makepeace Thackeray	A story in which a magic rose and a magic ring make the possessors seem irresistibly attractive.
Ruth	Elizabeth Gaskell	Ruth Hilton is a 15-year-old orphan when she is seduced and later abandoned by the wealthy Henry Bellingham. After giving birth to her illegitimate son she survives the stigma to become a heroic nurse.

S

Novel	Author	Synopsis
Satanic Verses (The)	Salman Rushdie	This is the infamous book which brought upon Rushdie the notorious death sentence, or fatwa, resulting in him seeking police protection. It is a novel which questions illusions, reality and the power of faith and is also a novel in which there are some passages that were interpreted by some Muslims as blasphemous.
Scarlet Letter (The)	Nathaniel Hawthorne	A young wife commits adultery and gives birth to her lover's child; as a punishment she is then forced to wear the red letter A on her bosom for the rest of her life. Her husband discovers the name of her lover and hounds him literally to death.
Secret Agent (The)	Joseph Conrad	Winnie is unaware that her husband is a secret agent but it is she who suffers most as a result of his activities when her simple-minded brother is innocently drawn in and killed. She then murders her husband and, afraid of the gallows, throws herself overboard from the Channel ferry.
Secret Garden (The)	Frances Hodgson Burnett	A young orphan girl injects life into a dismal family and gives them a reason to survive.
Swiss Family Robinson (The)	Johann David Wyss	The story of a family shipwrecked on a desert island.
Sylvia's Lovers	Elizabeth Gaskell	A novel which looks at the impact of the Napoleonic Wars upon the ordinary folk.

Novel	Author	Synopsis
T		
Tess of the d'Urbervilles	Thomas Hardy	Tess is seduced by Alex and gives birth to a child who dies. She then falls in love with Angel Clare and on the eve of her wedding confesses all to him and he as a result deserts her. Once more fate throws her into the arms of Alex which leads to murder and her eventual hanging.
Thérèse Raquin	Emile Zola	Thérèse is forced to marry Camille and in her unhappiness she turns to his friend Laurent; together they drown Camille and eventually each commits suicide.
Thorn Birds (The)	Colleen McCullough	Maggie Clearly falls in love with the local catholic priest, Ralph, and he finally gives in to her love. Ralph becomes a cardinal and dies shortly after finding out that Maggie's son is in fact his.
Three Men in a Boat	Jerome K. Jerome	This is a comedic account of a boating holiday taken on the Thames between Kingston and Oxford. It started as a travel guide but the comic element took over to make it the success it is.
Three Musketeers (The)	Alexandre Dumas, père	An adventure story in which a young man, by the name of d'Artagnan, leaves home to become a musketeer. This is a book which is also famous for the well-known saying: 'All for one and one for all.'
Through the Looking Glass and What Alice Found There	Lewis Carroll	This is the sequel to *Alice in Wonderland*. Alice wonders what it would be like on the other side of a looking glass and finds that she is able to pass through to an alternate world of pure nonsense.
Time Machine (The)	H.G. Wells	This is a social allegory set in the year 802,701 which describes a society divided into two distinct classes. The elitist and decadent class are called Eloi and the workers Morlocks.
To Kill a Mockingbird	Harper Lee	A young girl and her brother learn about fighting prejudice and upholding human dignity through the example set by their

Novel	Author	Synopsis
		lawyer father who defends a black man falsely accused of the rape of a white woman.
Tom Jones, a Foundling	Henry Fielding	One night a man named Allworthy finds an infant in his bed – it is a servant's abandoned baby. Eventually the servant marries and brings up the child who grows into a troubled young man.
Town Like Alice (A)	Nevil Shute	A novel describing the grim odyssey of white women and children in Japanese-occupied Malaya.
Treasure Island	Robert Louis Stevenson	An adventure story about pirates and buried treasure this book features the now legendary character Long John Silver.
Trumpet Major	Thomas Hardy	Set in the Napoleonic Wars this is the story of Anne Garland and the three men who each want to win her love.
20,000 Leagues Under the Sea	Jules Verne	A French scientist leads an expedition to destroy a sea monster which turns out to be a submarine.
Two on a Tower	Thomas Hardy	In the absence of her unpleasant husband, Lady Constantine falls in love with Swithin St Cleve. Hearing, wrongly, that her husband is dead she marries her lover. Circumstances part the two and when he returns he is shocked to find that she is no longer a young woman. She then dies in his arms shocked when he offers to marry her.
Typhoon	Joseph Conrad	Captain MacWhirr is convinced that his steamer will not survive the typhoon and so he confiscates the money of his 200 Chinese passengers.

U

Novel	Author	Synopsis
Ulysses	James Joyce	The work deals with the events of one day in Dublin as it follows the wanderings of two men through the city and their eventual meeting, with the various chapters corresponding to the episodes in Homer's *Odyssey*.
Uncle Tom's Cabin	Harriet Beecher	Uncle Tom, a black slave on a Kentucky

Novel	Author	Synopsis
	Stowe	farm, is sold to another owner. He is ill-treated and beaten but forgives his white masters.
Under the Greenwood Tree	Thomas Hardy	A comic novel introducing Hardy's village rustic who were to appear in his later works, this is the story of the love between Dick Dewy and Fancy Day mingled with both the fortunes and misfortunes of a group of villagers.

ʊ

Vanity Fair	William Makepeace Thackeray	Here we follow the interwoven story of two contrasting women, Becky Sharp and Amelia Sedley, watching their reactions to the rise and fall of their fortunes and their reactions and actions to and in various situations.
Vicar of Wakefield (The)	Oliver Goldsmith	The story of a good and philanthropic vicar who loses all his money and is then beset by misfortune after misfortune, until eventually when things can't get any worse all his misfortunes are resolved and his money returned.

ʍ

War and Peace	Leo Tolstoy	Set in the Napoleonic era this great 600,000 word epic tells the story of Russian society at that time through vivid description of war, personal stories and historical overviews.
War of the Worlds	H.G. Wells	Aliens arrive and start to kill humans and in the end are themselves defeated by germs.
Water Babies	Charles Kingsley	A series of moral lessons woven through the story of a young chimneysweep who runs away from his cruel employer only to fall into a river. Here he is transformed into a water baby and thereupon meets a variety of creatures.
Watership Down	Richard Adams	The rabbit's warren is about to be destroyed and so they flee in search of a new home.

Novel	Author	Synopsis
Waverley	Sir Walter Scott	Set during the Jacobite rebellion in 1745 it tells the story of Edward Waverley who becomes caught up in the political unrest, an unrest which crosses into his heart with him eventually choosing the gentle Rose over the politically active Flora.
Well-Beloved (The)	Thomas Hardy	A sculptor by the name of Jocelyn Pierston seeks the same perfection in a woman as he is able to sculpt in stone, but unsuccessful he eventually marries an elderly widow who has been 'chiselled by time'.
Westward Ho!	Charles Kingsley	Set in the Elizabethan period this tells the tale of seaman, Amyas Leigh, who wages war against the Armada and the Spanish Captain, Don Guzman, who is his rival in love.
Where Angels Fear to Tread	E.M. Forster	The impulsive young widow Lilia Herriton marries Gino Carella a match her mother frowns upon, tries to stop, but fails. She later dies in childbirth and her baby son is later accidentally killed.
Wind in the Willows (The)	Kenneth Grahame	A tale of four animal friends laced with lessons on morality for the young to absorb.
Winesburg, Ohio	Sherwood Anderson	This is a collection of short stories illustrating life in a small town.
Wings of the Dove (The)	Henry James	A wealthy American heiress, Milly Theale, is struck down by a terminal illness meaning that the motives of those who surround her are somewhat suspect.
Wives and Daughters	Elizabeth Gaskell	Centred on the families, the Gibsons and the Hamleys, where Mr Gibson, a widower, remarries for the sake of his daughter Molly. Initially it doesn't bring her happiness and there is much love entanglement to go through before the advent of happiness can dawn.
Woman in White (The)	Wilkie Collins	A thrilling Victorian drama novel which is vibrant with mystery in the form of a woman in white.

Novel	Author	Synopsis
Wonderful Wizard of Oz (The)	Frank Lyman Baum	Yes, there was a book before the film and everyone knows the story of the little girl who finds that right and truth has always been under her very own nose.
Years (The)	Virginia Woolf	Traces the history of a family from 1880 through to 1936.

THE OPENING LINES FROM CLASSIC BOOKS

It is said that no matter how long a book; how many words, how many lines, how many pages, the strength of the work can be judged by the opening lines alone. Maybe this is unfair but I do believe it is true. I also believe that this theory applies to many other things, people and situations too – think about it. First impressions – if your first impression of someone is poor, then it takes a lot longer for them to win you over; then there's that party, you know the one where you arrive and it's dead, dismal and dreary, the one where you wish you had never bothered to arrive in the first place and often leave before it gets going. For many people the same applies to the theatre too. My husband for example, who is a theatre fanatic like me, refuses to stay in his seat if a show doesn't grab him in the first 10 minutes. He says that it is he who has paid for the seat and so it is he who will decided whether to sit in it or not; this being based on the theory that if a writer can't be bothered to craft the top of the show to perfection then what's to follow will be inferior too. So in the world of literature it follows that the first taste should be the sweetest to tickle your classic taste buds to read on and enjoy, so here are the opening lines to many of the classics:

Quotation	Book	Author
Alice was beginning to get very tired of sitting by her sister on the bank, and of having nothing to do: once or twice she had peeped into the book her sister was reading, but it had no pictures or conversations in it, 'and what is the use of a book,' thought Alice, 'without pictures or conversation?'	*Alice's Adventures in Wonderland*	Lewis Carroll

Quotation	Book	Author
All children, except one, grow up.	*Peter Pan*	J.M. Barrie
As Gregor Samsa awoke one morning from uneasy dreams he found himself transformed in his bed into a gigantic insect.	*Metamorphosis*	Franz Kafka
Call me Ishmael	*Moby Dick*	Herman Melville
'Christmas won't be Christmas without any presents,' grumbled Jo, lying on the rug.	*Little Women*	Louisa May Alcott
Emma Woodhouse, handsome, clever, and rich, with a comfortable home and happy disposition, seemed to unite some of the best blessings of existence; and had lived nearly twenty-one years in the world with very little to distress or vex her.	*Emma*	Jane Austen
Happy families are all alike; every unhappy family is unhappy in its own way.	*Anna Karenina*	Leo Tolstoy
He was an inch, perhaps two, under six feet, powerfully built, and he advanced straight at you with a slight stoop of the shoulders, head forward, and a fixed from-under stare which made you think of a charging bull.	*Lord Jim*	Joseph Conrad
I am a sick man ... I am a spiteful man	*Notes from Underground*	Fyodor Dostoevsky
I have just returned from a visit to my landlord – the solitary neighbour that I shall be troubled with. This is certainly a beautiful country! In all England, I do not believe that I could have fixed on a situation so completely removed from the stir of society.	*Wuthering Heights*	Emily Brontë
I have never begun a novel with more misgiving.	*Razor's Edge, The*	Somerset Maugham
I was born in the Year 1632, in the City of York, of a good Family, tho' not of that Country, my Father being a Foreigner of Bremen, who settled first at Hull; he got a good Estate by Merchandise, and leaving off his Trade, lived afterward at York, from whence he had married my Mother, whose Relations were named Robinson, a very good Family in that Country, and from whom I was called Robinson Kreutznaer; but by the usual Corruption of Words in	*Robinson Crusoe*	Daniel Defoe

Quotation	Book	Author
England, we are now called, nay we call ourselves, and write our Name Crusoe, and so my Companions always call'd me.		
I wish either my father or my mother, or indeed both of them, as they were in duty both equally bound to it, had minded what they were about when they begot me; had they duly considered how much depended upon what they were then doing;—that not only the production of a rational Being was concerned in it, but that possibly the happy formation and temperature of his body, perhaps his genius and the very cast of his mind;—and, for aught they knew to the contrary, even the fortunes of his whole house might take their turn from the humours and dispositions which were then uppermost:—Had they duly weighed and considered all this, and proceeded accordingly,—I am verily persuaded I should have made a quite different figure in the world, from that, in which the reader is likely to see me.	*Tristam Shandy*	Laurence Sterne
In my younger and more vulnerable years my father gave me some advice that I've been turning over in my mind ever since. "Whenever you feel like criticizing anyone," he told me, "just remember that all the people in this world haven't had the advantages that you've had."	*Great Gatsby (The)*	F. Scott Fitzgerald
In that pleasant district of merry England which is watered by the river Don, there extended in ancient times a large forest, covering the greater part of the beautiful hills and valleys which lie between Sheffield and the pleasant town of Doncaster.	*Ivanhoe*	Sir Walter Scott
In the late summer of that year we lived in a house in a village that looked across the river and the plain to the mountains.	*Farewell to Arms (A)*	Ernest Hemmingway
It is a truth universally acknowledged that a single man in possession of a good fortune, must be in want of a wife.	*Pride and Prejudice*	Jane Austen

Quotation	Book	Author
It is this day three hundred and forty-eight years six months and nineteen days that the good people of Paris were awakened by a grand pealing from all the bells in the three districts of the Cite, the Universite, and the Ville.	*Hunchback of Notre Dame (The)*	Victor Hugo
It was a bright cold day in April, and the clocks were striking thirteen.	*Nineteen Eighty-Four*	George Orwell
It was just noon that Sunday morning when the sheriff reached the jail with Lucas Beauchamp though the whole town (the whole county too for that matter) had known since the night before that Lucas had killed a white man.	*Intruder in the Dust*	William Faulkner
It was love at first sight.	*Catch-22*	Joseph Heller
It was the best of times, it was the worst of times, it was the age of wisdom, it was the age of foolishness, it was the epoch of belief, it was the epoch of incredulity, it was the season of Light, it was the season of Darkness, it was the spring of hope, it was the winter of despair.	*Tale of Two Cities (A)*	Charles Dickens
Miss Brooke had that kind of beauty which seems to be thrown into relief by poor dress.	*Middlemarch*	George Eliot
My father's family name being Pirrip, and my Christian name Philip, my infant tongue could make of both names nothing longer or more explicit than Pip. So, I called myself Pip, and came to be called Pip.	*Great Expectations*	Charles Dickens
On an exceptionally hot evening early in July a young man came out of the garret in which he lodged in S. Place and walked slowly, as though in hesitation, towards K. bridge.	*Crime and Punishment*	Fyodor Dostoyevsky
Once there were four children whose names were Peter, Susan, Edmund and Lucy. This story is about something that happened to them when they were sent away from London during the war because of the air-raids.	*Lion, the Witch and the Wardrobe (The)*	C.S. Lewis

Quotation	Book	Author
Once upon a time and a very good time it was there was a moocow coming down along the road and this moocow that was coming down along the road met a nicens little boy named baby tuckoo.	Portrait of the Artist as a Young Man (A)	James Joyce
Once upon a time there were four little Rabbits, and their names were – Flopsy, Mopsy, Cotton-tail, and Peter.	Tale of Peter Rabbit (The)	Beatrix Potter
She waited, Kate Croy, for her father to come in, but he kept her unconscionably, and there were moments at which she showed herself, in the glass over the mantel, a face positively pale with the irritation that had brought her to the point of going away without sight of him.	Wings of the Dove (The)	Henry James
Someone must have slandered Josef K., for one morning, without having done anything truly wrong, he was arrested.	Trail (The)	Franz Kafka
Somewhere in la Mancha, in a place whose name I do not care to remember, a gentleman lived not long ago, one of those who has a lance and ancient shield on a shelf and keeps a skinny nag and a greyhound for racing.	Don Quixote	Miguel de Cervantes
Stately, plump Buck Mulligan came from the stairhead, bearing a bowl of lather on which a mirror and a razor lay crossed.	Ulysees	James Joyce
The drought had lasted now for ten million years, and the reign of the terrible lizards had long since ended.	2001: A Space Odyssey	Arthur C. Clarke
The past is a foreign country; they do things differently there.	Go-Between (The)	L.P. Hartley
The Time Traveller (for so it will be convenient to speak of him) was expounding a recondite matter to us.	Time Machine (The)	H.G. Wells
The year 1866 was signalized by a remarkable incident, a mysterious and inexplicable phenomenon, which doubtless no one has yet forgotten.	20,000 Leagues Under the Sea	Jules Verne
This is the saddest story I have ever heard	Good Soldier (The)	Ford Maddox Ford

Quotation	Book	Author
This is the story of what a Woman's patience can endure and what a Man's resolution can achieve.	*Woman in White (The)*	Wilkie Collins
Through the fence, between the curling flower spaces, I could see them hitting	*Sound and the Fury (The)*	William Faulkner
'To be born again,' sang Gibreel Farishta tumbling from the heavens, 'first you have to die.'	*Satanic Verses (The)*	Salman Rushdie
Well, Prince, so Genoa and Lucca are now just family estates of the Buonapartes. But I warn you, if you don't tell me that this means war, if you still try to defend the infamies and horrors perpetrated by that Antichrist - I really believe he is Antichrist - I will have nothing more to do with you and you are no longer my friend, no longer my 'faithful slave' as you call yourself! But how do you do? I see I have frightened you - sit down and tell me all the news.	*War and Peace*	Leo Tolstoy
When Farmer Oak smiled, the corners of his mouth spread till they were within an unimportant distance of his ears, his eyes were reduced to chinks, and diverging wrinkles appeared round them, extending upon his countenance like the rays in a rudimentary sketch of the rising sun.	*Far From the Madding Crowd*	Thomas Hardy
Whether I shall turn out to be the hero of my own life, or whether that station will be held by anybody else, these pages must show.	*David Copperfield*	Charles Dickens
You don't know about me without you have read a book by the name of *The Adventures of Tom Sawyer*; but that ain't no matter.	*Adventures of Huckleberry Finn*	Mark Twain

OTHER WELL KNOWN LINES FROM CLASSIC BOOKS

So the opening lines have enticed you further and you read on to to discover yet more and more gems. It is a lovely feeling to be able to knowledgeably quote lines from the classics or better still just drop them casually into the conversation; nothing makes you feel more well read – believe me, I know! My favourite quotation of all time is: 'Something will turn up' whenever the future looks bleak for me then out it comes followed by the words: as Mr Micawber would say! And then I feel, oh so intelligent, especially if I have to go on and explain from which book the saying originated and then when I can just drop in the name of the writer too, well that does it for me – Einstein move over, you have been usurped.

Quotation	Book	Author
A		
A lady's imagination is very rapid; it jumps from admiration to love, from love to matrimony, in a moment.	*Pride and Prejudice*	Jane Austen
A man can never do anything at variance with his own nature	*Adam Bede*	George Eliot
Actions are sometimes performed in a masterly and most cunning way, while the direction of the actions is deranged and dependent on various morbid impressions – it's like a dream.	*Crime and Punishment*	Fyodor Dostoevsky
B		
But beauty, real beauty, ends where an intellectual expression begins.	*Picture of Dorian Gray (The)*	Oscar Wilde
But, strangest of all, the very instant the shore was touched, an immense dog sprang up on deck from below ... and running forward, jumped from the bow on to the sand. Making straight for the steep cliff, where the churchyard hangs over the laneway to the East Pier ... it disappeared in the darkness.	*Dracula*	Bram Stoker
C		
Conventionality is not morality. Self-righteousness is not religion. To attack the first is not to assail the last	*Jane Eyre*	Charlotte Brontë
Curiouser and curiouser	*Alice's Adventures in Wonderland*	Lewis Carroll

Quotation	Book	Author
D		
Delicacy! A fine word for such as she! I'll teach her, with all her airs, that she's no better than the raggedest black wench that walks the streets! She'll take no more airs with me!	*Uncle Tom's Cabin*	Harriet Beecher Stowe
H		
He that is down needs fear no fall. He that is low, no pride	*Pilgrim's Progress (The)*	John Bunyan
How can I pray for you, when I am forbidden to believe that the great Power who moves the world would alter his plans on my account?	*Tess of the d'Urbervilles*	Thomas Hardy
How sad it is! I shall grow old, and horrible, and dreadful. But this picture will remain always young.	*Picture of Dorian Gray (The)*	Oscar Wilde
Humanity takes itself too seriously. It is the world's original sin. If the cave-man had known how to laugh, History would have been different	*Picture of Dorian Gray (The)*	Oscar Wilde
I		
I am no bird; and no net ensnares me; I am a free human being with an independent will	*Jane Eyre*	Charlotte Brontë
I did not bow down to you, I bowed down to all the suffering of humanity	*Crime and Punishment*	Fyodor Dostoevsky
I see that a man cannot give himself up to drinking without being miserable one-half his days and mad the other	*Tenant of Wildfell Hall (The)*	Anne Brontë
If all the world hated you, and believed you wicked, while your own conscience approved you, and absolved you from guilt, you would not be without friends.	*Jane Eyre*	Charlotte Brontë
If he has a conscience he will suffer for his mistake. That will be punishment as well as the prison.	*Crime and Punishment*	Fyodor Dostoevsky
If you please ma'am, it was a very little one	*Mr Midshipman Easy*	Captain Marryat

Quotation	Book	Author
It is a far, far, better thing that I do, than I have ever done; it is a far, far, better rest that I go to, than I have ever known.	*Tale of Two Cities (A)*	Charles Dickens
It is good to be children sometimes, and never better than at Christmas, when its mighty Founder was a child himself.	*Christmas Carol (A)*	Charles Dickens
It is in vain to say human beings ought to be satisfied with tranquility: they must have action; and they will make it if they cannot find it.	*Jane Eyre*	Charlotte Brontë
It is the eve of St George's Day. Do you not know that tonight, when the clock strikes midnight, all the evil things in the world will have full sway?	*Dracula*	Bram Stoker
It is very often nothing but our own vanity that deceives us	*Pride and Prejudice*	Jane Austen
It's no good fighting against Fate or trying to resist the smile of the angels.	*Madame Bovary*	Gustave Flaubert

L

Quotation	Book	Author
Life appears to me too short to be spent in nursing animosity or registering wrongs.	*Jane Eyre*	Charlotte Brontë
Love has no age, no limit; and no death	*Forsyte Saga (The)*	John Galsworthy

M

Quotation	Book	Author
Men are cowards before women until they become tyrants.	*Small House at Allington (The)*	Anthony Trollope
My dear boy, no woman is a genius. Women are a decorative sex. They never have anything to say, but they say it charmingly. Women represent the triumph of matter over mind, just as men represent the triumph of mind over morals.	*Picture of Dorian Gray (The)*	Oscar Wilde
My life looks as if it had been wasted for want of chances!	*Tess of the d'Urbervilles*	Thomas Hardy

O

Quotation	Book	Author
Off with her head!	*Alice's Adventures in Wonderland*	Lewis Carroll
Out of the frying pan into the fire!	*Tess of the d'Urbervilles*	Thomas Hardy

Quotation	Book	Author
P		
Prejudices, it is well known, are most difficult to eradicate from the heart whose soil has never been loosened or fertilised by education: they grow there, firm as weeds among stones.	*Jane Eyre*	Charlotte Brontë
S		
Saint abroad, and a devil at home	*Pilgrim's Progress (The)*	John Bunyan
Sentence first—verdict afterwards	*Alice's Adventures in Wonderland*	Lewis Carroll
Some of us rush through life, and some of us saunter through life	*Woman in White (The)*	Wilkie Collins
T		
Take care of the sense, and the sounds will take care of themselves.	*Alice's Adventures in Wonderland*	Lewis Carroll
Take nothing on its looks; take everything on evidence	*Great Expectations*	Charles Dickens
The best men are not consistent in good – why should the worst men be consistent in evil?	*Woman in White (The)*	Wilkie Collins
The children of the very poor are not brought up, but dragged up.	*Bleak House*	Charles Dickens
The man is silent, not because he would not have the words spoken, but because he does not know the fitting words with which to speak	*Kept in the Dark*	Anthony Trollope
The man who is insensible to the power money brings with it must be a dolt	*Lady Anna*	Anthony Trollope
The only way to get rid of a temptation is to yield to it.	*Picture of Dorian Gray (The)*	Oscar Wilde
The pitifulest thing out is a mob; that's what an army is—a mob; they don't fight with courage that's born in them, but with courage that's borrowed from their mass, and from their officers. But a mob without any MAN at the head of it is BENEATH pitifulness	*Adventures of Huckleberry Finn*	Mark Twain

Quotation	Book	Author
The tact of women excels the skill of men.	*Claverings (The)*	Anthony Trollope
The weak man becomes strong when he has nothing, for then only can he feel the wild, mad thrill of despair.	*White Company (The)*	Sir Arthur Conan Doyle
There is a limit at which forbearance ceases to be a virtue.	*Pilgrim's Progress (The)*	John Bunyan
There is nothing – absolutely nothing – half so much worth doing as simply messing about in boats.	*Wind in the Willows (The)*	Kenneth Grahame
There is nothing in the world so difficult as that task of making up one's mind.	*Phineas Finn*	Anthony Trollope
There was things which he stretched, but mainly he told the truth	*Adventures of Huckleberry Finn*	Mark Twain
They wanted to speak, but could not; tears stood in their eyes	*Crime and Punishment*	Fyodor Dostoevsky
Those who have courage to love should have courage to suffer	*Bertrams (The)*	Anthony Trollope

W

Quotation	Book	Author
We don't own your laws; we don't own your country; we stand here as free, under God's sky, as you are; and, by the great God that made us, we'll fight for our liberty till we die.	*Uncle Tom's Cabin*	Harriet Beecher Stowe
We're all mad here	*Alice's Adventures in Wonderland*	Lewis Carroll
What greater thing is there for two human souls, than to feel that they are joined for life – to strengthen each other in all labour, to rest on each other in all sorrow, to minister to each other in all pain, to be one with each other in silent unspeakable memories at the moment of the last parting?	*Adam Bede*	George Eliot
Women can resist a man's love, a man's fame, a man's personal appearance, and a man's money, but they cannot resist a man's tongue when he knows how to talk to them	*Woman in White (The)*	Wilkie Collins

Quotation	Book	Author
Y		
You are a wonderful creation. You know more than you think you know, just as you know less than you want to know.	*Picture of Dorian Gray (The)*	Oscar Wilde
You have killed my love. You used to stir my imagination. Now you don't even stir my curiosity	*Picture of Dorian Gray (The)*	Oscar Wilde

SOME OF THE WELL KNOWN CHARACTERS FOUND IN CLASSIC BOOKS

Sometimes when we read a book we become enchanted and enthralled not only by the storyline, but by the characters carrying that storyline. It is in these characters that we sometimes see ourselves, or maybe see what we would like to be; then sometimes we see characters who inspire us on to bigger and greater things, or who give us the courage to triumph over adversity. You see the stories we find in literature not only mirror lives and situations but also people, and that is the real fascination and is what draws us to books. Below you may meet your own personal hero, some you have forgotten and some you have never met before.

Character	Book	Author
A		
Aramis	*Three Musketeers (The)*	Alexandre Dumas père
Armitage, Jacob	*Children of the New Forest*	Captain Marryat
Aslan	*Lion, the Witch and the Wardrobe (The)*	C.S. Lewis
Athos	*Three Musketeers (The)*	Alexandre Dumas père
D'Artagnan	*Three Musketeers (The)*	Alexandre Dumas père
B		
Baggins, Bilbo	*Hobbit (The)*	J.R.R. Tolkien
Baggins, Frodo	*Lord of the Rings (The)*	J.R.R. Tolkienn
Baker, Jordan	*Great Gatsby (The)*	F. Scott Fitzgerald
Balfour, David	*Kidnapped*	Robert Louis Stevenson
Balfour, Ebenezer	*Kidnapped*	Robert Louis Stevenson

Character	Book	Author
Bates, Miss & Mrs	*Emma*	Jane Austen
Beck, Madame	*Vilette*	Charlotte Brontë
Benwick	*Persuasion*	Jane Austen
Bertram Family	*Mansfield Park*	Jane Austen
Bertram, Herry	*Guy Mannering*	Sir Walter Scott
Beverley, Colonel	*Children of the New Forest*	Captain Marryat
Beverley, Edward	*Children of the New Forest*	Captain Marryat
Bezukhov, Pierre	*War and Peace*	Leo Tolstoy
Big Brother	*Nineteen Eighty-Four*	George Orwell
Bingley, Charles and Caroline	*Pride and Prejudice*	Jane Austen
Bolkonsky, Andrei Nikolayevich	*War and Peace*	Leo Tolstoy
Bones, Billy	*Treasure Island*	Robert Louis Stevenson
Boulanger, Rudolphe	*Madame Bovary*	Gustave Flaubert
Bovary, Emma	*Madame Bovary*	Gustave Flaubert
Breton, John	*Vilette*	Charlotte Brontë
Bridehead, Sue	*Jude the Obscure*	Thomas Hardy
Brooke, Dorothea	*Middlemarch*	George Eliot
Buchanan, Daisy	*Great Gatsby (The)*	F. Scott Fitzgerald
Butler, Rhett	*Gone with the Wind*	Margaret Mitchell

C

Character	Book	Author
Caderousse, Gaspard	*Count of Monte Cristo (The)*	Alexandre Dumas père
Campbell, Helen	*Rob Roy*	Sir Walter Scott
Campbell, Mr	*Kidnapped*	Robert Louis Stevenson
Campbell, Robert Roy MacGregor	*Rob Roy*	Sir Walter Scott
Canty, Tom	*Prince and the Pauper (The)*	Mark Twain
Carew, Sir Danvers	*Dr Jekyll and Mr Hyde*	Robert Louis Stevenson
Carraway, Nick	*Great Gatsby (The)*	F. Scott Fitzgerald
Casaubon, Mr	*Middlemarch*	George Eliot
Cass, Geoffrey	*Silas Marner*	George Eliot
Castleford, Lord and Lady	*History of Henry Esmond, Esquire (The)*	William Makepeace Thackeray
Caulfield, Holden	*Catcher in the Rye (The)*	J.D. Salinger
Chaffanbrass, Mr	*Three Clerks (The)* *Orley Farm* *Phineas Redux*	Anthony Trollope
Charmond, Felice	*Woodlanders (The)*	Thomas Hardy
Cheshire Cat	*Alice's Adventures in Wonderland*	Lewis Carroll

Character	Book	Author
Churchill, Frank	*Emma*	Jane Austen
Clare, Angel	*Tess of the d'Urbervilles*	Thomas Hardy
Collins, William	*Pride and Prejudice*	Jane Austen
Comstock, Magenta	*Harry Potter Series (The)*	J.K. Rowling
Craven, Archibald	*Secret Garden*	Frances Hodgson Burnett
Crawford, Henry and Mary	*Mansfield Park*	Jane Austen
Crawley, Rawdon	*Vanity Fair*	William Makepeace Thackeray
Crimsworth, William	*Professor (The)*	Charlotte Brontë
Croft, Admiral and Mrs	*Persuasion*	Jane Austen

D

Character	Book	Author
D'Arcy, Fitzwilliam	*Pride and Prejudice*	Jane Austen
D'Arcy, Georgina	*Pride and Prejudice*	Jane Austen
D'Urberville, Alec	*Tess of the D'Urbervilles*	Thomas Hardy
Dalrymple, Lady	*Persuasion*	Jane Austen
Danglars, Baron	*Count of Monte Cristo (The)*	Alexandre Dumas père
Dantès père, Edmund	*Count of Monte Cristo (The)*	Alexandre Dumas père
Dashwood, Elinor	*Sense and Sensibility*	Jane Austen
Day, Fancy	*Under the Greenwood Tree*	Thomas Hardy
De Bourgh, Lady Catherine	*Pride and Prejudice*	Jane Austen
Dean, Nelly	*Wuthering Heights*	Emily Brontë
Deane, Lucy	*Mill on the Floss (The)*	George Eliot
Deane, Mr	*Mill on the Floss (The)*	George Eliot
Dedalus, Stephen	*Portrait of an Artist as a Young Man (A)*	James Joyce
Dent, Arthur	*Hitchhiker's Guide to the Galaxy (The)*	Douglas Adams
Derriman, Festus	*Trumpet Major*	Thomas Hardy
Dewy, Dick	*Under the Greenwood Tree*	Thomas Hardy
Dobbin, Colonel William	*Vanity Fair*	William Makepeace Thackeray
Doone, Sir Ensor	*Lorna Doone*	R.D. Blackmore
Doyle, Linnet Ridgeway	*Death on the Nile*	Agatha Christie
Dugal, Lady	*Lorna Doone*	R.D. Blackmore
Dumbledore, Albus	*Harry Potter Series (The)*	J.K. Rowling
Dupuis, Léon	*Madame Bovary*	Gustave Flaubert

E

Character	Book	Author
Eames, Johnny	*Small House at Allington* *Last Chronicle of Barset (The)*	Anthony Trollope

Character	Book	Author
Earnshaw, Catherine, Hindley and Hareton	*Wuthering Heights*	Emily Brontë
Earwicker, Humphrey Chimpden	*Finnegans Wake*	James Joyce
Eliza	*Uncle Tom's Cabin*	Harriet Beecher Stowe
Elliot, Anne	*Persuasion*	Jane Austen
Eppie	*Silas Marner*	George Eliot
Errol, Cedric	*Little Lord Fauntleroy*	Frances Hodgson Burnett
Esmond, Henry	*History of Henry Esmond Esq (The)*	William Makepeace Thackeray
Eva (Evangelina St Clare)	*Uncle Tom's Cabin*	Harriet Beecher Stowe
Everdene, Bathsheba	*Far from the Madding Crowd*	Thomas Hardy

F

Character	Book	Author
Fairlie, Frederick	*Woman in White (The)*	Wilkie Collins
Fairlie, Laura	*Woman in White (The)*	Wilkie Collins
Fairservice, Andrew	*Rob Roy*	Sir Walter Scott
Farfae, Donald	*Mayor of Casterbridge (The)*	Thomas Hardy
Farren, Molly	*Silas Marner*	George Eliot
Ferrars, Edward	*Sense and Sensibility*	Jane Austen
Finch, Atticus	*To Kill a Mockingbird*	Harper Lee
Finn, Phineas	*Phineas Finn & Phineas Redux*	Anthony Trollope
Flint, Captain	*Treasure Island*	Robert Louis Stevenson
Fogg, Phileas	*Around the World in Eighty Days*	Jules Verne
Forrest, Dr	*Railway Children (The)*	E. Nesbit
Fosco, Count	*Woman in White (The)*	Wilkie Collins

G

Character	Book	Author
Gandalf	*Lord of the Rings (The)*	J.R.R. Tolkein
Gatsby, Jay	*Great Gatsby (The)*	F. Scott Fitzgerald
Grainger, Hermione	*Harry Potter Series (The)*	J.K. Rowling
Gryffindor, Godric	*Harry Potter Series (The)*	J.K. Rowling
Gunn, Ben	*Treasure Island*	Robert Louis Stevenson

H

Character	Book	Author
Halcombe, Marian	*Woman in White (The)*	Wilkie Collins
Hale, Mr, Mrs Margaret & Frederick	*North and South*	Elizabeth Gaskell
Hallward, Basil	*Picture of Dorian Gray (The)*	Oscar Wilde
Hartright, Walter	*Woman in White (The)*	Wilkie Collins
Hawkins, Jim	*Treasure Island*	Robert Louis Stevenson

Character	Book	Author
Heathcliff	*Wuthering Heights*	Emily Brontë
Higgins, Henry	*Pygmalion*	George Bernard Shaw
Holbrook, Thomas	*Cranford*	Elizabeth Gaskell
Holmes, Sherlock	*Adventures of Sherlock (The) Holmes* (and other books)	Arthur Conan Doyle
Homais, Monsieur	*Madame Bovary*	Gustave Flaubert
Howard, John	*Pied Piper*	Nevil Shute
Hufflepuff, Helga	*Harry Potter Series (The)*	J.K. Rowling
Huntingdon, Arthur and Helen	*Tenant of Wildfell Hall (The)*	Anne Brontë
Hyde, Mr Edward	*Dr Jekyll and Mr Hyde*	Robert Louis Stevenson

I

Ishmael	*Moby Dick*	Herman Melville

J

Jakin, Bob	*Mill on the Floss (The)*	George Eliot
Jekyll, Dr	*Dr Jekyll and Mr Hyde*	Robert Louis Stevenson
Jenkyns, Deborah, Matilda and Peter	*Cranford*	Elizabeth Gaskell
Jennings, Mrs	*Sense and Sensibility*	Jane Austen
Jim	*Adventures of Hucklebury Finn*	Mark Twain

K

Karenina, Anna	*Anna Karenina*	Leo Tolstoy
Kimble, Mr	*Silas Marner*	George Eliot
Klesner	*Daniel Deronda*	George Eliot
Knightly, George and John	*Emma*	Jane Austen
Kutuzov	*War and Peace*	Leo Tolstoy

L

La Fleur	*Sentimental Journey (A)*	Lawrence Sterne
Ladislaw, Will	*Middlemarch*	George Eliot
Lammeter, Nancy	*Silas Marner*	George Eliot
Lanyon, Dr Hastie	*Dr Jekyll and Mr Hyde*	Robert Louis Stevenson
Le Fever	*Tristram Shandy*	Lawrence Sterne
Legree, Simon	*Uncle Tom's Cabin*	Harriet Beecher Stowe
Lennox, Mary	*Secret Garden (The)*	Frances Hodgson Burnett
Lheureux, Monsieur	*Madame Bovary*	Gustave Flaubert
Locksley	*Ivanhoe*	Sir Walter Scott

Character	Book	Author

M

Character	Book	Author
Mad Hatter	Alice's Adventures in Wonderland	Lewis Carroll
March Sisters	Little Women	Louisa May Alcott
Marner, Silas	Silas Marner	George Eliot
Medlock, Mrs	Secret Garden	Frances Hodgson Burnett
Middleton, Sir John	Sense and Sensibility	Jane Austen
Mock Turtle	Alice's Adventures in Wonderland	Lewis Carroll
Mondego, Mercédès	Count of Monte Cristo (The)	Alexandre Dumas père
Moran, Peter	So Disdained	Nevil Shute
Morland, Catherine	Northanger Abbey	Jane Austen
Morrel, Pierre	Count of Monte Cristo (The)	Alexandre Dumas père
Morris, Dinah	Adam Bede	George Eliot
Mowgli	Jungle Book (The)	Rudyard Kipling
Mulliner, Mr	Cranford	Elizabeth Gaskell
Murray Rosalie	Agnes Grey	Anne Brontë
Musgrove, Mr and Mrs, Charles, Mary (née Elliot), Henrietta and Louisa	Persuasion	Jane Austen

N

Character	Book	Author
Nemo, Captain	20,000 Leagues Under the Sea	Jules Verne
Newcome, Colonel Thomas	Newcomes (The)	William Makepeace Thackeray
Newcommen, Inspector	Dr Jekyll and Mr Hyde	Robert Louis Stevenson
Norris, Mrs	Mansfield Park	Jane Austen

O

Character	Book	Author
O'Dowd, Major & Mrs	Vanity Fair	William Makepeace Thackeray
O'Hara, Scarlett	Gone with Wind	Margaret Mitchell
Oak, Gabriel	Far from the Madding Crowd	Thomas Hardy
Obadiah	Tristram Shandy	Laurence Sterne
Osbaldistone, Francis	Rob Roy	Sir Walter Scott
Osborne, Mr	Vanity Fair	William Makepeace Thackeray

P

Character	Book	Author
Paget, Jean	Town Like Alice (A)	Nevil Shute

Character	Book	Author
Palmer, Charlotte	*Sense and Sensibility*	Jane Austen
Partridge	*Tom Jones*	Henry Fielding
Passenpartout	*Around the World in Eighty Days*	Jules Verne
Pendennis, Arthur	*Pendennis*	William Makepeace Thackeray
Pesca, Professor	*Woman in White (The)*	Wilkie Collins
Peter	*Railway Children (The)*	E. Nesbitt
Pew, Blind	*Treasure Island*	Robert Louis Stevenson
Phyllis	*Railway Children (The)*	E. Nesbitt
Poirot, Hercule	*Death on the Nile*	Agatha Christie
Pole, Miss	*Cranford*	Elizabeth Gaskell
Poole, Mr	*Dr Jekyll and Mr Hyde*	Robert Louis Stevenson
Porthos	*Three Musketeers (The)*	Alexandre Dumas père
Price, Fanny	*Mansfield Park*	Jane Austen
Prince John	*Ivanhoe*	Sir Walter Scott
Professor Moriarty	*Sherlock Holmes Stories*	Sir Arthur Conan Doyle

R

Character	Book	Author
Race, Colonel	*Death on the Nile*	Agatha Christie
Ransome	*Kidnapped*	Robert Louis Stevenson
Ravenclaw, Rowena	*Harry Potter Series (The)*	J.K. Rowling
Rebecca	*Ivanhoe*	Sir Walter Scott
Ridd, John	*Lorna Doone*	R.D. Blackmore
Roberta	*Railway Children (The)*	E. Nesbit
Rochester, Edward Fairfax	*Jane Eyre*	Charlotte Brontë
Rostova, Natasha	*War and Peace*	Leo Tolstoy
Rowena	*Ivanhoe*	Sir Walter Scott

S

Character	Book	Author
Schlegel, Margaret	*Howards End*	E.M. Forster
Seagrim, Molly	*Tom Jones*	Henry Fielding
Sedley, Amelia	*Vanity Fair*	William Makepeace Thackeray
Sedley, Joseph	*Vanity Fair*	William Makepeace Thackeray
Sessemann, Clara	*Heidi*	Johanna Spyri
Sharp, Rebecca	*Vanity Fair*	William Makepeace Thackeray
Shuan, Mr	*Kidnapped*	Robert Louis Stevenson
Silver, Long John	*Treasure Island*	Robert Louis Stevenson
Slytherin, Salazr	*Harry Potter Series (The)*	J.K. Rowling
Smith, Harriet	*Emma*	Jane Austen

Character	Book	Author
Smith, Mary	*Cranford*	Elizabeth Gaskell
Smollett, Captain Alexander	*Treasure Island*	Robert Louis Stevenson
Sorel, Julien	*Red and the Black (The)*	Stendhal
Sparkish	*Country Wife (The)*	William Wycherley
Square	*Tom Jones*	Henry Fielding
Stanley, Featherstonehaugh Ukridge	*Ukridge and Uncle Fred in the Springtime*	P.G. Wodehouse
Stenning, Phihllip	*Marazan*	Nevil Shute

T

Character	Book	Author
Temple, Miss	*Jane Eyre*	Charlotte Brontë
Thorpe, John and Isabella	*Northanger Abbey*	Jane Austen
Thwackum	*Tom Jones*	Henry Fielding
Tilney, Henry	*Northanger Abbey*	Jane Austen
Toots, Tilden	*Harry Potter Series (The)*	J.K. Rowling
Topsy	*Uncle Tom's Cabin*	Harriet Beecher Stowe
Towers, Captain	*On the Beach*	Nevil Shute
Troy, Sergeant Francis	*Far From the Madding Crowd*	Thomas Hardy
Tudor, Edward	*Prince and the Pauper (The)*	Mark Twain
Tulliver, Mr and Mrs Tom and Maggie	*The Mill on the Floss (The)*	George Eliot

U

Character	Book	Author
Uncle Tom	*Uncle Tom's Cabin*	Harriet Beecher Stowe
Utterson, Mr	*Dr Jekyll and Mr Hyde*	Robert Louis Stevenson

V

Character	Book	Author
Vane, Sybill	*Picture of Dorian Gray (The)*	Oscar Wilde
Venn, Diggory	*Return of the Native (The)*	Thomas Hardy
Vernon, Diana	*Rob Roy*	Sir Walter Scott
Villfort, Gérard de	*Count of Monte Cristo (The)*	Alexandre Dumas pére
Vronsky, Count Alexei Kirillovic	*Anna Karenina*	Leo Tolstoy
Vye, Eustacia	*Return of the Native (The)*	Thomas Hardy

W

Character	Book	Author
Wakem, Philip	*Mill on the Floss (The)*	George Eliot
Watson, Dr	*Hound of the Baskervilles (The)*	Sir Arthur Conan Doyle
Wentworth, Captain Frederick	*Persuasion*	Jane Austen
Western, Sophia	*Tom Jones*	Henry Fielding

Character	Book	Author
Weston, Mr	*Agnes Grey*	Anne Brontë
Wilcox, Paul	*Howards End*	E.M. Forster
Wilfred of Ivanhoe	*Ivanhoe*	Sir Walter Scott
Wilson, George B.	*Great Gatsby (The)*	F. Scott Fitzgerald
Winterborne, Giles	*Woodlanders (The)*	Thomas Hardy
Winthrop, Dolly	*Silas Marner*	George Eliot
Worldly, Wiseman Mr.	*Pilgrim's Progress (The)*	John Bunyan
Wotton, Lord Henry	*Picture of Dorian Gray (The)*	Oscar Wilde
Y		
Yeobright, Clym	*Return of the Native (The)*	Thomas Hardy

LITERARY TERMS

Each profession, from plumbers to brain surgeons, has its own language, a language which is peculiar to them and them alone. It is as important for a plumber to understand the uses of a plunger as it is for a brain surgeon to understand the uses of a scalpel. In the case of a writer, well he is quite unique in that he has a set of words to describe the use of other words, some of which have baffled the unsuspecting schoolboy for centuries! This section then will attempt to unravel the mystery of a selection of these words. However, please be aware that this is just the tip of the iceberg and that there are literally hundreds of just such words in an iceberg that not only refuses to melt but instead expands with the passing of time.

A

aesthetics	The nature and perception of beauty, especially as a part of the arts; those who subscribed to the 'aesthetic movement' in the late Nineteenth Century generally subscribed too to the affectations of eccentric speech, manners and dress.
alienation effect	Generally used in dramatic works where the intention is that the audience does not identify with the characters as portrayed on stage thus allowing them rationally to view a situation and analyse the story without feeling a part of it. It is a technique used by Bertolt Brecht in direct opposition to the personal identification encouraged by Constantin Stanislavsky.
allegory	This is used to describe a story or visual image with another second meaning hidden behind the initial literal meaning.
alliteration	A literary effect achieved by using several consecutive words beginning with the same or similar consonants.

allusion	An indirect reference to something – person, place, event etc. – which is not explained to the reader by the writer, but which relies upon the reader's own knowledge of that to which the specific allusion is made.
anachronism	This word is used to describe the misplacing of any person, place, thing or event outside of its correct historical time.
analogy	Analogies are used to illustrate an idea by using a more familiar idea that is in some way similar.
angry young men	This term was initially used by journalists in the 1950s to describe the authors and protagonists of novels and plays which appeared to resent, rebel and kick against the middle-class section of society of that time.
antagonist	This is the most prominent of the characters who oppose the protagonist hero(ine) in a dramatic or narrative piece of work.
apocalyptic	A word use to describe the revealing of the secrets of the future through prophecy.

B

bard	A term which since the Eighteenth Century has often been used to describe a poet and is in particular the word used to describe Shakespeare.
bibliography	The description of books: i. A list of writing by a particular author ii. The study of books as objects in themselves, e.g. paper, binding, page numbering, etc. iii. The list of books – used as reference books for the writing of another book – which is included to cite the point of reference
blank verse	Unrhymed lines of iambic pentameter.
Bloomsbury Group	A small and exclusive group of writers whose common link was that they were all friends of Virginia Woolf and her sister, Vanessa.

C

cacophony	A harsh, discordant and intrusive sound (onslaught on the ears).
canon	A body of writings recognised by authority; works by a literary author which scholars regard as authentic.
carpe diem	The meaning of this is 'seize the day'(make the best of the present moment) and comes from Horace's *Odes*, (I, xi)
circumlocution	A roundabout way of referring to something, rather than getting straight to the point.
codex	A book of ancient manuscripts.
colloquialism	Informal, everyday expressions generally used in speech rather than in formal writing.

coterie	A small group of writers generally bound together by friendship rather than by a particular literary style.

D

denouement	This is the clarification of the plot and tying up of the loose ends, usually in the final chapter.
dirge	Usually a song of lamentation in mourning for the death of someone.
donnée	This is a French word for something 'given' and is usually used to refer to the original idea or starting point of a writer's work.
double entendre	This is the French phrase for 'double meaning' and is used in English to denote a pun in which a word or a phrase has a second meaning (usually of a sexual nature).
dystopia	The opposite of Utopia, it is a unpleasant, fictitious world.

E

elegy	A formal, lyric poem generally lamenting the death of a friend or a public figure.
ellipsis	Generally the use of three dots ... to signify the omission of some text.
epilogue	The concluding section of any written work.
epistolary novel	A novel written in the form of a series of letters which are exchanged between the characters in the story.
eponymous	A term which is applied to a real or fictitious person after whom a place, an institution or something is named – an eponym is a name transferred from a person to a place or a thing.
everyman	In the world of literature the term 'everyman' has come to mean an ordinary man with whom every man can identify. The derivation is an English Morality play called – *Everyman*
expurgate	Means to remove objectionable material from a text (usually of a sexual or political nature).

F

faction	A work with factual contents presented as a fictional novel.
folio	A large-sized book where the size of the page is as a result of folding a printer's standard sheet of paper in half, forming two leaves – four pages.
fustian	Pretentious language.

G

genre	The French term for type which in the literary world translates into a category of work, such as comedy, tragedy, etc.
gothic novel	This type of novel is one of terror and suspense.

Grub Street	This was a street in London – it has now been renamed Milton Street – and was where impoverished writers were forced to live and write third rate books just to earn a living.

H

holograph	A document which is written entirely in the author's own handwriting,
homily	This is a sermon or a morally instructive lecture.
hyperbole	An exaggeration merely to emphasise a point.

I

iamb	A metrical unit of verse consisting of one unstressed syllable, followed by one stressed syllable.
idiom	A phrase which is impossible to translate literally into another language for the simple reason that its meaning does not match the said words.
incunabula	This is a word used for books printed before the Sixteenth Century.
inkhorn	This word dates back to the Sixteenth Century and is used when the language in a book is excessively literary or pedantic.
Innisfail	The romantically poetic name for Ireland.
interpolation	Used to describe a passage which has been inserted into a text at a later date by another writer – usually without permission of the original writer.
intonation	The pattern in the variation of pitch during a spoken piece.

J

jongleur	The French term for a wandering entertainer in Medieval Europe.

K

kitsch	Used to describe anything in the art world which is considered to be rubbish or tasteless.
Kit-Cat Club	A London club, with strong political and literary associations, founded in the early part of the Eighteenth Century.

L

legend	A legend is a story, or a group of stories, which are handed down through the years and generations, usually orally although many have now been committed to paper. The stories are usually about people, e.g. heroes and saints, as opposed to myths, which generally are based upon the stories of ancient gods.
leonine verse	This is a kind of Latin verse widely used in the Middle Ages.

197

libretto	This Italian word is used in English to describe the text – or spoken words – of a musical or opera, etc.
litany	Generally speaking this describes a long prayer chant.
literati	The collective term for educated people, especially writers or those studying or criticising such.

M

malapropism	A word which derived from the character Mrs Malaprop in Sheridan's play *The Rivals* (1775) and which means a confused and inaccurately comical use of a long word or words.
metre	The pattern of measured sound units which recur in verse.
morphology	The science of analysing the structure of words.
muse	A muse is the source of inspiration to a writer, usually represented as a female deity. In ancient Greece there were nine muses – nine sister-goddesses.

N

nemesis	Retribution or punishment for wrongdoing.
Newgate novel	Popular novels of the 1830s, which are based on the legends of Eighteenth Century highwaymen and other notorious criminals.
nom de plume	A pen name – a pseudonym – used by a writer for his published works.
novella	A fictional novel which in length falls between a short story and a full length novel.

O

obiter dicta	A Latin phrase meaning things said in passing.
onomatopoeia	This is the use of words in which the sound seems to echo the meaning of the word.
oxymoron	A figure of speech which combines two contradictory terms, for example bittersweet.

P

palaeography	The study and the deciphering of old manuscripts.
palindrome	A word which reads exactly the same from back to front as it does from front to back, e.g. deed.
Palliser Novels (The)	This is a term used to describe the political novels of Anthony Trollope.
Pandarus	In classical legend he is a son of Lycaon who assisted the Trojans in their war against the Greeks.
pandemonium	This is a word coined by Milton; the abode of all the demons, the capital of hell. (It is a word in common usage today and means noisy, chaotic and confused and is often used in conjunction with the saying: 'All hell broke loose.')
paradox	A contradictory statement or proposition.

paronomasia	A play on words, a kind of pun.
pastiche	A literary work made up of elements taking from various other writers.
pathos	The emotionally moving quality in a literary piece, appealing primarily to the emotions of sadness and pity.
patronage	The provision of financial – or other assistance – to a writer by a private individual or a public company.
pentametre	A line of verse consisting of five stresses.
periodical	A magazine published at regular intervals.
philistine	Generally used to describe someone interested in materialistic prosperity at the expense of intellectual and artistic awareness; someone who is not interested in culture.
plagiarism	The theft of ideas, for example the plots of a written piece, which are then passed off as one's own.
polysemy	A linguistic term used to describe a word which can have two entirely different meanings.
pot-boiler	A term used to describe a work written primarily to earn money.
protagonist	The chief character in a play or story.

Q

quarto	The size of a book or a page that is the result of folding a standard printer's sheet twice.

R

Renaissance	The re-birth of art, literature and learning which began in the mid 1400s and continued through until the mid 1700s.
repartee	This is used to describe a witty and fast moving response during a conversation and is usually used when the giver of an insult has it turned around to be cleverly used against them.
Restoration Comedy	A form of English comedy usually in the form of the 'Comedy of Manners' which flourished during the Restoration period in history.

S

S & F	A discreet description of popular modern fiction often used to describe romantic fiction and generally written for women – by women. The accent is on the materialistic side of life and tends to focus on the rich, with somewhat graphic details of their sex lives.
Sabrina	A poetic name for the river Severn.
semantics	The linguistic study of meanings in language.
silver-fork novels	Novels that were popular in Britain from the 1820s to the 1840s, they focussed on the fashionable etiquette of the upper classes during the period.
spoonerism	A term attributed to a phrase in which the initial consonants

	of two words have been swapped to create an amusing alternative expression. The name is said to come from the Rev W.A. Spooner (1844-1930), Warden of New College, Oxford who frequently mixed up his words. He is reputed to have told a student that he 'hissed my mystery lectures'. This can be deliberately used for comic effect.
syntax	A word to describe the way in which words and clauses are ordered to form sentences.

T

tetralogy	This is a group of four connected novels (or plays).
tract	A short pamphlet or essay presenting a religious, or political, argument or doctrine.
treatise	Used to describe a piece of written work on a specific subject
truncated	This is a written piece which has been shortened.
typography	The arrangement of printed words on a page.

U

Utopia	An imagined and idealistic form of human society.

V

variorum edition	Originally this meant an edition of an author's work which included the comments of others, including the editors. Now though such an edition can include other comments from the original manuscript through to various other versions.

POETS' CORNER

Whilst reading this book I am sure that you will have picked up on the comment, 'Buried in Poets' Corner, Westminster Abbey' and at the same time I am equally sure that most of you will be aware of the fact that this final accolade and acknowledgement of a writer's genius is afforded to only a selected few. However, for those of you not aware of this special English tradition, let me fill you in.

Poets' Corner, now one of the most well known parts of Westminster Abbey and which can be found in the South Transept of the Abbey, is the burial or memorial place of playwrights, poets and writers. The first poet to be buried there was Geoffrey Chaucer – and ironically it wasn't because he had written *Canterbury Tales* but was because he had been Clerk of Works to the Palace of Westminster. It wasn't until the Sixteenth Century that the tradition began in earnest when first a grander tomb was erected in

Westminster Abbey for Chaucer and then the great Edmund Spenser was also laid to rest nearby. After these initial burials of two literary greats there followed many more and, in addition, there came the special memorials too for the writers who were in fact buried elsewhere, but 'deserved' the honour of a Westminster Abbey burial.

The Literary Greats Buried in Poets' Corner include:

Browning, Robert • Camden, William • Dickens, Charles • Dryden, John • Hardy, Thomas • Johnson, Dr Samuel • Kipling, Rudyard • Masefield, John • Sheridan, Richard Brinsley • Tennyson, Alfred Lord

The Literary Greats Honoured by a Memorial in Poets' Corner include:

Austen, Jane • Betjeman, Sir John • Blake, William • Brontë, Charlotte, Emily and Anne • Burns, Robert • Butler, Samuel • Eliot, T.S. • Goldsmith, Oliver • Gray, Thomas • Hopkins, Gerard Manley • James, Henry • Keats, John • Milton, John • Ruskin, John • Scott, Sir Walter • Shelley, Percy Bysshe • Wordsworth, William

Although primarily this is a corner of England reserved for writers, it is not an exclusive corner, for buried there you will also find two actors: David Garrick, the Shakespearean actor, and a more modern actor, Laurence Olivier. The grave and monument of the composer George Frederic Handel can also be seen here. Then there are the graves of several of Westminster's former Deans and Canons to be seen too, as well as Thomas Parr who died in 1635 at the supposed age of 152!

Chapter Four

Classic Books for Children

A Mother Reading to Her Children

Give me the child until he is seven and I will give you the man.
An old Jesuit saying

Oh how true is this saying, for it is during those early formative years that the foundations of life are not only laid but are cemented into place. It is then that we are taught the social niceties of life, taught how to behave, or how not to behave in some cases; we are taught what to expect from people and from life in general and we are guided towards the most suitable route in order that we might secure happiness and success. If we are lucky during these formative years then we are also introduced to the world of books and thereby encouraged to develop a love of reading. Of course, we are totally unaware of all this early schooling, which is probably why we absorb so much and reject so little!

Having seen the wealth of classic books for adults it seems only fair then that we should now look at the same extensive wealth of classic books available to children. But looking at the books available for children is actually where the sense of fairness ends, for I have found that the children's library is visited almost as often by adults as it is by children! Think about the queues which form for the release of the latest Harry Potter book; are they made up exclusively of children? They most certainly are not. Is the fantasy that is *The Lord of the Rings* read only by the young? Definitely not! And what about Hans Christian Andersen? Well, I know from personal experience that I read his stories to my own children quite simply because I enjoyed them too! Then there is the genius that is Roald Dahl; he wrote for all age groups, and all age groups read the cross spectrum of his work. I think we adults, therefore, should be grateful to the writers of children's books and to the children themselves for sharing them with us!

So exactly what is the adult fascination with children's literature? Personally I think there is one advantage a children's book has over a book for adults, and that is that it is often more visually attractive than those written for adults. I remember my own dear mother blowing the saying: 'You can't judge a book by its cover' right out of the water when she insisted that as a child I always had beautifully bound books. She said an attractive book sitting on a shelf was actually calling out to be read. She believed that if the cover looked attractive then I would be more inclined to be curious and therefore pick it off the shelf to investigate further. Clearly then she thought that to a degree you could judge a book by its cover, in so much as the cover could be inviting, if not guaranteeing the quality of the hidden text between its covers. I can even remember that my favourite book had a beautiful red cover with gold writing – or maybe I am just shallow! But it is worth a thought and an interesting point is that many writers of both children's literature and adult's alike were, or are, also illustrators.

So let us now pay credit to those masters – of whom some people would say: 'Oh he only writes for children.' Remember that:

'In every adult hides the child'

These are the writers who open the doors to the joys of reading; these are the writers who have the responsibility of nurturing the literary intellects of tomorrow. And then when those little children have experienced the joys of literary discovery, they grow to realise that the world of books is a never ending, always expanding, treasure trove ready to entertain and inform the eternal curiosities of man.

The world of books feeds the hungry and curious mind

Hans Christian Anderson
1805-1875

'A humble genius and teller of fairy tales'

Hans Christian Anderson has been the most difficult of all writers for me to include in this book, the reason for this being, I am ashamed now to say, is that before I started my research I thought I knew all there was to know about Hans Christian Andersen; thought this would be a piece of cake, as they say. I mean wasn't he the chap who wrote *The Ugly Duckling*, *The Emperor's New Clothes* and *The Snow Queen* – and a few other stories granted; nothing difficult about that, right? Wrong. This man was so much more than the teller of fairy tales; this man was a genius.

From that point of realisation it seemed that every research route I travelled along would lead me further into the maze that was to reveal Andersen's lifetime of works. More and more gems seemed to appear from nowhere until I became both overawed and overwhelmed. I wrote a piece and scrapped it, wrote another piece and scrapped that too. In fact, I very nearly took Andersen out of the book altogether, quite convinced that I could never do the man justice and then I came across the wonderfully helpful Lars Bo Jensen at The Hans Christian Andersen Center in the University of Southern Denmark. He, his department and his country are obviously so proud of Hans Christian Andersen that it would be an insult to give up and so on I went!

Works by Hans Christian Anderson include:

It is impossible to include all of the works by Hans Christian Andersen, for they are too extensive; for that reason alone it is even impossible to include the majority of his works and so I have included a list by genre only. Be prepared to be both amazed and astounded at the outpourings of this humble genius.

Autobiographies (4) • Biographical Writings (6) • Collected and Miscellaneous Works (6) • Collections of Poems (8) • Cycles of Poems (6) • Drama (51) • Fairy Tales (212) • Fairy Tale Collections (38) • Minor Satiric and Humorous Writings (7) • Novels (6) • Other Prose (6) • Papers, Articles, Letters and Other Writings (42) • Poems (1024) • Separate Publications (37) • Travelogues (25)

And that, Lars Bo Jenson, told me is the simplified list. Sadly I do not have the word count available to me to go into the extensive classification really necessary for it to be a true representation of Andersen's works; but I do want to list just a selection of his fairy tales, for which he is so famous, by title – though unfortunately not all 212 of them! I am sure that many of you will recognise them as bedtime tales told to you by your parents, or tales told by your teachers during story-time at school. I defy anyone to read even this short list and not recognise several of the tales, for Hans Christian Andersen is actually a part of every child's life, and perhaps even a springboard to a later love of the written word.

Fairy Tales by Hans Christian Anderson include:

A-B-C Book (The) • Aunty Toothache • Bond of Friendship (The) • Days of the Week (The) • Emperor's New Clothes (The) • Farmyard Cock and the Weather Cock (The) • Flea and the Professor (The) • Gardener and the Nobel Family (The) • Girl Who Trod on the Loaf (The) • Goblin and the Grocer (The) • Golden Treasure • Iceman (The) • Little Claus and Big Claus •

Little Ida's Flowers • Little Match Girl (The) • Little Mermaid (The) • Marsh King's Daughter (The) • Money Pig (The) • Most Incredible Thing (The) • Nightingale (The) • Old Street Lamp (The) • Princess and the Pea • Red Shoes (The) • Snow Queen (The) • Snowman (The) • Stone of the Wise Men (The) • Story of a Mother (The) • Swineherd (The) • Thumbelina • Tinder Box (The) • Toad (The) • Ugly Duckling (The) • Under the Willow Tree (The) • What Happened to the Thistle • World's Fairest Rose (The) •

And that is just 35 of 'The Master's' Fairy Tales! So who was this man?

HANS CHRISTIAN ANDERSEN: The Writer and the Man

• Hans Christian Andersen was born into poverty on 2 April 1805 in Odense, Denmark
• His father was a shoemaker and his mother a washerwoman
• It was not until 1807 that the Andersen family had a permanent address
• In 1816 Andersen's father died
• Andersen's school attendance was sporadic in his early years but became even more so after the death of his father
• In 1818 his mother remarried
• Leaving Odense in 1819 he travelled alone to Copenhagen to try and make a living in theatre
• Jonas Collin, one of the Directors of The Theatre Royal in Copenhagen, became Andersen's guardian in 1822
• Collin raised the money to send Andersen to school, thus ensuring that he reached the necessary educational standard to be admitted to The University of Copenhagen
• A number of his poems were published in 1827
• Andersen graduated from Copenhagen University in 1828
• He initially wrote for the theatre but as we now all know this was not to be his artistic home
• Between the years 1831 and 1873 he spent a great deal of time travelling throughout Europe, Africa and Asia Minor and the impressions these travels had upon him are recorded in the many travel books he wrote, for example *A Poet's Bazaar*, *Pictures of Sweden*, *A Visit to Portugal* and *In Spain*
• Hans Christian Andersen's mother died in 1833
• In the year 1845 Andersen's novels begin to appear in English translations; some of his novels having already been translated into German, Swedish, Dutch and Russian

• He made his first trip to England and Scotland in 1847 where he found himself to be a celebrity of his time. It was then that he met Charles Dickens and it was also in this year that he read aloud to an audience from his fairy tales for the first time – of course Charles Dickens too travelled extensively reading aloud to an audience extracts from his own novels

• In 1857 Andersen returned to England and this time he stayed with Charles Dickens for one month

• In 1874 Hans Christian Andersen was made '*konferensråd*' which at that time was a high and prestigious Danish title, though is now obsolete

• Andersen suffered a lifetime of dental pain until he finally lost his last tooth in January 1873; in March of that year he got a whole set of new dentures. The fairy tale *Aunty Toothache* (1872) fittingly dealt with toothaches and false teeth

• After several years of serious illness, Hans Christian Andersen died on 4 August 1875 at Rolighed, the country seat of the Jewish merchant family Melchior. The Melchiors had taken care of him during the final period of his life

OVERVIEW OF HANS CHRISTIAN ANDERSEN

Hans Christian Andersen was born into a life of poverty in the Danish town of Odense, a life which was to be the stimulous for many of his later writings. The elderly, female inmates at the Odense Hospital (the workhouse) at that time told him folk tales that would prove to be the inspiration behind the tales he later created himself. His writing meant that he started life at the bottom of the social ladder and made the extraordinary climb to the top, with each rung being a testament to his literary achievements.

Generally speaking, even those who are not interested in literature, or even reading for that matter, know of Hans Christian Andersen, for the chances are that they have been told his fairy tales at some time or another in their lives, or maybe they have seen the enormously popular 1952 Hollywood musical film starring Danny Kaye which was based around the writer.

Hans Christian Anderson: The Film

Though the film is not a true biographical representation of Andersen but more a romantic story revolving around him, it has certainly captured the imagination and interest of many through the decades and, I am sure, even

207

stimulated some to read the real thing. On a different note, though still on the subject of the film, I for one was fascinated when re-watching the film, whilst I was researching for this book and pouring over numerous photographs of Andersen, I was astounded at the likeness between him and Danny Kaye. What a spectacular job the Hollywood Studio's make-up departments had done in visually transforming Danny Kaye into Hans Christian Andersen! You see, I am a real exponent of artistic cross-fertilisation, believing that one arts medium can truly enhance another, and here it seemed that Danny Kaye actually WAS Hans Christian Andersen, which in my mind is the first step in making the man and his stories come to life.

I believe that film lovers, those who don't generally enjoy reading, thespians – whoever – can, through the medium of their own artistic preferences, be stimulated into reading the works of any writer. At the same time, those whose preference is the written word can marvel at a piece as it comes to life before their eyes.

Enough of the film and back to Andersen the man, whose fame became truly international and grew rapidly from the 1830s when first his novels were popular in Germany, quickly followed by his fairy tales. In the 1840s he conquered Europe and America with both genre and from that moment on there was no stopping the rise in adulation of this extraordinary teller of tales. It is said that only the Bible has been translated into more languages than the works of Hans Christian Andersen, which has been translated into approximately 153 languages. As well as Danish of course, he himself spoke very good German, some Italian, fairly good French and some English – although the latter apparently very badly. Hans Christian Andersen has been called childish and naive by some critics. Well, if an underlying goodness and compassion; if an understanding of life and a caring of humanity which permeates his work can be classified as childish and naive, then I applaud those qualities and marvel at the example he has set to generation after generation through the underlying morality of his tales.

J. M. Barrie
1860-1937

The 'little' man who wrote for 'little' people
and who through his 'big' gift ensured that many
of those 'little' people grew too to be 'big'

Through Peter Pan J. M. Barrie gave the
gift of life to children

Works by J.M. Barrie include:

Auld Licht Idylls • *Jane Annie* [co author: Sir Arthur Conan Doyle] •
Little Minister (The) • *Little White Bird (The)* • *Margaret Ogilvy* •
My Lady Nicotine • *Professor's Love Story (The)* •
Sentimental Tommy • *Tommy and Grizel* •
When a Man's Single • *Window in Thrums (A)*

J.M. BARRIE: The Writer and the Man

• On 9 May 1860 James Matthew Barrie was born in the village of
Kirriemuir, Scotland as the ninth of 10 children born to David Barrie and
Margaret Ogilvy; he was known as Jamie

• When Barrie was seven years old his older brother, David, died in a skating accident on the eve of his 14th birthday. This tragic event sent Barrie's mother into severe depression and haunted Barrie himself for the rest of his life. Interestingly, Barrie's mother took consolation in her grief that her beloved son, David, would never grow up and so would remain a child forever. Barrie, eager to comfort his mother, tried in effect to become David, the son his mother had lost, and interestingly he stopped growing at the age of 14, the very age his brother had died. Barrie was then barely over 5' tall and very childlike in stature.

• He was educated at Glasgow Academy and then later at Dumfries Academy before entering the University of Edinburgh, where he was awarded an M.A. in 1882.

• In 1883 he began work as journalist for the *Nottingham Journal*, writing two weekly columns in addition to other non specific pieces; he stayed working on the *Nottingham Journal* for a further two years

• In 1885 he moved to London to begin work as a freelance journalist
In 1894 he married Mary Ansell, though stories have it that the marriage was never consummated and in fact it ended in 1909 when she began an affair with another writer

• 1897 was the year that was to begin the nurturing of *Peter Pan*, the seed sown by the death of his brother David, for that was the year in which Barrie first made the acquaintance of the Llewelyn Davies family whom he met in Kensington Gardens, London. Arthur and Sylvia Llewelyn Davies had five sons – only three when they first met – whom Barrie used to meet in Kensington Gardens; a deep and enduring friendship then developed

• In 1910 Barrie became guardian of the five Llewelyn Davies boys following the death of their mother – their father having died three years previously – whom he then brought up as his own sons

• It is said that the story of *Peter Pan* was based on, and evolved from, Barrie's friendship with the Llewelyn Davies family – as well as, of course, the initial inspiration being the early death of his brother, David:

> By rubbing the five of you violently together,
> as savages with two sticks to produce a flame,
> I made the spark of you that is Peter Pan
> J.M. Barrie

• Although *Peter Pan* was produced as a stage version in 1904, it wasn't until 1911 that it was finally published as a novel under the original title of *Peter and Wendy*

• In 1913 he was awarded a Baronetcy; he had refused a Knighthood four years earlier

• In 1915 George Llewelyn Davies, the eldest of the five brothers under the guardianship of Barrie, was killed in action during the First World War and then in 1921 tragedy struck the family again when another brother, Michael Llewelyn Davies, drowned with his friend in Oxford in what is thought to be a possible suicide pact
• In 1922 Barrie was awarded the Order of Merit
• He was appointed President of the Society of Authors in 1928
• In honour of his lifelong love of children, in 1929 J.M. Barrie donated the copyright from his work *Peter Pan* to Great Ormond Street Hospital. See details of this gift below in 'Barrie's Legacy Lives On In Great Ormond Street Hospital'
• 1930 saw him made Chancellor of the University of Edinburgh
• J.M. Barrie, the man who created the myth that is Peter Pan, died on 19 June 1937 leaving the world a legacy of childcare

BARRIE'S LEGACY LIVES ON IN GREAT ORMOND STREET HOSPITAL

J.M. Barrie loved children and had long supported Great Ormond Street Hospital for Sick Children (although the word Sick has now been dropped from its name), situated in London, and affectionately known as GOSH. In 1929 he was approached by the hospital to sit on a committee with the express purpose of helping to buy land to build a new wing, of which the hospital was in desperate need. Barrie declined the invitation saying that he hoped to find another way to help; that way as we now know was to make a gift of all his rights to his work *Peter Pan*, including all off shoot earnings from *Peter Pan*. He further requested that the amount raised by his gift should never be revealed and the hospital has forever honoured his last wish, as he honoured his 'little friends'.

Peter Pan is tangibly visible today throughout the hospital as a constant reminder of Barrie's generosity. He can be found in the guise of: The Peter Pan Café situated in the reception area of the hospital; The Barrie Wing; and The Peter Pan Ward. There is also a bronze statue of Peter Pan and Tinker Bell outside the hospital entrance; The Peter Pan Gallery houses editions of the book from all over the world and in many languages. Finally there is a plaque dedicated to Barrie in the hospital chapel.

When Barrie first donated his rights to GOSH, the copyright laws in force at that time in the UK stated that after 50 years they should, as such, expire. This meant that the bequeathed copyright first expired in 1987, 50 years after Barrie's death. However, the former Prime Minister, Lord

Callaghan proposed an amendment to the Copyright Designs & Patents Act of 1988, giving Great Ormond Street Hospital the unique right to royalties from stage performances of *Peter Pan* (and any adaptation of the play), as well as from publications of the story of *Peter Pan* in perpetuity which was wonderful news, not only for GOSH but for all those who love children and for the children themselves who, unlike Peter Pan actually want the opportunity to grow up. The situation regarding copyright, however, varies from country to country.

Peter Pan is the story of the boy who never grew up, so how fitting it is that Barrie should make such a generous gift to the UK children's hospital – Great Ormond Street Hospital – thus playing a huge financial part in ensuring that numerous children who would otherwise be robbed of the chance to grow up be given that chance by the world renowned hospital responsible for saving and prolonging lives of children, not only in the UK but from around the world too. To walk around the hospital and appreciate the help Barrie gave and continues to give through his very special gift is to appreciate that he has on many occasions given to a sick child the precious gift of life.

THE STORY OF PETER PAN

Peter Pan doesn't want to grow up and so he runs away from home. One night he visits the home of the Darling family who live in Bloomsbury. Peter Pan has a fairy attendant called Tinker Bell and both of them can fly – not unusual for a fairy, but it is for a boy! Adventures then follow when he teaches the three Darling children to fly too, enabling them to go with him to Neverland, where he lives with the Lost Boys who are protected by a tribe of Red Indians.

Wendy, one of the Darling children, becomes mother to the Lost Boys, but one day when Peter is away, they are all captured by the pirate Captain Hook. Peter comes to the rescue and Hook is eaten by a crocodile. Peter then takes Wendy and her brothers home and, after declining an offer of adoption by Mrs Darling, he leaves with the promise that Wendy will visit him every year to do the spring-cleaning.

Stage Plays by J.M. Barrie include:

Admirable Crichton
Boy David (The)
Dear Brutus
Ibsen's Ghost
Little Mary

Mary Rose
Quality Street
Twelve-Pound Look (The)
Walker London
Well Remembered Voice (A)
What Every Woman Knows
Will (The)

AND FINALLY

• Barrie also wrote extensively for the stage
• He was plagued throughout his life about his size – he was barely over five feet tall and was of a very slight build in a time when 'a man was a man' and expected to look a certain way and when deviance from the 'norm' in any way what-so-ever was frowned upon
• The most famous quote from Peter Pan – and probably known by most – is:

"Every time a child says
'I don't believe in fairies'
there is a little fairy somewhere that falls down dead."

• Although probably not quite so famous in the 'Well Known Quotes League' is another quote from Peter Pan about the direction to Neverland: *'Second to the right, straight on till morning'* more often than not misquoted as 'Second star to the right, straight on till morning' the word star actually being a Disney addition

Lewis Carroll
1832-1898

'Writer of children's novels, mathematician, photographer, and poet'

Major Works by Lewis Carroll include:

Alice's Adventure in Wonderland • Sylvie and Bruno •
Sylvie and Bruno Concluded • Through the Looking Glass and
What Alice Found There • Wasp in the Wig: A 'Suppressed'
Episode of the Latter (The) •

LEWIS CARROLL: The Writer and the Man

• Lewis Carroll was the pseudonym of Charles Lutwidge Dodgson who was born on 27 January 1832 as the eldest son, and third child, in the large family of seven girls and four boys born to the Rev Charles Dodgson and his wife Frances Jane Lutwidge

• He was educated at Richmond School, Yorkshire, before going on to Rugby Public School

• He went up to Oxford in 1851; sadly in the same year his mother died

• Carroll was an excellent scholar, of great intellect and with a superb mathematical mind

• It was in 1856 that he adopted the pseudonym of Lewis Carroll

• Carroll always had a great rapport and affinity with children, probably as a result of having eight younger siblings, and so had many children as friends in his lifetime, including the sons of the poet Alfred, Lord Tennyson, and of course the Liddell children who themselves were destined to become famous in their own right as the inspiration behind *Alice in Wonderland*

• The Liddell children – Alice Liddell, and her sisters Lorina and Edith – were the children of Henry George Liddell the Dean of Christ Church, Oxford and it was to these children that Carroll first told the story of '*Alice's Adventures Underground*' one day when they picnicked by the bank of the Thames. So enthralled was Alice by the story that she begged him to write it down for her, which he duly did and so a legend was born and Alice Liddell herself was immortalised

• Carroll gave the finished piece, 'Alice's Adventures Underground' to Alice Liddell at Christmas in 1864 – and thought that was the end of it; little did he know!

• In 1865 it was published under the revised title of *Alice's Adventures in Wonderland*

• In 1868 Carroll's father died

• 1872 saw the sequel *Through the Looking-Glass and What Alice Found There* published and dedicated to Alice Liddell

• During the Christmas of 1897 Carroll contracted bronchitis which gradually worsened, resulting in his death in mid January 1898

OTHER WORKS BY LEWIS CARROLL INCLUDE:

Verse

Collected Verse (The)

Hunting of the Snark (The)
Phantasmagoria and Other Poems
Rhyme? and Reason?

Mathematical Books
Curiosa Mathematica
Euclid and His Modern Rivals
Syllabus of Plane Algebraical Geometry (A)
Symbolic Logic, Part I & II [ed. by William W. Bartley III]

AND FINALLY
As well as being a mathematician and writer, Lewis Carroll was also an accomplished photographer.

Roald Dahl
1916-1990

Writer for both children and adults •
he had a passionate interest in the world around him from
the usual to the unusual and the mundane to the
unexpected • he was a master of suspense and a
creator and manipulator of the unexpected

ROALD DAHL: The Writer and the Man
• 13 September 1916 is the date Roald Dahl was born in Llandaff, Wales, to Norwegian parents Harald and Sofie Dahl
• Dahl's father died when he was just three years old
• His mother was a great influence on Dahl through her telling of stories and folk tales to all of the Dahl children; his father was an influence on his writing by example, for he was a disciplined diarist, keeping a detailed diary every day and Roald Dahl followed his example

• As a young child Dahl's education began at Llandaff Cathedral School after which, at nine years old, he was sent to board at St Peter's Prep School at Weston-Super-Mare
• From the age of 13 he was educated at Repton Public School
• Roald Dahl's first work for children was a picture book called *Gremlins* which was published in 1943. However, it wasn't until the 1960s that he started to write in earnest for children; up until that time he had concentrated on writing for adults, a fact which has been buried under the subsequent successes of his children's stories
• Initially he wrote short stories which were published in magazines
• Many of his short stories were televised in the enormously successful TV series *Tales of the Unexpected,* each with the famous unexpected final twist
• Like many writers he was interested in and passionate about so many things in life from breeding budgies to consuming chocolate – the latter of which I whole-heartedly approve
• In 1953 he married Patricia Neale and together they went on to have five children
• After his divorce from Patricia, Dahl went on to marry his second wife Felicity 'Liccy' Crosland with whom he stayed until his death
• In 1990 Roald Dahl was diagnosed with a rare blood disorder, myelo-dysplastic anaemia and on 23 November 1990 he died aged 74 years old

TRAGEDY AND COMPASSION

Roald Dahl's life was touched by an amazing amount of tragedy which he bore with an equally amazing amount of strength. His eldest daughter, Olivia, died when she was just seven years old after an attack of measles developed into encephalitis – inflammation of the brain. In another tragic event his four-month-old son, Theo, was brain damaged after a road accident. His first wife Patricia suffered three strokes whilst she was pregnant with their daughter, Lucy, and then just before his own death, his daughter-in-law, Lorina, died of a brain tumour.

Despite these tragedies, which would have destroyed lesser men, Roald Dahl showed great care and compassion in his lifetime, not only by helping and supporting his own family through their own tragic events but by offering support and help to other sick and disabled children too; to these children he gave both his money and even more precious, his time. That help and support has now been extended after his death and beyond his lifetime through the work of the Roald Dahl Foundation which was set up by his second wife and offers grants in three important areas:

a. literacy (because it was his own personal crusade)

b. neurology (because his own family had been so badly affected in this area)

c. haematology (because he suffered for many years with a blood disorder)

THE WORKS OF ROALD DAHL

Most writers have an area of specialty and an age group at which they aim. Some writers write only for children and some only for adults, whilst some write for both; then there is Roald Dahl. He writes for children and he writes for adults too, both with equal content of artistic strength and ingenuity. But the interesting thing is that his books for children are still read and enjoyed the second time around by adults; he also wrote for that most difficult of readerships – the dreaded teenagers! He was, and is, a writer loved and admired by all generations and one who has left a great legacy for future generations.

Works by Roald Dahl for children include:

BFG (The)	Orphan Sophie is snatched from her bed by the Big Friendly Giant and together they fight to stop all the other giants from tucking into the children of the world.
Boy	Roald Dahl's autobiography written for children so that they can see for themselves their favourite author when he was a child.
Charlie and the Chocolate Factory	Five golden tickets, hidden in chocolate bars, are set to change the lives of those who find them. A magical story with a moral, which has also been adapted into a hugely successful film – twice!
Charlie and the Great Glass Elevator	This story picks up where *Charlie and the Chocolate Factory* ended; that is, in the glass elevator with Charlie, Willy Wonka and the Bucket family who go on to have some incredible space adventures.
Danny the Champion of the World	Danny thinks he has the best Dad in the world, a dad who does everything a mother does; he then discovers that his dad has a secret.
George's Marvellous Medicine	George has a particularly nasty grandmother and so decides to concoct a medicine to cure her of her nastiness.
James and the Giant	James is a nine-year-old orphan who lives with his

217

Peach	greedy aunts. He dreams of going to New York where dreams come true and with the help of a giant peach and some insect friends he does just that.
Matilda	Matilda is an exceptionally bright young girl with supernatural powers which she uses to punish the bad people in her life.
Twits (The)	Mr and Mrs Twit are a nasty pair, each as bad as the other until finally they fall foul of a plot hatched by Muggle-Wump monkeys and the Roly-Poly bird.
Witches (The)	The Witches plan to get rid of all the children in England, but unfortunately for them their plan is overheard.

Works by Roald Dahl for teens include:

Boy and Going Solo	This autobiography carries on the Roald Dahl story for 'older young people', picking up the story where he left it at the end of *Boy*.
Roald Dahl Selection (A)	A selection of Roald Dahl short stories – suitable for 11 to 14 year olds.
Ten Short Stories	A special educational edition of Roald Dahl's short stories written especially for students of English literature and which includes various exercises to aid their studies.

Works by Roald Dahl for adults include:

Kiss Kiss	Eleven macabre stories exploring the sinister side of the human psyche.
My Uncle Oswald	A comic novel in which Dahl tells the story of Uncle Oswald, a Sudanese beetle and the gorgeous Yasmin Howcomely.
Tales of the Unexpected	A collection of 16 of Dahl's famous stories with the equally famous sting and a twist in the tale.

AND FINALLY

• In Roald Dahl's *The Witches*, the character of the grandmother is based upon his own mother – as his tribute to her
• Roald Dahl had false teeth since he was in his twenties

EXPERIENCE YESTERDAY'S WORLD OF ROALD DAHL TODAY

One place every child should visit at least once – and every child pretending to be an adult too, for that matter – is The Roald Dahl Museum and Story Centre in Great Missenden, Buckinghamshire which was created to house his splendid archive. This is an ideal outing for young and enquiring minds and is designed to stimulate creative writing in the young.

Great Missenden is the village where, from the year 1954, Dahl lived and where he wrote for an astonishing 36 years. He wrote all of his children's books in a writing hut, which he built in his garden – this fact puts me in mind of George Bernard Shaw and the revolving hut in his garden – a replica of this hut can now be seen at the museum, though the original of course remains at the home of Dahl's wife. Inside this replica hut can been seen a replica too of the writing board he made for himself. A word of warning to parents though: Be ready with a story when the children ask why they have to clean their bedroom floors when Roald Dahl apparently <u>never</u> cleaned his!

Brothers Grimm
Jacob Ludwig Carl Grimm 1785-1863
Wilhelm Carl Grimm 1786-1859

Two brothers blessed with both academic and literary prowess

Works (Collections) by the Brothers Grimm include:

Brothers Grimm Fairy Tales • Complete Brothers Grimm Fairy Tales • Complete Fairy Tales of the Brothers Grimm • Grimms' Fairy Tales • One Hundred Fairy Tales •

GRIMM BROTHERS: The Writers and the Men

• In 1785 Jacob Ludwig Carl Grimm was born on 4 January in Hanau, Germany to Philipp Wilhelm and Dorothea (née Zimmer) Grimm
• Jacob's brother, Wilhelm Carl Grimm, was born on 24 February 1786, in Hanau, Germany
• There were nine children in the Grimm family – eight boys and one girl (Charlotte)
• The brothers' father, who was a lawyer and court official, died in 1796 leaving behind his wife and six fatherless children (three children had died before him)
• The two brothers who, upon their success, became known as 'The Brothers Grimm' were educated at Marburg University where they both studied law
• It was whilst at University that the brothers met several people who were to influence and stimulate their studies into folk tales
• In1808 the brothers' mother died meaning that Jacob and Wilhelm, as the eldest surviving sons, then took on the responsibility for their remaining siblings
• To support his family Jacob took on the position of librarian at Kassel; he was quickly followed by Wilhelm
• In 1812 The Brothers Grimm published Volume One of *Kinder-und Hausmärchen* (Children's and Household Tales) containing 86 folk tales. Volume Two of *Kinder-und Hausmärchen* was published in 1815. This book had an additional 70 stories
• In 1819 the brothers received honorary doctorates form the University of Marburg
• In 1825 Wilhelm Grimm married Henriette Dorothea (Dortchen) Wild
• It was Wilhelm's wife and family who provided Jacob and Wilhelm with many of their folk tales
• 1829/30 saw the Brothers Grimm resign their positions in Kassel to take up positions as librarians and Professors at the University of Göttingen before moving on to the University of Berlin
• They eventually gave up their day jobs to devote time to their own studies and research
• Wilhelm Grimm died 16 December 1859, at the age of 73 years
• Jacob Grimm died 20 September 1863, at the age of 78 years

Fairy Tales by the Brothers Grimm include:

Cinderella
Death of the Little Hen (The)

Doctor Know All
Dog and the Sparrow (The)
Frog Prince (The)
Giant and the Tailor (The)
Glass Coffin (The)
Golden Goose (The)
Goose Girl (The)
Hansel and Gretel
Hare and the Hedgehog (The)
How Six Travelled Through the World
Idle Spinner
Juniper Tree (The)
King's Son Who Feared Nothing (The)
Lean Betty
Little Brother and Sister (The)
Little Peasant (The)
Little Red Riding Hood
Little Snow White
Love and Sorrow to Share
Mouse the Bird and the Sausage (The)
Old Beggar-Woman (The)
Poor Miller's Boy and the Cat (The)
Prince Who was Afraid of Nothing (The)
Rapunzel
Rumpelstiltskin
Seven Crows (The)
Sleeping Beauty
Snow-White and Rose-Red
Spider and the Flea (The)
Star Money (The)
Story of the Youth Who Went to Learn What Fear was (The)
Tale of One Who Travelled to Learn What Shivering Meant
Twelve Huntsmen (The)
Two Brothers (The)
Undutiful Son (The)
Wedding of Mrs Fox (The)
Wilful Child (The)
Wolf and the Fox (The)
Wolf and the Man (The)
Woodcutter's Child (The)

AND FINALLY

• The Brothers Grimm did not just tell a good story, they were, and are unique, in that they were true academics with a love of folk knowledge, language, of folk law, folk tales, songs and poetry which they collected, often by word of mouth, and committed to paper for future generations to enjoy. They preserved what could so easily have been lost to all – and what are actually too many to mention here!

Beatrix Potter
1866-1943

Artist • Storyteller • Animal Lover • Conservationist
• Preservationist • Farmer

Would I be wrong in saying that surely everyone knows the name Beatrix Potter? I don't think so! But it could have been such a different story if this extraordinary artist and storyteller had not also been a courageous and extraordinary businesswoman too.

WHERE DID IT ALL BEGIN?

Beatrix Potter's love affair with art and the natural world began when she was a small child. She was educated at home and so had little contact with other children, except for her brother Bertram who was six years younger than her. And so as a consequence of this somewhat solitary lifestyle her pets, of which she had many, became her friends and her drawings became her sanctuary, a way of expressing herself. She was fortunate that the natural flair she displayed for drawing was encouraged by her parents, and as a result she made many visits to the Royal Academy thus furthering the nurturing of this budding genius.

The date was September 4th 1893 when Potter sat down to write a picture letter to the five-year-old sick son of her ex-governess. His name was Noel Moore and he, as the recipient of that historical letter, now has a place in the history of literature for it was to him that Potter told the story of Peter Rabbit.

It was some years later though before she decided to write down the story in an attempt to have it published. In the year 1900 Potter sent a proposal for *The Tale of Peter Rabbit* to six publishers, all of whom incidentally turned it down! And so it was that in 1901, and with great self-belief, Beatrix Potter decided to publish the book herself. After it was published it was seen by Frederick Warne (one of the six publishers who had rejected the original proposal) and as a consequence he brought out *The Tale of Peter Rabbit* in the following year. It was an immediate success and so became the first of the now famous 23 little books for little people in a style and format that is recognised worldwide. So we must all be grateful to the courage of that young woman who believed in her ability and her work and who wouldn't take no for an answer.

MERCHANDISING

Today we are used to spin-offs in the form of merchandising from success stories but in the time of Beatrix Potter it was a relatively unknown phenomena, so the business side of this remarkable woman surfaced when she developed a merchandising side to her tales in the form of a Peter Rabbit Doll as well as Peter Rabbit wallpaper. She was indeed a businesswoman well ahead of her time.

The merchandising of Beatrix Potter's work is as far reaching as her work itself; buying into this it would seem usually begins with the traditional first dish for baby and then goes on and on with her much loved characters appearing on traditional tableware for children to ornaments, stationery and beyond. Add to this the bigger scale of themed gardens, museums etc., all dedicated to her work; throw in a ballet (1971) created by the great chorographer Sir Frederick Ashton and more recently a major motion picture starring Renee Zellweger as Beatrix Potter, and you will still just be skimming the surface of the Beatrix Potter story, or perhaps we should say industry?

BEATRIX POTTER: The Writer and the Woman

• Beatrix Potter was born in Kensington, London on 28 July 1886 to Rupert and Helen
• Hers was a wealthy family and they lived in the luxury of a large house
• She was used to servants and was herself taken care of by a nurse and educated by various governesses. It was a financially privileged background, but she saw very little of her parents and so her many pets played an increasingly important role in her life
• Her brother Bertram was born when she was six years old

- Bertram was not educated at home, like his sister Beatrix, but was sent away to school which of course intensified her isolation
- She developed her fascination with the countryside and its animals and flowers etc. whilst on family holidays to Scotland and the Lake District; it was on these holidays that she took a special interest in fungi
- In 1893 Potter wrote *The Tale of Peter Rabbit* in the form of a picture letter to a little boy that she knew had been ill for quite some time
- In 1901 Potter published *The Tale of Peter Rabbit* herself, it having been rejected by several publishers; she initially printed just 250 copies, which quickly sold out resulting in her having to print a further 200 copies
- After her book *The Tale of Peter Rabbit* was published by Frederick Warne these then developed more than a literary partnership with the publishing company, for she soon became engaged to be married to Norman Warne, the youngest of Frederick Warne's three sons. Tragedy soon struck, however, when Frederick died just a few weeks after their engagement. After this, Beatrix Potter remained single until she was 47 years old when she married her then solicitor, William Heelis
- In 1897 Beatrix Potter presented a scientific paper on the germination of spores to the Linnean Society
- As with her book *The Tale of Peter Rabbit* this paper was rejected although experts now consider that her thesis was in fact correct all along – will they never learn!
- In 1905 Potter bought the now famous Hill Top Farm in the Lake District of England which she used as the background for some of her tales
- In 1913 Potter married William Heelis
- Beatrix Potter was at one not only with art but with nature too and dedicated much of her later years to preserving the natural beauty of the Lake District where she holidayed as a child, by purchasing land, properties and farms which led to her becoming an expert in breeding Herdwick sheep. It seemed that whatever she touched led to an intensified expertise
- Twenty-two of Beatrix Potter's original drawings from her book *The Tailor of Gloucester* can now be seen in the Tate Gallery, London
- Beatrix Potter died 22 December 1943 in Sawrey in her beloved Lake District

Works by Beatrix Potter include:

Tale of Peter Rabbit (The)	The story of a naughty rabbit called Peter and his adventures in Mr McGregor's garden.
Tale of Squirrel Nutkin (The)	The story of a cheeky squirrel who lived on an island and who teased Old Brown, the owl.

Tailor of Gloucester (The)	It is Christmas Eve and an unfinished waistcoat is completed by some magical talking mice.
Tale of Benjamin Bunny (The)	Peter Rabbit and his cousin Benjamin Bunny get up to mischief galore in Mr McGregor's garden.
Tale of Two Bad Mice (The)	Lucinda and Jane were two dolls who, quite naturally, lived in a doll's house plagued by two bad mice called Tom Thumb and Hunca Munca.
Tale of Mrs Tiggy-Winkle (The)	A little girl called Lucie was forever losing her handkerchiefs, until one day she found out where they were going. They were being washed by Mrs Tiggy-Winkle the hedgehog washerwoman.
Tale of the Pie and the Patty-Pan (The)	Duchess the dog is invited by Ribby the cat for tea and is quite certain that she will be given mouse pie to eat and so goes to extraordinary unsuccessful lengths to prevent such an eventuality.
Tale of Mr Jeremy Fisher (The)	A story of how Jeremy Fisher, the frog, narrowly escaped from a hungry trout.
Story of a Fierce Bad Rabbit (The)	A story in which a naughty rabbit finally gets what he deserves.
Story of Miss Moppet (The)	Miss Moppet is Tom Kitten's sister and she is not very good at catching mice.
Tale of Tom Kitten (The)	A cat called Mrs Tabitha Twitchet has three kittens, one boy and two girls: Tom Kitten is a typical messy and naughty boy getting into a lot of mischief with his two sisters, Moppet and Mittens.
Tale of Jemima Puddle Duck (The)	Jemima Puddle Duck is a very innocent, and frankly not very bright, duck who finds that she needs the help of the farm collie dog, Kep.
Tale of Samuel Whiskers (The) – or The Roly-Poly Pudding	Mr Samuel Whiskers is not a very pleasant character, in fact he is a rather lazy rat who, together with his wife, catches Tom Kitten and very nearly turns him into a Roly-Poly pudding.
Tale of the Flopsy Bunnies	Benjamin Bunny, from earlier stories has grown up and is married to Peter Rabbit's sister, Flopsy. In this story we see their children, the Flopsy Bunnies being rescued from Mr McGregor and the pie-dish of his wife, Mrs McGregor.
Tale of Ginger and	A tom cat called Ginger and a terrier called Pickles

Pickles (The)	are shopkeepers whose habit of allowing customers to purchase on credit is the reason that they go out of business.
Tale of Mrs Tittle-mouse (The)	Mrs Tittlemouse is a very tidy dormouse and tries to keep her home just so, despite numerous uninvited visitors.
Tale of Timmy Tiptoes (The)	Squirrels Timmy Tiptoes and his wife Goody are busy gathering nuts when catastrophe befalls them.
Tale of Mr Tod (The)	A fox called Mr Tod and a badger called Tommy Brock are not very nice people and in this story Tommy steals Bouncer Bunny's grandchildren – the Flopsy Bunnies – in order to cook and eat them.
Tale of Pigling Bland (The)	There isn't enough food to feed hungry piglets so Pigling Bland and his brother Alexander go to market where they narrowly escape being captured and eaten by the evil farmer.
Appley Dappley Nursery Rhymes	This book was left unpublished for many years whilst Potter concentrated on the Peter Rabbit Tales, until finally she completed the work.
Tale of Johnny Town Mouse (The)	The country mouse, Timmy Willie, finds himself in the city but finds the cat frightening and the food strange. Whereas Johnny Town-Mouse, finds such things as cows and lawnmowers frightening.
Cecily Parsley's Nursery Rhymes	The title character in this second collection of nursery rhymes is a rabbit who brews ale.
Tale of Little Pig Robinson (The)	In this story we learn how the Pig in Edward Lear's famous poem *The Owl and the Pussycat* came to be 'in the land where the Bong Tree grows'.

EXPERIENCE YESTERDAY'S WORLD OF BEATRIX POTTER TODAY

Experience the beauty and tranquility of Beatrix Potter's beloved Seventeenth Century farmhouse – Hill Top in Ambleside, Cumbria – which on her death she left to the National Trust. It was at Hill Top that she wrote many of her tales and to step into her cottage is a bit like stepping into a time capsule. After a visit to the cottage then the next stop could be the nearby Beatrix Potter Gallery which houses original story book illustrations by Beatrix Potter as well as an exhibition of her life.

AND FINALLY
• Not only was Beatrix Potter a wonderful teller of tales, she was also a gifted artist of the natural world, an all consuming interest of hers since childhood
• By the end of her life Potter had bought 15 farms which she left to the National Trust, along with 4,000 acres of land which included cottages and other areas of beauty including Tarn Hows.

J.K. Rowling
1965 –

A writer of childrens books – but are they for children or for adults, that is the question?

J.K. Rowling

J.K. Rowling may have started off her literary journey with the intention of writing a book for children, but the destination she reached with her series of the Harry Potter books was a series of books for both children and adults. Harry Potter books have become somewhat of a cult phenomena, which is testimony both to her writing and to her creative skills.

J.K. ROWLING: The Writer and the Woman

• J.K. Rowling was born on 31 July 1965 in Yate, Gloucestershire as Joanne Rowling the eldest daughter of Peter James and Anne Rowling
• Twenty-three months later Rowling's sister, Di, was born
• The K in her name is taken from the first letter of her beloved grandmother Kathleen and acquired when the publishers asked her to drop the name Joanne
• Rowling was brought up in a house full of books, probably laying the foundations of the path she was to tread
• She wrote her first book when she was six years old. It was a book about a rabbit and was called – Rabbit!
• At the age of 11 Rowling went to Wyedene Secondary School where she met Sean Harris, to whom *The Chamber of Secrets* is dedicated
• It was when she was in her teens that she heard the devastating news that her mother had MS
• In 1983 Rowling went to Exeter University where she studied French – though really she wanted to study English!
• 1990 was the year that was destined to change her life forever. The tale of how the story for the first Harry Potter book came into Rowling's head is now almost as universally famous as the books themselves and a tale known surely by everyone. However, for those who have been living on the moon since the mid 1980s, here it is again: J.K. Rowling was travelling from Manchester down to London on a crowded train when the idea of a bespectacled, boy wizard – who didn't actually know that he was a wizard – first came to her. As she didn't have a pen with her, the idea grew and grew in her head as quickly as the train travelled south, but it wasn't until that evening when she arrived home and had a pen in her hand that the first words of *The Philosopher's Stone* were committed to paper
• 1990 was a year destined to change her life in another way, for as well as being the year that Harry Potter was born, it was also quite tragically the year that J.K. Rowling's mother died
• Rowling moved then to Portugal where she met and married her first husband, a Portuguese man, and where she gave birth to her daughter, Jessica
• The marriage however did not succeed and so with a failed marriage behind her and only a part completed manuscript of *The Philosopher's Stone* Rowling arrived back to live on British soil
• In 1996 Bloomsbury made an offer for *The Philosopher's Stone* and so it was that the J.K. Rowling success story really began and continues to this day

THE HARRY POTTER SERIES – A BRIEF SYNOPSIS OF EACH OF THE BOOKS

Harry Potter and the Philosopher's Stone	Harry Potter is the orphaned child of powerful wizards and has magical powers of his own that he knows nothing about until he is 11 years old when he embarks on adventures unknown at Hogwarts School for Wizards.
Harry Potter and the Chamber of Secrets	It is time for Harry's second year at Hogwarts School and he has been warned by house-elf, Dobby, not to return, but is Dobby friend or foe and what will the glimmering ink in a hidden diary reveal? The Chamber of Secrets is opened and a monster is let loose terrifying anyone who meets its gaze.
Harry Potter and the Prisoner of Azkaban	Harry is eager once more to return to Hogwarts and to be with his friends Hermione and Ron – just one thing – why have the sinister prison guards of Azkaban been called in to guard the school?
Harry Potter and the Goblet of Fire	The Triwizard Tournament between schools of magic is due to take place. Contestants, who have to be over 17 years of age, are chosen by the Goblet of Fire. Harry is too young and yet his name is thrown out by the Goblet and so he must take part as the magic is irreversible.
Harry Potter and the Order of the Phoenix	Harry is in grave danger. Who is watching him and why are his friends being strangely secretive? What is the Order of the Phoenix? So many questions but one thing is for sure Voldemort is out for revenge.
Harry Potter and the Half-Blood Prince	What is the purpose of Professor Dumbledore's visiting the Dursley's house in Privet Drive and what will happen when he meets Uncle Vernon and Aunt Petunia?
Harry Potter and the Deathly Hallows	Danger beckons Harry as he sets about locating and destroying Voldemort's remaining Horcruxes. He is afraid but must somehow find the strength within him to complete this seemimgly impossible task

THE TALES OF BEEDLE THE BARD

Just when we thought it was all over and despaired of there ever being another Harry Potter novel, along came a tangible link to the final book to keep all the Harry Potter fans happy and to stave off the withdrawal symptoms.

The Tales of Beedle the Bard is actually a plot device within the seventh novel – *Harry Potter and the Deathly Hallows* – of the Harry Potter series, in which the book is left to Hermione Granger by Albus Dumbledore in his will. It is in this bequeathed book that there are five tales, one of which contains an important clue.

The Tales of Beedle Bard can be described as a popular collection of wizardry and children's fairy tales.

A BRIEF SYNOPSIS OF EACH OF THE FIVE TALES

Babbitty Rabbitty and her Cackling Stump	The story of a king who wants to keep all magic to himself but to do this he must first capture and imprison all of the sorcerers in the kingdom and he must also learn magic. However, the only person willing to teach him is a fraud and so things don't go quite to plan.
Fountain of Fair Fortune (The)	Once a year, in a supposedly magic fountain, one person may bathe to have his or her problems resolved. Three witches hope to take advantage of these magical properties as does a knight they meet on the way. All problems are solved, not by the fountain but from within their own hearts.
Tale of the Three Brothers (The)	Three brothers make a magical bridge to cross an impassable river, but halfway across they meet the personification of Death who is angry that he has lost three victims. Pretending to be impressed by the brothers he grants them three wishes – though of course the wishes do not bring safe contentment!
Warlock's Hairy Heart (The)	A young and handsome warlock who has decided that he will never fall in love decides to find a witch wife to be the envy of everyone. But he has placed his beating heart in a casket and when he returns it to his body he finds that it is not as he wished and so he takes out the witches heart to replace his, but he cannot discard his bad heart and so both he and the witch die – with him holding both hearts in his hands.
Wizard and the Hopping Pot (The)	A kind wizard uses a cauldron to cure sick Muggles, but when he dies his son is not as kind and refuses to help a warty old woman. His cauldron then grows warts and becomes grotesque in every way until eventually the young wizard can take no more. He then finds that when he is prepared to help others, all is well with the cauldron again.

AND FINALLY J.K. ROWLING THE COMPASSIONATE

In 2005 J.K. Rowling founded The Children's High Level Group (CHLG) together with MEP Baroness Emma Nicholson of Winterbourne to help the one million children across Europe still living in large residential institutions. Most people believe that the reason these children are in such institutions is because they are orphans, a fact which is incorrect for only 4% are orphans, the remaining 96% are there because they come from poor families, are disabled, or come from ethnic minorities. They live in these institutions with little health care or education and with almost no human contact or stimulation whatsoever.

J.K. Rowling may be successful, she may be wealthy, but she is also most definitely compassionate for she has stepped in and is doing all she can through CHLG to help those children who are less fortunate than children you or I may ever meet, and have fewer opportunities to make their lives as fulfilled and successful as her own. *The Tales of Beedle Bard* was written to help these children and so for that reason Rowling has waived her royalties, and Bloomsbury, Scholastic and Amazon will donate all net proceeds to the Children's High Level Group (CHLG).

Johanna Spyri
1827-1901

Works by Johanna Spyri include:

Arthur and Squirrel • *Chel: A Story of the Swiss Mountains* •
Children of the Alps • *Children's Carol (The)* • *Cornelli* •
Dora • *Erick and Sally* • *Eveli: The Little Singer* •
Francesca at Hinterwald • *Gritli's Children: A Story of Switzerland* •
Heidi • *Jo: The Little Machinist* • *Jorli: The Story of a Swiss Boy* •
Leaf on Vrony's Grave (A) • *Maxa's Children* • *Mazli: A Story
of the Swiss Valleys* • *New Year's Carol (The)* •
Peppino • *Renz and Margritli* • *Rico and Wiseli* • *Rose Child (The)* •
Story of Rico (The) • *Tiss: A Little Alpine Waif* • *Toni the Little Wood
Carver* • *Uncle Titus in the Country* • *Veronica* • *Vinzi: A Story of
the Swiss Alps* • *What Sami Sings with the Birds* •

JOHANNA SPYRI: The Writer and the Woman

• Johanna Louise Heusser was born on 12 June 1827 in a Swiss Alpine village
• She was the fourth of six children born to Joh Jak Heusser and Meta Schweizer

- Her father was a doctor and her mother was the daughter of a pastor and writer
- Their home included a medical practice and a small clinic in the *Doktorhaus* (doctor's house) and over the church.
- Between the years 1833 and 1841 she was educated at a primary school in Hirzel as well as receiving private lessons from Pastor Salomon Tobler; between 1848 and 1843 she continued her education in Zürich
- In 1852 Johanna Louise Heusser married Johann Bernhard Spyri (1821-1884), a lawyer and editor of the *Eidgenössische Zeitung* thus becoming Johanna Spyri, the name by which she would be forever remembered
- In 1855 Spyri's son, Bernhard Diethelm, was born
- 1871 was the year in which her first story appeared, *A Leaf on Vrony's Grave* by J.S. Using only her initials, she continued to be a prolific writers of stories both for adults and children
- The inspiration for *Heidi* came when she holidayed with an old school friend, Anna Elisa von Salis-Hössli; it was after this holiday that stories about Heidi began to appear
- Tragedy stuck Spyri's family in 1884 when both her husband and her son died in the same year; her son was still a young man in his twenties at the time of his death
- Two years after the death of her family, Spyri moved to her last home in Zürich
- Johanna Spyri died on 7 July 1901

Short Story Collections by Johanna Spyri include:
Moni the Goat Boy and Other Stories
Pet Lamb and Other Stories (The)

AND FINALLY

- Although Johanna Spyri was a prolific writer of other stories, she is primarily remembered for her delightful novel *Heidi*, which has inspired films, drama adaptations and musicals and which I am sure has been an introduction to the world of books for many children. It was one of the first books I ever read as a child and so Spyri and her charming story of Heidi will always have a very special part in my heart and, as a consequence, in this book too
- There is a refreshing alternative to the commercial theme parks in Switzerland, where visitors from all over the world can now visit Heidi's village, Heididorf at Maienfeld, and where they will find themselves

transported back in time to the time of the story of Heidi when they visit Johanna Spyri's *Heidihaus* (Heidi's House)

J.R.R. Tolkien
1892-1973

Works by Tolkien include:
Adventures of Tom Bombadil and Other Verses from the Red Book (The) • *Farmer Giles of Ham* • *Fellowship of the Ring* [The first part of *Lord of the Rings*] • *Hobbit: or There and Back Again (The)* • *Legend of Sigurd and Gudrún* [edited by Christopher Tolkien] • *Return of the King (The)* [The third part of *Lord of the Rings*] • *Two Towers (The)* [The second part of *Lord of the Rings*] • *Tolkien Reader (The)* • *Smith of Wootton Major* • *Letters from Father Christmas* • *Silmarillion (The)* • *Unfinished Tales of Numenor and Middle Earth* •

J.R.R. TOLKIEN: The Writer and the Man
• John Ronald Reuel Tolkien was born on 3 January 1892 in Bloemfontein, South Africa to Arthur Reuel Tolkien and Mabel (née Suffield)
• His father emigrated to South Africa from Britain in the 1890s and was joined there by his new wife
• In 1895, when Tolkien was just three years old, his mother brought him and his younger brother, Hilary, back to England to visit their grandparents
• Tolkien never saw his father again for his father died of rheumatic fever soon after Tolkein, his mother and his brother left South Africa
• He was educated at King Edward's School in Birmingham where he was passionately interested in languages and as a result founded a club which met most days after school and was made up of like-minded individuals
• In 1900 Tolkien's mother was accepted into the Roman Catholic church and Tolkien himself remained a devout Catholic throughout his life. At this point Father Francis Xavier Morgan was a large part of the Tolkien family life

• In 1904 Mabel Tolkien died, thus leaving her two little boys orphans; Father Francis then took care of the material and spiritual needs of the two boys

• In 1911 Tolkien went up to Exeter College, Oxford to read Classics

• On 22 March 1916 Tolkien married Edith Bratt; this was a relationship which had initially started when he was just 16-years-old and Edith was 19 but had been halted by Father Francis, who was keen for Tolkien to concentrate on his studies, until he came of age

• Ronald and Edith Tolkien went on to have three sons together, John Francis Reuel, the first born who later entered the priesthood becoming Father John Tolkien; the second and third sons were called Michael Hilary Reuel and Christopher Reuel respectively; their only daughter, whom they called Priscilla, was the last of the Tolkien children to be born in 1929

• As a Second Lieutenant in the First World War, and as many other soldiers in the unsanitary trenches of the time, Tolkein contracted trench fever

• Tolkien was not just a gifted linguist and academic but he had a deep and consuming love of language and worked throughout his life at creating his own language – Elvish

• The great academic that he was, it was only to be expected then that after the war he would take up academic posts in the world of languages, including Assistant Lexicographer on the New English Dictionary, Reader in English Language at the University of Leeds, and later as Professor of Anglo-Saxon at Oxford

• In 1959 Ronald and Edith Tolkien retired to Bournemouth

• In 1972 Tolkien was awarded the CBE by the Queen

• Edith died on 22 November 1971 after which Ronald moved back to Oxford and into rooms provided for him by Merton College

• J.R.R. Tolkien died soon after, on 2 September 1973

• The Tolkiens are buried together

AND FINALLY

• In 1998 *The Lord of the Rings* was voted as Best Book of all time by bookshops and book clubs

• There is now a film based on *The Lord of the Rings* as well as a stage musical, thus making his words visual in every sense and accessible to those who perhaps would, or could, never read these extraordinary works for themselves

Chapter Five

Prizes Awarded for Literary Achievement

Recognition for achievement is so satisfying and, when one thinks about it, we enter this world on just that note, recognition for the achievement of being born! There we are not having yet seen the light of day and some one is saying, 'Well done, just one more push.' Though quite who is doing the pushing is debatable as, at nought minutes old, you are hardly in the position to say it was you!

This recognition for achievement phenomena continues throughout life, there was the prize for winning the egg and spoon race when you were just six years old, the new computer you were given when you passed the school entrance exam at eleven, and years later the diploma for passing your college exams.

So it comes as no surprise then to know that the literary world is not exempt from this recognition for achievement treadmill with its various prizes and awards to be had for the successful and acclaimed writer. There are many, many awards for literary success at varying degrees of recognition. However, we will look at only the three internationally renowned literary awards, known as the Nobel Prize, the Pulitzer Prize and the Man Booker Prize.

The Nobel Prize

Alfred Nobel
1833-1896

• Alfred Nobel was born in Stockholm, Sweden in the year 1833 to Immanuel Nobel and Andriette Ahlsell Nobel
• His father was an engineer who built bridges and buildings
• Alfred grew to be a man of great intellect and by the age of 17 years old he could speak and write in five languages – Swedish, Russian, French, English and German

235

The Nobel Prize was instigated by Alfred Nobel,
who was born in Stockholm, Sweden in 1833

• He was destined to be a renowned scientist, inventor, businessman and not least the founder of the Nobel Prizes
• Unlike many scientists Nobel waded into the arts; he was intensely interested in literature and wrote poetry and drama too
• In 1867 Nobel obtained a patent for dynamite
• During his lifetime, as well as inventing dynamite, he had by the time of his death 355 patents to his name; so he was 'the great achiever'
• His interests were far reaching and of a non exclusive nature in that he enveloped greatness and forward thinking in all areas; he was very interested in social and peace related issues and so his Nobel prizes became an extension and conclusion of a lifetime of interests across the full spectrum of greatness and achievement
• Alfred Nobel died at his home in San Remo, Italy, on 10 December 1896 leaving behind a special legacy in the form of a series of world renowned prizes in recognition for the various achievements of the future intellects destined to follow him
• In his last will and testament he wrote that much of his fortune was to be used to give prizes to those who had done their best for humanity in the field of chemistry, literature, peace, physics, physiology or medicine. It was a very controversial will, opposed by his own relatives and questioned by the authorities of various countries and it so wasn't until 1901 that it was finally accepted and the first prize awarded

THE NOBEL PRIZE IN LITERATURE

The following are past winners of the Nobel Prize in Literature.

Year	Recipient	Country	In Recognition
1901	Sully Prudhomme 1839-1907 (pen name of René François Armand Prudhomme)	France	'in special recognition of his poetic composition, which gives evidence of lofty idealism, artistic perfection and a rare combination of the qualities of both heart and intellect'
1902	Christian Matthias Theodor Mommsen 1817-1903	Germany (Born in Garding, Sleswick, then Denmark)	'the greatest living master of the art of historical writing, with special reference to his monumental work, *A History of Rome*'
1903	Bjørnstjerne Martinus Bjørnson	Norway	'as a tribute to his noble, magnificent and versatile poetry,

Year	Recipient	Country	In Recognition
	1832-1910		which has always been distinguished by both the freshness of its inspiration and the rare purity of its spirit'
1904	In This Year: The prize was shared i) Frédéric Mistral 1830-1914	France	i) 'in recognition of the fresh originality and true inspiration of his poetic production, which faithfully reflects the natural scenery and native spirit of his people, and, in addition, his significant work as a Provençal philologist'
	ii) José Echegaray y Eizaguirre 1832-1916	Spain	ii) 'in recognition of the numerous and brilliant compositions which, in an individual and original manner, have revived the great traditions of the Spanish drama'
1905	Henryk Sienkiewicz 1846-1916	Poland	'because of his outstanding merits as an epic writer'
1906	Giosuè Carducci 1835-1907	Italy	'not only in consideration of his deep learning and critical research, but above all as a tribute to the creative energy, freshness of style, and lyrical force which characterize his poetic masterpieces'
1907	Rudyard Kipling 1865-1936	United Kingdom (Born in Bombay, Br. India)	'in consideration of the power of observation, originality of imagination, virility of ideas and remarkable talent for narration which characterize the creations of this world-famous author'
1908	Rudolf Christoph Eucken 1846-1926	Germany	'in recognition of his earnest search for truth, his penetrating power of thought, his wide range of vision, and the warmth and strength in presentation with which in his numerous works he has vindicated and developed an idealistic philosophy of life'

Year	Recipient	Country	In Recognition
1909	Selma Ottilia Lovisa Lagerlöf 1858-1940	Sweden	'in appreciation of the lofty idealism, vivid imagination and spiritual perception that characterise her writings'
1910	Paul Johann Ludwig Heys 1830-1914	Germany	'as a tribute to the consummate artistry, permeated with idealism, which he has demonstrated during his long productive career as a lyric poet, dramatist, novelist and writer of world-renowned short stories'
1911	Count Maurice (Mooris) Polidore Marie Bernhard Maeterlinck 1862-1949	Belgium	'in appreciation of his many-sided literary activities, and especially of his dramatic works, which are distinguished by a wealth of imagination and by a poetic fancy, which reveals, sometimes in the guise of a fairy tale, a deep inspiration, while in a mysterious way they appeal to the readers' own feelings and stimulate their imaginations'
1912	Gerhart Johann Robert Hauptmann 1862-1946	Germany	'primarily in recognition of his fruitful, varied and outstanding production in the realm of dramatic art'
1913	Rabindranath Tagore 1861-1941	India	'because of his profoundly sensitive, fresh and beautiful verse, by which, with consummate skill, he has made his poetic thought, expressed in his own English words, a part of the literature of the West'
1914	In This Year: The prize money was allocated to the Special Fund of this prize section		
1915	Romain Rolland 1866-1944	France	'as a tribute to the lofty idealism of his literary production and to the sympathy and love of truth with which he has described different types of human beings'

Year	Recipient	Country	In Recognition
1916	Carl Gustaf Verner von Heidenstam 1859-1940	Sweden	'in recognition of his significance as the leading representative of a new era in our literature'
1917	In This Year: The prize was shared		
	i) Karl Adolph Gjellerup 1857-1919	Denmark	i) 'for his varied and rich poetry, which is inspired by lofty ideals'
	ii) Henrik Pontoppidan 1857-1943	Denmark	ii) 'for his authentic descriptions of present-day life in Denmark'
1918	In This Year: The prize money was allocated to the Special Fund of this prize section		
1919	Carl Friedrich Georg Spitteler 1845-1924	Switzerland	'in special appreciation of his epic, *Olympian Spring*'
1920	Knut Pedersen Hamsun 1859-1952	Norway	'for his monumental work, *Growth of the Soil*'
1921	Anatole France 1844-1924 (pen name of Jacques Anatole Thibault)	France	'in recognition of his brilliant literary achievements, characterized as they are by a nobility of style, a profound human sympathy, grace, and a true Gallic temperament'
1922	Jacinto Benavente 1866-1954	Spain	'for the happy manner in which he has continued the illustrious traditions of the Spanish drama'
1923	William Butler Yeats 1865-1939	Ireland	'for his always inspired poetry, which in a highly artistic form gives expression to the spirit of a whole nation'
1924	Wladyslaw Stanislaw Reymont 1867-1925 (pen name of Rejment)	Poland	'for his great national epic, *The Peasants*'
1925	George Bernard Shaw 1856-1950	United Kingdom (Born in Dublin, Ireland)	'for his work which is marked by both idealism and humanity, its stimulating satire often being infused with a singular poetic beauty'

Year	Recipient	Country	In Recognition
1926	Grazia Deledda 1871-1936 (pen name of Grazia Madesani, née Deledda)	Italy (Born in Nuoro, Sardinia)	'for her idealistically inspired writings which with plastic clarity picture the life on her native island and with depth and sympathy deal with human problems in general'
1927	Henri Bergson 1859-1941	France	'in recognition of his rich and vitalizing ideas and the brilliant skill with which they have been presented'
1928	Sigrid Undset 1882-1949	Norway (Born in Kalund- borg, Denmark)	'principally for her powerful descriptions of Northern life during the Middle Ages'
1929	Thomas Mann 1875-1955	Germany	'principally for his great novel, *Buddenbrooks*, which has won steadily increased recognition as one of the classic works of contemporary literature'
1930	Sinclair Lewis 1885-1951	USA	'for his vigorous and graphic art of description and his ability to create, with wit and humour, new types of characters'
1931	Erik Axel Karlfeldt 1864-1931	Sweden	'The poetry of Erik Axel Karlfeldt'
1932	John Galsworthy 1867-1933	UK	'for his distinguished art of narration which takes its highest form in *The Forsyte Saga*'
1933	Ivan Alekseyevich Bunin 1870-1953	Stateless domicile in France (Born in Voronezh, Russia)	'for the strict artistry with which he has carried on the classical Russian traditions in prose writing'
1934	Luigi Pirandello 1867-1936	Italy	'for his bold and ingenious revival of dramatic and scenic art'
1935	In This Year: The prize money was allocated 1/3 to the Main Fund and 2/3 to the Special Fund of this prize section		
1936	Eugene Gladstone O'Neill 1888-1953	USA	'for the power, honesty and deep-felt emotions of his dramatic works, which embody an original concept of tragedy'

Year	Recipient	Country	In Recognition
1937	Roger Martin du Gard 1881-1958	France	'for the artistic power and truth with which he has depicted human conflict as well as some fundamental aspects of contemporary life in his novel-cycle Les Thibault'
1938	Pearl Buck (pen name of Pearl Walsh née Sydenstricker) 1892-1973	USA	'for her rich and truly epic descriptions of peasant life in China and for her biographical masterpieces'
1939	Frans Eemil Sillanpää 1888-1964	Finland	'for his deep understanding of his country's peasantry and the exquisite art with which he has portrayed their way of life and their relationship with Nature'
1940	In This Year: The prize money was allocated 1/3 to the Main Fund and 2/3 to the Special Fund of this prize section		
1941	In This Year: The prize money was allocated 1/3 to the Main Fund and 2/3 to the Special Fund of this prize section		
1942	In This Year: The prize money was allocated 1/3 to the Main Fund and 2/3 to the Special Fund of this prize section		
1943	In This Year: The prize money was allocated 1/3 to the Main Fund and 2/3 to the Special Fund of this prize section		
1944	Johannes Vilhelm Jensen 1873-1950	Denmark	'for the rare strength and fertility of his poetic imagination with which is combined an intellectual curiosity of wide

Year	Recipient	Country	In Recognition
1945	Gabriela Mistral 1889-1957 (pen name of Lucila Godoy y Alcayaga)	Chile	scope and a bold, freshly creative style' 'for her lyric poetry which, inspired by powerful emotions, has made her name a symbol of the idealistic aspirations of the entire Latin American world'
1946	Hermann Hesse 1877-1962	Switzerland (Born in Calw, Wuerttemberg, Germany)	'for his inspired writings which, while growing in boldness and penetration, exemplify the classical humanitarian ideals and high qualities of style'
1947	André Paul Guillaume Gide 1869-1951	France	'for his comprehensive and artistically significant writings, in which human problems and conditions have been presented with a fearless love of truth and keen psychological insight'
1948	Thomas Stearns Eliot 1888-1965	UK (Born in St Louis, MO, USA)	'for his outstanding, pioneer contribution to present-day poetry'
1949	William Faulkner 1897-1962	USA	'for his powerful and artistically unique contribution to the modern American novel'
1950	Earl (Bertrand Arthur William) Russell 1872-1970	UK	'in recognition of his varied and significant writings in which he champions humanitarian ideals and freedom of thought'
1951	Pär Fabian Lagerkvist 1891-1974	Sweden	'for the artistic vigour and true independence of mind with which he endeavours in his poetry to find answers to the eternal questions confronting mankind'
1952	François Mauriac 1885-1970	France	'for the deep spiritual insight and the artistic intensity with which he has in his novels penetrated the drama of human life'
1953	Sir Winston Leonard Spencer Churchill 1874-1965	UK	'for his mastery of historical and biographical description as well as for brilliant oratory in defending exalted human values'
1954	Ernest Miller	USA	'for his mastery of the art of

Year	Recipient	Country	In Recognition
	Hemingway 1899-1961		narrative, most recently demonstrated in *The Old Man and the Sea*, and for the influence that he has exerted on contemporary style'
1955	Halldór Kiljan Laxness 1902-1998	Iceland	'for his vivid epic power which has renewed the great narrative art of Iceland'
1956	Juan Ramón Jiménez 1881-1958	Spain	'for his lyrical poetry, which in Spanish language constitutes an example of high spirit and artistical purity'
1957	Albert Camus 1913-1960	France (Born in Mondovi, Algeria)	'for his important literary production, which with clear-sighted earnestness illuminates the problems of the human conscience in our times'
1958	Boris Leonidovich Pasternak 1890-1960	USSR	'for his important achievement both in contemporary lyrical poetry and in the field of the great Russian epic tradition'
1959	Salvatore Quasimodo	Italy	'for his lyrical poetry, which with classical fire expresses the tragic experience of life in our own times'
1960	Saint-John Perse (pen name of Alexis Léger) 1887-1975	France (Born on Guadeloupe Island)	'for the soaring flight and the evocative imagery of his poetry which in a visionary fashion reflects the conditions of our time'
1961	Ivo Andric 1892-1975	Yugoslavia (Born in Travnik, Bosnia)	'for the epic force with which he traced themes and depicted has human destinies drawn from the history of his country'
1962	John Steinbeck 1902-1968	USA	'for his realistic and imaginative writings, combining as they do sympathetic humour and keen social perception'
1963	Giorgos Seferis (pen name of Giorgos Seferiadis)	Greece (Born in Smyrna, Turkey)	'for his eminent lyrical writing, inspired by a deep feeling for the Hellenic world of culture'
1964	Jean-Paul Sarte	France	'for his work which, rich in ideas

Year	Recipient	Country	In Recognition
	1905-1980		and filled with the spirit of freedom and the quest for truth, has exerted a far-reaching influence on our age'
1965	Mikhail Aleksandrovich Sholokhov 1905-1984	USSR	'for the artistic power and integrity with which, in his epic of the Don, he has given expression to a historic phase in the life of the Russian people'
1966	In This Year: The Prize Was Shared: i) Shmuel Yosef Agnon 1888-1970	Israel	'for his profoundly characteristic narrative art with motifs from the life of the Jewish people'
	ii) Nelly Sachs 1891-1970	Sweden (Born in Berlin, Germany)	'for her outstanding lyrical and dramatic writing, which interprets Israel's destiny with touching strength'
1967	Miguel Angel Asturias 1899-1974	Guatemala	'for his vivid literary achievement, deep-rooted in the national traits and traditions of Indian peoples of Latin America'
1968	Yasunari Kawabata 1899-1972	Japan	'for his narrative mastery, which with great sensibility expresses the essence of the Japanese mind'
1969	Samuel Beckett 1906-1989	Ireland	'for his writing, which – in new forms for the novel and drama – in the destitution of modern man acquires its elevation'
1970	Aleksandr Isayevich Solzhenitsyn 1918-2008	USSR	'for the ethical force with which he has pursued the indispensable traditions of Russian literature'
1971	Pablo Neruda (pen name of Neftalí Ricardo Reyes Basoalto) 1904-1973	Chile	'for a poetry that with the action of an elemental force brings alive a continent's destiny and dreams'
1972	Heinrich Böll 1917-1985	Federal Republic of Germany	'for his writing which through its combination of a broad perspective on his time and a sensitive skill in characterization has contributed to a renewal of German literature'

Year	Recipient	Country	In Recognition
1973	Patrick White 1912-1990	Australia (Born in London, United Kingdom)	'for an epic and psychological narrative art which has introduced a new continent into literature'
1974	In This Year: The prize was shared: i) Eyvind Johnson 1900-1976	Sweden	'for a narrative art, far-seeing in lands and ages, in the service of freedom'
	ii) Harry Martinson 1904-1978	Sweden	'for writings that catch the dewdrop and reflect the cosmos'
1975	Eugenio Montale 1896-1981		'for his distinctive poetry which, with great artistic sensitivity, has interpreted human values under the sign of an outlook on life with no illusions'
1976	Saul Bellow 1915-2005	USA (Born in Montreal, Canada)	'for the human understanding and subtle analysis of contemporary culture that are combined in his work'
1977	Vicente Aleixandre 1898-1984	Spain	'for a creative poetic writing which illuminates man's condition in the cosmos and in present-day society, at the same time representing the great renewal of the traditions of Spanish poetry between the wars'
1978	Isaac Bashevis Singer 1904-1991	USA (Born in Leoncin, Poland)	'for his impassioned narrative art which, with roots in a Polish-Jewish cultural tradition, brings universal human conditions to life'
1979	Odysseus Elytis (pen name of Odysseus Alepoudhelis) 1911-1996	Greece	'for his poetry, which, against the background of Greek tradition, depicts with sensuous strength and intellectual clear-sightedness modern man's struggle for freedom and creativeness'
1980	Czeslaw Milosz 1911-2004	Poland and USA	'who with uncompromising clear-sightedness voices man's exposed condition in a world of severe conflicts'

Year	Recipient	Country	In Recognition
1981	Elias Canetti	United Kingdom (Born in Rustschuk, Bulgaria)	'for writings marked by a broad outlook, a wealth of ideas and artistic power'
1982	Gabriel García Márquez 1928-	Colombia	'for his novels and short stories, in which the fantastic and the realistic are combined in a richly composed world of imagination, reflecting a continent's life and conflicts'
1983	William Golding 1911-1993	United Kindom	'for his novels which, with the perspicuity of realistic narrative art and the diversity and universality of myth, illuminate the human condition in the world of today'
1984	Jaroslav Seifert 1901-1986	Czechoslovakia	'for his poetry which endowed with freshness, sensuality and rich inventiveness provides a liberating image of the indomitable spirit and versatility of man'
1985	Claude Simon 1913-2005	France	'who in his novel combines the poet's and the painter's creativeness with a deepened awareness of time in the depiction of the human condition'
1986	Wole Soyinka 1934-	Nigeria	'who in a wide cultural perspective and with poetic overtones fashions the drama of existence'
1987	Joseph Brodsky	USA (Born in Leningrad, USSR)	'for an all-embracing authorship, imbued with clarity of thought and poetic intensity'
1988	Naguib Mahfouz 1911-2006	Egypt	'who, through works rich in nuance - now clear-sightedly realistic, now evocatively ambiguous - has formed an Arabian narrative art that applies to all mankind'
1989	Camilo José Cela 1916-2002	Spain	'for a rich and intensive prose, which with restrained compassion forms a challenging vision of man's vulnerability'
1990	Octavio Paz	Mexico	'for impassioned writing with

247

Year	Recipient	Country	In Recognition
	1914-1998		wide horizons, characterized by sensuous intelligence and humanistic integrity'
1991	Nadine Gordimer 1923-	South Africa	'who through her magnificent epic writing has - in the words of Alfred Nobel - been of very great benefit to humanity'
1992	Derek Walcott 1930-	Saint Lucia	'for a poetic oeuvre of great luminosity, sustained by a historical vision, the outcome of a multicultural commitment'
1993	Toni Morrison 1932-	USA	'who in novels characterized by visionary force and poetic import, gives life to an essential aspect of American reality'
1994	Kenzaburo Oe 1935-	Japan	'who with poetic force creates an imagined world, where life and myth condense to form a disconcerting picture of the human predicament today'
1995	Seamus Heaney 1939-	Ireland	'for works of lyrical beauty and ethical depth, which exalt everyday miracles and the living past'
1996	Wislawa Szymborska 1923-	Poland	'for poetry that with ironic precision allows the historical and biological context to come to light in fragments of human reality'
1997	Dario Fo 1926-	Italy	'who emulates the jesters of the Middle Ages in scourging authority and upholding the dignity of the downtrodden'
1998	José Saramago 1922-	Portugal	'who with parables sustained by imagination, compassion and irony continually enables us once again to apprehend an elusory reality'
1999	Günter Grass 1927-	Federal Republic of Germany (Born in Danzig)	'whose frolicsome black fables portray the forgotten face of history'

Year	Recipient	Country	In Recognition
2000	Gao Xingjian 1940-	France (Born in Ganzhou, China)	'for an œuvre of universal validity, bitter insights and linguistic ingenuity, which has opened new paths for the Chinese novel and drama'
2001	Sir Vidiadhar Surajprasad Naipaul 1932-	United Kingdom (Born in Trinidad)	'for having united perceptive narrative and incorruptible scrutiny in works that compel us to see the presence of suppressed histories'
2002	Imre Kertész 1929-	Hungary	'for writing that upholds the fragile experience of the individual against the barbaric arbitrariness of history'
2003	John M. Coetzee 1940-	South Africa	'who in innumerable guises portrays the surprising involvement of the outsider'
2004	Elfriede Jelinek 1946-	Austria	'for her musical flow of voices and counter-voices in novels and plays that with extraordinary linguistic zeal reveal the absurdity of society's clichés and their subjugating power'
2005	Harold Pinter 1930-2008	United Kingdom	'who in his plays uncovers the precipice under everyday prattle and forces entry into oppression's closed rooms'
2006	Orhan Pamuk 1952-	Turkey	'who in the quest for the melancholic soul of his native city has discovered new symbols for the clash and interlacing of cultures'
2007	Doris Lessing 1919-	United Kingdom (Born in Kermanshah, Persia)	'that epicist of the female experience, who with scepticism, fire and visionary power has subjected a divided civilization to scrutiny'
2008	Jean-Marie Gustave Le Clézio 1940-	France and Mauritius	'author of new departures, poetic adventure and sensual ecstasy, explorer of a humanity beyond and below the reigning civilization'

Year	Recipient	Country	In Recognition
2009-	Herta Müller 1953-	Germany (Born in Nitzkdorf, Banat, Romania)	'who, with the concentration of poetry and the frankness of prose, depicts the landscape of the dispossessed'

To many though, including myself, one Nobel Prize stands out as being humanely special and that is of course the Nobel Peace Prize which is awarded for persons or organisations who have promoted world peace. It is so wonderful that a man of such outstanding intellect in such a diversity of fields should recognise and value the achievement of those striving for world peace, so wonderful that it just had to be written down in this book about writers.

❦

The Pulitzer Prize

The Pulitzer Prize exists today as a direct result of the extraordinary Hungarian-born Joseph Pulitzer.

Joseph Pulitzer
1847-1911

• Joseph Pulitzer was born into a wealthy family in Mako, Hungary on April 10, 1847
• His father was a grain merchant of Magyar-Jewish origin and his mother was German Roman Catholic
• Pulitzer was educated by tutors and in private schools
• A the age of 17 years he wanted to join the army, but poor eyesight and poor health in general prohibited him from doing this
• His early – successful – career was as a journalist and he eventually became the owner of the *St. Louis Post-Dispatch*
• He became a hugely successful and dedicated, workaholic journalist; there is no doubt that today he would be both proud and pleased to know that in the Pulitzer Prizes more awards in journalism go to the exposure of corruption than to any other subject
• Joseph Pulitzer died in 1911 on board his yacht

250

In his will Joseph Pulitzer made provision for the establishment of the Pulitzer Prizes as his personal contribution to inspire excellence in the arts. He specified as to where the awards would go, but as a visionary he also made provision for development and changes in the awards and left instructions that in any year where entries fell below standards of excellence then the award would be withheld. Since its inception in 1917 the number of awards has been increased to 21 with the introduction of poetry, music, and photography as qualifying subjects.

THE PULITZER PRIZE FOR FICTION

The following are past winners of the Pulitzer Prize for Fiction.

Year	Author	Novel	Publisher
1917	No Award		
1918	Ernest Poole	His Family	Macmillan
1919	Booth Tarkington	Magnificent Ambersons (The)	Doubleday
1920	No Award		
1921	Edith Wharton	Age of Innocence (The)	Appleton
1922	Booth Tarkington	Alice Adams	Doubleday
1923	Willa Cather	One of Ours	Knopf
1924	Margaret Wilson	Able McLaughlins (The)	Harper
1925	Edna Ferber	So Big	Doubleday
1926	Sinclair Lewis	Arrowsmith	Harcourt
1927	Louis Bromfield	Early Autumn	Stokes
1928	Thornton Wilder	Bridge of San Luis Rey (The)	Boni
1929	Julia Peterkin	Scarlet Sister Mary	Bobbs
1930	Oliver Lafarge	Laughing Boy	Houghton
1931	Margaret Ayer Barnes	Years of Grace	Houghton
1932	Pearl S. Buck	Good Earth (The)	John Day
1933	T. S. Stribling	Store (The)	Doubleday
1934	Caroline Miller	Lamb in His Bosom	Harper
1935	Josephine Winslow Johnson	Now in November	Simon & Schuster
1936	Harold L. Davis	Honey in the Horn	Harper
1937	Margaret Mitchell	Gone with the Wind	Macmillan
1938	John Phillips Marquand	Late George Apley (The)	Little
1939	Marjorie Kinnan Rawlings	Yearling (The)	Scribner
1940	John Steinbeck	Grapes of Wrath (The)	Viking
1941	No Award		
1942	Ellen Glasgow	In This Our Life	Harcourt
1943	Upton Sinclair	Dragon's Teeth	Viking

Year	Author	Novel	Publisher
1944	Martin Flavin	*Journey in the Dark*	Harper
1945	John Hersey	*Bell for Adano (A)*	Knopf
1946	*No Award*		
1947	Robert Penn Warren	*All the King's Men*	Harcourt
1948	James A. Michener	*Tales of the South Pacific*	Macmillan
1949	James Gould Cozzens	*Guard of Honor*	Harcourt
1950	A.B. Guthrie	*Way West (The)*	Mariner Books
1951	Conrad Richter	*Town (The)*	Knopf
1952	Herman Wouk	*Caine Mutiny (The)*	Doubleday
1953	Ernest Hemingway	*Old Man and the Sea (The)*	Scribner
1954	*No Award*		
1955	William Faulkner	*Fable (A)*	Random
1956	MacKinlay Kantor	*Andersonville*	World
1957	*No Award*		
1958	James Agee	*Death In The Family (A)* (a posthumous publication)	McDowell, Obolensky
1959	Robert Lewis Taylor	*Travels of Jaimie McPheeters (The)*	Doubleday
1960	Allen Drury	*Advise and Consent*	Doubleday
1961	Harper Lee	*To Kill A Mockingbird*	Lippincott
1962	Edwin O'Connor	*Edge of Sadness (The)*	Little
1963	William Faulkner	*Reivers (The)*	Random
1964	*No Award*		
1965	Shirley Ann Grau	*Keepers Of The House (The)*	Random
1966	Katherine Anne Porter	*Collected Stories*	Harcourt
1967	Bernard Malamud	*Fixer (The)*	Farrar
1968	William Styron	*Confessions of Nat Turner (The)*	Random
1969	N. Scott Momaday	*House Made of Dawn*	Harper
1970	Jean Stafford	*Collected Stories*	Farrar
1971	*No Award*		
1972	Wallace Stegner	*Angle of Repose*	Doubleday
1973	Eudora Welty	*Optimist's Daughter (The)*	Random
1974	*No Award*		
1975	Michael Shaara	*Killer Angels (The)*	McKay
1976	Saul Bellow	*Humboldt's Gift*	Viking
1977	*No Award*		
1978	James Alan McPherson	*Elbow Room*	Atlantic Monthly Press
1979	John Cheever	*Stories of John Cheever (The)*	Knopf
1980	Norman Mailer	*Executioner's Song (The)*	Little
1981	John Kennedy Toole	*Confederacy of Dunces (A)* (a posthumous publication)	Louisiana State U. Press

Year	Author	Novel	Publisher
1982	John Updike	*Rabbit Is Rich*	Knopf
1983	Alice Walker	*Color Purple (The)*	Harcourt Brace
1984	William Kennedy	*Ironweed*	Viking
1985	Alison Lurie	*Foreign Affairs*	Random House
1986	Larry McMurtry	*Lonesome Dove*	Simon & Schuster
1987	Peter Taylor	*Summons to Memphis (A)*	Alfred A. Knopf
1988	Toni Morrison	*Beloved*	Alfred A. Knopf
1989	Anne Tyler	*Breathing Lessons*	Alfred A. Knopf
1990	Oscar Hijuelos	*Mambo Kings Play Songs of Love (The)*	Farrar
1991	John Updike	*Rabbit At Rest*	Alfred A. Knopf
1992	Jane Smiley	*Thousand Acres (A)*	Alfred A. Knopf
1993	Robert Olen Butler	*Good Scent from a Strange Mountain (A)*	Henry Holt
1994	E. Annie Proulx	*Shipping News (The)*	Charles Scribner's Sons
1995	Carol Shields	*Stone Diaries (The)*	Viking
1996	Richard Ford	*Independence Day*	Alfred A. Knopf
1997	Steven Millhauser	*Martin Dressler: The Tale of an American Dreamer*	Crown
1998	Philip Roth	*American Pastoral*	Houghton Mifflin
1999	Michael Cunningham	*Hours (The)*	Farrar, Straus & Giroux
2000	Jhumpa Lahiri	*Interpreter of Maladies*	Mariner Books/Houghton Mifflin
2001	Michael Chabon	*Amazing Adventures of Kavalier & Clay (The)*	Random House
2002	Richard Russo	*Empire Falls*	Alfred A. Knopf
2003	Jeffrey Eugenides	*Middlesex*	Farrar
2004	Edward P. Jones	*Known World (The)*	Amistad/HarperCollins
2005	Marilynne Robinson	*Gilead*	Farrar
2006	Geraldine Brooks	*March*	Viking
2007	Cormac McCarthy	*Road (The)*	Alfred A. Knopf
2008	Junot Diaz	*Brief Wondrous Life of Oscar Wao (The)*	Riverhead Books
2009	Elizabeth Strout	*Olive Kitteridge*	Random House

The Man Booker Prize
established 1968

The term the Man Booker Prize is generally shortened to the Booker Prize and still even shorter to the Booker. It promotes the finest in fiction by rewarding the very best book of the year in recognition of this. Man plc has sponsored the Man Booker Prize since 2002 with the prize money at time of going to press being £50,000.

So who is eligible to win a Booker? The criteria is as follows: The author must be a citizen of the Commonwealth or the Republic of Ireland and the book itself must be a full-length novel published in the year of the prize; it must be an original piece of work, written in English and not a translation; neither must it be self-published.

THE MAN BOOKER PRIZE FOR FICTION
The following are past winners of the Man Booker Prize for Fiction.

Year	Author	Novel	Publisher
1969	P.H. Newby	*Something to Answer For*	Faber & Faber
1970	Bernice Rubens	*Elected Member (The)*	Eyre & Spottiswoode
1971	V.S. Naipaul	*In a Free State*	Deutsch
1972	John Berger	*G*	Weidenfeld & Nicolson
1973	J.G. Farrell	*Siege of Krishnapur (The)*	Weidenfield & Nicolson
1974	Nadine Gordimer	*Conservationist (The)*	Cape
	Stanley Middleton	*Holiday*	Hutchinson
1975	Ruth Prawer Jhabvala	*Heat and Dust*	John Murray
1976	David Storey	*Saville*	Cape
1977	Paul Scott	*Staying On*	Heinemann
1978	Iris Murdoch	*Sea, The Sea (The)*	Chatto & Windus
1979	Penelope Fitzgerald	*Offshore*	Collins
1980	William Golding	*Rites of Passage*	Faber & Faber
1981	Salman Rushdie	*Midnight's Children*	Cape
1982	Thomas Keneally	*Schindler's Ark*	Hodder & Stoughton
1983	J.M. Coetzee	*Life and Times of Michael K*	Secker & Warburg
1984	Anita Brookner	*Hotel du Lac*	Cape
1985	Keri Hulme	*Bone People (The)*	Hodder & Stoughton
1986	Kingsley Amis	*Old Devils (The)*	Hutchinson

Year	Author	Novel	Publisher
1987	Penelope Lively	*Moon Tiger*	Deutsch
1988	Peter Carey	*Oscar and Lucinda*	Faber & Faber
1989	Kazuo Ishiguro	*Remains of the Day (The)*	Faber & Faber
1990	A.S. Byatt	*Possession*	Chatto & Windus
1991	Ben Okri	*Famished Road (The)*	Cape
1992	Michael Ondaatje	*English Patient (The)*	Bloomsbury
1993	Roddy Doyle	*Paddy Clarke Ha Ha Ha*	Secker & Warburg
1994	James Kelman	*How Late It Was, How Late*	Secker & Warburg
1995	Pat Barker	*Ghost Road (The)*	Viking
1996	Graham Swift	*Last Orders*	Picador
1997	Arundahti Roy	*God of Small Things (The)*	Flamingo
1998	Ian McEwan	*Amsterdam*	Cape
1999	J.M. Coetzee	*Disgrace*	Secker & Warburg
2000	Margaret Atwood	*Blind Assistant (The)*	Bloomsbury
2001	Peter Carey	*True History of the Kelly Gang*	Faber & Faber
2002	Yann Martel	*Life of Pi*	Cannogate
2003	D.B.C. Pierre	*Vernon God Little*	Faber & Faber
2004	Alan Hollinghurst	*Line of Beauty (The)*	Picador
2005	John Banville	*Sea (The)*	Picador
2006	Kiran Desai	*Inheritance of Loss (The)*	Penguin
2007	Ann Enright	*Gathering (The)*	Jonathon Cape
2008	Aravind Adiga	*White Tiger (The)*	Atlantic
2009	Hilary Mantel	*Wolf Hall*	Fourth Estate

THE MAN BOOKER INTERNATIONAL PRIZE FOR FICTION

A very young prize in this world of 'Recognition for Achievement' is The Man Booker International Prize with the first prize being awarded as recently as 2005. Awarded every second year it can be won by an author of any nationality, providing that his or her work is available in the English language with the first three winners being Ismail Kadare in 2005, Chinua Achebe in 2007 and Alice Munroe in 2009.

Chapter Six

Well I Never Knew That!

Bookshelves

Enthralling storylines between the covers
Fascinating facts behind the writers
And so the student of literature becomes the expert

When you 'know' all about the writer, then you're smart; when you 'know' all about their works as well, then you're really smart; so now you know a bit about both you must be home and dry then? If not an actual authority on the classics, you're getting there, and so others will justifiably admire you? Right? Wrong! You see you will find that the real experts or the real enthusiasts – on any subject at all for that matter – as well as knowing all the important facts on their subject, actually know all the quirky facts too, for this turns an area of study into area of fascination. For example you might know that Beatrix Potter wrote *The Tale of Peter Rabbit* but do you know how long it took to get the film *Miss Potter*, starring Renée Zellweger and Ewan McGregor, based on her life, from the script to the stage? Have you any idea by what nickname C.S. Lewis was known? The answer to both of these questions is, for most, quite probably – No! So here you can read on to find out all the fascinating facts you didn't know, you didn't know.

• The name and pictures of Quality Street sweets were taken from J.M. Barrie's illustrated edition of his play *Quality Street*. The play is more or less completely forgotten now, but not the brand he inspired!
• After his death Charles Dickens left something to each member of his staff in his will
• The Hollywood film *Miss Potter* starring Renée Zellweger and Ewan McGregor took 14 years to progress from the script stage to the big screen
• When no one wanted to publish *The Tale of Peter Rabbit* Beatrix Potter published it herself and sold it at one shilling a copy – that's five pence in today's money
• Louisa May Alcott's novel *Little Women* took her just two months to write – from May to July in the year 1868
• How many times have you said those well known words:

   'Oh! what a tangled web we weave
   When first we practice to deceive!

But have you any idea who penned those immortal words? They are the words of Sir Walter Scott, author – among other works – of *Ivanhoe*
• Agatha Christie wrote six novels using the pseudonym Mary Westmacott
• C.S. Lewis died on the same day as President Kennedy in 1963
• *Alice's Adventures Underground* was the original title for *Alice's Adventures in Wonderland*
• Anthony Trollope was what we would today call a workaholic; each day, before going to work at the Post Office, he wrote 2,000-3,000 words; rode to hounds mid-week and Saturday; in his life-time wrote seventy books; the day after finishing a novel he would start the next

• As late as the Twelfth Century books were so expensive that Winchester Cathedral swopped a Bible for a country estate

• Beatrix Potter really owned a rabbit called Peter and took him everywhere with her on a lead

• By the turn of the Twenty-first Century *The Lord of the Rings* by J.R.R. Tolkien had sold more than 50 million copies in 30 languages

• C.S. Lewis and J.R.R. Tolkien were close friends and it is said that J.R.R. Tolkien played a large part in the conversion of C.S. Lewis from atheism to Christianity

• Charles Dickens, famous for the eccentric characters he created, actually created almost one thousand named characters

• Charlotte Brontë was less than five feet tall

• D.H. Lawrence did not hold back on the description of Lady Chatterley's affair with the gamekeeper when he wrote *Lady Chatterley's Lover*, neither did he cut out the four letter words. The result being that the book was deemed unpublishable in England until 1960 when Penguin books published the full text. The result of this was a court case where they were prosecuted under the Obscene Publications Act 1959 and during which they were later acquitted after a celebrated list of high profile authors appeared as witnesses for the defence. This trial had a far reaching effect on writing and publishing in future decades

• Daniel Defoe was nearly 60 years old when he wrote his novel *Robinson Crusoe*

• During his lifetime John Galsworthy was honored with degrees from the Universities of St Andrews, Manchester, Dublin, Cambridge, Sheffield, Oxford and Princeton

• During the last ten years of his life John Bunyan wrote 40 books

• Each Nobel Prize consists of a medal, a personal diploma and a cash award

• Each year, on the anniversary of his death, a wreath is laid on Charles Dickens' tomb in Poets' Corner, Westminster Abbey, despite the fact that it is more than 100 years since he died

• Eleanor Roosevelt was a great fan of Roald Dahl and he was frequently invited to the White House

• Although Mark Twain started his novel *Adventures of Hucklebury Finn*, which was the sequel to *Tom Sawyer* in 1876, it wasn't until 1883 that he finished the work. This was because it was a bit of a stop-start situation; he would work on it for a while and then he would stop, to either work on or do something else

• Ever wondered for how long a writer works each day? Well each writer is of course different; some lock themselves away and don't reappear until their work is complete whilst others, like Roald Dahl, decide on how long they will work each day and then stick to it. Dahl wrote for two hours each morning and then a further two hours each afternoon. During each session he used six pencils, which he sharpened at the beginning of the session and which lasted for just two hours – he didn't like working with a blunt pencil

• Did you know where the saying 'rule of thumb' comes from? No? It's quite fascinating really because it comes from the law stating that a man could not beat his wife with anything thicker than his thumb – something that one needs to remember when reading some of the great Nineteenth Century novels. In that era it was believed that a woman's place was indeed in the home and 'under her husband's thumb'

• Haley's Comet could be seen in the night sky not only on the night that Mark Twain was born but also on the night that he died

• Charles Dickens' major novels were first published in weekly installments. This was because most people at that time couldn't afford to buy a full-length novel

• *Alice's Adventures in Wonderland* by Lewis Carroll was actually written for a 'real' child after Carroll took the three daughters of the Dean of Christ Church for a boating trip on the river followed by a picnic on the banks of the Thames, during which he told them stories. The children's names were Lorina, Alice and Edith and it was Alice who later begged Carroll to write down the stories. So out of this trip the book was born and the heroine was named after Alice

• Hans Christian Andersen was an archivists dream, for he rarely destroyed anything that he had written and so today his writings remain intact, including thousands of his letters

• In 1938 Hitler was short listed for the Nobel Peace Prize and in 1945 and 1948 Joseph Stalin, the Secretary General of the Communist Party of the Soviet Union (1922-1953), was also nominated for the Nobel Peace Prize for his efforts to end the Second World War

• In our preoccupation with refuse collection and recycling have you ever wondered about the origin of the strange name 'dustbin' – a name we take for granted and don't think twice about now? Well in Victorian times coal was the important fuel and creator of energy for it was coal that was used to create the steam that powered the factory machines and coal was burned for domestic and industrial warmth. The burning of all this coal of course created masses of dust-like ashes which were collected in bins – dustbins. These bins were then emptied once a week by dustmen and taken to dust yards. Charles Dickens' novel *Our Mutual Friend* is based on a dust contractor who owned one of these dust yards

• It took Gustave Flaubert five years to write *Madame Bovary*

• J.M. Barrie, the creator of Peter Pan, was himself, at barely over five feet tall, the height of a child. Was that the inspiration behind his book, or was the untimely death of his brother – who was denied the chance to ever grow up – his inspiration?

• The first publisher approached with the manuscript of *Pride and Prejudice* by Jane Austen turned it down

• It is said that the first full novel was written by a woman, Murasaki Shikibu, and was called *The Tale of Genji*. It tells the story of a prince in search of love and wisdom. It is also said that – to date – it is a woman who is responsible for writing the most novels; Dame Barbara Cartland apparently completed a novel every two weeks and had more than 700 novels to her name

• Charles Dickens wrote *A Christmas Carol* in just a few weeks

• In 1857 Gustave Flaubert was tried on the grounds that his novel *Madam Bovary* was immoral; he narrowly escaped conviction

• Jack was the nickname by which C.S. Lewis was known

• Jean-Paul Sartre who was awarded the 1964 Nobel Prize in Literature, declined the prize. The reason for this was because he had consistently declined all official honours

• John F. Kennedy was awarded the 1957 Pulitzer Prize in Biography for his book *Profiles in Courage*

• Lewis Carroll suffered from a bad stammer

• J.R.R. Tolkien wrote his children annual illustrated letters as if from Santa Claus. A selection of these letters was published in 1976 with the title: *The Father Christmas Letters*

• Louisa May Alcott shared the same birthday as her father, Amos Bronson Alcott, and almost ended up sharing the same 'death' day too; however she in fact died two days after her father.

• Mark Twain, the pen name of Samuel Langhorne Clemens, is actually a riverboat term meaning the line between safe water and dangerous water

• *Jane Eyre* by Charlotte Brontë was originally published using the pseudonym Currer Bell

• J.K. Rowling thinks that the best place to write is not in a library, nor her study, or even her living room; it is well documented that she likes to write in cafes, where there is a constant supply of coffee and the company of people around her – she obviously doesn't enjoy the secluded isolation that most writers crave

• Most people know that D.H. Lawrence's novel *Lady Chatterley's Lover* got the author into a lot of trouble but few know that his novel *The Rainbow*

was also seized by the police and declared obscene
- The earliest film adaptation of Charles Dickens's novel *Oliver Twist* was in fact a silent movie made in 1909
- Nevil Shute's bad stammer prevented him from being commissioned into the Royal Flying Corps
- Novelist Graham Greene, was also a first cousin of the author Robert Louis Stevenson, so I guess it is all in the genes!
- J.R.R. Tolkien drew his own illustrations for his novel *The Hobbit*
- Penguin sent 12 copies of *Lady Chatterley's Lover* to the Director of Public Prosecutions challenging him to prosecute, which he did – and lost – after a six-day trial at the Old Bailey
- Renowned as a 'very long' book, few people actually realise that the novel *War and Peace* by Leo Tolstoy is in fact a mammoth 600,000 words long
- Roald Dahl became interested in writing for children after making up bedtime stories for his own children
- Twice a year the North Yorkshire, English seaside town of Whitby hosts a festival of goths and part of the reason for this is that Whitby appears in Bram Stoker's famous novel *Dracula*
- *Jude the Obscure* by Thomas Hardy was publicly burned by the Bishop of Wakefield in the year it was published, 1895
- Most people know that Samuel Johnson wrote the first Dictionary of its kind in English, but did you know it included over 40,000 words?
- Roald Dahl was actually trilingual; he spoke English, Norwegian and Swahili. He learned to speak Swahili when he worked in Africa for Shell in the 1950s
- Rudyard Kipling was the first Englishman to receive the Nobel Prize for Literature
- Sir Walter Scott coined the phrase, 'Wars of the Roses' in his novel *Ivanhoe*
- Somerset Maugham never owned a typewriter but wrote everything out longhand
- The author, Anthony Trollope, is credited with introducing the pillar boxes to Britain – first in the Channel Islands in 1854 and then a year later on the mainland. Incidentally, they were initially painted sage green and it was not until 20 years later in 1874 that they were painted the now familiar red; a colour now known as 'pillar box red'
- Roald Dahl was 6' 6" in height
- The Brontës published their works under the pseudonyms of Currer (Charlotte), Ellis (Emily) and Acton (Anne) Bell (Brontë)
- Roald Dahl wrote to his mother once a week from the age of nine, when he was at boarding school, until her death 32 years later

- Somerset Maugham suffered from a bad stammer
- The concept that fairy dust was needed before one could fly was added to the story of Peter Pan at a later date, when it was reported that several children had injured themselves when they had tried to fly from their beds – and in some cases even from their windows. So I suppose it was an early health and safety issue that prompted the rewrite!
- *The Life and Opinions of Tristram Shandy* is the full title of the novel generally known by its briefer title of *Tristram Shandy*
- The stage version of *Oliver Twist* was appearing in no fewer than 10 London theatres before serialisation of the novel was even complete
- The term 'Big Brother is watching you' is taken from George Orwell's novel, *Nineteen Eighty- Four*, as is the term 'newspeak'
- There is circumstantial evidence that Charles Dickens and Ellen Ternan (his lover after he separated from his wife) had a child that died shortly after being born; however, there is no proof and so it will always remain circumstantial
- Since 1901 to date the Nobel Prize in Literature has been awarded to 104 persons
- To date only 11 women have been awarded the Nobel Prize for Literature, they are: Selma Lagerlöf (1909), Grazia Deledda (1926), Sigrid Undset (1928), Pearl Buck (1938), Gabriela Mistral (1945), Nelly Sachs (1966), Nadine Gordimer (1991), Toni Morrison (1993), Wislawa Szymborska (1996), Elfriede Jelinek (2004), Doris Lessing (2007)
- To date the Internet Movie Data Base (IMDB) lists no less than 23 screen versions of *Oliver Twist*, the first being made in 1919 and the latest in 2005 – with no doubt more to come
- *Treasure Island* by Robert Louis Stevenson was written during a family holiday when the weather was wet and Stevenson, wanting to amuse his young stepson, drew a map of an imaginary island and called it Treasure Island
- Westward Ho! in Devon is the only town in England to have an exclamation mark and was named after the book of the same name written by Charles Kingsley in the mid 1800s
- When *Charlie and the Chocolate Factory* was published in China, 2 million copies were printed – breaking all records
- When Roald Dahl attended Repton Public School a gift box would regularly arrive from the nearby Cadbury chocolate factory. Inside this box were new chocolate bar inventions which the boys were asked to eat and then deliver their verdict. The result of this was a lifetime love affair with chocolate and the seed for his future book, *Charlie and the Chocolate Factory*

• Yellow backs – these are cheap editions of novels; their name derives from the fact that they were bound in yellow boards. They were the railway novels of the 1870s and 1880s
• The first typewriters came on the market in 1874, four years after Charles Dickens' death, meaning that the great man himself, and all those great writers that went before him, were condemned to writing in longhand, with pen and ink too – or even a quill!

THE END

Bibliography

Deary, T, *Horrible Histories England*, Scholastic Children's Books, 2004

Lange, H, *90 Classic Books for People in a Hurry*, Nicotext, 2008

Gamble, N, *Favourite Classic Writers*, Hodder Wayland, 2003

Lloyd, J and Mitchinson J, *Advanced Banter*, Faber and Faber Ltd, 2008

Baldick, C, *Oxford Concise Dictionary of Literary Terms*, Oxford University Press, 2004

Drabble, M and Stringer, J, *Oxford Concise Companion to English Literature*, Oxford University Press, 2007

Walder, D, Literature in the Modern World, Oxford University Press, 2003

Davis, P, *Charles Dickens A to Z: The Essential Reference to His Life and Work*, Facts on File Inc, 1999

Hardwick, M & M, *The Dickens Encyclopaedia*, Wordsworth Editions Ltd, 1973

Alexander, M, *A History of English Literature*, Palgrave Macmillan, 2007

Grant, N, *Oxford Children's History of the World*, Oxford University Press, 2008

Websites:

www.britannica.com

http://www.tolkiensociety.org/tolkein/bibl2.htm

www.walterscott.lib.ed.ac.uk

www.anderson.sdu.dk/vaerk/register/index_e.html

www.eswsc.com

http://www.bbc.co.uk/history/historic_figures

www.litencyc.com

www.seeingjaneausten.com

www.louisamayalcott.org

http://charlesdickenspage.com/ (David Perdue)

Index

Index